CRITICAL MASS

Gunnar C. Garisson

SHAPESHIFTER BOOKS, SEATTLE

Published by
SHAPESHIFTER BOOKS
Seattle, WA 98106

FIRST EDITION
March, 2012

FIRST EBOOK EDITION
March, 2011
ISBN 978-1-4524-8899-8

Copyright © 2011 by Gunnar C. Garisson
All Rights Reserved.

ISBN 978-0615623016

Cover art by Remy Francis,
www.rembrandz.com

Manufactured in The United States of America

This book is dedicated to my mother, Carol, without whose enduring support, this project would have never taken shape. Also to my two wonderful children, David and Tyrin, and my beautiful wife, Deena, for being my inspiration and letting me bogart the laptop.

———————

"I believe that banking institutions are more dangerous to our liberties than standing armies. If the American people ever allow private banks to control the issue of their currency, first by inflation, then by deflation, the banks and corporations that will grow up around [the banks] will deprive the people of all property until their children wake up homeless on the continent their fathers conquered. The issuing power should be taken from the banks and restored to the people, to whom it properly belongs."

-Thomas Jefferson, 3rd President of The United States of America

"The greatest enemy of knowledge is not ignorance, it is the illusion of knowledge"

-Stephen W. Hawking

"If the school of free thought will ultimately bring on the fall of civilized man, then the fall of mankind is necessary, and therein lies the full length of its revolution. Mother Earth will tolerate us no longer than we choose to tolerate each other... What we call 'human nature' is nothing short of natural selection at its most convoluted level."

-The Alliance For Gaia

CRITICAL MASS

TABLE OF CONTENTS:

Chapter 1: Thorsson Krey

He had been running through the maze of city streets and broken down cars for what seemed like half of the night. Of the five who were chasing him, three were still right on his heels, occasionally yelling obscene threats at him. One had dropped out from sheer exhaustion before it started raining and another slipped coming around a corner and hit his head on the curb. His accomplices didn't even look back as his agonizing cry echoed through the deserted streets. The streetlights had long since been broken out, but light flickered down from the traffic on the matrix of overpasses above, reflecting off of the glass on the skyscrapers and the layer of water on the street, creating a bit of a psychedelic effect as his headset blasted one of his favorite thunderous songs, and he smiled, not even winded from the chase. Three were still right on his heels, because that was exactly where he wanted them.

The time was nigh, and for a moment he sped his cadence, causing them to accelerate desperately. He let the one who was closest reach out to grab the back of his jacket and almost get a grip on him before he dropped to one knee and hunched over forward with his head down, sending the man sprawling over him, face first, onto the pitted asphalt. The next in line, wide-eyed with his feet skidding on the wet pavement in a sudden attempt to slow himself, had his arms out to the sides, flailing around as if reaching for something to grab onto. In one fluid motion he pivoted around 180 degrees to the left on the balls of his feet, raising his center only slightly, and thrust a powerful punch with his right hand directly into the defenseless attacker's grossly over-exposed solar plexus. The man made a horribly deep wheezing sound as his feet lifted about six inches off the ground and he folded nearly in half, stopped right in his tracks, and dropped like a sack of potatoes to the street where he tipped over sideways in fetal position; alive, but unable to move.

The third man made no attempt to slow down, and actually lunged at him, hurdling over his fallen comrade in an attempt to tackle him while crying out in a blind rage as he flew through the air with his arms extended. Gracefully, he simultaneously caught the back of the man's left wrist and hand with his right hand, while pivoting to the left and stepping back with his left foot, just clearing the man's line of attack and dragging his momentum off course and toward the ground. He suddenly reversed the flow and twisted his attacker's wrist back the way it came, pivoting at the waist to the right, and backing up the motion with his left hand, dislocating his elbow with a loud snapping sound as he caught him in the face with his left elbow, sending him reeling onto his back a few feet from his partner. A large knife bounced out of the man's coat and clanged to a stop several inches from his head, but he made no attempt to grab it, and instead rolled toward his wounded arm, moaning in pain with blood oozing from his mouth and nose, quickly diluted by the pooling rain.

He stood fast, assessing the situation instinctively, though obviously clear of his attackers' immediate threat. His medium length hair, drenched from the rain, whipped an arc of water into the air as he spun his head quickly to the left and turned his attention back to the first man, who was already clambering up from his spill. He reached down to his waist and turned off his music. The man was looking over his shoulder, reaching into his coat for something, and desperately trying to get to his feet, when he ran right by him on his blind side, giving him a taunting pop on the back of the head on his way by. The man made it to his feet and produced the pistol he had been fumbling for.

"Freeze!" the man yelled, pulling the slide back and aiming at the back of his head.

He knew if it was loaded he would have been shot at a long time ago. He kept running, and after a brief pause by the gunman, the chase resumed. He darted in between two abandoned cars and up onto the sidewalk, running along the series of broken out and decaying store fronts on his right. Still gripping his pistol, the man winced as he struggled to catch up, his face badly gouged from the fall. Nearing a familiar intersection he noticed the light of approaching headlights from around the corner and was debating whether or not to alter his course when he heard the sound of a police radio and decided to press on.

As he rounded the corner, the cops in the patrol car barely glanced at him, rounding the corner in the opposite direction, nonchalantly, and passing right by his armed pursuer as well. The police had long since written off the entire underground as a liability, and were scarcely seen down here at all. Their job was primarily to protect the upper crust from the dregs that still lived here. In the daytime, in barricaded zones, it was not uncommon to see them protecting a truck delivering or receiving goods through underground warehouses or escorting city engineers as they conducted surveys of the infrastructure, but even then they were easily bribed into complete uselessness. One car? At night? These two must have been down here to buy drugs, arrange a hit, or kill somebody themselves. At any rate, they were completely uninterested in the lives of those who lived here, and that was fine by him.

———————

Things had not always been this bad. As a young boy, he could remember these streets bustling with life. It was an expanding hive of people, cars, and commerce more diverse than the mind could keep up with, and it was magical. At any time, day or night, you could walk these streets and still be surrounded by people. There was always crime, but people lived their lives pretty much oblivious to it. That changed at a pretty frightening rate.

There has been much speculation and controversy as to what point it was that it became irreversible, but the hard fact is that humans overpopulated the planet to the point of sociological and economic critical mass. Somewhere around 2048, less than ten short years ago, mankind had reached a global population of nearly 11.5 billion people before things got so bad that the growth actually flat-lined and the mortality rate finally equaled the birth rate. Despite all the warning signs and attempts to educate the masses by the conveniently ignored minority of people interested in sustainability in the 20th century, mankind marched merrily into the future, interested only in economic growth, while defeating even that possibility by throwing billions of dollars a year into programs designed to kill the weed by hacking off it's branches while the root continued to grow deeper and deeper.

The ensuing depression, also both economic and psychological, gave birth to the rampant practice of every desperate act man is capable of. While some innovative solutions had been found to address the environmental holocaust that was staring them in the face, the sociological condition was irreparable. With the middle class all but extinct, the rich needed to find a way to protect themselves from the poor, and a new kind of segregation was taking place in most of the major cities of the world.

Out of the ashes of the war torn inner-city jungles, cities were being constructed right over the top of themselves. Access to large buildings was being sealed from below, and a matrix of new freeways and viaducts was connecting them together at higher and higher levels. It started as an attempt to ease unbearable levels of traffic congestion, but evolved without resistance into a convenient way to leave the unfortunate ones behind.

Denial in every form pushed the poor further and further out of society. What started as being barred from employment at anything that paid livable wages, and being unable to open a bank account, quickly turned into class-based discrimination toward patrons upon entering a store to spend what little money they did have, and eventually, logistical denial of access to their world at all. The poor had been reduced to a barter system and a state of undeniable anarchy, where the strong survive, and the weak get trampled. Thorsson Krey flourished here. He and a very tight-knit family, known on the streets as The North Clan, had found numerous ways to get whatever they needed.

———————

He hooked left at the next intersection, the man behind him now breathing so hard he could hear him from ten feet away. There was an eight foot high concrete barricade across the entire width of the road, building to building. The man slowed as if to rest a bit, assuming the fight would take place here. Without looking back, Krey trotted up to the graffiti-riddled wall and leaped up, catching the top edge with his finger tips and vaulted over using his powerful forearm as a fulcrum. He landed almost silently, as the exhausted attacker scrambled to catch up. The beaten man clumsily threw himself over and landed with a loud thud, nearly losing his balance and falling over sideways before breaking into a run.

They were nearly to the next intersection by the time he was close again. Krey saw headlights again, but this time heard the whine of a high-torque cargo truck. He hurdled onto a row of dead cars parked along the right side of the road, running on the rooftops as the man jumped up to follow. The last one was a van and it gave him just the height he was after. He leaped up, out, and to the right, just as the truck was going by. He had enough momentum to clear it, but held back a little, then turned his body around in mid-air, came down right behind the moving truck and grabbed the bumper. He squatted and slid on his feet for a second or two, then let go, spinning around to face his opponent who had jumped straight over, hoping to land on him.

The unsuspecting man had not seen his maneuver, and was facing away from him, looking up the street to see where he went. Krey jumped silently at him and scissor kicked him right between the shoulder blades so hard that his head flew back with enough force to cut off the blood flow to his brain and knocked him unconscious in much the same fashion as a boxer's most menacing uppercut to the chin. The man sprawled forward like a rag doll, ten feet out into the street, where he skidded to a stop on his already wounded face. His gun flew a bit further, and finally bounced across the street, sliding under an old Volkswagen bug that was tipped onto it's side, impaled by a fire hydrant.

Laughter erupted from behind him, echoing through the buildings. Familiar laughter. He turned around, smiling, to see an old man through the broken out windshield in front of the van he had jumped off of, cloaked in a blanket and nursing a bottle of something nasty.

"Did you like that?" Krey asked sarcastically, bowing with his arms out to his sides.

"Man, that was that funniest fucking thing I've seen in a week!--- 'cept you made me piss my pants, mother fucker!" he exclaimed, still laughing out loud. "Jumpin' off a mother fucker's roof 'n shit...damn," he mumbled, laughing again.

"He'll be out for about ten to twenty minutes..." Krey said, gesturing at the dark lump in the middle of the road. "The Glock under the car is unloaded, but it should fetch you a few meals at Vinny's..." He turned and started to walk away. "You might want to make yourself scarce... These assholes have no sense of humor."

"Hey Dragon!" the old man called out.

Krey stopped. "Catch!" he ordered, grinning, and slowly reached into his pocket with his back still turned.

The old man, still in the van, raised a cup and tilted it toward him. Krey spun around, squatting low, and snapped a shiny quarter out from between his thumb and middle finger with his hand inverted up near his ear. The coin zipped through the air and landed directly in the cup from about 20 yards out with a dull thunk. The old man busted up laughing again.

"Sounds like you didn't do too well today, my friend..." Krey jabbed, turning to leave again.

"Already spen' it, brotha," he replied, tipping his bottle toward him and nodding with gratitude. "Already spen' it." Though most of the upper crust had made currency obsolete years ago with scannable implants and electronic funds, a buck was still a buck down here.

Krey walked off smiling and shaking his head, quietly murmuring to himself, "Thomas, Thomas, Thomas...."

Thorsson Krey was recognized by many, but few knew his real name. He was known on the streets as "The

Dragon," due largely to his intense fighting style and Norse tattoos, but in slightly tighter circles he was called "Thor." Even fewer knew where he and his family resided. They were known mainly by reputation. Well liked, greatly respected, and deeply feared, they conducted their business relatively unscathed because they weren't in the habit of creating enemies, and the enemies that chose them as targets were dealt with swiftly, and generally made an excruciating example of.

CHAPTER 2: THE NORTH CLAN

"We have to arrange a truce with them, it's the only way for both sides to continue getting what they need without a war!" she yelled, leaning forward in her seat and glaring across the table at the arrogant man in front of her. Her long, blonde hair was sweaty and sticking to the side of her face as she scowled at him.

He backed off, if only in mannerism, and shrugged sarcastically, "If it's a war they want..."

"Kait's right." They both turned to look at Tyr as he spoke calmly from his seat at the table, leaning back with a horn of mead in his hand. "A war with Central will not benefit us... even if we emerge unscathed. We must seek a truce, Uruz."

"I guess you're right," he sighed, throwing his overgrown arms to the sides and glancing at them both. She sat back ungraciously and stared at him with sullen eyes, unsurprised by his momentary inability to think clearly before responding with force. "But we can't let them think *we're* approaching *them* with a truce... that will make us look weak," he added, finally on the right track.

"That's exactly what Thor said." They now looked the other way as the slender man beneath the hat tilted his head up and spoke from the other side of the table, then lit a small brass lighter and took a long pull off his pipe, smoke coming out of his mouth as he added, "Right before he geared up and strutted out of here with a shit-eating grin on his face." He smiled as he spoke without ever really making eye contact.

"Where was he going?" Kait asked, a little concerned.

"Where do you think?" Uruz replied for him, grinning first at her, then Dagaz, who was still grinning as well, already pulling another hit from his pipe.

"He mentioned a shipment that was supposed to be kept secret. How he found out about it, I don't know, but I believe his intention was to observe and not get involved," Dagaz replied.

"Yeah, right!" Uruz blurted out, accidentally spitting a little mead across the table onto the side of Kait's face. "He doesn't think that far in advance!"

"At least *he* thinks!" Kait sneered, wiping the side of her face off with her sleeve.

Tyr sat up from his reclined position, laid down his empty drinking horn, burped proudly, and stated, matter-of-factly, "There *is* method to his madness... he is a creature of instinct, and is quite obviously blessed with a serious element of luck," They all chuckled in agreement, nodding as he continued, "Criticize him all you like for his apparent recklessness, but in the end he will most likely out-live us all." He loomed over the table, looking into each of their eyes, hers twice. She nodded, finally grinning herself.

"What exactly is it he hoped to accomplish?" She asked to the forum, eyes lowered to a point a few degrees down, and million miles away.

"Why don't you ask him yourself?" Dagaz offered, gesturing with the brim of his hat, up and to the right at the security screen showing Krey punching in his code for the front door as he looked side to side, smiling.

The door slid open sideways, emitting a windy sound as it glided on its well maintained tracks to reveal a rain soaked figure, head down, but looking at them all, walking in through the small corridor toward the inner security door that still separated them. He lifted his right arm and hit the panel and the heavy steel door shut quickly behind him, then he punched in the code for the inner door and joined the family.

"Top of the mornin' to ya!" he exclaimed, exchanging glances, but immediately returning to hers. She smiled, obviously relieved to see him in the flesh.

"We were starting to worry about you," Tyr spoke up, echoing from a point about twenty feet away where he was re-filling his horn directly from a tapped carboy, half full of mead, hanging inverted on a large brewing rack where several more hung, churning away at various stages of fermentation. At 5 to 10 gallon capacity apiece, depending on which carboy was being used, they were a long way from out, given the three or four that were finished and aging.

He pulled up his chair, tossing his wet leather jacket onto a hook on a stand to his right, and pulled his left hand through his drenched hair, exhaling heavily as he sat down. "That's a long, slippery slope, my brother. You'll go grey... or blind."

"No, that's from-" Uruz started.

"We get it, we get it!" Kait interrupted with a slightly disgusted look, blushing slightly.

Tyr laughed as he re-approached the table, returning his gaze to Thor. "This is true... this is true. A long, slippery slope indeed." He sat back down.

"Where's mine?" Krey asked, gesturing at Tyr's horn.

"It's all yours, asshole!" joked Uruz, slapping him on the back hard enough to make his head spring back like a rag doll. "And a fine batch it was indeed!"

"_Was_?" Thor asked facetiously.

"Well, you were gone all day..." Uruz slurred defensively, obviously more than just a little bit intoxicated.

Krey looked at Kait and grinned maliciously, then leaped from his seat and tackled Uruz right out of his chair onto the floor. They rolled about ten feet from the table, right by Dagaz who didn't even look up, cursing each other as they fought. Though Uruz outweighed him nearly two to one, it was far from one sided, and in a couple seconds, Krey broke free as if it never happened and yelled, "Where's my horn?!" as he walked purposefully towards the brewing rack.

Uruz staggered to his feet, laughing boisterously, and returned to his seat. "Grab me another one, brother!" he shouted back at Krey, who was already filling number three.

"So, how are things on the west end?" Thor asked, returning to the table and handing a horn to Uruz and Kait.

Kait spoke up. "We have a situation. Jerrick's generators have failed for the third time in a week, and he's blaming our computers. Their crop won't survive if it happens again, so I told him we would get him three more, even though we all know it's probably just an operator error or some kind of random network glitch. I don't have to tell you how it would affect us if we lost that food source..." she added, glancing over at Tyr, who nodded. "Anyway, he agreed to double our share if we can deliver in two days."

"Nice," Thor nodded, and smiled at her. "That will give us enough trading stock to fortify ourselves _and_ all of our allies for quite awhile."

She bowed, smiling, with one hand at mid-section, and one outstretched toward him, playfully inviting a kiss. He couldn't resist; taking, and gently kissing the back of her hand.

His relationship with her had been unorthodox, to say the least, for as long as he could remember. They grew up as neighborhood rivals, always trying to outdo each other, but friends to the end. Friendship became something resembling love, but there was always something platonic between them.

When a deal between her clan and a neighboring arms dealer went south, she was left alone, and was immediately taken in as family to the North Clan. He had learned so much more about her in the last three years, and had come to respect her immensely. She was both a warrior and a diplomat; a lady and a rogue. In this environment it was not uncommon for women to be as strong as men, as life down here demanded it. There had long since been no use for the self-affirming rhetoric of the twentieth century to do with equal rights and Nazi-feminism. Down here there was only truth and survival. She understood this better than anyone.

"Oh, get a fuckin' room!" Uruz sneered.

"We all need to get a room," Tyr yawned, standing up, stretching, "we have a lot of work to do tomorrow...."

"I'll have control chips for three cars calibrated by morning," Dagaz added, "but I'm gonna sit this one out." He pulled one last drag from his pipe, and exhaled, capping it and sliding it into his coat pocket. "You never told us what happened in Central." he said, turning to Thor, who was picking up empty drinking horns again.

"I stirred up a hornet's nest, and led them to Cane's neck of the woods," Thor chuckled, already buzzed from the mead. "When that war's over, they'll be begging us for help. Plus it will keep them busy while we take care of some of our business. It looked to me like they were trying to poach some of our electronics territory."

"You're sure nobody recognized you?" Tyr prodded.

"Let's just say they didn't see what they *thought* they saw." The sound of the rain hitting the concrete and steel roof was starting to become a loud drone, drowning the city in cold darkness. "Let's go topside!" Thor invited Kait.

"What's the matter, not wet enough?" Kait flirted.

"There's something you have to check out," he evaded, grabbing her hand and heading for the spiral staircase in the far corner. "See you guys in the morning...."

As the hatch opened, water cascaded over both of them, and they quickly leapt out onto the concrete slab. The roof was alive with dancing drops of rain hammering the half-inch layer of accumulated water like a meteor shower, illuminated in random symphony by flashes of lightning in the near distance. The city spanned for what seemed like an eternity, fusing with everything in its path. Cities that used to be in different states were now part of the same malignant west-coast tumor. He sealed the hatch behind them, punching in his code on the keypad, and turned to her. Already completely soaked to the bone, she held her arms out to the sides. "Well...?" she asked.

"Remember what I was telling you about energy fields and electricity?"

"Yeah, I've seen you do it... the stun gun... the security camera...."

"The same level of manipulation can be done regardless of the magnitude," he stated, matter-of-factly.

"What do you mean? What kind of magnitude?" she asked, puzzled and slightly worried.

Just then, a large flash of lightning lit up the sky, lingering long enough to cast noticeable shadows off of the surrounding buildings, then immediately erupted into a violent thunderclap that shook the very surface they were standing on. Her eyes widened with excitement, and he grinned with opportunistic sophistry.

"Fuck you! You didn't do that!" she laughed.

"I know, but that would sure be a cool trick..." he joked back. "No, seriously, check this out," he invited, jumping up and taking a seat on one of the large rectangular vent hoods. "Stay right there! No matter what you see, don't get too close!"

She stood with her arms crossed in preemptive skepticism and stared with a quasi-cynical look on her face, waiting. He closed his eyes and straightened his back, hands face down on his thighs, and took a deep breath in through his nose with his tongue on the roof of his mouth, then exhaled through his mouth with an audible hiss. He did this three more times, each time appearing more relaxed and centered. His arms slowly rose out to the sides with his palms turning toward the dark clouds looming overhead. It was then that she noticed the feeling of being surrounded by a field of static.

"THOR!" she screamed, stopping herself after one step toward him to see the flash of a giant column of light tied to the heavens engulf his whole body with a deafening crash. It was gone before she could breathe again, and through the residual flash blindness in her field of vision, she thought she saw his eyes glowing as he slowly opened them and lowered his arms back to his thighs.

"Everything vibrates at a certain pitch. Everything," he said shakily, as he slowly recovered, eyes widening and waning cyclically. "If you know what is about to happen, the pitch is easy to tune into. The rest is simply a matter of accepting it, and raising or lowering your own pitch to match it. You can't stop the force of a river through confrontation, but if you accept it's energy, you can alter or bend it's direction quite easily." The look on his face changed nonchalantly from teacher to student. "It's actually amazing how similar water is to electricity," he wondered, "They both follow the path of least resistance...."

"Jesus Christ, Thor!" she said, relieved, but totally blown away by his apparent lack of respect for the gravity of what just transpired, as she stood in the pouring rain with her arms wrapped around him, nervously laughing and crying at the same time.

They stood near the concrete knee wall for about an hour, taking in the amazing view of the city at night. As far as the eye could see in every direction was a sea of structure; cold, wet, and unforgiving, yet somehow beautiful in its vast, random complexity. Scattered throughout the maze of synthetic terrain were small pockets of activity: lights in buildings, cars meandering down otherwise desolate streets, and occasional wanderers of the night, searching for some kind of satisfaction... searching for a victim.

CHAPTER 3: MILK TOOTH

The cloaked figure walked slowly and deliberately down the alley between the two buildings toward an intersection that was near what used to be the old Sea-Tac/ Portland border, rain pouring like a fountain off of the cupped brim of his large hat. His car was parked behind a dumpster, facing the back road on-ramp to the viaduct that led north to the upper level of Seattle, well concealed in the darkness. He paused for a moment beneath an old awning and pulled a cigarette from his pack, lit it, then took a long drag, his slightly shaking hand replacing his lighter into the inside pocket of his dark grey trench coat. He exhaled the enormous cloud and watched as it rose upward toward the rooftops, illuminated at last by a beam of light radiating from a flickering streetlight on the corner, then flicked the nearly full length cigarette into a nearby puddle where it died with a quick hiss.

This area was well known for its underground nightlife, sometimes trafficked well past dawn by drunks, musicians, playboys, whores, and drug dealers. He heard the methodical thump of a live band a couple of blocks away, and unintelligible intermittent shouts and vibrant screams and laughter that made him suddenly tingle with lust and envy. He could feel the activity, yet was somehow excited by his secretive separation from it. Standing ankle deep in a large puddle near the entrance to the alley, he paused; gasping inside as the water made its way through his boots and chilled his feet with earthly presence. His breathing became shallower and faster. He was starting to feel alive.

His predator instincts sharpening as well, he paused with his nose to the wind like a wolf on the hunt becoming intuitively aware of oncoming prey slightly before the scent even hit its nose. He heard the footsteps and immediately knew it was a female in high heels coming from the left, and from the wildly erratic cadence, he could tell she was also very drunk. He swept to the edge of the wall, silent beneath the sound of the pouring rain, and hidden from view. He extended his awareness well beyond her staggering sound and noted only silence beyond her. She was alone. She was his.

As she cleared the corner, not even glancing to her right, he swept behind her, hooking the left side of her face and long, dark hair with his hand, and yanked her into the alley with a menacing grip, casting a true predator's nearly subconscious peripheral glance back the way she came to screen for witnesses. He had control of her right hand with his, and backhanded her entire body like a rag doll directly into the wall behind him. Her face slammed into the weathered cinder blocks with the force of a car wreck, and she blurted out a dull moan as he let go of her hand and coldly slammed her on the back in the same puddle he was standing in.

Down on one knee beside her, with his right hand calmly around her throat, he was exhilarated again by the feeling of the cold water soaking through his right pant leg, and he straddled her mid-section as she slowly twisted and groaned in the growing pool of water, trying very hard just to stay conscious. He leaned over her and pulled her torso up enough to get his arms around her back and neck and embraced her closely, pulling her near and tight, the blood from her injured face running freely down the side of his cheek as he rocked her side to side, humming to her softly as she quivered in fear, unable, or unwilling to make a sound.

He closed his eyes, sighed deeply, then let go, dropping her back into the puddle. The water splashed as she tossed her head back and forth, and she gasped as he pulled the large knife out of his already blood soaked trench coat. He was starting to feel alive again. He was starting.

CHAPTER 4: PILLOCK

"I'll get more 'n a couple meals for this..." Thomas grunted, reaching under the overturned car with his outstretched arm, trying not to spill his bottle with the other. "God dammit! Shit-ass fuckin' thing!" He cursed loudly as he set the bottle on the pavement and laid on his stomach, squirming inward. He finally got a grip on the pistol with his fingertips and proudly pulled his new treasure toward himself with a boyish smile. "Oh, I think you'll feed my hungry ass for *at least* a month," he mumbled, backing out of the niche he had crawled into.

He stood up, brushed off his already soiled and shabby clothes, then straightened his imaginary necktie in an over dignified manner, clearing his throat sarcastically. He stood as straight as his decrepit old bones would allow, given the many long years of sleeping in cars and under bridges with absolutely no medical care. "I'll take the steak and lobster tail and a glass of your best cognac, Sir," he said in a poorly faked English accent, smiling at himself and turning around blindly, "and the lady will have-"

"And the lady will have what?!" the voice boomed from right next to him.

Thomas nearly jumped right out of his skin as he completed his turn right into the man. His bloody face was shocking enough, but his penetrating glare made Thomas's knees buckle as he jumped back about two feet and pointed the pistol desperately at the man he had all but forgotten about. "Jesus tap-dancing Christ!"

"Give me my fucking gun!" the man demanded, stepping once directly toward him, and snatched it right out of his trembling hands with a powerful sweeping motion as Thomas tried in vain to squeeze off a round that wasn't there. The pull made Thomas lose what little balance he had, and as he fell toward his assailant, the man backhanded him across the side of his face with the butt of the gun, sending him sprawling across the sidewalk in front of the car.

Still in a lot of pain himself, the man started holstering his weapon beneath his damaged jacket as Thomas struggled desperately to put some distance between them. He was barely able to crawl, and fell of the edge of the sidewalk into the backed up gutter with a splash. "Dragon should've iced your sorry ass," he spluttered defiantly through the mixture of blood bubbles, gutter water and saliva that was oozing out of his mouth.

It was raining loudly, and the thunder was getting more frequent, but this definitely got the puzzled man's attention and he grinned, throwing his head back and looking up into the cloudy sky with his arms outstretched as if he suddenly had a great epiphany. "Dragon?" he asked, looking back at Thomas and smiling with an almost sinister calmness as he walked slowly toward the helpless drunk, cracking his knuckles.

CHAPTER 5: THE FOOD CHAIN

"Shhhh..." he said scornfully, his ear pressed tightly to the metal door at the top of the stairs. He heard the sound of footsteps slowly fading off to the right, and the whine of a sports car, probably a vintage 12 cylinder, fading out to the left and down the ramp. *"Let's go!"* he whispered, quietly turning the key in the giant brass padlock to the right with his other hand on the door latch. He pushed the latch down and opened the door a crack. Peeking out, he saw no movement and opened it a little further. Nothing to the left. He stood up, waving behind him for Tyr, Kait, and Uruz to follow, and walked nonchalantly out the door, all four dressed in contemporary business attire, carrying briefcases and suddenly chatting in character about the make believe goings on of their busy day, while following Mr. Krey to his target.

It was gorgeous. A brand new Thunderbird with all the trimmings. Krey carefully set his briefcase on top without missing a beat in the conversation and stepped aside from the driver's side door, allowing Tyr to produce his "key." One pass from the input gun loaded with Dagaz's trademark control chip, and the door opened, interior lights coming on to a warm invitation.

"After you, sir." Tyr gestured with his left hand, facetious after not detecting any traffic in the parking garage.

"But of course..." Thor entered the driver's seat, quickly grabbing the control chip from Tyr on the way in, and unlocking the other doors for his accomplices. "This is the part that always trips me out," Thor said calmly, as Tyr and Uruz shut the back doors, and Kait got in front. He pulled the trigger on the device while holding it over the ignition scanner. The car started right up and spoke, *"Good afternoon, Ms. Royer, what is your destination?"*

Uruz burst into laughter from his nose, trying to suppress it. "Ms. Royer?" he asked, laughing so hard he cornered himself between his seat and the door.

Knowing full well there would be no voice recognition going on, Thor was already going through the computer maps and picking a destination that would get them closer to the exit point.

"Starbuck's West. Estimated time of arrival is 12 minutes, thirteen seconds." The car accelerated toward the gate and everyone inside grew serious as they closed in on the manned security booth at the end of the ramp toward the entrance of the complex.

As they pulled up to the booth and stopped, the guard looked out at Thor and then at the car and punched some numbers into his computer, adding "Seventeen fifty-five," and gesturing his chin toward Thor's left wrist which was still hanging nonchalantly over the steering wheel.

Thor had already glanced at his name tag and responded, "Just put it on my tab, Kyle." His right hand was busy typing something into the computer, then scanning the small monitor by his right knee with the gun. The guard was busy typing as well and didn't see what he was doing. He stopped; looking puzzled for a second, and then turned his attention back to Thor.

"I'm sorry, I didn't get your name...."

Thor turned his head slowly and looked right into the guard's eyes. "But you see, my darling, that's the beauty of it," he smiled, winking at the guard, and seized control of the automobile, now reprogrammed for manual operation. He stomped on the gas pedal and slammed through the stop arm, screeching out of the parking garage and leaving the guard in a cloud of smoke.

Now Kait was laughing hysterically. He smiled and laughed along with her.

"Hard left!" Tyr called out from the back seat, his navigation computer out on his lap. Thor responded quickly. "Two blocks up, and take a right!" he called out again.

"Turn on the side scan sonar, GPS and radar! We have traffic at twelve o' clock!" Thor interjected, gesturing with his chin at the new flood of traffic merging onto the overpass ahead, while handing the control gun back to Tyr. "Maintain steering control. We only need the other cars to be able to read us..."

"Why not blend in again? You're going to stick out like a sore thumb!" Kait said.

"Last time we almost got caught. Anyway, I have an idea. Tyr, just feed that phony simulator route into the car's computer. I'll take care of the rest. All their roadblocks will be in the wrong places!" He accelerated boldly and headed straight for the congested ramp, grinning at Kait. She nervously returned his smile, then started to relax. Though he seemed to love surprising people with sudden plan changes, he usually knew what he was doing. He reached over and put one hand on her thigh, as if to reassure, then grabbed the steering wheel with both hands and zeroed in on the centerline of the ramp, still accelerating.

"Strap yourselves in!" he shouted as he bounded up the ramp. The other cars read his location and vector and parted from his path and each other's like a school of scared fish. At all times there was at least one meter between the cars and the three foot high side walls of the ramp and freeway. The nav computers just compensated for all surrounding changes and adjusted their car's position and trajectory accordingly. Reaching the banked left bend at the top of the ramp that hooked around to merge with the main highway, Thor was still accelerating, somewhat to the surprise of the other three. "How 'bout that side scan?" he asked seriously.

"How fast can the other cars react?" Uruz asked from the back, trying to mask the slight worry in his voice.

"Twice as fast as this car is capable of driving," Tyr answered.

"YEEEEEEE-HAWWWWW!" Uruz screamed, finally clicking on his seatbelt.

Thor smiled, turning into the bend at over 120 miles per hour. The car started to fishtail to the right, still parting through the middle of the other cars, until it was almost sideways; wheels squealing underneath them in a controlled harmonic tone. Thor had slightly let off the accelerator and had his head turned slightly toward Kait, who was clenching her armrest tensely, but obviously enjoying herself, and mouthed the words, "I love you."

> *I want to make you make me happy,*
> *and when the tables turn,*
> *I will become the fish,*
> *and you, my love, can be my worm.*
> *We'll troll along the greasy waters*
> *of discarded dreams, and we'll laugh*
> *as the cold world tears itself apart at the seams.*
> *And when the loneliness*

I pack around in bags like maggots,
Falls upon the floor and shatters,
crawling in ten thousand ways,
I would follow you to the ends of the earth,
or the highest mountain,
Just to see a half-assed smile
stretch across your jaded face.

And then the loneliness explodes inside my mind
and silence takes my thoughts before I speak,
and gives them to somebody quicker.
Another siren's call that beacons me to toy with fate,
and I see your face like a battering ram
as I slam my ship into the rocks again.

And when the ashtray of our love is finally full,
and butts are falling on the floor,
Will you believe? Will you release me?
Will you gently ease the hook out,
or will you just yank it
from my throat in cold indifference,
throw me back and try again?

I want to make you make me happy,
and when the tables turn,
I will become the fish, and you, my love...
my little worm.
We'll troll along the greasy waters
of forgotten dreams,
and we'll laugh as the cruel world
gets sucked into the sewer drain.

They came around the corner and straightened out.
Now it was a straight shot, nine miles into the heart of old

downtown Seattle. Kait was staring out her window at the cars as they were passing and caught a glimpse of an old business man spilling a drink all over the front of his expensive suit as his car's computer lurched him to the right to avoid contact with them. She burst into laughter and turned to the left to tell everyone about it when she was interrupted by Tyr's voice.

"So how do you propose we get to the west end garage? You punched in 'Starbuck's West,' remember? The cops will probably have the bridge levels blocked!"

"I know another way. I've mapped it out on foot a couple of times."

"Underneath? The old bridge is nothing but rubble! That quake left no passable route!"

"Or so it would seem," Thor added, already veering to the right toward one of the old downtown exits. The off-ramp, still in service as a cargo ramp for the heavily fortified industrial sector, pitched gracefully down and to the right, then turned sharply to the left and under the main highway before splitting into two channels. The left fork descended to become a large bridge over the industrial park, leading to a series of proprietary, one-way security gates for the companies below. Thor had already slowed down and turned onto the one on the right, which spiraled down all the way to ground level, where it led to the shipping docks.

"What the fuck are you doing?" Uruz yelled, suddenly very serious. "There's more security at the shipyard than there is downtown! We'll be caught for sure!"

"Just double check your seat belts, we're not going to the shipyard, and we're not getting caught!"

Tyr leaned forward a little "Bro, this is a nice car, but it can't fly..."

"Sure it can."

Kait clenched the door handle and the side of her seat as Thor widened his approach into the radius, then tightened it through, as close to the inside column as possible, and floored it directly at a gap in the concrete side rail that looked like it had been caused by some sort of recent collision. Tyr dropped the computer between his feet and braced himself, wide eyed, clenching his teeth.

The sound of the passenger side rear view mirror snapping off as it hit the edge of the railing was like a gunshot to the frozen crew... and then silence. Time stood still as the car flew through the air, slowly arching downward and forward, directly in line and underneath the double wide bridge above. It cleared the concrete by not more than two inches on either side, and was now heading for a large sandbar that had built up over the streets in the years since the big earthquake shut this area down. Kait gasped loudly and held her breath, wincing as it looked like they were on a collision course for the peak of the mound.

Thor already had his foot on the brakes, bringing the nose down in mid-air by arresting the inertia of the car's flywheel, as the back tires hooked the top of the sand and the car glided onto the backside of the mound, bouncing only a little more than a foot off the ground before some steering control was regained. Sandy mud flew everywhere and completely blackened the windshield in a matter of seconds. Thor held his course, turning into each fishtail as it happened, and after a few seconds the car came to a full stop. Kait was already climbing halfway out the window, scouting the area and reaching around the front to wipe off the windshield.

"HELL YES!!" Uruz yelled with a crackling voice, wide eyed in disbelief.

"Shhh..." Thor cautioned, pointing up at the large overpass above. "They're probably just starting to assemble, but we better play it safe."

"Safe?" Tyr asked, obviously more than a little upset.

"Hey, a lot of math went into that," Thor insisted, "not to mention, I paid some friends of mine quite a bit to lower the ridge and make sure this incline was clear of rocks and debris... You don't think I would've just winged that do you?"

Kait climbed back in and spoke sarcastically, but relieved. "I think you're having a cranial-rectal inversion, that's what I think!"

Tyr and Uruz laughed, finally able to breathe normally. Uruz slapped Thor on the shoulder to get his attention. "Do it again!" he yelled like a giddy child.

"I'll be driving the next one, thank you very much," Tyr interrupted. "Ground control to Monkey One, do you have a plan to get the rest of the way? It won't be long before this area starts getting a little hostile!"

"Relax and enjoy the ride, I've got the rest of it mapped out to the inch," Thor assured them, driving slowly down toward a small mudslide between two buildings. "Trust me."

"I fucking hate it when you say that," Kait snapped playfully, then started strapping on her shoulder harness and ammo clips out of her opened briefcase. Uruz started assembling something that looked more like a space cannon with a shoulder strap, while Tyr and Thor safety checked the hardware they were already wearing concealed beneath their suits. Thor pulled a small disc from his breast pocket and slid it into a small slot on the face of the car's navigation console.

"Takes care of all the usual suspects, plus, look what we get to watch in the meantime," Thor announced, as the computer went quickly through a re-formatting routine designed by Dagaz to keep the hardware completely untraceable, as well as make it user friendly right from the start for its new owner's purposes. "Beginning right...about...here!" he pointed, as the monitor suddenly switched over to display a map, moving in real time around a cursor in the center, mimicking the cars movements to the letter. "Pretty cool, huh?" Thor asked, swerving back and forth while pointing at the cursor, grinning like a kid with a new toy. "This was another Dagaz original I was able to coax out of him yesterday. Looks like he did a pretty good job..."

"He wrote this whole thing last night?" Kait asked.

"Not exactly. This is the map Jerrick's guys got me, done in tidal charting language on an old shipboard navigation program designed for use when integrating GPS with side scan sonar and radar. All he did was update the language for use with this car's modern equipment, and input the barrier data, and *voila*," he gestured flamboyantly, "our ticket to a hassle free afternoon!"

Kait flinched, smiling, but holding her hands over her ears. "La la la la la WHY THE HELL DID YOU HAVE TO USE *THOSE* WORDS!!!"

Okay, okay, I just have one question Einstein," Tyr interrupted facetiously. "How are we getting home?"

Thor smiled, knowing full well that after they made delivery of the nav computer, the flywheel generator would be pulled, along with its state of the art charging and solar power systems for use in underground facilities, as well as hydroponics farms across Jerrick's new grid, and there would be no more car. They would need other means to traverse the extremely hostile industrial district, then central, on the long trek north. One down, two to go.... "Trust me."

CHAPTER 6: CAUSE/ EFFECT

He had been staring at the monitor of his computer for so long he didn't even notice his cigarette had burned down to the filter and it was nearly dark outside his penthouse window. Yes or no? Accept or decline? Click no and everything remains the same; stagnant, corrupt, loyal to the machine, predictable and safe. Click yes and become wealthy beyond imagination; the server of justice, killer of giants... and hunted.

He had been in the shadows for so long while perfectly executing phase after phase of his corporate level vendetta, that he had almost lost track of the "why." It started as retribution for 10 years of loyal service ignored as soon as it became more convenient to use him as a Patsy for yet another global scam they had no monetary reason to have to pull off. It seemed the yuppies at the top of the ladder weren't rich enough, and actually needed *more* millions to get by, so they developed a quick, but unscrupulous method of skimming residual funds from every shareholder in a "maintenance" effort, and then billing them for the service, thereby laundering the stolen money... right through the department of John R.

Reid, Public Relations and Chief Financial Officer of Vector Beta Securities, Inc., one of the largest Internet security contractors in the world.

He could scarcely remember the days of being the "Golden Boy," the smiling "Yes man" doing PR work on TV for the booming company. His name and face had been drug through so much mire and public litigation that he had to move three times and change his identity on both paper and implant. Two plastic surgeries later, and people finally stopped pointing at him on the street and talking behind his back. Lesser men would have folded under the pressure they put him through.

Poor John was never even aware they were doing it. His public outburst of genuine surprise at the first of the inquiries may have been the only thing that saved him from an equally public lynching, but his standing with the public didn't last a week. Things got real complicated, real fast. Society loves nothing more than to see the blood of its heroes, and the evidence they framed him with was insurmountable. He was allowed, under a curtain of deceit, to keep his position in the company in exchange for his cooperation and his silence. The drawback? He was now James S. Stanton. The irony? James S. Stanton had *them* by the shorthairs. He had finally exacted his revenge and he couldn't even take credit for it.

Yes or no? Accept or decline? To be, or not to be? Complicated? Shit, things have never been simpler. He gasped as he let gravity take his hand's weight to complete the keystroke. The transfer started, confirmation appeared, and it was done. No way to stop it now... *bask in the moment.* He was overcome with primitive emotion, but not fear. It was simple, like before. His heart pounded, and he felt alive, like before....

He closed his eyes with his hand still on the keyboard and moaned; the picture still vivid in his mind, but losing warmth. He cried out loud as he could almost hear her voice cry out, and his right arm came up high, in a fist. He slammed it down on the small computer, smashing it into a dozen pieces and stared out the window across the sea of lights at the insomniacal flow of the city. Now he felt it. Now he felt alive. But something wasn't right. He needed more. He needed her....

CHAPTER 7: OLD WORLD WITHIN

Jerrick's place never ceased to be amazing, nor was it the same one visit to the next. Within the structurally reinforced walls of what used to be one of the west end's largest consumer retail malls was now growing an oasis of hydroponically nurtured crops of every kind. There were stores upon stores, full to the ceiling with every kind of food bearing, or medicinal herb producing plant known to man, running with a seemingly never ending array of interconnected irrigation, lighting, and airflow.

The whole mall was set up logistically for peak efficiency, and required little more than gravity to move the water from one job to the next, as there were catwalks built up in each room keeping plants in groups at over 100 different phases of growth within each room. Toward the extreme ends of the process were livestock annexes where the many types of farm animals were kept, living off of certain plants, while providing CO_2 and fertilizer to the others. A small, but technologically advanced control and battery room run by the nav. computers from the cars, several high efficiency flywheels, and a skeleton crew of well-armed workers were all that were necessary to run the show, but this place was also home to a great many friends and family of Jerrick's, and was usually booming with life.

What started as a way to feed his crew and their allies without depending on outside sources turned into one of the most stable and thriving businesses in the underground. Jerrick's iron clad security and loyal, family run infrastructure was more than enough to ensure they wouldn't be attacked by rival clans or nomads. Quite simply, no one wanted to damage this source of food, nor were they capable of running the multi-organizational operation themselves, for fear that they would mess it up and bring the whole west end back around into the state of gangland chaos and depravity that existed right after the great quake cut off all the old Alki Underground shipping passages.

His story spread, and some of the more organized clans and gangs from the other sectors adopted some of the same agricultural techniques to supply their own, but for the most part, as the underground population centers grew closer to extinction, it was still survival by whatever means arose; smash and grab, pillage and plunder, or try to skim from the upper crust without getting caught and exterminated. They had to face it, in a totally toxic environment, nearly devoid of natural sunlight, with putrid air and even worse water, it took a biological genius like Jamaican born Jerrick to keep the whole thing producing timely crops, year after year, and a man of his level of diplomacy to govern the results. Hell, if the underground would see reprieve in his lifetime, Jerrick would be King.

Krey and Jerrick had a lot of respect for each other, and were as close as brothers. It was not the least bit uncommon for the two of them to wander around the facility talking about whatever for hours on end. Tonight, something was different. Kait could not remember the last time Thor looked so serious. They were about 50 yards away, and up on a catwalk over some tomato plants, but she could see by his nervous glances that something wasn't right.

Jerrick hadn't stopped talking for quite a while, and now Thor was staring straight down, while bracing his weight on the handrails and tapping his right foot quickly and steadily. He did this whenever he was deep in thought, trying to solve something.

"What do you suppose this is all about?" Kait asked, nudging Tyr, who was preoccupied with the same nervous fidgety dance as Thor.

"Something doesn't feel right," Tyr said softly, peering up at her sideways with one eye showing from behind his long, straight hair. "Did Dagaz tell you why he sat this one out?"

"No."

"Something doesn't feel right," he repeated.

The old food court was now a very classy dining room and gathering hall with a stage. Uruz spent most of his time here when they were on these trips. Since North Clan family were some of the only visitors not required to check in weapons, Uruz would hang here, under the guise of *added security*, and frolic in the eclectic splendor of the best food in the underground, bar none.

At any given moment, there were over 10 different stations cooking, packaging, canning, bottling, dehydrating, or otherwise preparing for travel, fruits, vegetables, jerked meat, canned soups, hashes, and dozens of prepared whole meals for short range delivery, as well as military style MRE's for medium length storage, and dehydrated, vacuum sealed meals for the long haul. He found a reason to sample them all.

Everyone here was like family to the North Clan, so when they saw him coming, they joked and delivered, no questions asked.

"Hey! Pillocks! How 'bout some steak that tastes a little less like ASS?!!!" Uruz yelled, holding his plate up in the air, as if to send it back to the kitchen. Several people, who obviously didn't know him, looked his way, astonished, then over at the pair of Rasta's walking purposefully toward him, mumbling to each other while locking and loading their personal arsenals. The bystanders started to get worried, and ducked back a few feet, just behind a stone knee wall with leafy plants growing out of the top.

Uruz lightly tossed his plate on the table in front of him, careful not to spill it, but going for the "warbley coin" effect. Before it stopped warbling, he had pulled his enormous rifle/ grenade launcher from behind his back, removed the strap from over his head and shoulder, and slammed it on the table in front of him.

"Dat bes not be all ye got wif ye, Mon," yelled the one on the left, still marching toward him as he flipped his long, black dreadlocks out of his face with his neck muscles and pulled back the slide on his hand cannon, drawing down on Uruz.

"Corse not, Mon! Wuz plannen on shootin' ye wif me Johnson, YES, I!!!" Uruz mocked in crescendo as he pulled a dark bottle out from behind his back. He was making an excruciatingly contorted face while holding the neck with one hand and aimed it right at their faces with the bottom pressed into his crotch, when the cork shot off with a loud BANG!!! The cork whizzed right between their heads, and they all burst out laughing, exchanging hugs and handshakes.

"A bottle of my brother's newest mead, as I promised!" Uruz extended the bottle to the eager men, "WASSAIL! This one has a big kick and a little sparkle..." He gestured with his chin to the incident behind them with the cork, "as I'm sure you noticed."

"Tanks, bra," said Jaimisson, the younger one, as he reached out for the bottle, sliding his 9mm automatic back into its shoulder holster without losing eye contact.

"Any time! And don't even THINK about taking THIS back!!!" he exclaimed at Joyce, lunging out over the table to retrieve his half eaten plate of food before the older brother could reach it. "Seriously, my friends, that was the best steak I've had in an age. Thank you so *very* much," he added, humbly, while cutting another large bite with surgeon's care. "So," he inquired through a mouthful of food, gesturing at his plate, and then down the eastern hall, toward the livestock annexes, "who gave up the ghost?"

"Now ya know that's no polite, now, Uruz 'Tha Bull,' it were Bess, if ya needs ta know... it were Bess," Joyce answered while looking down at the floor with sad eyes.

"Vaya con Dios, big girl," Uruz saluted with his next bite on the fork, gesturing again at the eastern hall that branched out to the livestock annexes. "We honor your sacrifice. Please excuse me... Me barriet ugum le Al!" he added in Gaelic.

"Yeah, Mon, you sure *have* had too much to drink, now you're talkin' Gaelic to a dead cow," Jaimisson teased, nudging his brother and laughing hysterically.

"Got us dry ice packed on board this time?" Uruz asked, suddenly serious, and looking to roll up. "We almost lost half the beef because of an unexpected detour last time we went by water...."

"Got it," they both said, almost in stereo.

Uruz pulled his small, belt-clip managed palm radio off his waist by its thumb hole, held it up to the side of his face, and said calmly, "Monkey Two to Monkey One. Cut yo jibba jabba fools! This ship is ready to sail! These fine lads have packed us on ice!!!"

"20 minutes or so, bro, make sure you have the charts set up for Inside Sound/ via Deception Pass, sounds like Inside Lake Union is gonna be too hot. We might have a problem with Central. It's too soon to tell and too risky 'til we know. Besides, we need time to discuss a few things inside the tightest ring, I'll be there in a minute... Out."

"Roger that. How 'bout the rest of you? You with Thor?" Uruz asked.

"We're on our way... Out." Kait keyed in.

"No, we're on our way IN... Out." Tyr joked.

"Piss off..."

CHAPTER 8: VITAM PIRATAE LEIGO

Standing purposefully out on the end of the small schooner's retro-wooden bowsprit, Thor found himself engulfed in a moment of solace rarely afforded anyone in this troubled world. He was undeniably at home here. In this setting, in this singular purpose, he was home. His ancestors were Vikings, and it was obvious to the casual observer that this was simply in his blood.

He seemed to have a deeper understanding of the sea than of land, and intuitively knew his way around boats without ever needing so much as an explanation of any of the tools and equipment needed to handle a small craft in even the most adverse weather. If he had his way, there would always be a reason to launch a vessel and sail off on a journey, leaving behind all the troubles of this inflamed world. All that was left to want during moments such as these was the freedom to wander, but wandering without purpose, it would seem, was just plain suicide.

As if navigation wasn't tough enough with regard to currents, tides, depth, changing weather conditions in a constantly changing topography, there was the Coast Guard to consider. The very second one strayed outside the innermost shipping passages and tried for open waters, they would pop up on screen and be visited in a decisively hostile manner within minutes. If you couldn't show immediate documentation of purpose and current manifests, you would be boarded and towed, or blasted out of the water. Gone were the days of pleasure sailing, recreational fishing, diving and obscurity.... Due to the terrorist bombardment of our weakest regulated boarder, the coastal shipping ports, the government stepped in and put to a martial freeze any unauthorized activity resulting in a ship entering any port along either coastline.

There were limits to the accuracy they were able to maintain in keeping track of unregistered local skiffs, usually doing maintenance runs, tows, or charity runs. Their methods in this spectrum of the grid seemed to be based loosely on repetition analysis and pattern recognition software. This posed a possible solution by way of a complex series of feints and false starts, until the vessel was simply confused for another one of its class or treated as a lost cause, not worth the manpower or money to assist or investigate. Then they would simply fall into position in a shipping lane, and try not to attract any attention.

Jerrick loved it when luck of the draw gave him pros like Thor and his crew to pilot a shipment, with just as much of their own cargo on board to lose, headed to the same port as his big delivery... Some call it fate, he saw it as a chance for mutual gain. This way, The North Clan got a ride home, Jerrick got an important delivery taken care of, and he and the Clan could now settle their business with the delivery of just one more car.

The freedom to wander.... Had he not felt so soberingly upon his own shoulders the weight of those who depended on him more than they wanted to admit, he would have, on several occasions, turned his rudder to port and put the setting sun on his horizon for as long as his luck would hold. To have but a taste of true freedom, this kind of freedom, would be worth any risk of self one might fear. Not so when it comes to family loyalty and duty.

To this master alone are we all slaves. In this duty do we find our purpose, but not our freedom. Freedom is found only at the loss or abandonment of all else we hold dear. Still standing, head high and chest out, on the forward watch position on the bowsprit, with the wind and spray blasting him directly in the face, he cried proudly, his tears camouflaged perfectly by the water building up and naturally streaming sideways across his face. The freedom to wander? It would have to wait at least one more lifetime....

Through his oversized, antique, but very powerful rifle spotting scope, he was able to see for miles. They usually planned these trips for days covered by heavy fog to help hide their position from other ships, but truthfully the bigger concern on a clear day, especially in the narrower passages wasn't ships at all, but skiff pirates. Some had made an art form out of sniping as many crew members as possible from shore in the narrowest channels, usually in a current-fed inlet, before a bend or sand spit, effectively setting the craft adrift, then approaching the crippled craft with inflatable dinghies, heaving its cargo overboard and taking off with it on all-terrain vehicles.

Because there were still cases of misidentification, desperation, or arrogance leading to terminally bad decision making resulting in an attack on a North Clan skiff, they always proceeded heavily armed, and at high alert, but it had been a very long time since problems with anyone other than the Coast Guard had cost them a shipment. *All the more reason to be cautious....*

Tyr, now standing beside his younger brother, horn of mead appropriately in hand, spoke out calmly. "We've got the course you and Jerrick laid out augmented with some great smoke and mirrors... should get us home by nightfall if everything goes smooth," he added, quasi-facetiously, "You know..."

"...we could save a lot of time by cutting east through Lake Union?" Thor interrupted.

"What the hell is going on, bro?" Tyr insisted, putting his arm around Thor's neck and pulling him close in brotherly fashion.

"Let's go below." Thor gestured with his chin toward the pilot house door, hanging ajar in the cool breeze and gently thumping in rhythm at the over-painted jamb as the bow of the ample craft kissed at the small waves being sliced at beneath its hull.

The two stepped off the bowsprit and started toward the pilot house. Tyr gestured to Uruz as well, and he nodded, locking in their course into autopilot, then falling in behind them, leaving one hand on the wheel peg as long as possible, and staring back at it before reaching the small spiral stairwell leading below, as if he was afraid he would never see it again. They made their way down to the narrow landing to join Kait, who was already sitting at a table at the base of the stairs, going over some paper charts with a concerned look on her face. "Well," she shrugged, "we've never went so far out of our way to avoid someone before.... I just hope there's something in it for us, cause this ain't gonna be easy! It looks like part of the shoreline along the southern channel of the inside passage has changed dramatically!"

"Here's the long and veiny..." Thor started to announce, pounding once on the table as if he had a judge's gavel with his gaze slightly averted, obviously a little embarrassed to have to speak of this at all.

He laid it all on the line.... How he had intentionally interfered with a Central shipment, then allowed himself to be chased to another rival's territory with the intention of rekindling an old war to weaken both sides who were simultaneously challenging the North Clan's business relations on multiple fronts, as well as possibly uniting against the Clan in an all-out war. To divide them immediately seemed prudent, if done *very* discreetly. Through his sources, however, Jerrick had caught wind that after one preliminary attempt by Central to retaliate against Cane, a temporary truce had been called. Odd timing for a sit-down. Odd timing unless someone else had some new information that would change the face of the conflict....

Then there was all of Dagaz's strange behavior. They were family, and to even bridge this topic in any serious light was unthinkable. Yet who was missing? Who was always missing? He was always a trusted brother and right in the middle of anything the Clan had going on, but for some unknown reason, they had all noticed a change in his demeanor lately. More and more he seemed to disagree with the direction the Clan was taking, but rather than voice any alternate choices or solutions, he would just seem to sarcastically poke at the rest of the Family, then take his leave.

On several occasions Tyr, the sort of unofficial gravity of the brotherhood, tried to sit aside with him and counsel, but to no avail. Dagaz was as hard headed and neurotic as they come. He would choose when and where he needed to vent, and on who, but God forbid one should dare to offer him a solution or point out a problem on their own.... He was starting to alienate himself from each of them, one at a time, as if he had something planned. *But full blown betrayal? Inconceivable.*

Chapter 9: Predator

He took the off ramp leading to his parking garage on manual control and about twice as fast as he usually drove it. He was changing fast. The timid pushover who had made all the right choices in life and took all the right precautions to ensure that nothing ever happened that he would regret was dead. Murdered by his own id, he was becoming stronger by the day… but there was a price… a demand… a thirst.

He slowed slightly as he approached the security booth for his parking garage. "Hey Fritz!" he called out at the guard in the window; his left arm outstretched, palm up, to allow the man in the booth to scan his wrist with a small cordless wand.

"Good evening, Mr. Stanton," the automated voice called out in an official, yet somehow relaxing tone.

"Go ahead, James," Fritz nodded, raising the stop-arm to let him through. Stanton sped off, breaking traction just long enough to let out a cocky squeak from his tires as he B-lined for his favorite spot. When he pulled up, he blatantly double parked, nearly full straddling the spot to his immediate left that a woman in another car was just taxiing around the row to park in. He looked right at her, but made no attempt to correct the problem. Instead, he smiled as he got out of his car, armed his alarm, then wiped the BMW logo on the hood to a mirror polish with his sleeve.

She yelled at him through her car's PA speaker on the way by, somewhat afraid to roll down the window with night approaching, *"What the hell, asshole?!! Keep it on auto, you prick! You're too stupid to go manual!"*

"How's this for manual, bitch!" he yelled back, still smiling devilishly, and opened his trench coat, yanking out his semi-erect penis and waving it in her general direction. She swerved widely to the left and the right, seeing this through the rear-view mirror, then sped off, disgusted, nearly clipping the entire row of rear bumpers. "Yeah, you *better* run..." Stanton snickered to himself with a new expression on his face; one of sadistic self approval and satisfaction. This slowly morphed into a sinister grin as he strutted proudly to the elevator door.

His penthouse door slid quietly open on its tracks, and he entered. "Lights!" he yelled, and squatted, unnecessarily clapping twice as the lights came on, to amuse himself further. He flipped on the power to his computer, pulled the blinds to see the night lights emerging on the city, and lit up a cigarette, exhaling a long breath while leaning against the window jamb, gazing outside and waiting for his computer to finish booting up. He took a deep drag, held it for a few seconds, then blew it straight into the enormous pane of glass he was staring through, momentarily entrancing himself as the smoke billowed out 360 degrees in a great sideways mushroom cloud, putting a temporary haze on the breathtaking view. He took a couple casual steps back, his arms now up above his head, reaching for the ceiling, then locking his fingers together behind his head, cigarette still hanging out of his mouth, and uttered the voice command, "Big screen!"

As smoothly as the smoke was dissipating from view across the large pane of glass, the same screen that was already showing on his desktop monitor came into view across the entire width of the window, visible only from the inside, still leaving a view of the outside to either side of the screen through equal sized windows that spanned the rest of his lush living room.

"Street cams," he spoke calmly, something already changing in his tone. A menu popped up, overlaid on the large screen with the city flickering and moving as a real-time background. There were over twenty different locations listed. Some were identifiable intersections or topside landmarks, but many had names too ambiguous for anyone but him to identify. He was sitting up on the edge of his desk, reaching around the screen and manipulating several of the selections into split screen views when the phone rang, chiming through on his elaborate surround sound system.

"Answer!" he ordered. A click echoed as if in slow motion through the room. *Or was it through his head?* No one ever called him at home. Never. *No one even has this number,* he thought. Unless this was a random wrong number, they were onto him a lot faster than he had anticipated....

"Hello?"

"We know it was you.... You're a dead man!" the deep and dominating, but obviously mechanically altered voice bellowed anonymously at him from everywhere and nowhere at the same time, made twice as menacing by Stanton's state-of-the-art sound system... and then they hung up with a click that resonated in the room and in the depths of his head for a few seconds before gradually becoming the slamming of a heavy prison door to his recollection.

He had anticipated having to vanish into a haze of paperwork again, just not so soon. Almost everything was in place, liquidated beyond recovery by anyone not bearing his implant ID, but he had a growing and unresolved need that was holding sway over all other business in his life, and she was finally starting to reveal a pattern. Sooner or later, they all reveal a pattern to him; an invitation he knows *must* be intentional.

He sped up his layout on the computer, if only just a little, *almost* unshaken by the threat, but mostly just distracted by his current obsession. There were now nine individual views split evenly on the screen, all of various places in the underground... all of populated areas from discreet vantage points. He had absolutely no intention of anyone finding even one of his high resolution remote cameras. They were simply too incriminating. The signal they sent back to his laptop, as state-of-the-art as it was, would be as easy to trace as following a trail of bread crumbs. He could be triangulated as the receiver no matter where he was, even if he wasn't actively using that cam.

His ulterior motives were apparent in his designs long before his current preoccupation began taking hold of him. Being predominantly his own design contribution to the branch of Physical Building Security at his work, he had already made these things smaller than a crayon, and camouflaged as everything from a protruding nail head to the end of a twig on a bush at knee level. The only real danger to the indiscriminate use of his applications were random transmitter detection attempts, or "bug sweeps," to which there was no real defense except not providing anyone with a reason to bother. Two of the cameras showing isolated areas outside night clubs near the Border District had his particular interest tonight.

He watched intently in real-time for a while, laughing out loud as a young couple coming out of one of the area's tougher bars, nervously looking behind themselves as they fled, tripped and sprawled onto the populated sidewalk, causing quite a commotion. Too bad he couldn't get sound from this particular device, he smiled. He remembered planting this one in a tree-like vine, grasping its way throughout a lopsided chain link fence across the street and to the right about seven feet off the ground, to take advantage of wide angle 180 degree and dual side views. This bar was one of his favorite spots to find her. He had found her here before.... *Now he was starting to remember!*

"Number seven, review! Start, 8:PM. Reverse at 4X speed!" He watched intently, suddenly queasy with his own carelessness. He watched the large screen for a few more seconds, then planted one arm on the middle of his desk and slid across on his hip to the computer side, leaning forward toward the small monitor in "business stance," as he liked to call it, and crushed out his cigarette in the shiny brass ashtray to the right, never taking his eye off the square on the bottom-right. "Number seven, view spread, wide angle, zoom 150 percent!" He leaned in just a little closer, staring closely at the left side of the screen at what appeared to be the corner of the building the bar was in.

Suddenly, there it was! A woman came flying up off the ground from around the corner in the darkest part of the alley, off balance, with the unmistakable silhouette of a man attached to her side, grabbing her hair and guiding her, then he was gone and she was walking backwards down the sidewalk. He flinched and looked away. "Stop seven!" he yelled. He didn't want to see anymore, this would cheapen things... It would cheapen her. "Delete seven," he said somberly, still looking away. He heard the beep prompting him to confirm. "Delete seven!" he repeated forcibly. He typed a mad series of commands and the seventh window in his grid disappeared entirely. Out on the street across from the bar, miles away, a small plume of smoke rose up from the vine where the camera used to be installed.

He was almost done shutting down the last of the windows when suddenly he saw her. Her long blonde hair flowed like a goddess as she turned around to say something back to someone inside the club, then she was gone, off of the left side of the screen. "Number eight, view spread! Wide angle!" He slammed his fist down on the desk as the whole left side of the screen became obscured by the front bumper of a car, allowing him only the slightest glance of her hair whisping out of sight to the left, and the back of her knee high leather biker boot, as her heel kissed him goodbye... "FUCK!" He slammed his fist down again, feeling it all start welling up inside him again. "God dammit-SHIT!... FUCKIN' BITCH! GOD DAMMIT!...FUCK!!!" he screamed until he was hoarse, spinning around twice, out of control, and throwing his chair randomly across the floor toward the front door as he lost his balance in every possible way.

He sat on the floor, sobbing, and reached in his breast pocket for another smoke. He lit the filter accidentally, then as he let it drop from his slobbering lips to lay smoldering on the floor next to a pile of broken glass from a small picture frame, he grew very silent, staring miles away through unwiped tears. He would find her. He would teach her. He would regain control.

CHAPTER 10: INTUITION

Kait hardly said a word the whole way back. After they got the bread truck that Jerrick set up for them unloaded just into the airlock-style foyer of the North Clan stronghold and waved the driver off, she slipped off without saying anything to anyone. Although this actually bothered Thor just a little, she didn't do it to play games or make him worry, that was simply beneath her. She was having a genuine problem with the whole Dagaz issue. This was compounded further by the fact that he wasn't home when they got back. She simply couldn't stand to hear any more speculation about the man who, until very recently, had been a brother to them all... beyond suspicion... beyond perpetration.

She could not conceive of what may be going on with him, but she sensed something wasn't right. She sensed this for quite a while and kept it to herself, not wanting to believe it was anything big. Then there was this whole matter with Central. It was starting to remind her of when she was young. Things felt so uneasy toward the end. There were no identifiable warning signs. No flashing red light, no booming voice of warning to pull back and defend. Just an uneasy feeling... *like this one.*

She thought that going to see a show at her usual Friday night hangout in the Border District would pacify her a little, but instead it kind of made it worse. All night she had the gnawing sensation of being watched. Not just the usual hot-chick-being-ogled-at-a-show kind of watched, but something else... something altogether wrong. She even left a little early and took a different route back up north than she usually did, just in case.

The sensation intensified as she left the club and started down the sidewalk, her hard soled leather boots clacking on the sidewalk echoing 'til they sounded like two sets of feet, and the cool night air blowing through her hair magnified the tingling up her spine and the back of her neck. It wasn't like her to get freaked out over nothing, so she kept a vigilant eye all around her to make sure she didn't have a tail. Thor was going to meet her at the old Qwest Field for a "meeting of the minds," over some gladiator football in about an hour, but this was one time she wished he was along for the entire walk.

———————

She met Dagaz shortly before her entire family was killed, and even then it was as if he came to her on purpose; on some level aware that she would need them all in the end, and, more personally, where she was in her own philosophical journey. It was this "coincidence" that had always left an unspoken bond between them, never requiring analyzation or further discussion, but simply understood.

He approached her outside a street deli where she squatted, picking through the spoils of a scuffle with two attackers that started just up the road and came to a stop right here. Dagaz saw the whole thing from about a block away, but to his surprise, before he could get 10 feet closer to assist, she had both of them sprawled on the ground, unconscious, and was going through their pockets and stashing their weapons and valuables in her coat. He approached, smiling, with his hands open and out to the sides at about hip level. She had already glanced at him once as he was crossing the street and so far saw no reason to exchange looks with him. "Can I help you?" she asked, sarcastically.

"Nice work.... Kait, is it?"

"That's right. And who might you be?" she replied, still not looking up at him as she busily finished rifling through the second man's front cargo pocket on his pants. She counted semi-silently through about twenty dollars' worth of small bills, and shoved all of it, along with a small cache of coins into a leather pouch hanging from her belt and stood up, whipping the hair from her eyes with a sideways motion of her neck and looked at him squarely in the eyes.

"Name's Dagaz." He offered his hand to her, and she shook it, nearly making him flinch from pain. He had a very effeminate way about him, almost as if he was gay, yet there was something very non-pretentious about him. Though he was very non-threatening, physically, being all of 5' 10", yet no more than 130 lbs., soaking wet, he projected some sort of inner strength that she felt she could confide in. She intuitively felt he could be trusted, and he seemed familiar to her, like they had met before. He was wearing an amulet that looked like an Icelandic version of Thor's Hammer with a Celtic Trinity knot in the center, something she grew up seeing a lot of among the members of her rival, but kindred clan to the north. Then there was the Norse connotation in his nickname..."Dagaz," the Futhark rune for prosperity among the Vikings. She could immediately tell that he was North Clan, though she didn't recall seeing him with Thor before.

"How do you know my name?" she prodded, starting to walk away from the scene, but gesturing for him to follow. He accepted, looking back a couple times to make sure the men on the sidewalk weren't coming around yet.

"I know who you are. Thor speaks very highly of you," he grinned, one eye catching her stare from under his wide rimmed, fedora-style leather hat.

"You know Thorsson Krey!!?" she tested, smiling widely, "prove it!"

"Aaaah, hmmm, lets see..." He scratched his chin between his thumb and forefinger, playfully. "Wow! This is actually harder than I thought," he added, glancing up at her while she grinned playfully back at him. "I got it!" he blurted, and started digging through his pants pockets. He produced an old piece of letter sized paper that was folded to pocket size somewhat randomly, and yellowed from age. He began to carefully unfold it, looking at her and nodding with a cheesy grin as if he had a rare treat in store for her.

She smiled widely in anticipation, even though she had a pretty good idea what he was about to show her. "I think I know what that is..."

"Oh, yeah?" he probed, holding back the readable side from her until the right moment while reviewing its contents himself.

"Yeah, if it's what I think it is, my copy is in even rougher shape," she smiled. The writing was revered by Thor as not only a philosophical gem of enormous value to anyone involved in the martial arts, but also because it was one of only a few surviving pieces of his family legacy, passed down from his father's father, when a small group of them were forced into hiding shortly before the great quake. He left it, and a few other important artifacts, including the recipe for his then famous "Allfather's Mead," with his brother Ragnar, who stayed behind to watch over the remaining family, including Thor's mother.

Around the time the government attempted to corral its people into population centers for easier control, the entire "blacklist" was being executed. "The Powers That Be" did not want to be challenged by any charismatic uprising at such a volatile time and were ready to do whatever was needed to prevent this from happening. The Clan headed, at first, for an area near the Alaskan/ Canadian border with the intention of drawing others to their cause and living the way God intended, while making whatever difference they could from there. The small band of radicals were never seen again, but rumors and tales surfaced from time to time of this "Alliance For Gaia" from the far north, a group of environmental warriors branded "terrorists" by the government, striking the heart of the industrial beast over and over, with repeated success and a growing following. Every time a new story reached the mainland, it brought a proud smile to the orphans of the North Clan.

The original paper, still in Ragnar's possession after all these years, bore the crest of the North Clan, the same crest that Thor proudly brandished on his arm as a tattoo over his right bicep: a circular pattern of ravens surrounding drinking horns that are arranged to form a trinity knot in the center, with Futhark runes in a circular band around the outside forming, in Norse, what translates into, "Know Thyself, But Know That We Are Among You." The rest of the text, copied, but handwritten all in capital letters, read:

ACTIVE MEDITATION (OR "CENTERING")

DURING COMBAT, OR AT REST, DISTRACTING WAVES OF ANXIETY OR OTHER FORMS OF MAD, MIND RACING CAN BE EASILY ELIMINATED BY

SIMPLY AND CONSCIOUSLY REDUCING ALL THOUGHT PATTERNS TO THE "INSTINCTIVE" LEVEL; FULLY AWARE, BUT VOID OF INTENT, THEREBY ELIMINATING CONSCIOUSNESS OF SELF, AND WITH IT ANY DISTRACTING TENDENCIES TOWARDS OVER-ANALYZATION ONE MIGHT POSSESS, WHILE HEIGHTENING EXTRA-SENSORY PERCEPTION AS WELL AS OVERALL AWARENESS, THUS LOWERING REACTION TIME AND CREATING AN ENVIRONMENT CONDUSIVE TO THE EXCHANGE OF ENERGY. TRUE FOCUS ALSO COMES FROM THIS STATE; ASSERTED, BUT NOT <u>INTENDED</u>. IF THE ACT OF FOCUSING IS REFLECTED ON BY THE MIND CONSCIOUS OF SELF, THIS PRODUCES 'CONCENTRATION' (WHICH IS NOT THE SAME THING, AND IS, MORE OFTEN THAN NOT, COUNTER-PRODUCTIVE). IT IS ESSENTIAL TO KEEP THIS CENTER WHILE MOVING, BUT WITHOUT CONTINUED CONSCIOUS PRACTICE, EXPECT TO HAVE TO 'RE-CENTER' AND 'RE-CENTER' OFTEN AS YOU BECOME AWARE OF OLD PATTERNS OF THOUGHT TAKING OVER. EVENTUALLY, EVEN JUST <u>BEING</u> CENTERED BECOMES INSTINCTIVE. THIS IS NOT ABSCENCE OF THOUGHT, BUT SIMPLY ABSCENCE OF <u>CONSCIOUSNESS</u> OF THOUGHT. (THINKING ABOUT THINKING IS A MENTAL TRAP MUCH LIKE TWO MIRRORS FACING EACH OTHER...) FEEL. IDENTIFY AND ACCEPT THE FLOW OF YOUR OPPONENT'S ENERGY. ACCEPT ALL SURROUNDING ENERGY AND PULL IT TO YOUR CENTER. THE RESULT IS THAT THIS CENTER THEN BECOMES THE CENTER OF YOUR UNIVERSE, QUITE LITERALLY. THIS IS POSSIBLE BECAUSE AN INFINITE CIRCLE ALSO HAS INFINITE

CENTERS. THIS IS THE TRUE BALANCE. TRUE CALMNESS. WHEN ROOTED THROUGH THE ENERGY OF THE EARTH, IT MANIFESTS THE IMMOVABLE AXIS *AROUND* WHICH ALL HOSTILITY MUST TRAVEL.

Thor had given her a copy of this when she was nothing more than a teenager with an attitude problem. He was several years her senior, and had always been fond of her, kind of like a sister, but kind of something else. Having come of age fairly close to each other, they grew up aware of each other's trials and tribulations, and Thor, a martial artist since childhood, had taken a particularly keen interest in her combat training. You just didn't last long on these streets without a serious edge, and though she certainly was never lacking in physical or mental toughness and fighting prowess, he considered it his personal duty to train or at least impart upper level skills and techniques upon all his inner circle of friends and family.

She was a major concern of his ever since her family died. He vowed to look after her, and made it a mission to train her to a degree that brought her to rival his own skills. He was always worried about her. So much so that it concerned her that he might know something she doesn't. For the most part, she tried to just remain honored and flattered by his over-protectiveness, though at times it bugged the shit out of her. It was torture to him as well.

He wasn't just that way with her, it was with everyone he cared about. It was as if something out of his control, and really, really bad happened, possibly in another life, to all the people he cared the most about, and he was powerless to do anything about it. Sometimes it nearly consumed him. The irony was that she was the one who had all the reason in the world to feel that way, but was comparatively laid-back. It had only been three short years since her family was torn apart right before her very eyes, and already she was as socially adjusted as could possibly be expected in a place like this....

She was almost there, hopping up and down through the street-wide layer of concrete blockades, then the eight-footer outlining the perimeter of lower-level street access around what used to be a ground level parking lot, and the stadium itself, along with a dozen out buildings, utility sheds, storage facilities, and the like. It was far too confusing of a layout, from an engineering standpoint, to seal up entirely. Just like most of the upper crust, it would never be 'rat proof.'

She followed his instructions to the letter, and ended up at what looked like an un-screened culvert, about 4 feet in diameter, with about one foot deep of semi stagnant, chunk ridden, fly infested filth oozing out and into the adjacent drainage ditch that smelled like it came from the rotting carcasses of a thousand syphilitic lepers who lived out their final days on a diet of nothing but bad eggs and humus. "No bloody way!" she exclaimed out loud, seriously wishing she hadn't bent down to try and look through it.

"Yeah, that's what I thought!" Thor boomed out from right above her, sitting on top of the retaining wall, legs dangling as if he had been there for a while, even though she was sure she looked up right before she bent down.

"Holy shit, Thor! You scared the bujeesus out of me!" she smiled up at him, left foot across the small stream, right foot in front of it, and her right hand now keeping her stable by bracing against the retaining wall. "Where the hell did you come from?"

He made a sort of flamboyant gesture with his right hand, starting down around his feet, fingers down, and wiggled them up, slowly dissipating the movement, palm now up around eye level, as if it was a burst of smoke... "POOF?" he offered, less than mysteriously.

She grinned. "Well, tell me you can *poof* us in *there*, Quagmire Boy," she gestured up toward the stadium, "cause there is no fucking way I'm goin' through that shit!"

"Yeah, I know," he said, a little more serious, "hop up here!" He offered his hand, stretching down to her. She leaped up and caught his wrist, and he, hers. They both curled biceps in unison, as if rehearsed a hundred times, and he swung her up and to his left, where she landed right on her butt on the top edge of the cold, concrete wall. There was a 10 foot high chain-link fence with a spiraling razor wire top rail about a foot and a half behind them, giving them the perfect place to lean back and relax. "So what are you, anyway, about a size 6...?" he quietly inquired, putting his arm around her and pulling her softly, but firm to his side.

"Yeah," she responded, smiling at him suspiciously, out of the corner of her eye, "but you know that already...why would you ask me such an odd question at a time like this?" she asked, wondering, at first pass through her mind if maybe he hadn't bought her something, yet he seemed to be here without a package of any kind...

"Yeeeeaaaaahhh, it's just..." he dragged out, over acting a mysterious look around in all directions, meant to capture her gaze as well, and then he stopped on it... grinning... waiting for her to catch on that there was a bag bearing the North Clan crest behind her and to the left a bit, nearly hidden from view, about 10 feet back on the *other* side of the fence! It was immediately afterwards that she turned back toward him and realized Thor's boots were wet....

She spun her head around and just barely had time to catch sight of his devilish grin. "Oh, SHIT!!!" she yelped, interrupted by Thor pulling her right off the wall, and guiding their drop right into the soup with a disgustingly muddy

"SPLOICH" as they landed almost up to their knees in such a position as to splash the whole front of Kait's clothes, but leaving Thor nearly unscathed. Fearing retaliation, he quickly lifted her up and into the mouth of the shallower concrete culvert, laughing hysterically as he realized the bog had suctioned one of her boots right off, and she was now standing bare-foot on one leg, wet knee high boot on the other, with her lost boot between Thor's legs, splashing in the mire as it filled up with murky liquid. She looked like she was in shock, but spoke frighteningly calmly. "New clothes?" She gestured with her chin up towards the fence and bag. Thor nodded, grasping at his left side from laughing so hard, but couldn't stop even long enough to answer her verbally. He still had his right hand on her leg, and bent down to grab her soaked boot with his left.

He stood up, pouring the carrion out of the boot and smiled, humbly, still on the verge of serious laughter. "May I see your foot, M' Lady?"

"Why certainly, my Lord," she replied cordially, with an unusually assertive grin on her face for someone soaked with putrescence from head to foot. Then, there was the sideways re-positioning of her bare foot, deep down in the muck, grabbing as much of it as possible...

"Oh, SHIT!!!" He barely had time to flinch.

CHAPTER 11: OBSESSION

Almost everyone, when it really comes down to it, is a creature of habit. Even the most spontaneous person: unemployed, single (especially single people), young, radical; even the most "free" person, when you look close enough, will follow some sort of trackable pattern. Some people are so utterly habitual that the only thing that really distinguishes one day from the next is the relative spontaneity of the unusual people they encounter.

In her case, however, it wasn't the where, it was the when that was eluding him. The others were easy. He would simply hang out in, or near, an underground club for a few consecutive nights, and out of the many prospects, each complete with its own unfolding drama, she would emerge. This time things were different. He couldn't rely on her being anywhere at any particular time, he only knew that on certain nights, she would show... taunting him. Flirting with him in her every movement; her every glance was an invitation. He watched her leave each time, and each time he better understood where she was coming from. The last time, he was stifled by a car blocking the view of his camera, but he had a hunch where she was going.

He crossed the street and B-lined for the intersection just down the street from the club. He could feel the bass tones pumping through his chest, slowly fading as he got further and further down the street. His heart started racing as he passed the small alley he frequented the other night, the chalk outline fading with the raindrops into an unidentifiable blemish reminding him that he was still alone. He let the long end of the yellow crime scene tape, still attached to the brick corner, slip out of his fingers like a beloved cat's soft tail as he passed the alley's edge, and turned his head, only briefly, catching the last glimpse of it whipping quietly back into the darkness to be forgotten altogether.

He had been so lost in emotion, with his attention diverted, that he didn't notice the dark shape in the black town car across the street slowly snuff the light from his cigarette, staring at him through a partially rolled up, rain speckled window. The man continued to watch only him, in spite of the small flurry of foot activity within the club's proximity that was making him blend nicely in his fedora and trench coat.

Stanton strolled, a little more purposefully, the rest of the way up the street and took a quick right at the intersection. He was sure she probably turned this way, as he never saw her up the main road from here, coming or going. The other man slowly opened his door and stepped out, shutting it behind him while continuing his stare toward the corner about 50 yards away.

Around the corner and about a half a block down the sidewalk, Stanton saw what he was looking for... a medium diameter drainage downspout, banded right to the brick wall every three feet with a small steel strap; the whole thing running from the roof, right into a drainage hole in the sidewalk. He had an uneasy feeling all of a sudden, so he made very quick work of attaching a remote cam neatly hidden close to the wall, concealed within the hardware along the three foot high band, and pointed down the road toward the on-ramp.

If his hunch was correct, she was from up north, and was walking the girders underneath! He had heard of such a thing, but it would take someone of extreme conditioning and dexterity to pull it off for any kind of prolonged hike. *Were the hell else could she be going?* The only thing past the overhead highway in this direction was an old abandoned granary, knee deep in pigeon shit. A few people stayed there in the winter, but looking like her? With groomed hair and nice clothes? Not likely. They were almost exclusively hardcore street people with nowhere else to go. She wasn't exactly topsider material either, but she was definitely doing better than that.

He smiled, pushing the small remote button on his keychain, activating the camera. Time would tell.... His car, parked just clear of the back-road that led to the dumpster alley, was already unlocked, warmed up, and pointed back at the on-ramp for northbound. Just before he reached the top of the ramp, he stared hard into his rear-view mirror all the way back down the dark and deserted side street, focusing on the lit up corner, and gasped, actually feeling his heart skip a beat and a chill go up his spine as he saw the unmistakable silhouette of a man emerge on foot from the other street and stop, looking right up at him as he rounded the corner and sped north.

Chapter 10.5: For Life...

They stood together underneath the cascading falls of the underground drain water collector for the elaborate stadium fountain display as it poured over the seemingly random geometry of the concrete ledge; the shimmering lights reflecting in from all around this modern art masterpiece as the water found its way down from all directions to pool up over their feet across a large, high density translucent pane, visible from inside the highway tunnel below them. Having stripped away their dirty clothes and discarded then on a ledge to be soaked further, they both stood under a small shower of cascading water that was noticeably warmer than the rest, having pooled shallowly over a series of high intensity lights above, before meandering down a series of drop-offs and ending up here. From deep inside the fountain they could see the flash and unidirectional streaks of car headlights shining through the shallow layer of swirling water at their feet, creating a light show to rival the Aurora Borealis as it combined with the lights from above in a vibrant display of moving art, continuously repainting every inch of the walls, ceiling and their faces and bodies as they washed away the last of the sludge from the tunnel.

The atmosphere... the fresh water pouring over her already erect nipples... knowing that passing cars could see their anonymous forms through the light pane from overhead... it was all too much for her to handle, and she surrendered to it completely; her knees nearly buckling beneath her as she pulled herself to him and locked her legs behind his waist. She reached up through the water and grabbed onto the edge of the spillway, teasing his lips with her reddened nipples, then looked down at him, straight through the eyes she understood like no other, and with her long blonde hair soaked and ensnaring both their bodies from head to waist, they unleashed years of unresolved passion and desire in one seemingly never-ending kiss, both of them instantly peaking to a state of suspended and prolonged orgasm unlike anything either of them had ever experienced.

They had messed around before, drunk on mead, and held back some part of themselves in a concerted effort to keep it casual. *For the good of the Clan... for the good of their long standing friendship....* There was a line in the sand they both knew should never be crossed. Screw the line in the sand. This was anything but casual, and things would never be the same again.

Chapter 12: A New Dawn

To the sound of faint laughter and growing activity, he awakened... confused, but not hung-over. He sat up in bed and smiled as he realized the source of his confusion. He reached over to his right and gently put his hand on the mound of covers next to him to make sure he didn't dream anything. She mumbled something sweetly, then rolled slightly towards him, putting her warm, muscular leg over his and groped upwards toward her pillow, pulling everything slightly toward herself. His mind had already quickly whisked through the events of last night, and he was instantly hard again, as if the very touch of her skin at all was some kind of powerful aphrodisiac he could neither resist, nor would ever again care to.

The voices were Uruz and Tyr. If Dagaz was here, he was either still asleep, or staying very quiet. Thor could tell by the quiet tone and cadence of the conversation that there was business being worked out, and decided, with all the will power he could conjure, to let her sleep and join the conversation below. He stealthily slipped his leg out from under her without so much as a stir, then sat on the edge of the bed waiting for the blood to flow back to his head so he could get dressed. For a moment, he heard the slightest stir out of her, then he realized.... The business end of his Katana was being held all the way across his throat from behind. "I don't think so," she said softly, but insistently, as she forced him to slowly lay backwards, legs still hanging off the end of the bed, and she grasped him with her left hand, kissing him upside down as she put the sword aside and pulled herself slowly down the length of his body without an inch of air between them, pausing only briefly as her breasts passed over his anxious mouth.

Downstairs, Uruz was leaning back in his chair; empty breakfast plate on the table to his right and a tall mug of something resembling coffee in his hand. Tyr was pacing the floor, coffee in hand, wearing the million mile gaze he usually had on when a good plan was coming together. Though they were both smoking rolled tobacco, there was still the strong aroma of breakfast in the air when Thor popped the hatch to his attic style loft and started winding down the spiral stairs into the main living chamber of the stronghold.

Sausage, fried potatoes, eggs...and yes, bacon, sweet bacon. First taste of the spoils of a successful trip to Jerrick's. Fresh meat, produce, milk, eggs, soap, paper products, leather goods... hell, it wouldn't be long before these guys started their own clothing line! For those who had anything to barter, or any skills to bring to service, they brought civility back into a world of thieves.

"It lives!" Uruz shouted up at him, raising his glass high.

"Brother... " Tyr nodded, also gesturing with his mug.

Thor grinned, exchanging glances, but hardly the conversationalist first thing in the morning. He meandered into the kitchen nook, nose in the air, following the food aroma to its source. "Aaaaahhh," he sighed, reaching the source of the bouquet. "Christ, I just sounded like Dagaz for a second!"

"Aaaaahhh, yeaaaahhh, you did," Tyr prodded.

"So who won the game?" Uruz practically yelled, in his usual fashion.

"Me," Thor smiled. He was chopping up some garlic on the counter, getting ready to pitch it in the gourmet style omelet-for-two he was quickly preparing, while the scent of fresh coffee already filled the air as scalding hot steam erupted out of the small espresso maker to his right with a powerful hiss.

"Yeah, that's what it sounded like twenty minutes ago!" Tyr jabbed, beating Uruz to the punch. Thor finally emerged from around the corner with a deliciously prepared omelet, center-piecing the giant breakfast plate. It was stylishly surrounded by a side of bacon, toast, fruit slices, and a toasted bagel with cheese, along two mugs of coffee he skillfully gripped through the fingers of the same hand.

Thor smiled at both of them devilishly with raised eyebrows, then eloquently spoke, "You'll forgive me if I don't join you gentlemen for breakfast...."

"Certainly, certainly," Tyr mimicked.

"Hey, bro..." Here it came. Uruz, thick as he was, remained astonishingly hard to deceive. "Have you seen Dagaz... *Or Kait*?" he added, looking right through him with a cocky smile on his face. Thor started grinning uncontrollably, partially at Uruz's keen perception, and was just about to answer him when the hatch to his loft opened again. All three of them stopped what they were doing right in their tracks and stared. Tyr knew from the very second her leather boot touched the top stair tread that it was Kait. It took Uruz about a second or two longer, in spite of his allegations, as if he didn't believe his own eyes.

"No Dagaz, huh?" she asked casually, as if nothing out of the ordinary was going on. Thor smiled and paused at the table, then sat down the food, waiting to see what she was going to do. Tyr and Uruz both stood, frozen solid, with their mouths wide open. "Yeah, that's what I thought...." She smiled coyly at Thor, approaching him directly, rather than being seated. She was fully dressed, as if going somewhere.

"No breakfast?" Thor offered, tilting the obviously tandem plate toward her as she approached.

"Maybe just a little..." She leaned toward his ear, picking a toasted bagel with cheese off the plate, "I have something I need to do," she whispered, running her fingers down the inside of his arm as she walked slowly away, finally breaking contact at his fingertips... finally looking away. "I'll see you guys later!" she said out loud, heading out the double security door. Thor watched her walk off, getting smaller in the security monitor, until he couldn't see her at all.

He doled out half the food onto another plate, then slid it like a Frisbee over to Uruz, knocking his empty plate about an inch over, then looked up, realizing Uruz and Thor both still had the same blank expressions on their faces. "What?" he smiled through a mouthful of eggs and bacon. "So, do we have a plan for J's next car?" he transgressed, changing the subject to snap them out of their sudden stupor. Still no response... "Oh, come on, man, you all knew it was inevitable!" he laughed. "It's not like you didn't see it coming!"

Uruz sat back in his chair, looking at Tyr, and they both started laughing hysterically. Uruz grabbed up the breakfast plate, started shoveling food in his mouth, and exclaimed through a mouthful of eggs, "That's putting it mildly *mmm*shmuhshmack* what took you so long?" he smiled, reaching for his coffee as a couple crumbles of egg fell from his mouth and he tried vainly to catch them.

"You know what took me so long," he scolded, "she's no ordinary girl!"

"Respect, that's what," Tyr added. "I don't care, it was a long time coming.... It's a perfect match."

"Anyway, " Thor eluded, "J's car..."

"Yeaaaahhh," Tyr said softly.

"Aaaaaahhh," Thor added, looking slyly at Uruz, who glared at him, quasi-judiciously, then smiled, saving it for a future conversation.

"We were thinking it might be smooth," Tyr stepped up, "given that we don't know where Dagaz is, if we go for another 'Hack & Drop Shipment Authorization' from our good buddies in law enforcement. They have multiple impound yards within reasonable proximity, so as long as you're up to the computer work in Dagaz's stead, *including a control chip,* we can seize the drop cargo in running condition without needing to disable more than two people... a truck driver, and maybe an accomplice or trainee."

"Up to the hack? Shit, who do you think taught Dagaz how to do it? Albeit, the control chips were pure genius, but I have his software for that...." He gestured toward their community terminal controlling mead production. "No problem. When do you think we should do it?"

"Tomorrow," Uruz said.

"Got it. I know what Jerrick's after... consider it done."

CHAPTER 13: A NEW DAY

She set off on her usual route: past her old family's home to quietly pay her respects, down by the overgrown tent city between the train tracks and the river, near the old industrial district which was still home to many small families with young kids who she often paused to play with, then right over the heart of the underground valley via a series of nearly impassable girders, beams and webbing that kept one with acrobat's skills, such as her, well above all of the many threats on the way south to the Border District. She sat for hours at one of the high points along the way, staring off to the south at the only mountain in sight in this direction... a giant snow-capped volcano rising out of the smog shrouded horizon, towering above even the ring of clouds lingering down a good distance from its rounded peak. Seemingly dead as a post, she remembered growing up hearing stories about how it erupted at the onset of the Great Quake, causing a river of mud to wash away several miles of city like it was nothing. Looking out into the valley now, it appeared that the whole area was built right over the top of the disaster as if it never even happened.

Nothing but busy little ants rolling progress right over the top of each other, not even stopping to mourn the fallen or reflect on the foot that toppled the hill in the first place. *What was our place in all this madness?*

Sometimes she marveled at the grandeur that seemed to elude them all... the unfortunate ones, the downtrodden, the have-not's. Thinking about how much greener the grass must be for those who were born into privilege and didn't have to constantly struggle just to obtain the most fundamental necessities sometimes brought her to tears. She would sit and daydream about what it would be like to live in one of those protected townhouses. No real challenges at all... just a sterile, aerosol existence with all your freedoms traded off for safety and predictability.

She smiled. *They can fucking have it!* Sometimes she just needed to remind herself that the grass is always greenest where the dogs are shitting. Her lifestyle is what made her into who and what she is, and she wouldn't trade that, or anyone in her life, for all the money and security in the world. She stood carefully on the edge of the giant angled I-beam and stretched, judging from the sun's position in the western sky that she should probably hurry up if she was going to reach the club before the music started.

There was a new band playing that she couldn't get enough of. She yearned to bring Thor with her tonight, but she knew he would be needed at home. Without Dagaz, he was the only one capable of doing all of the tech-work necessary to pull off the next job. She wasn't sure which way they would go, but they would undoubtedly need a control chip programmed, and Thor was the computer guru for anything else they might encounter.

The God's honest truth was that she needed to get out of there as bad as he needed to stay. Things wouldn't be so awkward in a day or two, but there was no way she was about to hang around this morning and subject herself to total bombardment. Though she was very comfortable with taking things to a new level with him, it was still a huge change for both of them, and would require a little bit of time to process.

She jumped up to the webbing above her and grabbed it with her hands. Hanging from this position, all her aches and pains stretched right out of her and she pulled herself up to chin level about twenty times before doing an artistic, but risky dismount back onto the large I-beam below. She started running gracefully along the beam, counting the angled webbing as it intersected in V shapes every 50 feet, divided every other V by a vertical column; twice as wide as the beam.

She slid her back toward the first of each member, figure-8-ing through them, but alternating angles. When she got to the columns, she jumped up to the flange above her head that separated it from the upper webbing, hooking around it on alternating sides, keeping this symmetry all the way down the viaduct while the steady stream of traffic flowed almost silently up above. This was the routine that kept her in such tremendous shape. Her gymnast physique, in combination with her years of combat training, both with Thor, and without, was the reason the rest of the Clan didn't have to worry about her safety too much. She was, quite simply, nearly unbeatable in a hand to hand fight, as her seemingly countless victories had proven, time and time again.

Up ahead in the distance, nearly impossible to see in the setting sun were the taillights of someone coming down the off ramp near the club where she was headed. As the buildings beneath her started growing in size again, and the commotion below became more than just an occasional derelict scavenger, she started to slow things down instinctively, falling out of obvious peripheral sight and stretching her own awareness much further out. Staying just to one side of the main girder, she started her decent; the underside of the off ramp itself providing the perfect layout of concrete and structural members for a quick and natural route to the street below.

Under the full veil of darkness now, she sped her cadence instinctively as she became excited by the drum beat emanating from the club, growing steadily louder as she approached. Once on the street level, she adjusted her entire vibe, so as not to reveal where she came from. Proactive defense strategy had kept her alive so far, and with very few altercations that she didn't see coming in advance. She knew quite well that even an inferior adversary could pose a grave threat if handed the element of surprise.

Inside, the energy was booming. The band was absolutely intense; playing something in between the most grinding, punch-heavy industrial punk rock, and retro, bluegrass/ rockabilly with hook after hook that had the small mob of 100 or so out on the floor in a state of swirling slam dance frenzy and eating out of the palm of their hands. The underground music scene was tremendous. Most of these bands had no way to record their music, no chance of ever being heard by the mainstream, and no way to get paid beyond the scraps these small clubs offered, but they created and performed original and inspired music night after night in places such as this, all up and down the west coast out of the pure love of their art.

This was pure culture. Pure art reflecting the times; undiluted by the transgressions of mass media. No mass-production for efficiency, no sterilization or censorship to appease the status quo, and especially no tailoring or selling out the raw integrity of the art to make it palatable to the masses to increase profits. Though sometimes it seemed that it was nearly impossible to grasp hold of something you liked and retain it, some groups managed to produce their own recordings on computer, store most everything online and distribute it all over the free world, then give out or trade flash chips at their shows that could be played on even the cheapest digital music player.

This was the extent of the music world without the aid, involvement, and control of the global record companies that had all but destroyed the true nature and soul of the art. This is why frequenting these clubs and keeping this scene alive was so important to so many.... Not everybody had a computer anymore. Hell, most people down here grew up without even the benefit of electricity. Kait had built up quite a collection of music, rivaled only by Thor's, and they were both constantly turning each other on to new groups. This was one to show him, for sure, she thought, smiling and nodding her head to the grinding beat.

She was in a playful mood, but ever since the last time she was here, she kept having the same intermittent sensation of being watched. Off and on it gnawed at her like an itch you can't scratch. She pretty much dismissed it all together because every time it happened, no one was in sight, at least no one that seemed to be paying attention to her... *but then she saw him!*

Out of the corner of her eye she saw what appeared to be Dagaz, turning his head down and away, hiding his gaze under the rim of his trademark fedora, and disappearing swiftly into the cluster of people around him! *No*, she thought, rationalizing. *This can't be, he doesn't even know about this place, not to mention its relative distance from home....* He would have to be following her, and why would he do that? If he just needed to speak to her alone, he would have stopped her miles ago. *It had to be someone else!*

She meandered around the club, trying not to seem too obvious, but looking everywhere. He had to have been just leaving the restroom when she spotted him. Perhaps that's all he was doing in the first place, and now she feared he might be on his way down the street, taking the mystery of his disappearance with him. "Look out!" she yelled, the sound of her voice nearly drowned in the pulsating music. She bolted for the door, knocking several people off balance as she shoved her way out.

Outside the wind was starting to howl; a damp odor taunting her nostrils, and she knew it was going to rain. In fact, there was quite a storm on the way indeed. Coming in powerful, short gusts, the wind was tossing pieces of trash to and fro all over the street. She looked as far as she could see in both directions and didn't see hide nor hair of Dagaz. She quickly jogged to the left for about half of the block until she reached a small gap between buildings, leading through to the trash alley behind the club... still nothing. It was possible she was just seeing things, or he got in a car with someone and they were just gone. What she did know is that it was going to get very nasty out, very soon.

She went back in the club and quickly bought up the recordings from both bands that were playing tonight, seriously complimenting the Psycho-Billy band she got to hear tonight, and supporting the other on blind faith. She had just enough money on her to buy two copies of each. Even though she and Thor traded freely and copied each other's music, she wanted him to have his own copies of the cover art, which was almost as phenomenal as the music. Thinking about him, she started to miss him immensely, and she honestly wasn't sure if she liked that or not. Either way, it certainly wasn't something she was used to.

She swung the door open again, this time a little slower, nodding at the bouncer and taking a right instead. Another glance around revealed nothing but a few cars parked along the road as usual. She started down the sidewalk; gusts of wind hastening in frequency and intensity. They were hitting her from behind and this was starting to irritate the shit out of her, as it was blowing her long hair right into her face.

She was in a bit of a vortex between buildings, and it seemed no matter which way she faced, the wind would hit her from the back. She was just leaving the pavement, a few feet into the grass by the railing for the off ramp she would climb when she finally had enough and decided to head home.

Reaching into her right side cargo pocket on her pant leg, she suddenly had the intense feeling that someone was behind her. Before she could turn around, a gust of wind blew the leather fedora right past her leg where it spun around and rested a few feet out in front of her. She smiled, able to breathe again, and continued tying her hair back. "So, where the fuck have you been hiding out?" she called out loud, speaking well over the volume of the wind, but still not turning to look at him.

No answer. She was overcome with a sudden bad feeling, and started to spin around to see what was wrong with him, when, YANK! Her head was jerked straight back from her pony tail, pulling her momentarily off balance. Why would he do this? She dug her heel, regaining some posture, then reached back, grabbing the hand he was holding onto her with and pinning it to her head. She breathed in and squatted low, twisting her frame and pivoting on the balls of her feet with his hand trapped. His arm was twisted all the way under, 180 degrees, when she could finally see his face.

She gasped when she realized this was not Dagaz! She stood all the way up, nearly breaking his arm, then took one step back. As his weight bore down on his lead foot, she suddenly released his hand and thrust a powerful kick right into his kneecap, breaking the joint straight back. His screamed echoed off the surrounding buildings, but no one was around to hear it. He mumbled something unintelligible, the passed out from the pain, quaking on the ground in his long trench coat.

She stood above him, wide eyed, catching her breath, and looked around her. Threat contained. She knelt over him, finished tying her hair back, then started checking his pockets. He was some sort of wealthy topsider. Going through his wallet she found over $150 in various denominations, enough to enjoy any of the many guilty pleasures of the underground, but pretty much worthless up top, where implant scan was the currency of choice, and several retail cards, also worthless without scanning his wrist implant. Jackass probably came down here a lot, looking for prostitutes and was going to try to rape her. She resisted the urge to pummel him further in his sleep, and twisted around to see where that hat of his went; one hand still on his chest.

The sound was unclear, kind of like a hum from way down inside your head.... Everything shook sideways and smelled strange. She couldn't control her mouth and briefly had the sensation of biting her tongue. A strange echo, like several different voices all trying to say the same word, but from different starting points, rambled on in her head, then everything faded to darkness.

He laid on his back gasping for air; the pain in his leg nearly unbearable. The spring loaded cuff-stunner he grabbed her wrist with was designed to shock until turned off by the remote side, which was still in his hand. Struggling hard to get to his feet, he fumbled the transmitter grip. It fell to the ground next to her rapidly convulsing body. He had no intention of turning it off anytime soon, and he smiled slightly through the pain at the way he stole victory from the jaws of certain defeat. In the blink of an eye, the verdict was changed again.

"James Stanton!" the voice boomed from right above him. His heart missed a beat and he jerked with his whole body so hard that he literally crumbled back to the ground, scrambling to roll onto his back so that he could get a look at who was behind him. The man was wearing black business attire from head to toe, his arm outstretched toward him, holding a TC Contender single shot competition pistol with night sights and a silencer, leveled motionless right between his eyes. Stanton's mouth popped open, but he was unable to make a sound.

CHAPTER 14: THE SCORE

Thor, Tyr and Uruz waited impatiently in the living room of the stronghold for the phone call to come in. The "overflow" impound drop shipment, authorized last night by Thor, posing as the over-crowded impound yard under the parking tower where they got the last car, would insure that the next car impounded would be towed to a location just up the street instead of the impound yard. The success of this sort of scam was in its originality. The powers that be simply didn't expect a hack for something like an impounded car, not to mention the security was lax for things they really didn't give a shit about, and they didn't give a shit about some poor bastard's illegally parked vehicle. By the time the real truck came to pick up the order, they were gone.

"It's 7am, where the hell is Kait?" Thor fumed, pacing the floor in the opposite direction as Tyr's "coffee waltz."

"Settle down, she's a firecracker, bro, you trained her, she can take care of herself... Probably got stuck spending the night somewhere to stay out of that storm. She's always down in Border goin' to shows, you know that." Uruz slapped his back, now pacing a little himself.

"She'll show, don't worry bud, just keep your mind on the job," Tyr scowled. "You got the chip we need, right? It sounds like it's gonna be a brand new BMW... Probably with all the trimmings, knowing most of the uptown scum that could afford that car! They're always temperamental, though. Seems like the owners just *have* to reprogram all of its accessories with their own macros... messes up everything for us!"

"Not this time, baby!" Thor smiled, starting to lighten up. "Got it handled. Needless to say, I didn't get a lot of sleep last night...."

"You know," Uruz pondered, "we might want to think about reprogramming the lock someday soon...." He gestured at the front door.

"Why now? We got two AWOL," Thor stated.

"Yeah, we need for them to come in safe.... I'm just not feeling good about *shit* right now. I don't know why." Both of them looked up at Tyr, to see his reaction, but he was already headed to the phone, as if he sensed it coming.

Sure enough, just before he got to the computer desk, the soft buzz of their phone monitor software went off, and he casually reached over and hit the speaker button. *"Northgate Towing,"* the incoming voice said, stern but quick.

"Yeah, we need you guys to come and pick up a car and take it to overflow, north side," stated another voice, probably a police dispatcher.

"What time? We're real busy...."

"As soon as you can, this morning. It looks like we've got a shuffling disaster on the horizon."

"Alright. We can send a truck before we open, we have a couple of guys in your area. How about 8?"

"We'll try to have it ready."

"Try hard. If not, it'll set us back all day...."
"Alright, thanks."

Both sides hung up, then Tyr pushed the button to disconnect. "Easy money, let's go!"

"A *shuffling disaster*?" Uruz smiled, giving Thor a small shove.

"Yeah, they're gonna have fun with that shit! I couldn't resist. I wish we could tap their security cameras and make a movie out of that fiasco!" He paused, giving Tyr a scheming look with one eyebrow raised, his wheels suddenly turning.

"Don't even think about it, bro!" Tyr laughed, punching in a code on the keypad by the side door. The door slid open, revealing another airlock-style security door, double coded in both directions. They piled in the small foyer, waited for the door to slide closed, then checked the twin monitors before punching in the code for the second door. One showed the front entryway and the other showed the inside of the roof hatch, so that you couldn't accidentally leave another point of entry open when leaving this way. Both were closed and they were good to go. Tyr entered the second code, and they stepped out into the garage. They weren't in the habit of keeping personal vehicles, so the room was more of a shop than a garage, but they did keep the crown jewel of their operation: a high-torque diesel tow truck, capable of pulling a house off its foundations.

Thor was in a nearby cabinet, digging through a stack of door magnets. He came to "Northgate Towing" and tossed them sarcastically at the side of the truck, to a dull "whump" of a noise as they stuck almost perfectly in place. Tyr was adding new license plates over the top of the old ones, and Uruz was digging through a closet and grabbing coveralls with his right arm, while rummaging through a gun cabinet with his left.

"Any special requests?" he asked.

"I'll take twin 1911's with a shoulder harness, and a backup PPK with an ankle holster," Thor replied quickly. "Two clips per gun. Same belt, silencer for PPK in pouch."

"Good choice, Winch-man, and how 'bout you, Point?"

Tyr scratched his chin, then replied, "Silenced PPK, inside chest holster with one extra clip, and a stun wrench."

"Packing light? Do we have an optimist in our midst this morning?" Thor prodded, still fumbling around with the door magnets. "Give me a bug wrench, too! That thing saved my ass before!"

"Better make it two clips," he smiled.

Uruz pulled out a final gun, his favorite, a pistol grip Benelli twelve gauge automatic with 3 inch magnum hollow point sabot slugs. "And the other winch-man will take... this!" He released the action, sending a round into the chamber, then laid all the hardware across the nearby staging table, and tossed them each their coveralls. They scrambled into position with military precision and were on their way within minutes.

Tyr drove, taking a kind of roundabout route through the maze of building bases, protruding beneath the almost solid layer of suspended roadwork above. He needed to make sure that they would approach the building from the same direction as the access tunnel from above that the police would have made available to them. Uruz was riding shotgun, and Thor was in the back seat of the crew cab. They all had their weapons hidden completely inside their coveralls, and were casually bullshitting with each other as if nothing unusual was going on.

"All I'm saying is that if I didn't have shit for a future, just the same old corrupt government, devastated environment, dead-end job as another link in the machine, no girlie... Why not do it? In another 100 years, things might just be better!" Uruz pondered.

"And what exactly gives you that impression?" Tyr challenged. "Our track record over the *last* 100? Come on, bud, face it, they're just writing checks they'll probably never have to cash!"

Thor laughed with him, "Yeah, I say freeze all their sorry, rich asses, then have a huge game of pool out in space with the capsules! *Rich Man's Escape*, my ass! More like *Chickenshit's Way Out!* I say, good riddance, anyway! They're the people who are the most directly responsible for the sorry state we all live in.... They're scared shitless of us, and without the slave labor they still get from the hoards of poor bastards in the outskirts, they would never be able to prosper the way they do! They will always need a working class to exploit. I say more power to 'em! Freeze every knob-gobbling one of 'em and ship them all off this rock! Maybe then we'll be able to breathe again!" He threw his arms out to the sides in grandiose fashion, intentionally over-dramaticizing his point like a preacher on a soapbox. "Can I get an Amen?!"

"Amen, my brother, amen," Uruz said with a proud nod, reaching back over his armrest with an outstretched fist for Thor to bump. "What's that shit cost, anyway?"

"Why, you saving up your spare change?" Tyr poked, looking back at Thor with a grin.

"Yep! No, seriously any clue?"

"A whole lot more than anyone sane could come up with... Let's face it, even your standard rich guy would not be welcome in a small room full of those fat-cat billionaire swine elitists that bankrupted this country before the war. *Global Bank of the World... New World Order...* shit, everybody bleeds, and they all spilled theirs all over the ground when the Earth scratched that itch with the great quake! All men sure *aren't* created equally, but in the eyes of God, they sure can be destroyed equally!" Thor ranted further.

"Yeah? So what's that shit cost, anyway?" They all laughed again while Thor, finished rolling a cigarette, lit it and took a deep drag, blowing a huge cloud at the back of Uruz's head. "Gimme a drag!" Uruz demanded.

"Cops!" Tyr blurted out.

"Where?" Uruz asked, frantically. Thor looked up from where he was checking all his clips down in his lap. He glanced around for a moment, then he smiled.

"Cops! You said, *Gimme a drag...* Cops! They're a big drag!" Tyr joked in a cheesy manner, lightening the mood a little from Thor's cynicism. "Anyway, gentlemen, we're almost there... Game faces!"

———————

Tyr pulled up to the main bay door showing on the otherwise plain looking, window and doorless structure, rising up to what would be 10 stories or so before it took on the characteristics of a normal skyscraper. The base was built out about two feet thicker than the rest of the building, until about street level above. This meant it was here before the quake, then retrofitted to enhance stability and quickly provide iron clad security against the entire underground population. The ensuing food riots and destruction caused by our own military on surrounding buildings provided an immediate excuse to build in this manner, effectively shutting out the poor, but truth be told, the reason most government buildings were still standing was that they were built this way from conception.

This was probably one testimonial to the common belief that the government saw all of this coming a long time ago, and did absolutely nothing to prevent it. It was simply part of the destabilization necessary to institute its built in savior... The World Bank. Complete financial control through debt-based slavery and a pre-engineered global bankruptcy. These buildings, as with most of the government's property, were impenetrable. Even the door could withstand any foreseeable means of forced entry, including explosives. Only one thing could open the jaws of this iron clad cash pot....

Tyr finished backing up to the door and hit the horn twice. Open sesame! The huge steel door started rolling upward, exposing an increasing gap from the ground up. Through the rear-view mirror, Uruz could see one pair of boots, a worker, probably operating the door. Tyr looked back through his and saw black shoes, black pants. A cop. Uruz was already slowly bailing out of his side, coughing naturally and blowing a large snot-rocket out of his nose with one finger over the other nostril.

"How many?" Thor asked quietly.

"Two. One cop... my side."

"Time?"

"7:45 on the nose."

Thor cleared his throat, then grabbed a clipboard with manifests made up on it for a prop, mainly to give the cop something to look at besides the contour of their clothes, and what they may or may not be carrying under them. He proceeded around the front of the truck, tapping Tyr's window with the edge of the clipboard as he saw that the car was already in position behind them, and he wouldn't need to drive any further. Tyr bailed out behind him.

"How you doin'?" Uruz nodded to the worker, who returned the nod, but didn't speak. Judging from the type of overalls he was wearing, he was probably a trustee working off his sentence from the city jail. There were likely to be a few more of them milling around, but for now it looked like just these two guys and the cameras to work around.

"That was quick! You guys are early," the officer muttered, looking down at the folded over newspaper in his right hand while balancing a steaming hot coffee in his left.

"Yeah, well, we got a lot to do today," Tyr responded, mirroring his attitude as the car was slowly raising into position on the large flatbed. Thor was up on top, guiding the sleek BMW into position while Uruz worked the winch motor from the ground. Tyr was fumbling in his front pocket for the small input gun loaded with his control chip, when he noticed the cop staring right at him.

"You might need these!" The officer tossed Thor a set of keys with a remote alarm/ ignition on them. "The dumb bastard apparently left these in the ignition down in the Border District, with his drunk ass blocking an off-ramp!"

Thor caught them without looking away from what he was doing, and immediately pushed the alarm button, starting to worry about time. The alarm chirped loudly, flashing the lights twice. Not real sure whether or not the other button was even for the ignition, Thor pushed it. Instead of the motor turning over, the trunk popped open about six inches. He chuckled, a little embarrassed, and walked to the rear of the car to shut it. Tyr was approaching the cop as if to make chit chat, but he had his eyes fixed on Thor. The cop, glued to his newspaper again, was leaning with his right side on the truck. Uruz was recruiting some help from the inmate tightening down the straps when he saw Thor looking down into the trunk.

From where he was standing on top of the truck, his mind immediately raced through the subject of whether or not the two cameras, up and behind him could see the body; twisted sideways with one leg snapped 90 degrees the wrong way at the knee, and a bullet hole in his forehead. He quickly shut it, bearing down with his shoulder into it, as if to insure that it stayed shut. He locked eyes with Tyr, face flushed from shock, and gestured with his eyes at the cop, then away to their egress route. Tyr read his level of concern and acted immediately.

"Watch out!" he yelled, gesturing wildly toward the back where Uruz was fastening the last tie down. His arm came up, nailing the officer's coffee from the bottom, spilling it all over his face and chest.

"Shit!" the cop yelled, blinded for a moment as Tyr pushed right past him toward Uruz and Thor, who had already jumped off the back.

"What? What did I do?" Uruz yelled back.

"Holy shit, man, I thought you lost it for a second," Tyr acted out.

"Yeah, I saw that, too! Damn!" Thor added.

"What the hell, guys! God dammit! You burnt my eyes!" the cop yelled, desperately trying to wipe himself off with his newspaper. "Wait right here, we still got paperwork!" he added, bolting for a restroom to get cleaned up. "God dammit!!!"

"Shit, I'm sorry, man!" Tyr yelled through the door to him. Turning his attention to Thor, he muttered, *"What the fuck? What is it?"*

"A body!" Thor whispered back, trying to keep from looking nervous to the cameras.

Uruz, knowing something was going down, was in tight, with his back turned, also trying to look natural, but mainly keeping an eye on the trustee, who was waiting just under the bay door for the officer to return. Uruz pulled his "bug wrench" and pretended to be tightening something on the ratchet holding one of the straps down over the front wheel.

"Should we turn it in and abort? So far, it's not our problem," Tyr posed, nervously watching the garage for the officer who, from the sound of it, just cleared the inside security door and was only moments away.

"No time!" Thor said aloud, pointing down the street at the real tow truck, which had just rounded the corner just up the street. "Fire it up!" Uruz saw it, too, and was already standing strategically close to the inmate, but in the blind area of the cameras, just under the jamb of the doorway. Thor walked toward the door opening, flipping his wrench around in his hand casually as he approached the officer.

The cop, obviously still upset about the coffee incident, marched straight toward Thor, with a clipboard in his hand. "So," he spoke up, matter-of-factly, "I'm going to need you to fill out these two form-" He shook violently, the clipboard falling to the ground as Thor held the stun wrench directly under his chin with his right hand, while yanking his head back with his left. He cut off the charge, then quickly thrust kicked the side of his right knee, down at an angle, sending him into the ground, unconscious, with an injury that would buy them even more time after he came to.

Uruz, only a second behind him, hit the inmate in the ribs with his wrench, knowing full well a trustee wouldn't risk his status to help them, and probably with only a short sentence left, had no interest in running. The stunned officer crumbled just inside the door, but Uruz had to quickly pull the inmate a couple feet in from where he dropped, still twitching, as Thor hit the button to close the bay door without a moment to spare. The Northgate tow truck was just pulling up. Tyr had pulled the driver's side door magnet off as he got in, but the lone driver of the other truck looked a little confused as he approached. Thor jumped in with Uruz right on top of him, pretending for the cameras to be waving goodbye to the pair so a chase wouldn't be immediately dispatched.

They waited until they got clear of the first turn on their mapped out egress route before anyone could even speak. Tyr slammed on the brakes after looking everywhere to make sure no one was looking. "Plates and magnets!" Uruz bailed out, running to the back and popped off the rear license plate, exposing another one. Thor quickly rolled down the window and reached down, peeling the large Northgate Towing logo magnet off the door, and tossed it face down on the floorboard with the other one. Uruz did the same to the plate as he got back in, the two of them pulling a retractable cover the entire length over the BMW. They sped off, looking in the rear-view, and up above at the suspended matrix, but it was obvious after a couple blocks that they got away with it. No flashing lights, sirens, gunshots, or reports on the scanner. Uruz laughed first, and they all breathed a little easier, temporarily forgetting that they were hauling a dead body in the back of a stolen car.

CHAPTER 15: IRONY

All three of them were pacing the floor now. The stolen car could mean enough heat, but the body of a topsider? Outside a police station? Nearly ten minutes elapsed before anyone finally broke the ice.

"Are you sure the cameras didn't have line of sight? I mean, they use fish-eye and wide angle for entryways," Tyr asked again, nervously.

"Positive! If they did, I would have felt it from where I was standing," Thor assured them. "Anyway, I've got a funny feeling about this...." He jumped back up on the truck and pushed the button in his pocket. The trunk popped open. Tyr and Uruz climbed up to join him, finally more curious than worried.

They all stood and stared at him. He was a pretty well-to-do business man in his 30's or early 40's. He was wearing a long, expensive looking, but thoroughly soiled trench coat, $300 leather dress shoes, and a very expensive watch, which Uruz was already peeling off his wrist. He laid sideways in the trunk with a broken leg, a bullet hole in his forehead, and a hat and briefcase next to him.

"I'm not positive, but I think I might know who this is," Thor said softly, almost whispering even though their entire dwelling was a soundproof fortress.

"Who?" Tyr looked up at him, surprised.

"Remember the guy who shut me down when I tried to hack Vector to get those security codes for the car dealership uptown?" Thor asked, scratching his chin.

"Yeah," Uruz laughed, "he almost cooked your computer before you could get back out! That was funny!"

"Fuck you! No, I'm serious...."

"The Fortune 500 whiz kid.... Yeah, John Reid, or something. This ain't him," Tyr concluded.

"I think it is."

"Just look at him! His face was printed all over the world, that's *not* him!"

"No, no, no, an AFG site I check out a lot reported that he went into hiding, got his name changed... plastic surgery... the works."

"The Alliance For Gaia... *a conspiracy site!*" he mocked, "Those guys do more than anyone to expose corruption, but still... what makes you think *this guy* is him, just because Reid disappeared?"

"Because they had *his* picture," Thor smiled, pointing at the corpse in the trunk and realizing this was probably one of the most corrupt business men on the planet. He reached in and turned him over, checking his pockets for a wallet. To his surprise, nothing. *But why was all of this other stuff intact?* His ID must not be of any concern because he still had all his teeth.... Thor grabbed his left wrist and squeezed in with his fingertips, rubbing around in a circular motion just behind his watch line. He nodded and tossed the man's arm back into the trunk. "His chip is still intact. Someone was probably going to dispose of the car and everything in it, but got interrupted somehow.... They made no attempt to cover their tracks otherwise."

"Did the AFG site know his new name?" Tyr asked.

"Yeah... Stanford, or Stanton or something. We can probably pry that thing out and tell for sure." He gestured at the man's wrist. "It's the same software we use for the control chips."

"If you do that, the thing will be useless after that.... Wasn't this guy rich as shit?" Tyr posed, raising an eyebrow invitingly. "And it's safe to assume not very many people know he's dead... *or alive*, for that matter."

"What are you suggesting," Uruz teased, "dragging him up topside, and running his arm through a banking terminal in front of God and everyone?"

"If one of us has his blood type, they could implant it... theoretically," Tyr schemed, starting to sound a little too serious.

"Judging by the looks of things, that would have to be very soon," Thor speculated, "and we'd have to do it here." He grabbed the briefcase out and shut the trunk. "First things first!"

"To the nutcracker!" Uruz yelled. They hopped down and cleared off a small area around a table vise on the workbench next to the truck. Thor set the case sideways in the jaws of the giant vise, with the front plate just below the seam and the rear one just above it, and started cranking the large handle to the right. It started to cave in immediately and when he heard the crunch, he knew the lock was broken. He pulled it out and opened it. They were all huddled around it like kids at Christmas, but the result was a bit anticlimactic.

Instead of tightly packed stacks of hundred dollar bills, there was a small laptop computer and a stack of disorganized folders and paperwork. They started going through the stack, paper by paper, and realized it was a bunch of tracking documentation showing a serious case of creative math on someone's behalf; embezzlement to the tune of over 60 million dollars, with enough supporting information to literally hang somebody in court. Somebody named Kennick. Over and over the paperwork showed funds bled from nearly every deal Vector Beta was involved in, then corresponding amounts, broken up neatly into over ten different offshore accounts, added together always totaling the amount of discrepancy.

"Judging from the looks of things, he was going to turn this Kennick guy in, but got shut down before he had a chance to," Thor observed. He scratched his head for a moment. "Either that, or he was going to blackmail him...." He pulled the laptop gently out of the case, cradling it under his arm for safekeeping. "This is nice! It's my guess there's a lot more of the same on this thing. Bro, can you still do blood testing with that scope of yours?"

"Sure. I'll get right on it before he dries up and this is all for nothing!" Tyr looked concerned. "Are we sure we want to be doing this?"

"It's not like the guy who shot him is going to ask the cops to see the surveillance tapes... nor would it tell them anything if they did!" Uruz speculated, growing increasingly enticed by the thought of how much they stood to inherit if they played their cards right.

"Are we sure about that?" Thor asked, playing Devil's advocate.

"Are we sure about anything? Who cares? I say it's worth a shot!" Uruz said, smiling at Tyr.

Tyr looked up from setting up a staging area for the blood tests, "I'm gonna need my kit from inside, anyone need anything?"

"A tall horn of mead. Better make that two," said Uruz, gesturing at Thor, who looked lost in thought, a million miles away. "He's missing his honey."

Thor smiled without breaking his trance-like stare. "Nice one..."

"We better hold off on that, at least 'til we determine if one of us is going to bleed." Tyr called out from just inside the first security doorway.

"So what type are you?" Uruz asked Thor.

"Heterosexual," Thor said without batting an eye, his attention turned back to the paperwork in the briefcase. Uruz burst out laughing. Thor finally smiled, "Type B positive," he said. "How about you?"

"I have no bloody clue," Uruz said somberly. "I remember my mother talking to a doctor about it when I was little. They thought I had the plague and were going to try a transfusion."

"You are the damn plague!"

Tyr was gathering up the equipment he needed from the inside cabinet beneath the computer desk when he noticed the hatch to Thor's loft apartment was open about two or three inches. He looked all around himself, quickly, then called out, "Kait!" He paused a moment, then took a couple steps closer, cupped his right hand in the shape of a bull horn, then tried again, directing it right at the loft this time. "Kaitlyn! You up there?" He paused again. This time, when he didn't get a response, he quietly slid Thor's Colt 1911 .45 auto out of the computer drawer, unlocked the hammer safety, then quickly negotiated the spiral stairs, pistol out front, and peered into the room.

Somewhat to his surprise, no one was there. He expected to see Kait asleep, at the very least, after being out for so long. Thor never left his door open. He un-cocked the pistol, shut the door carefully, then came back down and started gathering up the supplies again. Coming in through the doorway themselves, Thor and Uruz met him halfway with a confused look on their faces at the sight of the drawn weapon. "Did you leave your door open this morning? Any chance at all?" Tyr pointed at the loft with the pistol, obviously still disturbed.

"No."

"You're sure?"

"100%. It's just the way I exit... Unless I got shit in my arms and have to balance through the opening, I *always* pull the latch as I start around the first set of stairs. Maybe Kait has been back. It's shut now," he observed, "you been up there?"

"Yeah," Tyr said kind of slowly, starting to get a little lost in thought.

Thor looked all around the family room and computer desk for some clue. "I'm going to look for a note real quick," he said, pointing up at the loft, "you guys probably better get the lab set up for this, we're losing *a lot* of time! I hope it still works! Our bodies might reject the implant anyway, but the chances are certainly much better the fresher the situation is, you know what I mean?"

"Totally. Were on it," Uruz said, already grabbing things out of Tyr's arms to share the load.

"You know, I'm gonna check the entry log real quick," Tyr spit out, nearly dropping the remaining gear into Uruz's arms and bolting for the front door. The door to the garage slid shut behind him and he started pushing buttons on the control pad, as Thor disappeared into his room upstairs.

"Nutters," Uruz muttered, standing in front of the entry pad to the garage doors. "What am I supposed to key in my code with, my beak?" he asked, sarcastically, lifting up the huge armload of stuff to display.

"Shit, I'm sorry, bro." Tyr quickly typed a series of numbers into the pad by the front door, and the slider in front of Uruz reopened. "Cool?"

"Nice trick! You're gonna have to show me that one." He walked into the security foyer, and the first door slid shut behind him.

Upstairs, Thor could find nothing, but something still wasn't right. There was some kind of odor in the air that he recognized. It was very faint, but it was there. Being upstairs, he was used to dismissing that sort of thing, because everything found its way up here, but this was fresh, like smoke. Pipe smoke. He checked his ashtray to make sure it wasn't some random cigarette, like one of Kait's cloves, or hybrid hydroponic tobacco/weed farm abominations, but nothing turned up. No, he knew this smell. It was faint, but he knew it.

Following a hunch, he walked over to his fire safe. Hidden in a secret place where the floorboards fit together like a Chinese box, there was a small safe the size of a briefcase that held the original four brothers' most sacred, irreplaceable items. Photographs, papers, jewelry, etc., and the only ones who knew the combination, or even the whereabouts of the safe itself were Thor, Tyr, Uruz, and Dagaz. Feeling sick to his stomach from an intuitive vibe he couldn't wrap his mind around, he quickly dialed in the combination and popped the safe open. He felt flush and had difficulty breathing for a moment as his instinct turned out to be true. Everything in the safe that belonged to Dagaz was missing! "What are you seeing? Anybody come in while we were out?" he yelled loudly down at Tyr, quickly putting the safe back together and stowing it away.

"Nope, no one! Something's kind of strange, though," he started to process.

"What's strange?" Thor asked, wanting more pieces of the puzzle before throwing this out on the table.

"Well, it shows one entry and exit today, but-"

"We went out by way of the garage," Thor interrupted. "Who do you see on the monitor?"

"That's just it... no one! Why would she... did Kait leave a note?"

"Nope. It wasn't Kait."

"Dagaz? No shit... he knows how to program the security recorder, but why the hell wouldn't he want us to know he was here?"

"I don't know, but he took all his shit out of the fire safe, too."

"Really?!" Tyr exclaimed, both surprised and disgusted. "What the hell did we ever do to him? He's been our brother for years and now he's gonna run out on us as if we were total strangers? *Son of a bitch!*"

"Yeah, I know, and without even saying a word. Something doesn't add up. This just ain't like him."

"Fuck all," Tyr concluded. "There's nothing we can do about it right now, we'll talk about this later." He punched in the code and they both entered the foyer for the garage. When the second door opened, they were both a little surprised to see that Uruz had set up most of Tyr's mobile lab right on the flat bed behind the car, and was busy prepping the body for the extraction. "Damn, bro!" Tyr smiled.

"I pay attention," Uruz said, proudly.

"Alright, pay attention to this, " Thor smiled, rolling up his sleeve, "Tyr needs blood from all of us."

Tyr finished hooking up the computer and fired up the software for blood analysis he kept for emergency donors and transfusions. In most cases, there was no getting to an actual uptown hospital during an emergency, nor would any of them help you if you didn't have proper credit, so people on the street got pretty good at playing doctor and passing training on from family member to family member. Those with connections like the North Clan just took it to a higher level. What they couldn't pay or barter for, they stole. That's what it took to care for their own.

As he was loading in the last slide into his scanner, Uruz started getting pissed. He was done poking the corpse for blood, and was pulling out a large knife out of his boot in sheer frustration. "I'll get some God damn blood," he sneered.

"Watch where you do that! We don't want it contaminated with bile or other body fluid, just blood," Tyr advised.

Uruz tried several common points on the body, but came up dry. "Its already all coagulated!" he whined, throwing his arms up in frustration. "Fricken goat cheese!"

Thor smiled and pointed to the inside of his left thigh. "Go for the femul artery. It's got the largest inner diameter. It's likely still fluid in there." Uruz nonchalantly stabbed into the man's leg and twisted his blade sideways, as if he was dealing a lethal wound to a live opponent. This time there was blood. He reached out and over zealously snatched the small syringe from Thor's hand, then easily extracted a full tube of blood from just what was still spewing directly out of the wound. "Alright, now cork that wound before the area we need dries up entirely!"

"That is, if it hasn't already," Tyr added.

"Aye," Uruz mumbled through a mouthful of chocolate.

"Hey! Where the fuck did you get that?" Tyr inquired, gesturing at his mouth with a gloved hand. Uruz grunted and pointed casually at the trench coat of the dead man, crumpled into the corner of the trunk.

"Pocket," he mumbled through chocolate blackened teeth.

"You sick bastard!" Thor laughed. He was way too much of a germ-a-phoebe to handle eating anything while there was loose blood all over the place.

"What? He won't be eating it. Screw it."

"That's not the part that bothers me," he explained softly, looking over at Tyr, who was smiling, but busy punching keys like a madman. Thump! He hit "enter" with authority, then stood up straight, stretching his back side to side as the computer analyzed the three samples. Finally, it stopped. Tyr pointed at himself, Uruz, then Thor, calling them out.

"A negative, A negative, and B positive." He pushed a drop of blood from the dead man out onto the glass slide, then put a top pane over it and carefully loaded it into the small scanner, throwing the other three into a bowl of alcohol for cleaning. This time no one spoke. They anxiously stared at the screen, waiting for the results. If it matched any of them, it would be possible, as long as the host body didn't reject it and go into toxic shock, to carefully cut out the man's implanted ID chip, fuse it in line with the new blood vessels, and have fully functioning access to the man's entire topside identity.

One would be able to access bank accounts, credit lines, pass through security doors, gain VIP treatment at public events, etc. Facial recognition software could still be a potential problem out in public, but as long as an ambient scanner didn't get both sets of data at the same time, the discrepancy would go unnoticed. The trouble was that they had become more and more common. They were mounted in every storefront, bank terminal, street corner and drive thru. The one saving grace was that although they were getting pretty sophisticated, they still required line of site to use.

The solution was to implant the chip in a location on the body that the scanner couldn't see unless one wanted it to, but where one could fool someone who was watching into thinking they had just scanned the government issued left wrist implant. There were many ways to accomplish this, but surely one of the best was the palm of the opposite hand. It could be presented by pushing up the left sleeve with the right hand in the correct position, a wave, picking up an object, etc., but more importantly it could be concealed very easy, as there were all kinds of reasons why a scan might not show anything, but a positive with the wrong name would be catastrophic. The prison barges off the coast were teeming with thieves who tried to kill someone for their implant.

The computer finally finished chewing on the sample, and after several inconclusive passes, produced a positive result. Tyr looked up at Thor. "B positive." Uruz stopped chewing and, for a moment, you could've heard a pin drop.

"Well I'll be a cocksucker's lunch," Thor said, slightly overcome by a head-rush of seismic providence. "Bring me two horns of mead! Let's get this done!"

Tyr worked on the implant while Uruz worked on disposing of the body and dismantling the car. They had a furnace that was created to be a multipurpose steam generator/ forge/ heat source and was truly a work of art. Designed and built into the structure by his grandfather's generation of North Clan, it was capable of heating the entire building through the conduction of heated water through a pipe network built into the entire floor. The main reservoir was heated in a tank just out of sight above the fire, but in front of the chase for the flu.

Due to its positioning, the water was heated at an extremely efficient rate. The temperature could then be controlled by how far the damper that allowed the conduction of water was opened. Its own heat would cause the circulation to commence, slowly heating the plasticized concrete floor to the desired temperature. Due to its high thermal mass, it would stay at that temperature long after the fire was extinguished. The super-hot exhaust shaft leading out to the roof had a series of resistance based turbines that were spun by the heat and smoke and produced a flow of electricity to a huge battery array in the adjacent storage room.

The capacity as a metal forge was built in to the design by way of its deep capacity and forced air bellows that could be operated to increase the heat dramatically. They possessed a full array of casting tools and sand boxes, allowing them to manufacture metal tools, parts, and weapons in pretty much any shape or material desired. Uruz stoked the fire with the bellows and tossed the man's body into the open chamber, along with several bricks of press-fuel they had left from the winter, courtesy of Jerrick's organic compost, to speed the process and mask the smell coming out of the stack. A fairly good amount of the car could be dealt with in the same manner, in large casting pots, and the non-combustible alloy retained in bricks. First he needed to strip off what they needed to keep, which were, in this particular case, some very high dollar components. Jerrick would have to receive this one piece mail. It was simply too hot.

Tyr was finishing up. The procedure seemed to work perfectly. All that was really required biologically was constant blood-flow through the device. Whether or not Thor's body would reject the implant, only time would tell. Now it was time to lay low for a day or two and let things cool off a bit. *Yeah, right....* This was not something Thor was exceedingly good at. He was already wrapping the incision on his right palm with a thin layer of gauze and covering that with a leather fingerless glove. "Where the hell are you going?" Tyr asked him.

"Hunting." He shook Tyr's hand with his left hand, keeping the sore right one close to his body. "I've got some questions that need answered."

"Yeah, I suppose so." Tyr let go of the hand shake and grabbed him by the scruff of the neck, pulling him in for a rough, big-brotherly hug. Uruz, seeing what was happening out of the corner of his eye, stopped working temporarily and walked over toward them. Tyr smiled, "I suppose I'd go with you, but someone has to keep this derelict out of trouble!" He pointed at Uruz with his thumb.

"What is this, the Vacillator 500 over here? Get the fuck out of here, you're buggin' me!" Uruz sneered, shoving Thor back about two feet, "Come here, pillock!" He reeled him back in for a bear hug, stopping only after he got an audible grunt out of Thor. "Oooooh shit! Sorry, bro," he said, momentarily forgetting about the implant. "Let me see it!"

"It's wrapped," Thor said, showing him the hand with the gauze.

"Right palm... interesting," he said, holding Thor's hand by the wrist, and nodding at Tyr. "Take care of yourself out there. There might be people gunnin' for us over this shit," he advised. "You know, she's gonna come back right after you leave...."

"It's not just her."

"Well what, then?" Uruz pried, starting to get annoyed at Thor's stubbornness.

"Dagaz was here," Tyr interjected.

"When?"

Thor spoke up. "Today, during the small gap when we were gone. Tells me he was watching us and waiting. He even tried to cover his tracks!"

"He also grabbed the last of his personal shit out of Thor's fire safe!" Tyr added.

"Jesus," Uruz said somberly, "you don't think he would sell us out would he? I mean, this is Dagaz were talking about, right?!"

"Never trust a man who has lost his faith," Thor answered. He walked over to the side door, still needing a thing or two from inside.

"Wait!" Uruz yelled. He reached into the cab of the tow truck and grabbed Thor's harness, stretching toward Thor with the twin .45's . "I know you usually pack light, but do this for me...."

"Thank you," he accepted, grabbing them with a nod and a smile. "Take care, my brothers, I'll be back!"

Outside it was starting to get dark. There were an unusually large number of cars on the streets above, possibly another football game, or some other public event getting ready to begin. This meant a higher than normal degree of ambient light flickering about. Thor had his attention focused on the faces of those he passed, hoping to see something he could use... someone who could tell him something.

She had only been missing for a day and a half, but every fiber of his being told him something was horribly wrong. The worst thing was the timing. Had she allowed herself to get too close, to show too much of herself to him, and now she was running as a defense mechanism? *Impossible,* he told himself, but he had to entertain any and all possibilities. The worst case scenario seemed almost just as hard to swallow.

She practically had eyes in the back of her head, and was a certifiable nightmare in a fight. It was conceivable that someone finally got the drop on her, but not very likely. At any rate, he would have to retrace her steps as close as he could guess them to have been, and pray for the best. His main area of focus, of course, would be the Border District club scene. He had been there a few times with her and knew some of the people who knew her quite well. If she was OK, they would almost surely have seen her in the last couple days.

When she needed to think, she came here... the infamous Bar-muda Triangle: a series of clubs and pubs along a three-street triangular hub of unabashed, uncontrollable drunken mayhem that appealed strongly to only the truly deranged and wild at heart. With this, of coarse, and in the absence of any kind of real law enforcement, came the type of sick bastard behavior leading to the highest rate of murders and disappearances in the Great Northwest, earning the region its colorful name.

There were a total of over 10 bars in the three street junction between Casino Rd., a concrete canyon named Shotgun Alley, and an ongoing shanty town that slowly morphed into a converted strip mall lovingly referred to as Hell's Ditch. To approach the junction from any of these thoroughfares at night was foolish and time consuming, to say the least. He decided to go straight to the Triangle via Kait's monkey bar route under the viaduct.

He went this way with her before, and was familiar enough with it to negotiate its challenges even with his new handicap to protect. Somewhat hidden, and easily defensible, this was to be their own private tryst on the off chance that they were to ever get separated in any of the outbreaks of violence that erupt in the Triangle. There were several sections of bridge, stretching on for what seemed like miles, where the ground was far enough away that a fall would be fatal, and though she was at least as coordinated as Thor, he still scanned the ground as he traversed along, hoping against all odds that he didn't spot the product of a rare mistake.

It was totally dark by the time he reached the off-ramp leading to the cluster of lights and music. He quickly scaled down and headed for the club he remembered going to with her before. Hell's Kitchen was a progressive, cutting edge to retro punk and industrial metal bar. The loud atmosphere precluded idiotic small talk, pickup lines, and any other sort of meaningless bar rhetoric, and left only pure animal lust and magnitude as a basis for hooking up with people of interest. This was the way both of them always preferred it, so this became their unofficial favorite watering hole. The irony was that without as much drunken conversation, there were less fights breaking out here than at other more halcyon venues nearby.

Inside, people were starting to amass as the band onstage set up their gear for a show. The large, bearded bartender didn't really know Thor personally, but he definitely remembered him after the fight that broke out about a month earlier. Several guys had it in for Thor, and he danced around them with a beer in his hand, narrowly evading punch after kick after punch, throwing these guys into each other, the walls, and the floor with the smallest effort, and without directing even one attack at them, he had all of them exhausted and incapacitated on the floor without spilling his beer; the entire population of the bar watching and cheering him on.

The immovable axis around which all hostility must travel. It was an exercise in nothing short of pure Zen. He had even been seen on numerous occasions walking, almost in slow motion, right through the center of the mosh pit, a swirling vortex of spontaneous, undirected violence, without so much as even the slightest physical contact with any of the numerous flailing participants. At times he would almost seem to anyone looking to be an apparition, floating through the slam dance, completely unaffected by it. Though his exploits up north had not become known to everyone down here, it was safe to say he enjoyed a bit of mysterious notoriety in this area as well. The bartender smiled as he approached, making his own version of a martial artist's ready stance. "Hey Drunken Master! What can I get you?" He gestured at the rows of bottles behind him.

"Oh, nothin' tonight, man. I was just wondering if you've seen Kait in the last couple nights...."

"Kait? You mean the hot blonde who's usually with you?"

"That's the one!" he smiled back. "You seen her?"

"Oh, yeah! She was here the night before last." The burly man glanced around, starting to look a little concerned. "I haven't seen you here in a while. Do you know what's been happening around here?" he asked, leaning over the bar toward Thor.

"No! What?" Thor asked out loud with his palms up and out to his sides, starting to get a little upset.

"Three girls killed in three weeks. All within a couple of blocks of here," he spoke up, jabbing his large index finger down onto the bar hard enough to shake nearby glasses. One down the street in Hell's Ditch... a prostitute, and the other two within a block of here."

Thor looked concerned; almost sick. "Are they related?"

"What?"

"Was it the same fucking guy?!" he snapped.

"I don't know, I don't know. They say the first one was raped and beaten. The second was knifed, and the third... Well, I guess they didn't leave her body, but people saw a guy attacking her, then a second guy showed up and there was some kind of gunfight and everyone scattered. Later on, the body was gone. The second girl was a customer of mine," he sneered, as if wanting revenge, "but no one got a look at where the third one came from. This happened well after I remember seeing, what was her name? Kait? After that, I think...."

"Where did it happen?" Thor asked, a little more temperate.

"Right in front of the overpass, around the corner."

"Did anyone see the shooter?"

"Briefly. They thought he was a cop, and got scared. I think it was a professional hit.... There was never anyone on the scene... no investigation."

"Thanks, man." Thor tossed a couple bucks into the man's tip jar, then slapped him on the shoulder and started to walk off. "Thanks."

"No problem," he yelled over the band starting to do a sound check. "Hey! One more thing, I almost forgot!" Thor turned around and looked at him. "Some guy was asking about her, too. I wanna say three, maybe four days ago.... Skinny guy wearing a black trench and a wide brimmed leather hat. Almost a cowboy style hat. Said he was her brother," he started to remember, "...but she told me her family all died when she was a kid."

"They did." He walked off, clenching his fist over the implant, over and over, trying to numb himself to the pain and gain strength. *Dagaz! What the fuck are you up to? If you touched one hair on her head....* He marched with a purpose to the overpass he came down from. This had to be the spot the bartender was talking about. He started combing the ground, one end of the street to the other for clues... anything that would tell him what the hell happened.

He got all the way across the street without anything of note entering his single-minded field of vision, then he saw it... a small, black hair-tie with a silver Celtic eternity knot fastened to it. He picked it up slowly. This wouldn't ordinarily be of too much interest except it was he who gave it to her, along with a long explanation of its meaning, on her birthday last year. There was a small cluster of long, blonde hair still stuck in the metal part. She used to complain of it pulling her hair when she took it out, but she loved it so much she used it all the time, anyway. His heart sank and tears started welling up in his eyes, as he knew it had to be her that the bartender spoke of. *What had she gotten involved in? A professional hit? Was the other man Dagaz? What the hell was going on?*

He cried out in pain, rage and frustration so loud that he could hear dogs begin to bark way off in the distance down in Hell's Ditch. *Pull it together, man.* He started combing the whole area around where he found the hair-tie for more pieces to the puzzle. It was dark, but there was just enough light coming from around the corner to see the ground. He bent down in the grass, growing knee high next to the old pavement. He could see some pretty big spots of blood on the ground, and was busy scraping the coagulated mess with the back edge of his knife in the hopes that he could somehow compare DNA between the hair and the blood to make sure the blood came from her, when he saw something shiny in the grass. It was the remote handle to a pair of stun-cuffs!

He had seen them demonstrated, but never actually owned the device. This was a hugely expensive piece of hardware. He realized he could probably safely rule out some derelict street attacker at this point. He was fiddling with the grip on the thing when he noticed something else. He parted the grass carefully and took a closer look, blinking just to make sure he wasn't seeing things. It was a black leather wallet.

He quickly opened it, and came one held breath away from passing out from shock when he saw the picture on the ID card affixed to the inner flap. The name on the card was James S. Stanton... *it was Reid! It was the man in the trunk!* He dropped the wallet, scrambling backward as he gasped for air. He started to hyperventilate, and had to focus hard to come back without losing consciousness. *Slow down... Breathe.* He slowly regained his composure and became aware that he was rubbing the implant bloody. The glove was off and the gauze was peeling, already soaked in blood from the activities that brought him here. *Just Breathe....*

None of this made very much sense, but it was definitely time to find out as much as he could about "James S. Stanton." All he knew for fact was that Reid was dead, and it would not be reported. No, now *he* was Reid, or "Stanton." Better yet, now he had Stanton's address! For all he really knew at this point, Kait could still be alive. He had to hope, but his instinct did not reassure him.

First order of business, find out what this bastard was worth. He snatched up the wallet, tucked it in his pocket, and started the long trip back up north. With any luck, the banks would be opening right about the time he got back. He would need to get cleaned up and prepare to adopt his "topsider" persona before he could get within twenty feet of a banking terminal, but in spite of extreme exhaustion and sleep deprivation, he was confident he could pull it off without a hitch.

Going topside was always a risk. Though there was a huge percentage of harmless sheep to camouflage one's presence, the level of intolerance for your fellow man had reached an unprecedented threshold. The paranoid establishment culture would panic and report you on site if they thought for one second that you were homeless. To them, that simply meant that you were there to steal whatever they had, or worse, were some sort of psychotic deviant that escaped its restraints, and needed to be rounded up immediately to be put back on your side of the fence. Either way, you had absolutely no business around them, and would be forcibly removed or detained in police custody at the slightest whim of one who had money and power.

The primary difference is that the poor generally refused to accept the implant of a chip, as it was actually illegal to be a vagrant. So many scans took place in the course of any day, even just walking around or shopping, that it would raise red flags to the police immediately just by being broke. If your chip revealed a zero balance, you could be detained and investigated. If one didn't have their own home and income, they were immediately remanded to a state run facility for the welfare of derelict citizens, where all their basic needs were taken care of, but they were immediately put into whatever position the institute saw fit for them to strengthen the work force and contribute to society in exchange.

It was communism with an electric gift-wrap, because once in this system, there was no chance for advancement, as there was no income. The cost to house and feed the citizen always exceeded the petty amount the job that they were assigned to do would pay. It was either live in this prison for the unfortunate, or the relative freedom, but absolute uncertainty of the underground. Escaping the commune really wasn't hard, if one decided to go underground, as they didn't spend a whole lot of money keeping up any of the facilities or infrastructure of the project, but as with any oppressive government, it was simply better to avoid any entanglement or exposure in the first place, if at all possible.

CHAPTER 16: REVELATION

Tyr and Uruz were back inside the stronghold. Uruz was rifling through the paperwork in the briefcase, and Tyr was glued to the dead man's laptop. He had it connected to his own, using his software to break through any encryption he encountered. Having already made it through a challenging password series required just to boot the damn thing up, Tyr was perusing his hard drive, looking for pieces of the puzzle.

It was just odd that a man of Reid's stature would end up in a situation to try to blackmail anyone. He was wealthy beyond imagination already. Certainly it wasn't just about the money... maybe it was a personal strike. Either way, at this point, it didn't really matter, except that the contents of the briefcase were still intact, and probably still incriminating to someone. *Perhaps it wasn't blackmail at all.* What if he was simply going to blow the whistle on some high level corporate corruption? They killed him, but somehow were stopped short of destroying the evidence. *That would mean they would most certainly be looking for it... and that would put everyone in danger!*

He stumbled onto a program named "Cams" and opened it up. A menu popped up listing a number of locations. He punched one in, and started laughing hysterically as the screen came up, "Hey bro! Check this out!" Uruz leaned over and burst into a fit of guttural laughter, snorting profusely as the screen showed a gigantic woman in her mid to late 50's struggling tenaciously to get into a pair of pants in a dressing room somewhere. He looked at the time caption in the corner of the screen and suddenly realized it was a live feed. "This is in real time! Holy shit!"

"Reid, you sick, perverted fuck! I love it!" Uruz chuckled, finally regaining his composure. "What else does he have?" he asked eagerly.

Tyr punched in link after link, laughing at the man's audacity. Some of them showed bathrooms from the ceiling vent, some were of different intersections and street side views around town, but they were all obviously very candid. After checking out nearly all of them, they were growing bored with the whole thing and almost closed the program when Uruz saw a link toward the bottom of the list that interested him.

"What's H.K.? One and two... check those out," he said. Tyr clicked on the link for "H.K.-1," and was kind of caught off guard to see the front door of Hell's Kitchen in the Border District. "Hey," Uruz exclaimed, "I know that place!"

"Yeah, me too. I haven't been there in a while, but I'd bet dollars to donuts that that's exactly where Thor went yesterday! What a trip!" Tyr suddenly felt a chill go up his spine. He quickly punched in the second link and saw a shot from along the side of a building, down a street he didn't recognize, at an off ramp. Cars were flying by overhead on the freeway, but nothing was going on at street level. It looked like a ramp that probably didn't see much use.

"I know *that* place, too!" Uruz yelled out. "It's right around the corner from the bar. What a strange spot to put a cam... I like the dressing room better!" He reached out to change the link, but Tyr grabbed his wrist, sensing something strange about this. "What?" Uruz complained. "You're not going to see him pop up in it unless you could rewind it... which you can't."

Tyr scratched his chin, then opened his eyes wide, pointing at Uruz. "No shit! Bro, that's it!" He dropped down a menu on the player and started looking for recorded files. Sure enough, he found an entire database full of them. "Jackpot!" he exclaimed, and clicked on the last date recorded. The laptop was dead when he started, and so was its owner, so he assumed it was probably receiving a signal up until the battery died. The screen that popped up, oddly enough, was of the same view from that particular camera. It was night time....

He watched for about three or four uneventful minutes before he looked closer and realized just how enormous the file actually was. He clicked on the progress bar and dragged it to the right, speeding through the recording until finally, there was movement. He pulled back just a bit, then waited, letting it play out. Suddenly, a figure appeared from the left side, walking away from the camera. It was a woman. "Jesus Tap-dancing Christ!" he yelled, slapping Uruz entirely too hard with the back of his hand.

"Fuck!" Uruz yelled back, annoyed at the attack and rubbing his arm where Tyr slapped him as he turned his attention toward the screen. His scowl became a look of shock similar to Tyr's as he saw who was walking across the screen. "That's Kait!" He turned to Tyr, who was nearly catatonic, eyes and mouth wide open, but unable to speak. They both jumped back suddenly as they saw that she wasn't alone, and then watched in horror as she was attacked from behind, disabling her attacker only to have the verdict changed by a stun gun of some kind.

The resolution was fair, but the light was poor, and she was a long way from the camera, still, they could visibly tell she was still twitching from the stunner long after a third man entered the scene from the left, fired one shot right into the attacker's forehead, then walked away, somewhere off to the right. She laid there twitching with the fallen man on top of her for what seemed like forever, while her brothers sat powerless in front of the monitor, still not believing what they were seeing.

"What the fuck?" Tyr finally said, still staring at the screen with unblinking eyes. A couple more minutes passed, then a car pulled up. *It was the BMW they just dismantled!* The shot in the head... The kick by Kait, bending the attacker's knee straight back... *The guy on the ground was Reid himself!* They watched on to see the man with the gun, dressed all in tactical black, similar to a swat officer, pull up close to the bodies, then get out and pop the trunk open.

He threw Reid in the trunk, then grabbed the case and computer out of the passenger side and threw them in with him. He shut the trunk, then walked slowly over towards Kait, who was still on the ground, shaking violently. Even if she had survived this far, the ongoing shock at that voltage would turn her into a vegetable.

Tyr and Uruz were both red with rage, gritting their teeth and wanting so much to look away, but continuing to watch just the same as the man leveled his pistol at her head. Suddenly there was a flash of muzzle fire from just off to the left, in the darkest part of the alley, well off the road. The man dropped to his knees, then folded over backward, almost on top of her. Tyr's mouth was wide open again.

A pair of figures emerged from the darkness dressed in military gear. One covered the street back toward the camera while the larger one knelt above Kait, disconnecting whatever was shocking her, then checked her pulse. He made a gesture to his partner with his hand open, back and forth across his throat like a knife, and Uruz yelled out loud, grabbing hold of Tyr by the clothes with his fists.

Tyr sat with his jaw clenched, tears welling up in his eyes, and closed his fists so hard he started cutting himself with his own fingernails. The huge man hoisted her onto his shoulder, fireman style, then took off back into the dark the way he came. The smaller man grabbed the apparent hitman the same way, but seemed to be having some trouble. Repeatedly he dropped the man, who seemed almost to be rooted to the ground. Suddenly there appeared to be commotion coming from the direction of the camera and the second man dropped him, also disappearing back into the alley after his partner. People were converging on the scene, but they must have arrived too late to see what really happened, so they didn't understand the relevance of the car, and left it in the middle of the road, blocking the off-ramp.

This was all starting to make a small amount of sense to them when they were snapped out of their deepened thought by a very loud bang on the front security door. They looked at each other, surprised and alarmed, especially given what they just witnessed. Uruz was scrambling for guns, while Tyr wiped his eyes and quickly shut the laptop with the program still playing. *Nobody comes here uninvited! Nobody!* The only people who even knew where they lived were the small handful that lived in tight pockets directly around this area, and they all knew better than to drop by unannounced. *"BANG! BANG! BANG!"* They heard again.

"Catch!" Uruz was still in the gun cabinet, not trusting the situation for a moment. He tossed Tyr a short shotgun, then grabbed another one for himself. They were kept loaded, but he strapped a bandolier with about 50 more shotgun shells attached to it around his neck and shoulder. *Now he was ready....* Tyr got there right before him. Looking at the monitor, they could only see the top of a hat. It looked like Dagaz. Only problem is, Dagaz wouldn't knock. Tyr cocked the pump on his shotgun to chamber a round. Uruz did the same, realizing he hadn't already.

Tyr pushed the intercom button and spoke in a loud, concise tone, "Step away from the door and identify yourself!" The person with the hat stepped back about three feet, and looked up at the camera. It *was* Dagaz, but he had a gun pointed at his head from the right, and a different set of hands holding him still by his lapel and the back of his neck on the left. "IDENTIFY YOURSELVES RIGHT NOW, MOTHER FUCKERS!" he yelled considerably louder and more violent. He was still stewing about Kait, and not in any mood for games.

The men backed up further. He could see it was Cane. He was the unofficial ruler of the U District; a ruthless dictator who was rising to new heights of power all the time due to his complete lack of ethics. He was one of the few underground bosses who had actually wreaked enough havoc to get the attention of the Governor and his anti-terrorism SWAT teams.

The man on his left was his brother, T. It was assumed, due to the fact that the man was over six and a half feet tall, that the "T" stood for "Tiny." No one was really sure because T didn't speak to anyone but Cane, and only then by whispering in his ear. It was pretty much common knowledge, however, that they were not a pair to be trifle with.

"We're here to speak to Dragon!" Cane spoke up, glaring into the camera, and forcing the gun a little harder into Dagaz's temple.

"Come on in," Tyr said softly, attempting to control the tone of the encounter. He hit a button, and the outer security door slid open. The front foyer was "L" shaped, so before they realized there was a second door, they had already shoved their way inside, and Tyr silently shut the first door behind them. They came defensively around the corner and became agitated when they realized they were trapped.

"Open this door or you'll be mopping up your skinny friend! I'm not fucking joking!" Cane yelled fiercely, ramming the gun up under Dagaz's chin and nearly choking him with it.

Tyr spoke calmly into the com, trying to manipulate their mood, as well as take some of their attention off of Dagaz and pull it towards the door. "Take it easy, Cane," he said softly and slowly, "I'll be able to open the door in three seconds...." He pushed a button on the panel, but not the one for the door. He could tell by Dagaz's increase in chest size that he was holding his breath already. "One... Two... Three..." He waited for just another second, then he looked at the monitor and smiled as both men crumpled to the floor without a fight. The gas was an invisible, odorless compound Tyr had been perfecting out of a few different household chemicals. He hit the exhaust fan, waited a couple more seconds, then opened the door for real.

"Whew!" Dagaz exhaled, then breathed in fresh air, trying to regain his composure. Uruz stepped in and gave him a big bear hug, lifting his feet off the ground. Tyr scooped up their weapons and patted them down revealing a couple knives and an ankle pistol. He still wasn't sure what to make of Dagaz's disappearance, or his sneaking in when they weren't there, so he decided not to say anything to him about it just yet. It was just good to see him alive.

CHAPTER 17: A WOLF IN SHEEP'S CLOTHING

He sat on the high point of the railing on the way back, listening as the dull hum of the occasional early morning traveler passed in Doppler overhead. He sat, thinking of Kait and remembering her laugh, her smile, her fight and her unquenchable energy. He sat for so long he barely noticed the occasional dull hum turning into a crescendo of interwoven, bidirectional rush hour frenzy on its way to feed the machine. He stood up, stretching, and started to walk toward the north end again, staring off into the horizon as the sun peeked up over the mountains.

On this particular stretch of road there wasn't much development out to the east. It was mostly marshland, a putrid byproduct of a failed ecosystem, and was deemed an indevelopable wasteland. This made for one of the most stunning sunrises Thor could remember seeing in a long time. Off in the distance he could see the tops of the Cascades through the sea of morning mist and hazy smog. To the west, an unseasonably warm blast of sunshine reflected off of the manmade ridge of buildings, mirroring the eastern skyline with its majesty; manifest destiny forcing fingers of new growth upwards toward the sky like the plates of the earth, colliding in critical mass to produce unprecedented beauty through uncalibrated rage.

Walking down the underside of the freeway, suspended high above the valley, he paused; taking it all in. The duality of his own existence seemed to resonate stronger in this place. He truly was a child of both worlds. Without the constant circle of death and rebirth, destruction and reinvention, he lacked purpose... yet somehow he longed for the solitude and harmony of nature.

To take his rightful place with his family in the fight to preserve what little natural beauty there was left on this infected planet would certainly be a purpose worth living for, but he was here and they were a world away. He wouldn't have the first idea how to even go about finding them and scarcely believed they were even still alive. Those that got away back in the day to carry on with that fight were nothing but ghosts to him now. He wanted to believe that the reports and rumors he heard about their deeds were somehow true, and not just the wishful thinking and fictional rhetoric of idealistic morons with too much coffee in their systems and time on their hands, but he had to consider the source of information.

The old ones, the true Alliance For Gaia, were not coffee shop philosophers and sidewalk commandos, but men and women of action. The people he had met in this life with that kind of integrity and honor could be counted on his fingers, and to lose even one was a tragedy to lament. He approached the metropolis, rising up before him on all sides with the energy of a self-perpetuating cancer, and took in his last unafflicted breath for today, feeling just a little bit smaller than he did just a moment ago.

He already knew what banking center he wanted to use. There was a small branch just above the parking garage he and his friends visited to get the first car, the one they delivered complete to Jerrick. He even grabbed the key to the security door at the top of the stairwell before he left home. Somehow he always knew they would have future dealings with this building, though no one, not even the North Clan, would be foolhardy enough to try hitting a bank.

For one thing, since almost everything was done electronically anymore, the only currency to be stolen would be in the form of personal treasure found in safety deposit boxes. The gold and paper money kept in lieu of capitol was typically held in much larger, seriously well-guarded facilities. This was more like a glorified ATM; a mostly automated center for the disbursement or reallocation of one's wealth.

Withdrawal was more or less unnecessary, because the money always had somewhere to go. Payments of any kind could be made, or cashier's checks issued, but the eradication of physical currency put a hasty stop to the practice of armed robbery. You had to have an implant to even get past the initial entryway scanning field, and after that, you had to have direct business to engage in.

To the best of Thor's knowledge, this was one of the last remaining stations that still hadn't incorporated facial recognition software in collaboration with the signal output from the implant. Plastic surgery was very common, so this software was inconclusive, at best, but would still warrant an interrogation by security involving the need for further identification. By a twist of pure fate, he had this man's ID, but they looked nothing alike, so to use it for this purpose would be very dangerous. If he was sniffed out, they would assume he killed Mr. Stanton, and given his social status and reputation as an underground "terrorist," he would be hard pressed to prove otherwise.

He climbed the last tier of steel reinforcement at the mouth of the parking structure, hopped over the concrete knee wall, and entered the stairwell marked for use as "utility access only." At the top of the stairs he used the key like before, peeking out before making a public appearance, then wrapped his weapons in his under shirt along with the key and his new wallet, looking around for a good place to leave them. In case something happened, he didn't want to compound his problems. All he had on himself was the freakishly ordinary looking suit he was wearing and the gloves covering the implant. He used the two foot long gauze strip that field dressed his wound to help tie the other stuff together and secure it under a stair tread for safe keeping, then stepped out of the utility door and donned a pair of sunglasses he had in his pocket.

As he walked nonchalantly toward the front of the building's lobby, he sensed a scan already taking place. He didn't know if it was manual, or ambient, like the implant scanners, it just felt different. It had a different pitch. He pretended to drop something, then looked about, head down, as he continued to walk forward.

He just cleared the plane of the front doorway when he heard, in a soft female voice coming from all around, but somehow loud enough only for him, "Good morning, Mr. Stanton. Welcome to World Bank, Branch 98372." He sighed, looking back up. If there would have been a problem with a facial scan, he would have known by now. Test #1 complete. The implant was functional and transmitting just fine. Now, to find out what kind of assets this chump still had left.

Thor knew that at one time, when he was actually caught trying to hack this asshole, the guy was very well off. Since that time, he had sort of fallen from grace, so to speak. It was very possible he was well paid for his silence and cooperation, as the Alliance website claimed, even after his downfall, but equally possible that he was gullible enough to allow it to be taken from him. The bastards set him up as the fall guy for all of their crooked dealings, then actually had the gall to reinvent him as another front man, because he was so good at it, and proceeded to try to do it again the next time the penny dropped and too many bureaucrats stood to lose their fortunes.

He had been in bed with all of the snakes of the earth: The Bilderberg Group, The Trilateral Commission, the despotism of the World Bank itself; the New World Order responsible for the artificially engineered global bankruptcy that had driven the world into the state of emergency it was in, and still maintained the mother of all puppet shows to keep the silent masses of brainwashed sheep from revolution for as long as it took the elite to live out their greedy little lives.

Thor was next in line behind a disgustingly obese sod of a lawyer, yapping incessantly on his phone as loud as if he was speaking to everyone in the room, obviously impressed with himself and in love with the sound of his own voice. Time seemed to be standing still and Thor was actually becoming physically nauseous from being in this environment for too long.

He could smell the putrid effervescence of a garrulous snooch of a woman, probably in her mid-50's, no doubt the product of upper-middle class pseudo-social climbing, having turned "new money" wealthy after the reshuffling of the plates; now a pompous, insecure fashion disaster engaged in "twaddle-speak" and the over-donning of entirely too much cheesy perfume. She was two people behind him, pouring some serious drama into her telephone "look at me" charade, the person on the other end obviously having to fight to get a word in, edgewise.

Off to either side were two guards, standing with blank looks on their faces. They were armed with some kind of wand with electrodes on the end. Probably not a fun thing to get hit with, but neither guard looked like he had the gumption to use it, and likely, never had.

Two of the five stations opened up at once, and the guy in front of him took the one on the left, not missing a beat in his long winded conversation. Thor walked up to the one on the right, pulling off both gloves, as if he needed to do so just to write something down. Higher level encryption was used for sensitive materials, such as court records, bank accounts, etc., and weren't subject to ambient scans, but required purposeful close up scanning of implant data to ensure privacy and accuracy.

Thor saw the table top scanner pointed down on the left side of the booth, and pulled up his left sleeve, keeping his right hand open and pointed up, so it would read the chip without blowing the facade. He saw confirmation on the screen that it took, and he breathed a little easier, but he was not ready for what he saw next, and actually choked a little on his own saliva as he struggled to keep his composure... *The balance in his account was over 47 million euros!*

He stopped the transaction as fast as he could, instantly paranoid that someone would see it, even though they would have to be right behind him. Something was making him jumpy. He put his gloves back on while the screen reverted back to its default welcome, looking forward for something shiny to cast a reflection backward so he wouldn't need to turn around, when he became keenly aware of a presence directly behind him. As suddenly as he noticed it, he was jolted into staring at the ceiling, shaking intensely as he struggled to tune into the frequency of the blast. Everything faded to black. He fell out to the sound of a faint voice...

"Is this him?"
"Yes..."

CHAPTER 18: A SNAKE IN WOLF'S CLOTHING

Cane and his brother were tied and cuffed, sitting in chairs with their heads slumped over, still very much unconscious. Dagaz finally plopped in his usual seat at the table and exhaled, apparently ready to speak as the immediate work was done. "Thank you," he said with a hokey smile, nodding at both of them as they looked at him scrutinously. "I'm sorry for bringing them here; I just didn't know what to do. As you can see, they kind of had me by the short and curlies...."

"Yeah, how exactly did *that* happen, anyway, bro?" Uruz asked first.

"Where's Thor?" Dagaz asked, evading the question.

"Taking care of some business," Tyr eluded, "how did these assholes get you in this position in the first place?"

"Alright, listen... I went to negotiate a truce with them because of what Thor did to them. Some people I know told me that Central had information that it was Thor that did it and not Cane. I wanted to get Cane back on our side before Central could form an alliance with them. What I didn't know is that Central had already made peace with Cane, and was planning a hit on us. At that point, I was already there and could only talk my way out of it by laying the bullshit on thick, and offering to bring them to Thor to discuss it in person. I'm just glad you were here, or this whole thing would've backfired!"

Yeah, you're laying the bullshit on thick right now, aren't you? Tyr thought to himself. "The only problem is, now they know where we live! We'll never be safe!"

"Would you rather I was dead?" Dagaz yelled, melodramatically.

"Bro, you should have never even went... We have to back up each other's plays, for better or worse!" Uruz scolded.

"You know what...? Fuck this shit! I get a gun put to my head, and all you're worried about is... You know what...? Fuck it! I'll be in my room." Dagaz stormed off with the transparent pretentiousness of a child throwing a temper tantrum for being called a liar after getting caught telling a lie. "How long until they wake up?" he said in an almost normal tone, just before reaching his doorway.

"Depends," Tyr answered, "probably about an hour." Dagaz tried to muster up one of his fake smiles for the sake of pleasantry, but in the end, it only served to further the awkwardness of the moment, and he turned and walked into his room, shutting and locking his door behind him.

"And then he leaves us with *this* present," Uruz joked, pointing at the two men, "a gift fit for a King...." Tyr smiled, trying not to laugh out loud.

They heard the beep of the front security door being opened. "Hey! Thor's back!" Uruz yelled, caught in the middle of pouring a horn of mead from the rack.

"Well, it's about God-damn time!" Tyr added, realizing it had been almost a full twenty four hours since he left them, and as bad as it pained him, Tyr was dying to show him the recorded video of Kait. He wondered if Thor already knew or not.... They listened as the second series of code was being punched in.

He glanced over at the doorway from where he was seated in front of their prisoners, and watched the door slide open from the strange angle this created, not able to see him coming in from the foyer. An arm emerged from around the corner and tossed a small package out onto the floor with a dull thud and the crinkle of its brown paper wrapping as it took an awkward roll or two toward them, then the door slid shut. Uruz was already done pouring his drink, and was nearly back to his seat near Tyr.

"Speaking of presents... " Uruz grinned, started to walk over toward the package.

"BRO! WAIT!-"

The explosion picked mighty Uruz up completely off his feet and sent him flying straight backward over the table and into the giant rack of 5 gallon carboys, spilling half of them onto the ground, and completely shattering the other half from the blast. The two restrained men were the closest to the bomb, and were subsequently cut in half as the fiery shockwave spread out into the large room like a giant expanding halo. Their bottom halves, still secured to the chairs they were sitting on, lay randomly strewn, smoldering beneath the metal table, still bolted to the floor.

Tyr managed to cover his head just before the blast and turn away, but was still blown all the way into the open area below the spiral stairs leading to Thor's room and the roof. He crawled for the stairs, barely conscious, but deafened and in a serious state of shell shock. Just as he reached up to grab the rail and pull himself up, the loft hatch blew downward from another blast, and gunfire erupted from the top of the stairs. He looked back to see if it was Dagaz they were shooting at only to see he hadn't even opened his door to help!

Uruz was unconscious, getting shelled to pieces by the automatic rifle fire. The one who threw the first bomb was now coming through the front door with three more men right behind him. As they zeroed in on him he screamed at the top of his lungs, knowing they had all been betrayed. "DAGAZ!"

Chapter 19: Pinched

It was chilly and the sky was grey. The hillside was devoid of most plant life, save for a short tundra carpeting on the ground with the occasional small flower or patch of weed. Basketball sized rocks scattered here and there broke the monotony of the landscape, which seemed to roll on into the distance, unchanged, but for some reason he could not focus on it. Suddenly a loud squawk sounded high above him and he turned his head to see what it was. The majestic bird, a bald eagle if his eyes did not deceive him, flew right overhead, gliding smoothly on its tremendous wingspan, and headed out over the crest of a nearby hill. He quickly followed. Upon clearing the hilltop, he could see a small house, a log cabin, he realized as he drew closer, standing alone in this barren diorama. He started walking toward it.

Almost as if being yanked off his feet by a giant rubber band, he was jolted out of this scene to the hazy awareness of a terribly bright light. *Am I dead?* Now he was starting to remember... *The bank! The person behind him!* He shook his head hard a couple times to clear his vision. Looking around, he quickly realized he was in a holding cell, a 7' x 7' concrete room with no furniture, no windows, nothing but a metal speaker cover directly overhead that undoubtedly had a small camera installed behind it with the speaker. He got hit from behind with a stunner! He smiled. *Those cowardly bastards!* They would never have gotten away with that one if he had seen it coming... *damn! The body... The chip!*

He quickly reached for his right palm with his left to confirm that it was still there. At least they hadn't figured that one out. The legitimate authorities must have been after Stanton as well for whatever he was doing that got him killed. *What a glorious mess.* Either that, or they did have facial recognition software at that bank, and they got a good look through the cameras at the police station after all.... *That would almost be worse,* he thought to himself.

Thor had been caught before, so they were aware of his existence, and he was even right under the cameras at one point before he realized it and adjusted his posture to blend in with the crowd. He could only hope that they didn't have anything concrete on him, or this could be really bad. Usually they used tactics like this just to mess up whatever it was you were trying to accomplish, and the trial was nothing more than a formal chance for you to hang yourself. They simply didn't have the resources to investigate underground crime, until it interfered with their own interests, then they usually just sent in the cleaners. They would certainly love to get a strangle hold on the entire North Clan if they could ever locate them, so his guess was that they would let him go immediately and try to track him to their hideout. If they didn't, then he would start to worry.

He stood up and started to stretch. He went through each muscle group as if this was the warm up for a rigorous training workout. For all he knew, he had all the time in the world, so why not. Starting with his legs and mid-section, he pulled himself into each of the deep stances and held, having an uncharacteristically difficult time centering his mind and controlling his breathing since he was seriously disturbed and spiritually off balance. His new found attachment to Kait had weakened him just a little. Had he been centered, with his mind only on the task at hand, he almost definitely would have been able to prevent his own capture.

Things usually happen for a reason... 47 million euros. He smiled again. He couldn't help but be distracted by that. Shit, he would be able to take care of the Family for the rest of their lives! He would have the resources to hunt Kait's attacker to the ends of the earth. For the first time in his life, he would have the finances to be free. First he would need to get out of this mess in one piece. Out of here....

He softly and purposefully stepped to the corner of the room, turned around toward the steel door, then knelt in seiza position, on his knees, buttocks on his calf muscles, with his toes pointed straight back, tops of his feet on the floor. His back was totally straight, and he had his arms relaxed, elbows out slightly, with the palms of his hands on his thighs, fingers to the inside at just shy of a 45 degree angle.

He started to meditate, breathing with his tongue on the roof of his mouth as he inhaled through his nose, letting it drop off as he exhaled out of his mouth with long, slow breaths. Within a few repetitions he was beyond worry. Beyond planning, overanalyzing, contemplating... he was beyond any actual "thought" at all. A newborn child enters the world in this state, then, as the very first truth of the world around him reveals itself, opening the floodgate to the sensation of a hard and unexplained slap on the ass from the first face you see, it is lost forever. We train ourselves to get back to its simplicity, to achieve enlightenment... true Zen, but we can only connect with it as a visitor. We know too much, and still we chase the Dragon's tail in every facet of our lives.

Minutes turned into hours, hours seemed like days, and it wasn't long before he lost all track of time. Wanting nothing more than to see an end to this waking nightmare of sterile imprisonment, he played on. He knew damn well they were trying to break him down... to wear him out. They obviously didn't know anything about him at all if they thought they had the power to do that.

CHAPTER 20: A CIRCLE REVEALED

"Clear!" Tyr heard in the distance, like it was coming through a tunnel, or in some kind of surreal movie. Sprawled out face down on the floor, he closed his eyes, pretending to be dead. He was shot up pretty bad, but still he drew breath. None of the bullets pierced vital organs, but he knew he would die very soon of blood loss from the many gut and limb shots that sent him reeling. The last thing he remembered seeing before he closed his eyes was Uruz flat on his back, almost unrecognizably charred from the bomb blast, and shot so full of holes that there was a 10' diameter pool of blood under and all around him and a large chunk of skull bone missing; brain matter exposed. Tyr was screaming on the inside, but he held it in for all he was worth. There was just one thing he needed to see.

The knob turned slowly on Dagaz's door, and Tyr watched intently through just a bloody slit of an eye as the four heavily armed assailants leveled their weapons at the door and waited. "Hold your fire!" The voice commanded from inside, then a hand emerged, holding a small badge on a chain. It was Dagaz's fake badge he used to boast about using to fool topsider lemmings into doing whatever he pleased.

The men diverted their weapons and stood at attention as Dagaz emerged from the room. *What the hell was his play? He's going to get himself killed!* Tyr's heart sank as he saw the look in Dagaz's eyes. For the first time ever he realized he was now seeing the real Dagaz. His nervous, pretentious nature was not just his personality, as they had always believed, but the byproduct of a charade that had fooled them all for years... *The badge was real!*

"Good job, men." He was now strapped with a standard police issue Glock 9mm, and was wearing his badge around his neck for all to see. He had a larger one they had never seen before clipped to his waist.

"All the rats in one hole?" the shooter at the top of the stairs spoke up as he hopped off the last run of stairs to join them, nearly stomping on Tyr's bloodied and outstretched hand as he remained still.

"Not exactly...." Dagaz paced the floor, looking dissatisfied and increasingly nervous. "Krey's not here. I just got word that he's been arrested, so we'll deal with him on our terms... and the welcoming party from Central is late, as usual." He had a strange shakiness to his voice. "Stay vigilant! This is far from over."

"How are they getting in? If they think they are going to hit the Clan on their own ground, they can't be planning on just knocking on the front door...." another one of his men speculated.

"I sold them the code. I programmed the door to accept this new code, but with a three second delay, and an audible warning on our end only. They'll be walking into an ambush. Just stay cocked and locked, when it happens, we'll only have three seconds of warning to be in position. There's no delay on the second door," Dagaz said, matter of factly. "I've been living in this nightmare for years, waiting for the right time to strike at the heart of this monster! We are taking the heads off of three major branches of organized crime in this city, and putting a stop to decades of insurrection. My own mother was killed by a thug from the underground looking for a place to hole up after a failed robbery! This shit has to stop! If they can't play by the rules, then there's no place in society for them to operate! Keep your eyes open, men, we have two out of three, this ends tonight!"

Son of a bitch! He shows up shortly before the same type of shit goes down between Kait's family and their rivals, and then it escalates into a full blown tactical strike that cost her everyone she loved? The only reason they missed her was an anonymous party that Dagaz also went to! It was right after that when he formally introduced his self to her. That son of a bitch set up her clan, too! He set this whole fucking thing into motion years ago!

Tyr's heart sank and his emotions welled from shock to disappointment, to sadness, to pure rage. He only had one play. He and Thor had wired the mead operation and computer desk with explosives when they were both up all night on one of their conspiracy tangents, and told no one. They both carried the means to detonate, but the charges were little more than it would take to destroy all evidence of their operation. They would have to be close... *very close.* To his good fortune, they assumed he was already dead and not a threat, as neither of them even managed to pick up a gun and fire a shot.

He was able to slowly flip up the cover on his watch, and hit a small switch. From where he lay, he could see the small red light come on beneath the desk. Most of the equipment was obviously destroyed in the blast, so they weren't interested in it just yet, but rather they were busy digging around in various backpacks, closets, drawers, etc. He knew they would come around to it, he just hoped it would be Dagaz who got too close. He held on with all the strength he could muster, finger ready on top of the small button that would let loose their avenger.

CHAPTER 21: THE TRUTH, THE WHOLE TRUTH, AND NOTHING BUT THE TRUTH

He and his family members had always tried to live their lives with decency and honor. They found whatever way seemed karmaeically sound to acquire what they needed to get by, but never walked on those less fortunate to do so. When they had to steal, they did so without killing, and only stole from people or businesses that could take it. Almost the entire topside was insured against theft, especially cars. By stealing one's automobile, you were essentially buying them a brand new one.

They did whatever they could to teach this philosophy to other, slightly more rash or depraved souls who didn't understand karma, or were beaten down for so long that they simply didn't care anymore. He and his family lived this way because it was the right way to live, not because there was any personal benefit for them in it, not for profit, not due to zealous fear-based religious duty, but simply because it was right.

They always fought the good fight, and for that they were still harassed, insulted, beaten down, locked up, and then insulted some more, only to be finally released when it was no longer profitable to keep them.

Thor had spun his wheels in this mire his entire life, and for those reasons alone, for freedom and a chance to find like-minded people, he *chose* to remain outside of society. He saw no worth at all in any of the ideals they *pretend* to value, or any of the superficial, materialistic attachments that motivate them. For the most part, he viewed them as an exponentially expanding virus eating away at anything and everything *he* holds dear.

One of the most difficult things he has ever had to do in his life was to sit there and lie, pretending to agree with the simpleton bullshit that was being heaped upon him in syphilitic piles, then kissing the ass of an inferior intellect, just to get them to leave him alone. The animosity he felt for the so-called leaders of this pestilence could not easily be quantified.

At this point, he figured he had been in his cell for about 24 hours without any contact. No explanation, no food, no water, and shackled in restraints that bound his wrists to his ankle cuffs with a three foot chain. They obviously didn't know much about his resourcefulness in combat! That was like giving him a weapon! It was apparent to him now that they didn't actually have anything on him. This whole process was just a big shakedown.

If they did know who he was at all, it was because of a facial scan somewhere that he must have walked right into, but they didn't have shit for evidence against him, or they would already have him before a judge. Once he did finally go, they would most likely just be giving him a formal chance to hang himself, to confess to *anything* just to make *all this horrible treatment* stop.... What they didn't realize was that he would *not* be broken, least of all by them! He was, however, becoming irritable and anxious on a very deep level. Something down in his core just didn't feel right, and he knew he needed to get out of this place as soon as possible.

They had interrupted what, by all rights, should have been an opus morning for him to bask in the moment and plan out the future of his new kingdom in front of an uptown coffee shop somewhere, taking in an uptown view, and checking out some uptown tail. He grinned at the irony... He made a conscious decision right then and there to be as big a nuisance as possible from now until his release, when he would go directly back down to the dungeon where he belonged.

He looked up, seeing the speaker/ microphone/ camera and grinned. "All right! I did it! I did it all! I confess! I'll sign anything, just please, please don't throw me back in the underground!" he yelled, having a hard time keeping a straight face. He wondered if any of these bastard sons of the computer age were even aware of Brer Rabbit. They all grew up watching movies and playing video games on huge, high resolution holo-screens. *Did the people up here even read anymore? Who cares!* His bait was gobbled up. The large steel door buzzed unlocked, then started to open, slowly revealing a man in a detective's three piece suit and two guards, armed with the same kind of stunners that the security guards in the bank had. He knew its pitch, now, but did not see it as being prudent to fight deep inside a facility like this one.

"Mr. Krey," the detective spoke up. "We've been wanting to have a talk with you for some time." His heart missed a beat. He was relieved as hell that the man didn't say "Stanton," but now there was just the question of how much, if anything, they knew. "It seems you've been placed at the scene of a few rather heinous crimes, Krey, but if you formally confess, it will be taken into serious consideration with regard to your sentence...." Thor just sat and silently stared at him.

"Look, asshole, your friends already confessed, and they've implicated you! Yeah, that's right! We already know exactly how it went down, we just need to see it on a formal document so we don't waste any more of the court's valuable time. Your cooperation will definitely help bring leniency to your sentence!"

Thor smiled. *Where the hell do they find these guys?* He exhaled, and looked down at the floor as if he was thinking about coming clean.

The officer continued, "Look, man, I'm not the enemy. I'm trying to do you a huge favor here... They're calling you a terrorist! I know you're not a bad guy... You probably just made some bad decisions and feel like now you don't have any choices left, but if you don't show some remorse and confess, the judge is going to have no choice but to give you the maximum sentence. You could be looking at being locked up for the rest of your life. Is that what you want?" He leaned down toward him, trying to look into his eyes. "I said, is that what you want?!?" he yelled, slamming his open hand against the wall, palm down.

"Shit, I'm sorry, were you still talking?" He smiled, politely, getting some satisfaction as he could see the man's face actually turning from white to red. "I was busy writing a poem. Check it out!" He recited it for the man, adopting a thick, but very convincing Irish brogue.

> *"My mind has gone and run away,*
> *I hope that I won't miss it...*
> *...and if ya see me hairy arse,*
> *well, ya know that you can kiss it."*

He cracked up laughing at his own joke so hard he fell over sideways out of his seiza position, then spoke out, still in character with his Irish accent,. "What did you say your name was? Mr. McFullo'shit? Sounds Irish... Do you have a little Irish in you? Do you want some? Piss off, Boyle," he taunted further, "Can't you see I have a lot going on, here?" He started laughing again, this time, right in the man's face, who was still leaning down toward him. He took the bait again. Thor cringed a little as the enraged man pulled back his fist and drilled him right in the face with a strong right cross, just above his left cheek, then stormed out of the room, followed by the guards. There was no doubt this would leave a shiner.

He fell over laughing hysterically as they left him alone again. Now he would have some leverage to use in his sure-to-be-senseless court proceedings. However this was to play out, he thought, it would probably behoove him to keep his mouth shut in the presence of the judge and just go for sympathy points. He wasn't going to convince this person to see things his way, nor was he likely to even listen to reason, but he did have the power to remand him to further evaluation, which would keep him incarcerated for up to 72 more hours! This would not do. He would bite the bullet and keep his thoughts to himself, even though this was something he was not exceedingly good at....

No sooner was he back into a state of centered meditation, when the door opened again and in walked another man in a three piece suit, followed by the same two guards. They carried in a collapsible table and two chairs and began setting it up, one chair on his side, and the other straight across from him. "Cigarette?" he offered, taking a seat.

"Sure," Thor replied, trying not to sound too anxious, though he couldn't even remember the last time he smoked a "tailor-made" factory cigarette instead of the home made, roll your own tobacco from underground hydroponics or houseplant style growing operations. A rare treat like this was almost worth getting pinched in the first place. *Almost.*

"Let me see that eye..." He leaned forward, then shook his head in obvious disapproval of the officer's tactics. "Jesus." He reached out, offering Thor a flame.

Thor inhaled deeply; eyes closed. He held the smoke for a couple seconds, then exhaled and sat down, leaning way back in his seat and smiling skeptically at the man with his arms crossed over his chest in a somewhat dignified manner, despite the shackles. "Good cop, bad cop?"

"I'm not a cop, I'm your lawyer."

"What the hell do I need a lawyer for? I didn't do anything!"

"Well, at this point, they have a sheet a mile long on you... they just need to show that you're remorseless and untreatable to obtain a life sentence, or a death sentence. If you can explain each of these offenses to me from *your* point of view, I will make sure they remand you to a clinic for 'treatment.' You and I both know you're not crazy, but you may have to play their game to get out of this."

"To be sure," he nodded, taking another long drag, "to be sure." This was the biggest pile of steaming excrement Thor had ever had the privilege of standing knee deep in. "Do you have a pen? I can start by writing a couple things down...."

The man's face lit up just a little too much. "Sure!" He reached into his suit jacket inside left pocket, revealing just enough of his shirt that Thor could see the strap of a shoulder harness style holster; the gun, no doubt, probably locked in one of the small weapon lockers outside the processing area for use by all of the cops. He produced a pen and offered it to Thor, extending his hand with the pen between two fingers, like a cigarette.

Thor reached for it, acting nervous, and intentionally rammed the back of his hand into the point of it, knocking it to the floor off to the man's right. The man turned and squatted, leaning over a bit without offering his backside to Thor, as any cop would instinctively do. This gave him just the angle he needed to see the small belt clip badge beneath the man's jacket, hidden way off to the right side, as any right handed person would probably wear it. Thor reached back out, this time offering his left hand, palm up to the officer.

"Sorry about that...." Thor played along, pretending to be genuinely unaware of the man's true identity.

"No problem." The officer looked at the guard to his left, then waved him closer. "Get my client a pad of paper, please." The guard nodded nervously, looking up at Thor just before he walked off toward the door. "Look, you're going to have to be as concise as possible, there's not much time left... They have you scheduled to go to court at 8:30! It's 8:00 right now."

"Got it!" Thor smiled and winked, making a clicking sound in his cheek as he pointed a finger pistol at the man and dropped the hammer. "What do you call a million dead lawyers at the bottom of the ocean?"

The man grinned. "What?"

"A good start!" The officer belted out the beginning of a genuine laugh, then pulled back as the guard came in with a small notepad about the size of a trucker's wallet and handed it to Thor.

"OK!" He exhaled hard into the palms of his hands and rubbed them together with the pad out in front of him, then picked it and the pen up and leaned against the wall and started writing. "Details, details..." he muttered. The officer smiled proudly a tiny bit, trying not to let it show.

Unbeknownst to most, Thor was actually an avid cartoonist, and given the circumstances, he could not resist. He quickly drew a comedic rendition of the man, exaggerating all of his prominent features, down to the excessive hair on the back of his hands, and his uni-brow. He depicted the man's hand placed palm down on a bible, while the other hand pointed at you, mouth open, making some kind of point to a judge, or somebody. The caption at the top of the page said, "How do you know when a lawyer is telling a lie?"

The officer was semi-distracted, talking to both guards about their families, etc., basically making small talk enough to make Thor feel comfortable writing down all the information he could muster. He turned over the paper and started on picture #2. It was exactly the same, even down to the body positioning, but instead of a bible under his right hand, he was holding a pair of cuffs, and instead of making a point with his finger, he was pointing a pistol at you. Through his open jacket, Thor even depicted the man's actual harness and badge in their proper places. The caption, answering the one on the previous page, was "His lips are moving!"

He shut the notebook and tossed it across the table toward the men, then sat back in his seat and yawned, genuinely unconcerned at this point what they did from here; they didn't have shit on him, and they didn't realize the implant was even done. One of the guards finished looking at it and burst into laughter.

The detective stood up without even looking back and banged on the door to be let out. "Keep on laughing... you can joke all the way to the commune with all the other worthless pieces of human trash!"

"At least they're still human, you backstabbing robot errand boy!" Thor retaliated, making the noise of a sheep just in time as the steel door slammed shut with a loud echo.

The courtroom had lost any personality or dignity that had been handed down in tradition over the centuries. All that remained was a sterile, plastic reflection of the institute the judicial system had always so proudly revered as the last outpost for truth to be revealed and justice to be dispensed. In keeping up with the social deterioration and complete martial intolerance, the modern courtroom had become nothing but a processing venue with a synthetic aire of false justice where the strays could be put back in line, and the obsolete, eradicated.

The room was divided right down the middle by a wall of see-through, bullet proof composite, a table and two chairs on the defendant side, and a large desk with what looked like a King's throne, set several feet higher than grade, with the usual State flag and National flag on either side of the Judge's chair. There was one chair for a bailiff to the side toward the entry door, and that was it. No witness booth, no jury box, no audience seating, just one case at a time, judged and sentenced by one man, in front of a camera on both sides of the glass.

At any given time, there were over 100 of these courtrooms dispensing judgment at the same time, taking up a quarter mile long wing of the jail/ district court building in every major district in the city, and they were all televised. The position of City Judge could be applied for by anyone without a criminal history, with only a simple, ambiguous psychological test to decide one's moral aptitude for the position. Needless to say, many self-serving wing-nuts with their own vigilante style agendas managed to get past the screening and were able to destroy just as many undeserving lives before their discrepancies were reported and investigated.

He was still in shackles when the two guards shoved him in the tiny room and slammed the door behind him. The bailiff on the other side hit a button on the wall and some lights came on in Thor's corner. He hit another one, and there was an ambient hum in the air, coming from the speaker above him. "Can you hear me, bud?" the bailiff asked, looking at Thor. Thor nodded. "Out loud, please." he said, a little louder.

"Yeah, 10-4!" he spoke aloud.

"Thanks. You're our first of the day. Just powering up." he said, in a friendly sounding voice.

"Just oiling the jaws of the money machine... right?" Thor smiled.

"You got it!" the man joked back, half smiling. He heard the loud click, then looked sideways behind him, toward the door. The door started to swing open.

"All rise!" he spoke aloud; a complete formality since Thor was the only one in the room and he had never sat down in the first place. In walked a 5'5" pudgy little toad of a man, bald on top, but with stringy, greasy strands of hair combed over the top in a failed attempt to conceal it. He sat down, tossing his oversize robe out to the sides in what looked to Thor just like a short, ugly woman's curtsy.

"Be seated!" the bailiff said even louder, trying to camouflage the smile he had because of Thor's facial expressions. Thor was bug eyed, like a curious cat. This self-important, pompous little twit wouldn't make eye contact with Thor no matter which way he leaned, but rather, sat there, gazing around the room as he shuffled his paperwork into submission, projecting the most pretentious vibe Thor could ever remember feeling. He gave up trying to lock eyes with the fool and sat back, a slight smile unavoidably toying with his lips.

"Mr. Krey, is it?" the judge asked, *still* not making eye contact.

"Yes *IT* is!" he responded, a tad over-zealously, and as sarcastic as possible.

"A simple 'Yes, Your Honor,' or 'No, Your Honor' will do, please."

"Ahhh!" he said back, eyes wide open, mouth wide open, head back, and then he shut down like a robot, "I'm sorry." he said, closing his eyes and slumping his head all the way forward, facing down at the table.

The judge didn't even look up to notice his self-entertainment. "You have been remanded to our custody for consideration of your alleged crimes against the State, some of which have been quite heinous in nature and destructive in magnitude. You have failed numerous attempts to be tailored as a functional *blah bluh blee bluh blah....*"

> *You seem quite ridiculous*
> *On your self-appointed pedestal.*
> *Flawless powers of observation,*
> *Why don't you use them on yourself?*
>
> *Rude and condescending,*
> *Don't speak as if you ever knew me.*
> *Another critic with a work in progress,*
> *A portrait of hypocrisy...*
>
> *Kill your own demons,*
> *I've got mine on the run.*
> *The evil things you think you see me do*
> *Aren't hurting anyone.*
>
> *I'll never say "Your Honor,"*
> *You sick, self-righteous piece of shit.*
> *Stroking yourself behind your desk*
> *From the pompous throne on which you sit.*
> *Just remember, little man,*
> *If you find you're playing God for sport,*
> *There may come a day*
> *When you find yourself inside my court!*

"....*blah blah bluh ble boo* bluh b-but if nothing changes, the next time we see you in here, you will receive a mandatory jail sentence of at least one year! If you are caught trying to circumvent the commune program and branch out on your own before you have demonstrated adequate means to do so, it will be considered another escape from processing, and will be punishable by one year's incarceration. Is this abundantly clear?"

"Yes."

"Yes... what?" the judge prompted, fishing for something he didn't deserve.

"Yes… it surely is," Thor said.

Outside the weather was beautiful. The sun was out and there was hardly a cloud in the sky. A nice cool breeze flowed in from somewhere out west, the gentle aroma of fresh cut grass and flowers mixing with the odd bouquet of the sea. Gulls complained high in the sky, still submerged well below the ever expanding skyline, halfway up to the tops of the man-made peaks, or halfway home, as Thor liked to see it, either way, he could see why this was considered prime real estate.

He took a huge breath in, savoring the fresh smell of smog-free air, and started humming the music to the song he made up in the courtroom as he slid down the steel column, one boot on each side, slowing his descent to the parking garage below. Above him, still basking in the sunlight of an otherwise uneventful morning, two guards lay peacefully unconscious in front of a building with a small fountain and sign that read "Northgate Serenity House, Dept. of Social Reinstatement." One had his left wrist cuffed to the other man's right ankle, and the other man was cuffed to the sign post. Somehow the smaller man's stun baton, still held tight in his other hand, was half engulfed in the larger man's butt cheeks, his pants pulled down around his ankles.

Chapter 22: So Help Me, God

Tyr continued to lie in a pool of blood, losing feeling in his extremities. His vision was starting to blur and he didn't know how much longer he would be able to hang on. The only thing keeping him going was revenge, and the only reason Dagaz hadn't noticed he was still alive was his own cowardice. He simply would not look at either of them. They had faced death together, philosophized for hours by a fire, hunted together, shared each other's dreams, hopes, and fears. What kind of two faced monster could have faked all of that, or experienced it for real with the kiss of Judas waiting just around the corner. He realized now that he didn't know him at all. This creature was nothing more than a doppelganger that needed to be punished for killing their friend.

He was having a tough time keeping his thoughts straight, and an even tougher time seeing clearly through the dried blood encrusted on his one, barely open eye. His long hair was strewn over his head and face, giving him the appearance that he was totally face down. He looked around the room again and again, trying to make a clear assessment of the situation. Two of the men were hovered around the computer terminal, trying to make heads or tails of the information there, but there really wasn't anything they could use. Dagaz had still not noticed the laptop, sitting closed on Kait's old chair on the mead rack side of the table. He was unfortunately keeping his distance from the entire blast area. He was extremely nervous and wouldn't stop pacing the floor in front of the security monitor. Then Tyr heard it... a couple small 'clang' noises, deep inside the building structure.

He was lying with his left ear almost touching the vertical steel tube that made up the spiral staircase to the roof, and had noticed this affect before during a hailstorm. It carried resonant sound like a railroad rail foretelling of a coming train. There was someone on the roof! *Central had not taken the bait....*

The sniper from the stairs was now by the front door, talking quietly to Dagaz, two men were still at the computer terminal, and the other two were heading for the garage, just realizing they would need a code for the door. Overhead, Tyr could just make out the sound of the loft hatch being cracked open about a centimeter. He grinned, waiting to see Dagaz fall over dead, but it never happened. *What are they waiting for?* He was about to push the detonator, take out two of them, and get the party started himself, when it dawned on him, they were waiting for others to get into position... *The garage!* The alarm Dagaz had been waiting for sounded quietly, and they all scrambled into position, lining up side to side behind the half-way point of the room, like it was the OK Corral! Guns drawn and focused on the front entryway, they waited for the second door to slide open to spring their ambush.

They heard the metallic slide, but were shocked when they realized the sound was coming from their right side, not in front of them. Three men opened fire from the garage door with pistols, one squatting and the other two standing behind him, then, as they scrambled to regain line of site to return fire without hitting each other, two more opened up on them from the loft hatch with automatic rifles. It was a complete bloodbath, flawlessly executed. They dropped like confused little flies; the betrayer, betrayed. It was poetry in motion, and Tyr couldn't help but smile, as painful as it was.

They stood over the bodies, finishing off one of the two closest to the bullet-ridden computer station with a shot to the head. Dagaz was lying awkwardly twisted over the top of one of his men, bleeding from numerous wounds, and trying to mouth something to the assailants as they came toward him. He looked scared and surprised, obviously not as confident in his three way coup d'état as he was a few short minutes ago. He looked away from the gunman as he leveled his pistol right at Dagaz's face. When he turned his head sideways and cringed in fear, he suddenly realized he was looking Tyr right in the eyes, and he was *not* dead... in fact, he was smiling. A snapshot of poetic justice... frozen in time.

One of them gestured to the mead racks and laughed as he said something to his buddy in an almost unintelligible dialect, somewhere between French-Canadian, Jamaican, and early twenty-first century urban "Ebonics." The other laughed, pulling the trigger and ending the life of the blubbering Judas with no more importance or thought given this, as to the random swatting of a fly. The two men at the top of the stairs joined their friends, gloating on and on, apparently assuming what they did here to be the death of the North Clan, as they were unaware of the Police Task Force involvement altogether. If not for this, Tyr probably would have thanked them, but as it turned out, the rats really were all in the same hole... and they were standing *so close* to the cheese....

Chapter 23: Scorpio Moon

All the way home from downtown, Thor was overcome with a dark feeling. Something wasn't right. Nothing had felt right since Kait disappeared that day, but he was used to rifts in the grand design working themselves out for the good of all, so he usually just bit the bullet and rode it out. He had a gnawing in his gut surrounding her fate that was clouding all other things. He would have to take on faith the fact that there was nothing more he could do for her, besides investigate any involvement the former owner of his new identity may have had in her disappearance. There was some kind of connection there, but instinct told him it was not much more than a coincidence. She simply wasn't involved with anything shady that a scumbag like Stanton would be involved in. It really made little sense at all. Then there was the money....He couldn't wait to tell Tyr and Uruz that their troubles were over forever....

He started to approach familiar territory: the old cemetery where Bruce Lee, and his son, Brandon, were both buried. He and Kait spent many hours sitting by the hill where the headstones used to stand, quietly paying homage to the fallen masters. Then there were the old floating bridges that used to connect the ground level freeways on the east and west; still great fishing platforms out over about a third of the lake, the rest sitting quietly at the bottom since the quake.

And finally, the crown jewel of the Northern District: the experimental communal valley known as Madison Valley; now just a failed wasteland of would-be upper level homes whose owners tried to remain interwoven into the fabric of underground society long after the segregation started. A noble effort, to be sure, but indefensible, and very soon run into the ground for all the greenhouse and hydroponic natural food production that was meant to be shared with the same ruthless assholes who ended up destroying it. Now, it was a valley of broken down homes and shanty villages stretching from the skyscrapers at the top of the hill, to the waterfront of Lake Union.

As he drew closer to home, the hair started standing up on the back of his neck. A nagging pain and rotting nausea swept over him like the flu. He started noticing people he recognized: a child here, a mother there, whispering... pointing... looking away... looking troubled. He came over the crest of the ridge and entered into the dark maze of the city again. Walking westward, directly into a faint breeze, he started to notice the smell of burning plastic, gunpowder, wood, etc.. This was very obviously more than just a family staying warm by a trash fire. *Now he was deeply concerned.* Just blocks away, he broke into a run.

It smelled like a house-fire. This was not too uncommon, and due to the physics of the situation, this was one of the rare times the powers that be got involved in any underground problems. It wasn't really that they cared, they just didn't want it to spread upward into their world. They would usually try to pull in on a viaduct above it, and combat the fire from there. This was usually pretty effective, as they had the resources to keep flooding it as long as it took, and weren't worried about what additional damage that may cause, only that the fire was out.

He could already see the flashing lights on the freeway that ran above their house, and his heart skipped a beat as he realized that it had to be very close to their place, indeed.... He sped up into a full blown sprint. As he came around the corner, only one block from his house, he started seeing debris in the street. *Damn*, he thought, *that would've taken one hell of an explosion.... A gas-main? The chop-shop up the street with all their paint?*

He saw a young family standing out in front of their place in the loft of a neighboring shop. He had spoken to them on many occasions. He had even saved their son from a serious beating by some wandering gang members from Central some time ago. They could see what was going on from their angle, but he wasn't quite there yet. The son ran up to Thor and grabbed his leg, hugging hard and crying out loud. Thor comforted him, but tried to pry away. He needed to see what was going on. The wife looked at Thor, crying, then buried her head into her husband's chest and shoulder. Thor's heart sank. *No!*

He ran up to the corner and paused, stepping out and looking through already tearing up eyes to see the smoldering remains of the North Clan stronghold, flaming up into the sky while fire trucks up on the overpasses showered streams of water down at it from above. In the street was debris of every kind, evidence that some kind of large scale explosion had taken place from inside and blew everything out. He could see smoldering body parts, and a complete body or two lying in the road, and though none of them appeared to be family, he screamed at the top of his lungs; his powerful voice echoing his agony and rage throughout every bit of the Northern District.

He rushed up, as close as he could stand, and tried hard to see inside. The entire area surrounding the old computer terminal and meadery was gone, as was everything for about fifty feet in every direction. It didn't take Thor two seconds to realize that the boobytrap he and Tyr had placed had been detonated. What he didn't know was if Tyr did it on purpose, or if it was set off by something else... He certainly didn't expect anywhere near this level of damage from what they had rigged, even if the initial blast set off a secondary one fueled by hundreds of gallons of twenty percent alcohol mead bottles... This was just catastrophic!

The entire loft was missing, blown to small bits all over the street and the freeways above. No one could have survived, not even from the garage, which was flaming up pretty good right now. *And who were these other people?* He could tell from the additional bodies that something big went down, *but what?*

He dropped to his knees, crying hysterically as everything he knew, everything he held dear, crumbled and crackled in the fires of destruction right before his eyes. All his purpose; lost. All his philosophy, now as meaningless as the drunken rants of the most laughed at derelict in Hell's Ditch. As his despair slowly transitioned into anger, in the midst of all the noise, human and machine, and the crackling of the fire, he faintly picked up on a familiar cough off to the right, just into the alley. He sprang up, running off balance for the noise as if afraid he would lose it completely. He ran right through a thick wall of smoke and steam and stumbled as he almost stepped right on him!

"Ragnar?" he said, extremely surprised, yet ecstatic to see a familiar face! His Great-Uncle, one of his Grandfather's brother's, who happened to be the Godfather of Thor's mother, was laying in the alley before him, one side burnt severely, and a couple obvious bones broken, propped up sideways against the wall. Still, he seemed more pissed off than broken, being as resilient as they come; truly a modern day Viking. He was one of the Old Ones: the Elite Family, most of which went into exile to regroup in the woods and try to bring the fight back to the government after the herding began in the wake of the great earthquake. Ragnar and a handful of others stayed to look after the young ones and those not strong enough to make the trip.

"Thor!" he laughed, hurting himself further, but unconcerned about his own pain. "My God, boy! Odin be praised! I thought for sure you were dead!"

He grabbed Ragnar's forearm with his right hand, hugging him with his left, such as was their family custom. "What the fuck happened here? Where's Tyr and Uruz?"

"Yeah..." he looked down, somberly, choking back the tears, then gathered his composure and exhaled hard, coughing some more. "Everyone is dead... GONE!" He slammed his fist down hard on the street. Thor nodded briefly, then looked down at the ground, tears welling up some more as Ragnar continued ... "I followed that turncoat, Dagaz to a secret meeting he set up with Cane and T! I figured he was trying to fix that thing he was babbling about when I ran into him about a week ago... something about you starting shit between Central and Cane... Anyway, he made a weird comment about just taking them both out while we had the chance, and I assumed the 'we' he was referring to was us, The North Clan! Now I know it wasn't!" He coughed hard, this time, a little blood came up in his spit. "FUCK!"

"Take it easy, we need to get you some help," Thor said.

"Fuck easy! You need to listen up, lad, don't you worry about me..." he smiled, through a half burnt auburn mustache and thick beard. He grabbed hold of Thor's lapel, and pulled him right up to his face. "Dagaz was a cop!" Thor smiled in disbelief. Ragnar slapped him right across the mouth, just hard enough to get his *full* attention. "Dagaz *was* a COP!! He died in the blast. I think Tyr set the whole thing off. I followed Dagaz and Cane here from a meeting with Central! He was playing all of them! I think they all thought he was betraying The North Clan, when he was actually bringing all the sheep in for slaughter! The son of a bitch got Cane and T inside by pretending to be their captives, I saw it, and I was looking for a way up to the roof to help, when I saw troops dropped on top from a chopper. I hid here and watched. I didn't know what the hell to do, and then here came Central right up the street with 5 or 6 more, and jimmied the garage door. Before I could do anything, it turned into a fucking free for all!

"I ran for the front door, intent on doing *something*... shooting my way in if I had to... then the whole place blew! I woke up over there," he pointed, "and your lady friend and her boy hid me from the cops. The last thing I saw was Tyr and Uruz on the floor and a cluster of men surrounding the computer terminal... They were dressed like cops, but I think it was Central. Tyr smiled when he pushed the button... son of a bitch killed them all!" He laughed fondly, then erupted into a fit of coughing that nearly choked him.

"There's no cops down here... not yet," Thor told him.

"They're already gone! They ran into the fire in zoot suits, then came back out with some sort of briefcase." He coughed violently, spitting up several small puddles of blood this time. "Then they just left...."

"Briefcase, huh? Silver?" Thor asked, suspecting the one they pulled out of the trunk.

"I think so, originally. It was pretty scarred from the blast. What the hell was it?"

"Just something we found. Sounds like maybe it had a tracking beacon... Uruz was supposed to have incinerated it as soon as he checked out its contents...." Thor scratched his head, then swept his hair over the top of his sweat covered scalp from front to back as he exhaled, trying to piece it all together. Through the wall of smoke they could hear a lot of new commotion. The sound of people gathering was getting louder, and now they could hear the sound of two police cruisers pulling up on the scene. Several doors opened and shut, and there was even the sound of weapons being cocked. A radio squawked something they couldn't make out.

"Yes, sir, were here. He's been spotted at the scene, but I don't have a visual..." one officer spoke up. There were footsteps and yelling coming in their direction.

"You need to go, Lad." Ragnar wheezed, shaking his hand and forearm, and holding the back of his hand with the other, he added, "Don't worry, just follow your heart, boy. It'll be all right. I love you. Now take this, it belongs to you... Get out of here now, I'll cover you!" He handed Thor a piece of paper, it was the original writing from his grandfather. He tucked it away safely in his pocket.

"Come with me, God-dammit," he whispered, angrily. "You're all I got left!"

"I promised your mother I'd protect you, now go!" He shoved him to his feet and pointed to the dark end of the alley, away from the smoke. Thor nodded, a tear still in his eye, then bolted down the alley, and out the other end. He could hear some commotion behind him, some yelling, then a couple gunshots.

From nearly two blocks away, safely obscured by smoke and shadows, he heard Ragnar's famous battle cry... a deep, resonant yell that echoed through the whole area, sending a chill up his spine. Warriors of their stature were a dying breed; lost to technology, and to the ages gone asunder.

As far as he knew, he was now the last of a breed apart, the last of his Clan, and the last of his family.

Where the other Old One's were, he didn't know. Not even Ragnar knew their fate. All that was known was that last time anyone heard of The Alliance For Gaia, they had taken refuge far to the north, and were recruiting followers to their cause to bring about revolution in a grand way. There were rumblings through the grapevine, then there were legends, too fantastic to be true, then there was silence. To go looking for them, he feared, would be an exercise in futility.

He ran all day and into the night. Mostly it was aimless running for the sake of clearing his mind and burning the frustrated, vile energy that was welling up inside him. From time to time he stopped and vented, cutting loose on a street sign or window, parked car or fence. *What the hell was going on? Why now? Why them?* None of this made any sense at all. If Dagaz was a cop, then everything he did and said for the last several years of their family's life together was a lie! *Why them?* They really weren't involved in anything that noteworthy! Aside from attracting more people to their way of life, all they were responsible for was the occasional theft of a car! This was common practice all over the city every day, and many of the robberies took place at gunpoint and resulted in the harming or slaying of the victim! Surely there were bigger fish to fry.

Was it about vantage point? Did they just need a contact in the underground? This would make more sense, but then why them? Why The North Clan? It had to have something to do with the Alliance and their blood ties with it...The other clans destroyed in the wake would suggest some kind of direct attack on underground organizations. They were always trying to send cops down here to snuff out the gangs as soon as they got too powerful. The problem was that they were too paranoid and no one ever got inside any of the main organizations. Every time they attempted it, the officer was sniffed out and killed.

They had never tried with the North Clan. Possibly because they had no reference for what made them tick, or perhaps they simply couldn't see a reason to risk it, but for whatever reason, Dagaz was the first and only attempt. That was why he succeeded. Everyone stopped looking for it. They let their guard down, and when a seemingly kindred spirit emerged from the shadows, needing help from them as well, but obviously capable on a number of useful fronts, he was welcomed as a member of the family without any further suspicion.

It worked so well because it was never *them* he was after. They were the obvious only channel for possible intel about the true location or activities of the AFG, probably the government's public enemy #1 if they knew the half of it. Then there was the North Clan's loose affiliation with the ruthless, toothless twosome: The Meña Brothers, Cane and T. Growing up in the U District, it didn't take them but a couple decades of extreme poverty to figure out a different way... *fear based control.*

They attracted the destitute young, needing order as much as money. Cane offered both, for a price... loyalty. His henchmen would kill anyone, anytime, for any reason. Having very strong connections in cocaine trafficking, their influence, as well as aftermath spread more and more uptown, threatening the wealthy both physically and financially. To even join his gang required a blood in; a random murder perpetrated in broad daylight uptown for the pure sake of proving one's commitment, while leaving himself as guilty as everyone else in the gang. Though his influence was starting to affect even their own ranks, the police, for the most part, wanted to kill him themselves.

Last, but certainly not least was Central, a self-perpetuating group of all black entrepreneurs and drug dealers. While not quite as ruthless as Cane's Latino-based organization, they operated autonomously, with no identifiable leadership, and were therefore extremely hard to track or bring down. The police tried for years to get any number of people brought in to break down the machine for them, but had little or no affect. It was a mystery how they even managed to function at all, yet function they did, with a fairly high degree of organization.

Dagaz was put right in the center of the whole tumultuous mess because he was the perfect mole. He had an extremely analytical mind, but a quiet and non-threatening demeanor, so he would ever remain in the shadows, quiet and trustable, but eyes open all the while to the best way to facilitate his own agenda, while able to break into character at a moment's notice and laugh, cry, share time, dreams, troubles, and even give advice to those who he called "brother," or "sister," but had every intention of abandoning one day. Thor cringed in actual physical pain at the thought of his brothers dying at the hand of this soulless coward; incapable of honor.

He stopped running for a moment and realized he was only a few blocks from the old Seattle Waterfront. As a child, during better times, he used to come here to spend time looking at all the sailboats. Now it was not much more than a giant accidental levy, caused by the collapse of the old Highway 99 viaduct, a massive double layered suspended highway of concrete, steel, and asphalt running the entire length of the downtown waterfront, that collapsed at the onset of the Great Quake, actually creating a huge levy that effectively broke the tsunami that hit a short while later, during the aftershocks. It was a tangled mess of steel re-bar, railing, concrete chunks, pre-stressed slabs, and automobiles that was nearly impassable, but he climbed the hill on many occasions just to watch the sunset from the best seats in the underground.

Tonight, he just wanted to be alone, and this was as good as it gets in that regard. He felt literally like a huge chunk of his midsection had been ripped out; leaving a hole that would never be able to be filled. He did not see from here why he would even want to try. It was not his nature to be a nihilist, yet he suddenly identified strongly with the misanthropic assholes he had always criticized for their bleak outlook on their fellow man, even in a place like this.

His only reprieve from the ache he felt in his gut and arms was the thought that it was Tyr who blew the device they built for exactly this sort of problem, and ultimately got the last laugh. He lifted an imaginary horn to his fallen brothers, wishing with all his heart he could have shared their fate. He cursed Dagaz, walking on, then stripped him of his name and title of brother, never again to be spoken of. He was a ghost to him now… not even a memory.

He reached the crest of the tallest part of the rubble, a section toward the center of the levy, then paused and looked back toward the city. The view was amazing. It was a panoramic masterpiece of lights and shapes, reaching up toward the sky in some areas, succeeding in others. Still early by uptown standards, traffic was booming, leaving streaks of color and white light flickering on every surface of every building, casting shadows over the tops of shadows. This was always a pleasant distraction, but he needed more.... He looked out toward the old bridge to Alki Beach that they traversed underneath to get to Jerrick's.

There it still was, just a silhouette sticking up into the night sky, the gutted out remains of an old observation tower, jutting up out of the debris at about a 15 degree angle, a mangled and twisted reminder of the tsunami that placed it there, it has served as sort of a new landmark in the underground ever since. On many occasions, Thor scaled up to the booth to hang out and take in a sunset. There was no glass, and the whole thing was tilted, but it was a relatively safe shelter, and you could see for miles out past the islands and peninsulas of the inner sound. As late as it was getting, the real show was to the east. He scaled upward, thinking of Kait and how she used to race him to the top. He sped up, using all his tricks as if she was there right then, and he smiled, tears welling up again. "I love you." he said aloud, for the first time... for the first time acknowledging the very real probability that he would never see her again, either.

He reached the pinnacle and sat down with his legs hanging down and swung them softly back and forth. He mulled it all over and over in his mind, but no attempts at reason or understanding lessened the pain one iota. This was a void that could never be filled. Many times throughout the course of the previous day, he had looked on his pistol with the warmth and favor of a much needed friend. For as much as it seemed this would end his suffering, he could not dishonor their memory with such a cowardly act. Then there was the matter of Ragnar's sacrifice... He would not return the gift of life Ragnar gave him with his heroic last stand, covering his escape until his last breath was spent, with a selfish act of cowardice like committing suicide. No matter what else life throws at him, no matter how bad it gets, he refused give up. He vowed right there, right then, to stay the course and honor all of them by living an epic life in their memory.

Standing high on the top edge of the man-made precipice, overlooking the wilderness of colossal peaks and valleys with his back to the ocean, he relaxed his eyes and let the scene become what it should have been all along. The tops of the tallest buildings became mountain peaks, covered with snow and ice, shrouded in a neck-high ring of hazy cloud cover. The deep valleys, blanketed in darkness, were still alive, radiant with the energy and unseen movement of nocturnal predators going about their rituals in the shadows. The activity of the foreground became a blur of trees swaying in the wind with all manner of vegetation depleting into the sand and boulders of the coastline.

Looking up, he couldn't remember a time in the recent past when he could see so many stars! When you spend so much time submerged below a concrete jungle, it is easy to lose perspective. Staring off, deep into space, he wondered how many worlds have come and gone without our influence... *without our infection*. He allowed himself to linger in between worlds for a long time, imagining what it would be like to live in a world this pristine; a world whose value was never quantified, but rather nurtured in symbiosis by every inhabitant fortunate enough to call it home. The wonders of its true nature unmolested by humanity, frozen in still life artistry, yet alive with vibration; the ebb and flow of its collective spirit, resonating in perfect pitch the harmony of thousands of individual tides, each no less grand than the whole, itself. Leaning back into a pocket between two planes of sheet metal, he slowly faded off, high in his nest, with his mountain range as a backdrop for a night full of dreams about freedom that would never be his.

He awoke to the first rays of light shooting through the cracks between buildings. It had been clear all night, so he woke up shivering, the steady breeze coming in off of the water amplifying the cold. He curled forward, breathing down his own shirt at the neck, trying to absorb more of the sun's rays. He got his bearings and received his first gut wrenching wave of nausea for the day over the loss he had endured. Stretching his arms out to the sides as far as he could, he looked over his shoulder to the east. The cold waters of Puget Sound spread out from here like a giant lake, but you could almost see right down the Strait of Juan de Fuca as it headed out into the Pacific Ocean like a massive river.

As a child, he had fished these waters all the way to the mouth of the Strait, La Push, a unique area of surfable beaches, rich history, and intense energy. He would often stay there, camped on Second Beach for days on end, feeling as if there was no civilization outside that world. The marine ecosystem had been so horribly polluted and interfered with by way of military sonar, tidal generators gone awry, and dumping, that the whole fishing industry was put on indefinite hiatus due to an almost steady state of red tide contamination. He wondered if they ever recovered, being right on the western seaboard. Close to the Olympic mountain range, it was even rumored that there were still huntable deer and elk. Probably just a myth, he figured. Either way, he now lacked the means to travel there. *Or did he?...*

He smiled, scratching his hand to make sure it wasn't a dream, he suddenly remembered the implant. He could go just about anywhere he wanted with that kind of money... *and be hunted...* His smile faded. He knew they didn't, as of yet, know that he possessed Stanton's ID, but someone was undoubtedly aware of the fortune, probably the poor bastards on the embezzlement paper trail in the briefcase, and by now, it was safe to assume they knew of his survival.

This went beyond the corrupt police, he was sure of that much. Central didn't have helicopters. *Whoever dropped in on Dagaz's little coup probably had that case wired,* he thought. They were aware of all the other elements, and simply made sure they were the last ones in the building. There would probably be nowhere to go where they couldn't eventually find him. Besides, a life of looking over your shoulder is no life at all. The real question was the money.... There was no bank in his name, or Stanton's where that much money would remain safe.

If it was still there now, it was due only to timing, and luck of the draw as to who got killed at the stronghold. If the ones who really knew what was going on were there and were killed in the blast, it would take them a while to put it back together, but they eventually would. That much he could count on. So where to go from here? He could hole up at Jerrick's place and work on rebuilding... but anyone he came into contact with right now would probably be put in grave danger. It was only a matter of time. Jerrick may have been on their list anyway, given their source of information   .

He needed a safe house right now, and the time to sort things out. *Time for a taste of uptown life. How nauseatingly intrepid.* He took a good look around, then lunged himself over the edge of the booth face and started sliding, fireman style, down one of the poles that made up the internal mast. Carefully keeping the point of friction away from his implant, he swung around a couple more vertical members and a large welded gusset plate, and he was down, bolting through the rubble with the intensity of a wolf on a hunt.

Piecing things together in his head, he knew he had a lot of stops to make in order to pull this off without a hitch, so he made haste. First order of business, he would need some new clothes. He needed to blend in... at this point, his life pretty much depended on it. The best place he could think of to shop for clothes without attracting too much attention in his present attire was one of the larger malls. Filled with kids trying their best to look like they came from the streets instead of uptown suburbia, he stood half a chance at getting in and out unnoticed.

These places were usually packed with people, which made facial recognition scanners obsolete. They all had numerous booth-style banking kiosks, so with any luck, he would be able to check fund availability before reaching a counter and putting himself at risk. He came down the backside of the levy toward the city with a newfound sense of focus. They took away everything he loved, but they had not succeeded in breaking him. As he lived and breathed, he swore on the graves of his brothers and sisters, he would not give them another chance to try.

CHAPTER 24: PHOENIX RISING

If there was one thing Thor had mastered in all his time in the underground, it was getting uptown without being noticed. To stay for long, undetected, that was another matter entirely. Fear tends to heighten the senses of the indigenous lemmings, giving them an almost superhuman ability to sniff out an outsider based on nothing but visual appearance. It has something to do with their innate preoccupation with physical beauty. Their entire culture seemed to be based on it, and everything in their culture was produced, bought or sold... including physical beauty. Since their daily routines no longer involved the strenuous physical activity that made one's body more and more defined and beautiful, they had to supplement ways to do so. For the right price, you could look nearly any way you wanted.

Even their art was structured such that people who had the look that the masses revered would succeed, and the rest, regardless of how good they were, could spend their entire lives trying to make it and never succeed. It got so bad in the mainstream that there was eventually only one adopted, formulaic approach to music, commercial art, and movies that was considered "sellable," and could be produced, at little or no risk of rejection, by the in-house artists working for the corporation. All that was needed to package it up and spoon feed it to the population was a pretty face, and those were not hard to come by.

Thor had always been nauseated by this aspect of life up here. You couldn't escape it. It was everywhere. On billboards. On the sides of buildings. In the malls. And yes, in the air... replacing the polluted ambiance of life, nearly devoid of the sounds of nature that were drowned out by the commotion of man. A constant seamless bombardment on the God Box, the one way window to mainstream enslavement of the mind; formerly a device for the free exchange of ideas, information and entertainment known as television, it had become a corporate owned and harvested mind-blast of proprietary collusion and advertisement with just enough fruit to keep the user from succumbing to scurvy of the mind.

Even the Internet, where you at least had to "pull" what you wanted to experience, rather than have it pushed on you, was getting tedious, at best. Awash with an all-time high of commercial redundancy, it had reached a point of almost complete uselessness. Never had he imagined a time or place in all of history more in need of an artistic renaissance.

To take supply and demand out of the equation seemed the only way to give it back its integrity, but then, without profit, who in this money driven culture would lift a finger to produce it? How much your value system changes when you remove money from the equation. What becomes truly priceless are the things no one can take from you. He had seen more diversity, intelligence, inspiration, and yes, beauty, in the graffiti on one wall of an underground pub's restroom than in the entire topside put together... *and the music?* The music of the underground, running the gamut of emotion and primitive energy, was a force to be reckoned with....

There were many things Thor would miss about the underground if forced to live out his days in this sterile environment, not the least of which was being able to walk from point A to point B without being stared at like a leper. He couldn't figure it out. It was like whatever it was that made him stand out was obvious to these people at a respectable distance, regardless of the fact that he was literally surrounded by people wearing almost the exact same clothes he was. The kids up here loved to piss their parents off by dressing like street kids: ripped up pants, leather, the works. It gave the "wannabe's" a little fake street credit, as well.

Girls seemed attracted to this level of "comfortable danger," yet, if the genuine article passed in front of any of them, they could immediately sniff out the difference, and would turn up their noses and walk away without a second thought. Just a touch of realism in the right places was all it took. The rips in the clothes centered over recent rips in the skin, the leather, shiny and weathered into armor, complete with scuffs and blemishes, and an overall tilt toward function and away from fashion. However close he thought them to appear, he couldn't shake the feeling of eyes on him coming from everywhere.

He looked down just a touch, so as not to make eye contact with anyone and proceeded up the wide entryway stairs leading into the mall. There were hundreds of other people walking into the mall, most of them young people moving in small groups of ten or so. He picked out a group that was a little taller than him, but dressed similarly, and fell in behind them, moving in the same direction.

As they approached the large double doorway, he noticed a metal detector/ implant scanner, manned by one security guard. He had never been back to the stairwell to retrieve his weapons, so he should be alright, he thought, taking off his fingerless gloves to expose the implant underneath. As he crossed the guard's path, he kept him looking at his eyes, instead of his face, and thinking only of himself... "Everything staying calm this morning?" Thor politely asked with an insider's smile, using a trick meant to invoke feelings of camaraderie in complete strangers; a manipulation best used when there's no time to discuss things further and a decision about you is being made based solely on first impression....

"So far, so good, bro," replied the guard as Thor passed through the detector without a sound. He had his palm showing nonchalantly, while appearing to be using that hand to expose his left wrist. In either case, the passing was uneventful, which is what he was after.

"With any luck it'll stay that way. Keep up the good work!" he said, nodding, with a double thump on the counter with his fist on his way by.

"Thanks," he concluded enthusiastically, obviously starved for conversation at his job.

At first glance, he walked through the mall's open food court, a odge Podge of fast food and pseudo-gourmet trendy cuisine, and Jerrick's place flashed into his mind.... *Had they really evolved that much?* This didn't really look any different than the last time he was in one of these places, *and yet...*

Then it happened. Just as he walked past the storefront on his left, exiting the food court, he heard a soft voice speak to him. *Directly* to him, without an audible sound! It still drew his attention to the store, but had no identifiable source! It said *"Would you like to try on some shoes, Mr. Stanton?"* At first he jumped nearly out of his skin, but quickly realized what must be happening. Though they had all joked that someday it might come to this, he hadn't actually heard of it yet, but then, he didn't really know anyone with an implant. The chip somehow was engineered to transmit his personal bio-rhythm to the advertiser's computer so that it could transmit audible messages back to him, and *only* to him, directly into his brain, progressively tailored for likes and dislikes by his own evolving demographic file.

They had been using chip-based ambient audio marketing for some time, but as the stores got more and more crowded and noisy, it became hard to hear the ones that were pinpointed at you. Sometimes just standing too close to another person got confusing enough. It was proven that too much noise, even quiet, ambient background chatter, actually affected the stores' bottom line, as people would have a tendency to get irritable after a while, and lose interest in spending money. This kicked the artificial telepathic marketing research into full gear.

This was one of the flagship malls, but Thor knew this would spread like a brushfire, and the ramifications were frightening to think about. Just like the all-encompassing convenience of the implant, this technology would be supported, no, *embraced* by the masses as a huge easement on the otherwise stressful lives of consumers. Only then, when it was literally everywhere, and had impregnated the mainstream with convenience's bastard son, would the true danger be realized. If they can tailor the message to have an identifiable voice, how hard would it be to eliminate the voice altogether, and only project the message? *Now our own heads weren't private?* He knew things up here were bad, but he had no idea just how far it had already gotten.

He sat down on a bench in the middle of the wide corridor, stores all up and down both sides, with people coming and going in and out of all of them. For the most part, they seemed happy, oblivious… even serene. He held his left hand tightly over the right, afraid to let go for fear of thoughts that weren't his own entering his head again. As with most things regarding loss of privacy or big brother, the only way it was really going to adversely affect someone is if they allowed themselves to become a target, *right?* We already succumb to every kind of poke and prod they impose on us, so *how is this different?*

He knew he was only temporarily playing Devil's advocate in an attempt to see both sides so he didn't grab a knife, cut out the implant, and do a 180 right back for the underground, but the facts were the facts, and this technology was fucking dangerous! *Know Thine Enemy... Know Thyself.*

Out of the corner of his eye, Thor caught a glimpse of a group of kids, aging from 14 to 18, playing recklessly in front of one of the jewelry kiosks out in the middle. It started fairly harmlessly with a shove or two, then escalated quickly into a squabble between two of the older ones. The big kid on the left reached back and made a fist, getting ready to hit the scruffy looking kid on his right, when they all suddenly dispersed, staring toward the ground in random directions.

Quite suddenly, and without provocation, they all shot off on their individual tangents quietly, slowly, *and at exactly the same time*, as if someone had flipped on a switch! They each took just a few steps, some of them bumping into other people and each other, as if they couldn't see, then they seemed to snap out of it, looking around, finding each other, then taking off through the mall as if nothing had happened! Thor's jaw dropped open. He looked all around them, but saw no security telling them to disperse. As a matter of fact, he saw no security anywhere!

He had a pretty good idea what just happened, and it scared the shit out of him. To be sure, he would need to test a theory. He walked into the shoe store right next to him. In case something went south, it was close to the exit. He went into a quiet isle where it looked like there were no cameras. He picked up a random pair of children's shoes and opened up the inside of his jacket. He reached up, intending to drop them into his inside pocket, when....

He suddenly realized he was standing in front of a row of woman's shoes with his nose all the way inside one. It felt similar to waking up from surgery, momentarily unaware of where you are, or even *who* you are. He grinned, unable to identify the tickling sensation in his extremities. He suddenly became aware of people on both sides of him. He realized he was standing in a pretty busy aisle, and there were women laughing at him. He smiled, pulling his nose out of the shoe, and laughed as well, seeing the humor in the situation. He nodded at the women and backed out of the aisle, trying to figure out where he just came from. "Ladies..." he nodded again....

"Pervert!" one of them scoffed under her breath. *Wow, what a rush!* He realized he had walked over to the next aisle and half way down it before stopping. He knew now this technology had already advanced much further than he had originally feared. He needed to get what he came for and get the hell out of here!

He quickly went down the men's shoes isle. He was in desperate need of some new tread. The boots he lived in were coming apart at the seams. As he walked down the aisle, all he saw was one pair after the next of the silliest looking, cheaply made, low ankle quasi-sport abominations he wouldn't be caught dead wearing. Finally, when he had just about given up hope, he stumbled onto a blast from the past. Right before his very eyes were a pair of retro-looking Doc Martens calf high steel toe boots. They looked just like the ones he remembered some of his older family members wearing, except they seemed to be making them a lot more heavy duty now. These were definitely him, and they were even his size.

He put them on; tossing his other ones in the trash, then went to go pay for them. That was when he noticed that there was no checkout in the store... anywhere! He figured you were probably supposed to pay on your way out of the mall, but after what just happened, he was a little afraid to try to walk out of the store with them. He still had the tags in his hand, so he couldn't be accused of stealing, then bravely headed for the entryway. When he was just about to clear the threshold, he closed his eyes and cringed....

"Thank you for your purchase, Mr. Stanton. You have been charged 283 Euros for your transaction," he heard directly into his head again. It made him jump, but he was actually relieved. To do the rest of this anonymously, without the scrutiny of a checker at the end, was somewhat comforting. He stepped out of the store back into the busy corridor and stepped up to an information sign. It was touch screen and holographic, with a 3D isometric map of the whole building, so he didn't have too much trouble figuring out where all the stores he would need were located.

He figured it would probably be relatively safe to spend just one night in Stanton's own house, at least safer than having his account pop up on the computer at a motel. Here, everything was under one roof, so even if someone figured out what really happened to Stanton after he was killed, he would be gone before any of these purchases were observed. They simply wouldn't be looking here.

He arrived at Stanton's residence with a full stomach, nice clothes and a million dollar smile and paid the Autocab with a swipe from his wrist when prompted. He shut the door and it sped off on its GPS guided preprogrammed course. He had a pretty good feeling the police hadn't been here.

The only ones who know he's dead are the one's (or one) who killed him. To the rest of the world, he was a ghost anyway. It looked like they found what they were looking for, so why not? He got on the elevator and pushed Stanton's room number from the billing address on his account. It was, of course, different from the one on his ID. A man like him wouldn't advertise, but would definitely want his correspondence regarding his money.

The elevator moved up for quite a while, then turned 90 degrees to the right, and started moving to the right. It traveled a few more seconds, then turned another 90 degrees to the right and stopped. The door slid open to reveal two more sliding doors with the seam in the middle. He started to worry, as nothing was happening. There was a button on the door. He set down a bag, and pushed it with his left hand. He could barely make out the sound of a doorbell inside. His eyes opened wide... *the implant!*

He set down the other bags, then pulled back the glove on his right hand. The doors slid immediately open. He scooped up his bags and entered; the doors closing behind him to complete darkness. He heard a faint noise from behind that he knew had to be the elevator being whisked off at high speed to a neutral location. "Lights!" he yelled, but had no luck. "God Damn voice recognition...." He reached into his pocket and fished out a lighter. Striking it he cupped the small flame and looked around. The place had been thoroughly tossed. Everything had been gone through, but there was no evidence of a police investigation. He turned his attention to the wall by the entrance and flipped on the light switches. He decided that if this place was now his, whether he kept it or not, he wanted to clean it up at least enough so that he could think straight.

He started putting away the papers that were all over the floor, randomly to be sure, into a file cabinet by a large desk, then into the desk drawers themselves after that filled up.

Inside the desk was a loaded Colt .45 1911 combat government model, just like the ones he had always carried. "Well, he had good taste," he muttered, pulling open another drawer.

This one revealed something that made his blood curdle! There was a brand new pair of shock-cuffs, with the detachable remote handle exactly like the one he found at the scene where Kait was taken! Stanton's involvement didn't make sense until now. *He must have been the one with the stunner....* It was her body that was gone, and the cuff itself was missing too. Stanton attacked her, then was killed by the man who was stalking him! He felt sick all over again when he realized he was using the identity of the piece of shit that probably killed the love of his life! He only wished he knew for sure.

Still rummaging through Stanton's things, he switched on his computer. When prompted for a password, he simply scanned his implant over the electric eye, and it continued booting up. Thor couldn't help but admire the hardware, this thing was state of the art. He accessed the routines that governed the house, first. He overwrote the voice recognition software to accept his voice instead, then looked up all existing commands and routines. After seeing what he saw in the mall today, he became very interested in security and privacy. He reprogrammed the computer for uni-directional operation and disabled any remote access by establishing a new, hard-line only firewall. Without wireless capability, nobody could use his activity as a homing pigeon.

All he needed now was to know what the police knew. He hacked, almost effortlessly, into the police mainframe, as they had done many times before, and started searching for reports or assignments pertaining to Stanton or the Clan. He came across a special division assignment pertaining to underground organized crime, but it was a reference only, the files nonexistent on the mainframe. To hide it in this manner meant collusion with the FBI, NSA, or CIA, who he would *not* be trying to hack, tonight or any other night!

There was not one word about Stanton. No missing person report, no criminal history, nothing. This was good, no matter what his decision was for the rest of his life, but he couldn't imagine living in this sterile, spoon fed head-trap of a world any longer than he absolutely had to. He was going mad from the volume of his own thoughts, and didn't foresee finding one truly like-minded person up here, so he finally gave in to morbid curiosity.

"God Box!" he yelled to his freshly programmed voice computer. The blinds collapsed and a very large screen was revealed, flickering on to a menu channel. Thor couldn't help but smile and clap. "Popcorn!" he yelled, then looked around, just entertaining himself. He surfed the channels, imaginatively asphyxiated, until he passed out from sheer exhaustion, face down on the desk, to an onslaught of mind-bending dreams.

> *I see a world gone to shit around me*
> *And a herd of people who could really care less*
> *Bred to believe that this*
> *"All Knowing, All Seeing" governing machine*
> *hears the voice of the people,*
> *and thus, they're rendered powerless....*
>
> *I see a chance for a future*
> *where the greedy bastards who took our world*
> *are forced to give it back,*
> *but this will never happen 'til the silent masses*
> *of sleepwalking puppets are ready to admit*
> *that things are not as they seem on the TV set,*
> *and the bloated man's wreaking of media cover up.*

Walls blind our eyes... spoon fed crooked lies...

Bloated mound of apathetic neuro-dialysis
Farting mass of pseudo-mental paralysis
Saturate
Bow down to corporate, mind-fed security
Bridging life and death and life through obscurity
Saturate
All day, whining, dining, selling, buying,
fucking leave me be!

Can't get up, can't break free!
Can't get up, can't break free!

No God Box

He awoke, more terrified than refreshed, and vowed
never to activate this damnable device again as long as he
lived.

CHAPTER 25: CHRYSALIS OF FATE

Upon waking, Thor realized there would never be an environmental revolution in his lifetime. What he witnessed on channel after channel, program after program, was nothing but elevated doses of the same maniacal garbage for the mind that caused things to digress to this point in the first place. One stupid, pointless distraction after the next, saturating the general public to the point of desensitization while the world slowly choked. Apparently he had stayed up all night last night, and was face down and asleep on the desk for most of the day, television rambling on and on. He even woke up with a small remote controller stuck to his forehead, leaving a deep imprint.

Across the planet, in even less fortunate places, things were utterly chaotic at best. Mankind was losing control altogether. There were wars, diseases, and human rights catastrophes he was never even aware of, and the world was in *much* worse shape than he had ever speculated. The problem had accelerated right past the point of reversibility probably before he was even born, and was still gaining momentum!

The only revolution that would occur would have to happen after an *extreme* drop in human population. We were becoming an itch in so many different ways, it was inevitable now that Mother Nature would be scratching it *very* soon....

He had thought about it long and hard, and what would have seemed like complete idiocy not two days ago, was fast becoming his only real option. He must have seen the commercial a hundred times last night, played repeatedly in the middle of the night for the insomniacal loser demographic who had no real life anyway, and would gladly pay big money to roll the dice on their future. *"Suspended Sunrise"* from CryoKinetics Inc. was the suspended animation program offering its purchasers a new lot on life; a chance to see the future open up right before their very eyes and to sidestep the impending doom that was staring them in the face. Given his recent turn of events, he had to admit this suddenly had a certain appeal to him.

He used to balk at the very idea, but now that he sat here, knowing full well that the predictions were correct, how could he consign himself to oblivion? He had made a pact with himself on the memory of his family not to squander his life, but rather, to live it to its fullest potential. How could he fulfill this vow from a sinking ship? There was nothing for him here... he had to come to terms with that, first. This world was as alien to him as it would feel to a person from the dark ages stuck in this glorious modern mess of honorless, money worshiping opportunists; blind to everything that truly matters. Not only would he never be happy here, he would be damn lucky to survive for much longer at all. He finally made the hard decision to follow through with a plan to liquidate everything and check into this program at once.

He looked the place up on the Internet. He had to admit, they had a pretty enticing pitch. He was actually starting to get fairly excited about this decision. Luckily the company was centered in Old Seattle, not 30 minutes by Autocab, even less by light rail or commuter train, and the night was still young. With any luck, he could make all the necessary preparations before dawn and be at their steps by the time they opened for business.

He opened up the filing cabinets again, this time to see what assets Stanton had, and to help organize them for liquidation. To his surprise, and relief, it looked like Stanton had been doing quite a bit of this already. The only thing left that wasn't already attached to his account was a sell order on the townhouse itself, and apparently there had already been three offers on it! It looked as if Mr. Stanton was getting ready to disappear again, but as fate would have it, he didn't quite make it in time.

Thor went about the rest of his business quickly and efficiently. He transferred all the money to another account, one of *his* choosing, then closed the old one. He then opened a new account in Jerrick's name and put 100,000 Euros into it. This was more than twice the amount owed by the North Clan. Now he could vanish with honor.

He put in the order to accept the largest offer on the house and have the money put directly into the new account, as he would not be returning here, regardless of tomorrow's outcome. It was just too dangerous to stay any longer... this situation was becoming a ticking time bomb. All it would take was Stanton's killer looking in on any of his assets or interests, including implant activity, to find out if he was in the clear, and Thor would be hunted. It was very likely that he was already.

He decided to make himself scarce for the remainder of the night. It was an excellent time to pay the orphans and widows of Hell's Ditch a visit they would never forget! He figured he would undoubtedly need *some* money when his little nap was over, but 47 million? *Come on!* He couldn't even wrap his mind around that kind of money, but he knew he could change a lot of lives forever and still not even put a dent in what he needed to get by for the rest of his life. He put Stanton's pistol in his pants, stuffed his clothes and his new computer into a large, expedition style backpack he found in Stanton's closet, then headed out the door, pausing briefly to look back one last time at a life that might have been.

Upon his arrival at CryoKinetics, Inc., he was immediately greeted by security in the form of plain clothed, over-polite agents whose job, in addition to welcoming you, opening your doors for you, and generally kissing your wealthy buttocks, was to sniff out, before you reached the front door, anyone who wasn't serious about their services and fully capable of footing the bill. It was an elitist clientele who weren't hard to spot a mile away. Luckily for Thor, their privacy protocol was as strict as it gets.

Being the subject of much controversy, they were constantly being subjected to reporters and legitimate investigators trying to infiltrate the operation posing as potential clients. Having also fallen under the scrutiny of everyone from the Paparazzi to law enforcement, they were in the habit of evicting anyone who attempted any outside inquiry as to the identity of any of their clients. Upon entering into one of their packages, you simply ceased to exist to the outside world. For the right add-on price, one could even purchase the option to have a staged death, complete with legal certification, obituaries, even funeral arrangements. The options were as vast as a client's list of reasons to do this in the first place.

Though there were plenty of rich, fat old men and women signing up in order to roll the dice again in the hope that the world would be better in the near future, there were a growing number of new clients who were doing this based almost solely on influence from the fear-based advertisement they liked to air immediately after any kind of terrorist attack or nuclear accident hit the news. The extremely wealthy were very easy to scare in this regard, because these were almost the only scenarios that no amount of money could buy your way out of.

The other large group were those afflicted with terminal disease. This was primarily a last ditch effort by them, hoping that medical technology would surpass their condition, and they would come out of suspended animation to find that the disease was now treatable. This was a gamble that required little provocation or salesmanship.

The one common bond? They were all dirty, rotten, filthy-stinkin' rich! If you had to ask the price, you couldn't afford it. In fact, the second screening on the way in, in the guise of a security booth, was a banking terminal. Potential clients were screened for total net worth before any real time was even invested in speaking to them.

Thor set down his pack before walking into the booth and nodded at the guard. "I would like an inventory slip for that, sir," Thor stated politely.

"Absolutely, Mr...."

"Stanton."

"Mr. Stanton, very well, Mr. Stanton, do you have any weapons or hazardous materials to declare?" he asked, typing things into his computer terminal.

"Yes, sir, I do. I don't go anywhere without my guns," he gestured toward the backpack leaning on the table leg by the guard, "and there is a priceless sword, as well."

"Just lay the whole thing right here, please," the guard said sternly, pointing to the conveyor belt in front of him that led to a large airport-style X-ray box. He finished typing a few more things, then printed up a receipt and handed it to Thor.

"Here's your claim slip, we'll keep it locked up safe until you leave," he added with a smile and a nod. Another man was already approaching him from the left.

"Mr. Stanton, please enter your financial information as prompted," he said, waving his arm politely, palm up, toward the banking terminal. He smiled and stood patiently with his other arm bent behind his back as Thor proceeded into the booth. He exposed the chip as he approached the screen, and just like in the mall, a voice spoke directly to him without making an audible sound. "Welcome to World Bank, CryoKinetics branch. Please sign on the screen to authorize CryoKinetics, Inc. to view your balance in order to proceed."

They had been sizing him up since he stepped out of the cab. With the myriad of programs available, he figured it was just their way of finding out just how much you had to work with before they invested any time in you, due mainly to the wide price range for their services. He also figured they were greedy assholes who would pitch you the absolute highest priced package once they had that information. He figured right.

The man's expression changed dramatically after he left the terminal, and it was painfully obvious they were prepared to kiss about 40 million Euros worth of ass. The man held out his hand, and Thor reached out and shook it firmly, looking the man right in the eyes. "Hi, my name is Dr. Frederick Casey," the man stated, "I'm one of the founding members and Senior Cryophysicists onboard. I will be guiding you through the process and assisting you in the selection and safe implementation of the Suspended Animation package that best suits your needs... First off, Mr. Stanton, could you please tell me your age?"

"Twenty-five," Thor said somberly. The man's eyes widened, as if he was having trouble believing it, but also having trouble thinking of something to say to challenge it.

"It's not the years, it's the mileage," Thor joked, beating him to the punch.

"Very good. Well, you appear to be in better shape than most of our clients, but if you choose to do this, you will need to undergo a physical examination prior to suspension," he added.

"You mean *Cryogenic Re-animation?*" Thor asked.

"No. Same concept, different magnitude... The use of cold temperatures is used in conjunction with a type of plasma transfusion to produce a state of *near suspended animation*. There is no way to bring someone back after cryogenic freezing. That's just science fiction.... We only use it to preserve tissue for transplant, like in the case of cadavers in storage for future thaw and use. Unfortunately, freezing the brain still amounts to irreversible death. We simply take things down a few notches so the effects of aging, muscle atrophy, etc., even over hundreds of years, are negligible. It's basically no more complicated than a bear hibernating through the winter." He winked and gave Thor a cheesy smile.

"A bear doesn't get a plasma transfusion..." Thor joked.

"You haven't spent the last 6 months hoarding nutrients in your body... besides, you're going under for a little longer than a winter, I'd imagine," he answered with a teacher's grin and a pat on the shoulder. The man started walking toward a set of double doors, waving Thor to follow. "Come with me."

This guy's good, Thor thought, already feeling a little bit more relaxed about the whole thing. They walked through the lab where most of the new research was still being done. Summing him up fairly accurately, the Dr. opted to give Thor the "No Bullshit" approach to marketing. He was right to do so, but Thor still had to make a concerted effort not to reveal the fact that he really had no choice, it was just a matter of which program to choose and for how long.

Dr. Casey broke it all down. After insuring that Thor was comfortable with the procedure, he went on to explain how the clients would be cared for oblivious to the transgressions of man. Nuclear War could erupt, and so long as there was something to come back to, they would survive it. This would be possible because the Cryo-tubes, as they called them, the life-support capsules that housed the clients, were *not being stored on the Earth!*

They existed, untouched, nay, untouchable, by the rest of the population, suspended not only in time, but in space; orbiting the Earth in a giant, armored, and thoroughly EMP shielded satellite capable of holding life support air and temperatures at this augmented level for nearly a millennium before requiring any kind of refueling or recharging. Fully automated and unmanned, it was the single most expensive piece of hardware ever assembled by mankind, and once a month, it got larger. It was predicted around the lab that at the rate they were signing up, it wouldn't be long before most of the population was on board and the thing would be so huge it would actually be visible in the night sky and eventually affect our tides, magnetically, like having another moon.

"Why not just build this on the moon?" Thor asked, obviously intrigued by the whole thing, but still a little skeptical... after all, this process seemed to erupt out of nowhere, and hadn't been implemented long enough to speak to any of the "satisfied customers." *The oldest customers were still sleeping!* There was only speculation and logic to rely on in order to make an educated judgment about it.

"That's a very good question, Mr. Stanton..." he paused, "If something was to happen on Earth, and there was nobody here to guide you back, leaving the moon would require a take-off, with a large fuel burn and real-time trajectory input in order to get home. All that would be needed to fall from orbit is a slight nudge, and then sit back and watch the orbit decay. The individual tubes are outfitted already to handle the heat and impact of re-entry, as well as support life for a time in the event that there is nothing to come home to, but also contain homing beacons to triangulate their position just in case things are still civilized. Every possible event that could be imagined has been factored into their design and built in as a safeguard."

"So it would seem." Thor was definitely intrigued by the whole thing, yet there was something this man was hiding.... "I'm ready! I just have one question, Doc, and I want you to be totally honest with me... otherwise, I walk."

"Certainly... anything."

"Have you ever lost anyone?" Thor asked, looking him directly in the eyes.

Dr. Casey took a deep breath, *hopefully not preparing a politician's answer,* Thor thought. "When we first started this, about three years ago, we were filling in the last part of the first ring on the satellite with a shuttle full of clients, when we experienced some kind of magnetic interference. As the new clients were being assembled into the housing structure, which is the giant, revolving ring surrounding the satellite, used to simulate gravity by using centrifugal force, something went horribly wrong. The new tubes didn't attach magnetically after they were locked in place around the ring, due to some sort of bizarre interference, probably a solar flare or something, and the lock-down failed.

"No one had any idea that anything was wrong until it was too late. The installation was believed to be complete, so the ring rotation was restored. As it picked up speed, the problem became apparent and the order to abort was issued, but it was too late. The centrifugal force had risen past the level manageable by the docking locks on the tubes alone, and almost all at once, they started breaking off and flailing in random directions into space. The shuttle only had enough fuel to retrieve 5... *5 people out of 40!* The other 35 are still flying through space, frozen solid. It was the worst day in CryoKinetics history... 35 lives lost, and years of research and development nearly wasted over a freak occurrence!"

"Nearly? How the hell is it they didn't bankrupt you in court? The families of the victims, I mean." Thor asked.

"Well, Mr. *Krey*, is it? As *you* well know, discretion is the better part of valor... There are times in life where the greater good can be best served without the eyes of the world upon you. Wouldn't you say?" the doctor smiled, offering a handshake. *Aaaah, the politician's answer...* Thor paused for just a second, unsure how the good doctor knew his real name, then burst into laughter, grabbing his hand firmly while looking him in the eyes.

"Yes, I would, Doc, yes I would. Thank you for your honesty."

"And you for yours," Dr. Casey replied, walking him toward another door. When they reached it, he gestured for Thor to enter without him. "We do everything we do around here under the *strictest* code of anonymity. No one will ever know you walked through this door unless *you* told them, and even if you did, they'll be dead and buried long before you wake!" He laughed as Thor entered the room without him. The sign on the door read 'PROCESSING.' He turned and paused for a moment, then nodded at the doctor and finished walking through. "By the way, those 35... None of them had families to speak of," he said as they parted. "And they all signed on for a century... Vaya Con Dios, Mr. Stanton!"

"You too, my friend! I'll say, *Hi* to your great granddaughter for you," he joked as he walked into the processing room. As the door shut behind him, he could hear Dr. Casey greeting some more prospective clients.

This room was basically little more than a lobby with an interviewing booth and a waiting area, but the decor was something to behold. The entire room, floor to ceiling, was designed to look as futuristic as possible. On all planes, walls included, there was first a layer of translucent composite, softer than glass, defining the inner shape. Then there was an offset of about 9 inches between this layer, and a semi-mirrored backer plate, creating an air gap between the two planes that left the illusion that you were suspended in the air, just above the floor, and that all the wall hangings and decorations were hovering in midair, just off of the walls.

The gaps for the ceiling and walls were filled with some kind of smoke with can lights recessed behind it, lighting up all the swirls caused by natural convection, as well as vibration from ambient sound waves in the room. The floor, which was also illuminated, was filled, not with smoke, but with water, also vibrating light designs onto the walls and ceiling from the footsteps being made. There were chairs along two of the walls, suspended above the floor and attached blindly to the wall about another 9 inches out, leaving the illusion that they were floating.

The light seemed to come from everywhere and was set at a very relaxing level, but was bright enough to do business. Three prospective clients sat in chairs, while a fourth was behind the booth, being interviewed. There was a soft, relaxing, yet warmly complicated musical composition streaming from a phenomenal, 3D surround sound system. It was just loud enough to drown out the voices in the booth, but not overbearing.

Spanning the short, translucent partition wall adjacent to the reception desk was a large motif, elaborately airbrushed onto a post-modern, 3D relief of itself depicting a shamelessly utopian version of the metropolis they now lived in. It was clearly lacking all the obvious problems of today, and was infinitely more advanced. Thor smiled, admiring the artwork more than the marketing savvy or clearly overoptimistic appraisal of their current sociological condition.

Behind him and to his right, Thor could feel eyes on him. It was a young couple, maybe in their 30's, and the energy they were throwing off was repulsive. The man was busy being judgmental, pompous and simultaneously jealous of Thor, while his wife sat terrified, not receiving the positive reinforcement she obviously needed to make a decision this big on her own, and was bickering at him under her breath without coming up for air. He had no use for this kind of Co-dependent, high maintenance garbage in even his loosest circles, and there was no way, suspended or not, that he was going to spend the next 100 years anywhere near these idiots....

"Hi, my name is James," Thor said, turning toward the man and offering his hand, "I'm an undercover investigator for the NSA. What have you guys heard about the proliferation of company stock value without adequate reinvestment in the security of the investors, or the acceptable survival rate of the clients? That would be you, on both counts," he said, pointing at both of them. "Nevermind.... How about the recent shuttle disaster that left all 100 of its clients floating through space in their frozen caskets?" He looked frighteningly hard into the woman's eyes during the last question. "Nothing? Not surprising." He exhaled loudly and turned away from them, trying to act angry.

"Come on, honey," the man whispered, losing the battle with his tough-guy charade. She got up so fast she knocked the paperwork from his hand, sending it sprawling across the floor. Thor bent down to assist. "That's q-quite alright, sir. I've g-got it," he stuttered, grabbing everything in one messy pile and bolting for the door with his wife, almost running into her as she turned to look back at the interviewing booth. The door slowly eased shut with a click.

Thor looked slowly over at the man in the end seat, smiling. The man looked at him for just a moment with a straight face, then burst into laughter. Thor cracked up as well, finally unable to keep up the act. "Thank you!" the man interjected, still laughing uncontrollably. "NSA... fuck me!!" Thor relaxed a bit, finally taking a seat, and waited for his turn to speak to the organizer, who was just wrapping it up with a man in his late 60's, well dressed, well spoken, but very obviously racked with some kind of degenerative bone or muscle disease, as he could barely stand, even on crutches. The man who was here before Thor, probably in his 50's, bounced by him with the vigor of a teenager. On his way by Thor, he offered up a "high-five," which Thor proudly took, still smiling about the other two. "Fuckin' NSA," he mumbled, smiling back.

"Hello, welcome to CryoKinetics," the young woman said softly to the man. "Where are the two that came before you?" she asked.

"Oh, they had second thoughts, anyway, I'm Kieran McGinn," he said in a thick Irish brogue. "I believe it was you I spoke to on the phone.... " They walked off toward the back and into the booth. Thor couldn't put his finger on it, but there was something very familiar about this man. For now, he considered that to be a good omen.

He sat in his chair, breathing deep and slowly slipping from a state of meditation to one of aimless daydream, something he had been conditioned not to do, but given the circumstances, it seemed almost unavoidable. He already knew he wanted to go under for one century. Given the rate of world change and the momentum the rate seemed to be gaining, anything more would be an absolute crap-shoot. Even that 100 might only serve to blind their eyes to their own demise, but at least there was hope, something not on the spreadsheets for those alive now.

It was strange to be anxious and in a hurry to be nearly frozen for 100 years, but to them, this time was said to pass nearly instantaneously, like an almost dreamless night. One minute, you're here, and the next.... They would be asleep before they left the Earth, and asleep 'til they got back. Lacking the manned facilities at the station, it was currently safer to bring them out of their slumber back here. *Ain't that a bitch!* Thor thought, *I finally get to go into space, and I'm going to be asleep the entire time!* Aside from what they could expect as far as assistance from the company upon awakening, about the only thing to discuss was payment.

Two more people came in the door just as the lady was wrapping it up with Mr. McGinn, so Thor stood up, stretched, and started walking toward the counter. "Hi! Welcome to CryoKinetics, Mister...?" she prompted, offering Thor her hand.

He shook it firmly, locking eyes with her, before replying, "Stanton, James Stanton." He almost lost it again. Trying hard to keep a straight face, he vowed that when he awoke, the first thing he was going to do was change his name back legally!

The inside of the booth was actually another banking terminal, set up for immediate processing of payment. She explained that given one hour from payment till the point of no return, people had a tendency to take their decision making a little more seriously. In the past, too many people left the facility, and never came back for their scheduled departure, then, despite signing a contract, would still expect a refund, due to the exceptionally large amounts they dealt with. One hour. No more… no less.

It was also just as important to have time to be at ease with your decision, so as not to be in a polluted state of panic when the procedure starts. In the end, he was surprised to find that the whole thing would only drain half his account.... He had assumed they would try to find a way to embezzle it all. *Oh well,* he thought, *the day is still young.* He didn't really expect to wake up and find that he was still in control of the rest, given the fragile state of the economy, nor did he really care, given the manner in which he came to possess it. His only real regret is that he wouldn't have time to set anyone worthy up with more of it, but the faces he brightened last night in Hell's Ditch with the chunk he spent already would be in his mind for 100 years.

He spent the next hour in the waiting room, off in his own corner, in seiza; eyes locked a million miles away in deep meditation. Deep breath in the nose with his tongue on the roof of his mouth, strong breath out the mouth, exhaling all the bad energies he had been packing around. He had no intention, whatever the future held, of bringing a load of hitch-hiking negativity with him. His mind had to be clear and his spirit centered. He did not move for the rest of the wait.

He sprang up out of seiza and onto both feet, simultaneously, then walked over to the door, the others in the room looking at him curiously. A moment later, the door opened and two doctors stood there, waving at everyone to follow. They walked down a long hallway with doors on both sides until they reached a large double door at the end. On the other side was a large lab, with rows of high tech looking beds down each side... 40 in all. The last 8 were dressed out with sheets, wires with electrodes, an I.V. tree & tubes, and each had a high tech diagnostic and monitoring machine and computer next to it, as well as a short curtain offering a small degree of privacy to each client.

On the wall, at the foot of each bed, was a sphincter style airlock, undoubtedly where the patients were fed into the cryo-tubes. Thor, being about as claustrophobic as they come, had one thing on his mind after seeing this. "Are we asleep before, or after, we get put into those?" he asked, pointing at the airlock closest to him.

"Before, and you'll be out before you wake... *trust me,*" one of the doctors spoke up, gesturing for Thor to grab that bed. The other four patients were escorted to stations of their own.

Trust me... I fucking hate it when people say that, he heard Kait's voice say in his head.

"I know, right?" he said out loud.

"Excuse me?" the doctor said, puzzled.

"Oh, nothing! Just talking to myself."

"All right! At least you'll be able to keep yourself company!" the doctor joked.

"Yeah, I think they charged me double, though," Thor joked, getting a few laughs from the other patients. "Maybe I should've asked about group rates...." They laughed again, a little harder.

"We have a comedian in our midst," one of the female doctors spoke up.

Thor took a sarcastic bow, "Yep, I'll be performing right here for the next 100 years...."

"At least you'll have steady work, right?" McGinn chimed in.

"To be sure, to be sure," Thor smiled.

"Somebody hurry the hell up and freeze me now," the old man said with a grin as he claimed a bed by tossing his jacket across it.

The doctors had them all tucked in, stripped down to their shorts, and wired for sound, with electrodes stuck all over their chests, forehead, and arms. They were all given an I.V. differing in color, probably due to length of suspension, body chemistry, etc.. All at once, Thor felt the rush of the initial medicine taking effect. It was definitely a euphoric of some kind, possibly Dilaudid or something similar, mixed with Valium, meant to take the edge off of acute pain and trauma. He smiled a big, cheesy grin at the doctor as she took his vitals again. He couldn't remember the last time he felt this good. He was just about to ask her what the drugs were for when she pulled two enormous needles out of her box of supplies and started hooking them up to tubes and to the machine. "Oh shit!" he laughed, unable to completely care what they were about to do. He started staring at the ceiling and then cracked up again.

"What?" she asked.

"What?" He jumped back to reality, noticing the softness in her eyes, the smoothness of her hair and skin, the warmth of her touch as she felt his forehead and arms.

"You're cold," she said.

"You're sexy," Thor slurred, unable to focus completely. She smiled, then pulled out the first of the large needles, sliding it into his left arm. He winced, remembering now that they said something about a plasma transfusion.... *Shit, that hurt.* She came around the other side with the other one.

"How about something sexy for this side, too," she said sarcastically. He flinched again, but laughed a little inside as he heard the moans and groans of several of the other clients who didn't have anywhere near the threshold for pain that he did.

"Symmetry is... symmetry... was... sexy... is..." He suddenly realized he was going cross-eyed and seeing double. He could still understand what he was hearing, but couldn't speak clearly. He heard the door open again, and then the familiar jingle and hard-step of Doctor Casey. *"Doc!"* he called out with his eyes nearly closed. *At least he thought he said it out loud....*

The doctor walked slowly around the room, checking out the status of each of the clients, then started giving what sounded like a very well-rehearsed speech, assuring each of them that they were doing the right thing for their given situations.... How they would go down in history as partners in this "never before tried" pinnacle of modern science; pioneers of the future, like Lewis & Clark, bravely charging forward to the next frontier, freed from the confines of conventional living.... Thor faded off in mid speech, most likely the doctors' true intention, but to the sound of his own music, echoing in his head.

> Cast aside what you'd like to see,
> and you'll suffocate in your apathy
> And I'd like to show you what the difference is
> between the one who survives, and the one who lives
> They say "Fate condemns the undetermined mind," no,
> Fate can KISS MY ASS this time!

He faded out of consciousness to the same dream he has had off and on since he was a small child... It was chilly and the sky was grey and darkening. He was standing on a hillside devoid of most plant life, save for a short tundra covering on the ground with the occasional small flower or patch of weeds. Basketball sized rocks scattered here and there broke the monotony of the landscape, which seemed to roll on into the distance, unchanged, but for some reason he could not focus on the horizon.

Suddenly a loud squawk sounded high above him and he turned his head to see what it was. The majestic bird, probably a bald eagle, flew right overhead, gliding smoothly on its tremendous wingspan and headed out over the crest of a nearby hill. He quickly followed. Upon clearing the hilltop, he could see a small house: a single story log cabin standing alone in this barren diorama. He started walking up the hill toward it.

Almost as if being yanked off his feet by a giant rubber band, he was jolted straight up the hill, stopping abruptly at the front door of the cabin. The dream always ended before he got this far, but this time the door was cracked open a bit and the house was obviously abandoned, so he entered. The house was cold and dark, but enough light made it in to see around. Everything inside was either rustic wood and patinated brass, almost black with age, or glass, some panes broken, some not.

A few steps down the dark hallway toward the living room and kitchen he became aware of a huge wolf behind him, coming out of one of the back bedrooms. It was black and stood chest high to him at the shoulders. Its head was slightly down and it kept its distance, but continued to follow him. For some reason he did not fear it, but rather, made a calm decision to avoid it and find another way out of the house.

He took a left turn at the end of the hallway into the kitchen, and the wolf went right, into the living room, but kept a constant eye on him as if not wanting him to leave. He could see its head through the interior windows and over the living room knee wall, here and there, always staring at him with those eyes…. He started looking around for a weapon, just in case.

The kitchen looked fairly run down and empty, but clean. There were some old supplies: oil lamps, pots, pans, old coffee cups, etc., but no knives or silverware. There was a window over the sink and one open on the top half of a Dutch door that looked like it hadn't been opened for a while. He turned back to see the wolf enter the room slowly, baring its teeth. For some reason he was still not afraid, and the wolf's teeth began to fall out onto the floor, bouncing around and falling into cracks in the hardwood until he couldn't see them at all. When he looked back up, the wolf was gone.

He heard a noise behind him and spun around to see a giant bald eagle sitting on the ledge of the open window. It suddenly flew off and he ran to catch up, getting stuck on the door for a moment. He broke free of the house and ran to catch up with the bird, now flying straight out over the tundra, but he couldn't make progress. No matter how hard he ran, time just seemed to go slower. It continued slowing as his field of vision narrowed smaller and smaller, then faded to blackness and silence....

CHAPTER 26: AWAKE

First there was the *sensation* of light... a warm glow, starting from a mere pinhole in the darkness, then growing larger. Then came cold beyond cold, and slowly becoming aware of his own body, then himself. Pain. He cringed, suddenly aware of some kind of sound... possibly himself crying out. The pain was nearly unbearable. He tried to call out, but couldn't move his mouth. The light was now becoming unbearable as well. He could feel his eyelids moving and tried to focus on that. He was becoming aware of people moving around him, but he still couldn't hear right. There were muffled noises and voices coming from nearly everywhere, but he couldn't make out any words or even tell what language they were speaking.

"How are they coming along?" the male doctor asked one of the two females that were assisting with the patients.

"This one's moving.... He keeps trying to speak. Should I give him another shot of adrenaline?" she asked.

"Do it! What about the other four?" he yelled while preparing something in a vial over by the sink.

"This one's not responding!" yelled the other woman. Neither one was dressed like a nurse or doctor, but more like some sort of soldier.

"That's what I was afraid of, " the doctor grunted, shoving his way past her with a syringe full of some kind of dark liquid. "I keep telling the asshole! We're going to lose every one of them!" He shot the fluid directly into the man's heart, slamming down hard to puncture the chest.

Thor's vision started to widen slightly, and he began to make out a set of eyes. Female eyes. Beautiful, like the eyes of an angel, unblinking and cutting through the haze with a softness he could feel even through his desensitized numbness. The contours of her face and hair began to take shape. She was starting to smile. "He's coming around!" she yelled out, turning to the other two, who were busy pumping on the chest of the older man, who still wasn't responding. She looked back down into his eyes. "Hang in there, it'll pass…. You're doing great!" He could just make out the stinging sensation of her grabbing hold of his hand. He tried to grab back, but couldn't even tell if he had moved at all. He grunted something audible, but unintelligible from the strain. She leaned down with one ear to listen. He clearly grunted out one word….

"Kait…."

He dozed back off, his arm falling off the table from exhaustion after he had managed to lift it up towards her. The military uniform she was wearing had a small device attached to the lapel that looked like a rectangular metal clip with a button on both ends and some sort of speaker or microphone perforation across the face. It made a chirping sound and she squeezed the ends together to stop it. She squeezed again and spoke into it, "I'll be right there." She turned to the doctor and said, "This one's exceptionally strong... be careful with him, I'll be back to check them out in a while, but right now I'm needed upstairs." She started walking toward the automatic door, stopping briefly to correct her partner's hand position while she gave another patient an injection. The other woman nodded in compliance.

The automatic door slid open and another doctor walked in, punching something in on the touch-screen of his electronic clipboard without really looking up.

"Hey Red, how's it hangin'?" she said sarcastically, intentionally bumping into his arm as she strutted right by him on her way out the door. She didn't even look back as he fumbled the clipboard, nearly dropping it.

"Bitch..." he mumbled under his breath after he regained control. The other doctor shook his head and smiled.

"I heard that!" she yelled as the door slid shut behind her. "Pompous little twit," she mumbled to herself. There was a corridor heading in both directions, an elevator door off to the right, and a wide stairwell with handrails on both sides directly in front of her. She started hiking up the stairs, effortlessly taking them two at a time.

She had the body of a gymnast; muscles overdeveloped in all the right places, accentuated perfectly by her skin-tight uniform, and flexing rhythmically as she powered her way up two more flights of stairs to the top. She reached it, still not out of breath, and opened a large metal door at the top.

Inside was some sort of equipment locker room. It was little more than a hallway; well lit with another door on the far end. There were large cabinet doors along the wall on both sides, and narrow locker-style doors up higher. She walked directly to one on the right about half way down, and put her right index finger on a small scanner on the handle. It popped open and she began pulling things out.

She pulled out a harness and strapped it on over her shoulders. It held several utility pouches and several clips of ammunition. She opened a locking case and pulled out a pair of long automatic pistols, then carefully slid them both into place in the harness and locked them down. She put on a short cut jacket with built in armor and communication capability, and finally, the icing on the cake: a long gun with a folding stock and pistol grip that she strapped around her waist in a belt holster that rode the length of her right thigh, waist to knee, the belt itself containing all manner of equipment case and tool imaginable. Her jacket was decorated like that of an officer of some rank, and she wore it proudly; standing up straight and checking herself in the mirror inside her locker door before she shut it and proceeded toward the other door.

On the other side was a large room leading to several different areas. The hallway turned into a ramp to the right, and straight forward it widened and turned into a ramp heading into a storage warehouse with a large bay door open on the far side of it. She paused for a moment, then sighed, staring up the narrow ramp corridor to her right and then proceeded straight forward, walking up the ramp into the dark warehouse.

The sound of her boots clacking on the hard floor echoed throughout the deserted room. There were shelves of stored goods, weapons, crates of equipment, dry food, etc., stored from floor to ceiling on metal shelves as far as the eye could see in the dark. She was about halfway through when there was a yell from the hallway behind her. "Sky!"

She stopped, turned around, and held her hands out to the sides, palms up. *"Yes?"* she responded, sarcastically.

"Sky! They need you upstairs as soon as possible! Where are you going?" the uniformed man asked nervously.

"To hell in a handbasket... and I'm taking the scenic route." She turned away from him and started to walk toward the open bay door again. "Tell him I'm on the way up."

"Aye," he said, formally saluting her, even though her back was turned already.

When she reached the doorway she paused, breathing and stretching for a moment inside the cargo bay as if preparing for something. She pulled one end of an air filter tube out of a pouch on the left shoulder of her jacket and fitted the small clip on the end of it to her left nostril, breathed deeply a few times, then walked outside. With her back to the door, she faced a large, open concrete patio with a surrounding knee wall, about three feet high, with spotting scopes mounted here and there, and a few steel panels laid out on the deck, covering utility access points for maintenance. She walked out in the open, stretching her arms out to the sides and taking in the breathtaking expanse of the surrounding panorama.

It was nearly dark outside, and the contrasting colors were creating a masterpiece of awe inspiring beauty. The clouds were sweeping in low, and in strips, swirling in tight knots here and there like a child's ribbon lost to a windy day.

She approached the side of the open deck, gazing out over the landscape to the mountain peaks in the distance. Untouched by mankind, the harsh, jagged points deteriorated into rolling hills of orange sand, stretching as far as the eye could see. The top half of the goddess, Sigyn, dipping just below the horizon with her colorful rings, dominated the already impressive view, as the enormous planet consumed nearly half of the visible skyline, shielding the world from danger with her unyielding loyalty and holding sway to the overbearing demon's head looming in close, just on the other side. High above, her twin wolves, Vali and Nari, play relentlessly in the night sky, circling the planet and each other, caught in an eternal struggle of dominance and submission until Ragnarok begins.

The voracious dust devils, some as large as a house, were tearing up the plains, spending themselves entirely as they bombarded the base of the mountain ridge, and each other, in a violent cycle of death and rebirth. Following one of the larger ones, she leaned out over the edge and looked straight down, losing sight of it as they passed by overhead, her vision obscured by the magnetic disruption emanating from the underside of the massive ship, hovering nearly a half mile above the planet's surface. She turned back toward the bay door, spotting the stairwell leading up several tiers toward the bridge, then waved at the Captain and two of his Lieutenants, who were standing outside on the mezzanine and started the long climb up to the top of the pilothouse.

When she got there, they were already back inside. She held her hand over a scanner on the outside wall and an airlock door slid quickly open. She stepped in, pulling off her nose filter and letting it retract; winding back up into its pocket. She opened the inner airlock, then stepped inside the bridge. "Hello.... Did you miss me?" she joked. When she didn't receive the warm reception she had expected, and in fact, was hardly noticed at all, she knew something was awry. She walked directly over to Captain Parnell, who was busy talking to one of his navigators, a skinny Ensign named Eriksson.

She came up to them in mid conversation, but was able to make out, "Just map it out... If I'm not mistaken, that will still put us ahead of the caves before the eclipse."

"Aye, aye, Sir!" the young Ensign saluted proudly, his extremely young age showing through in the crackling of his mid-pubescent voice.

"Sir! Captain Parnell, Sir! Lieutenant Commander Davies reporting for duty, Sir!" she mocked, smiling an insider's smile at the Captain.

He grinned back, trying not to let the Ensign notice too much, "Cut the shit, Sky, like you'd show me that kind of respect.... Anyway, Bjorn is a top notch navigator and cartography expert... we're lucky to have him onboard!"

"Show you that kind of respect? You get what you give, my love," she smiled.

"You would do well to remember that yourself... Anyway, we-"

"What?!?" she interrupted loudly, with a strange look on her face. "What's that supposed to mean?"

"It means, shut up and listen, dammit! About an hour ago, we ran some preliminary numbers and we are still way short on crystal, *and* we're approaching eclipse way too close to what we believe may be the largest Sand Dragon nest on the planet."

"What are we going to do about it?" she asked.

"Straight to the point, that's what I love about you," he said, patting her on the shoulder.

"Well?"

"We're altering course as we speak, and getting another Carrier ready for harvest, and to be used as a wingman, if necessary."

"What do you mean, 'if necessary.' If *what* is necessary?" she asked, becoming agitated.

"What do you think? In case were attacked on a large scale," he replied. "They get more and more bold with their attacks each time! We wouldn't be able to defend against a large assault if our shield failed! We're just a mining vessel... a Carrier rigged out for harvesting, not for battle," he elaborated. "It's kind of one or the other!"

"A mining vessel stripping an ecosystem of its fundamental resource with no regard for our hosts. Sound familiar? Gee, what's next? Declare war on them for defending themselves? Why the hell are we cutting so close to their nest? Why not double back, for God's sake?" she yelled.

"Orders, that's why. We don't have the crystal to leave this system, and every hour we're here our fleet burns more and more of it fighting this bizarre gravity out in orbit! They're affording us one more harvester.... *One!* That's it. We have to speed up our collection rate, even at that, or we'll never make it, and every one of us will eventually power down and die out there before we can get to the next system. This is just where we happen to be in this planet's rotation, so suck it up... *we have no choice!* They're all depending on us! What I need you to do is oversee the mining ops yourself. No one can motivate people like you can, Sky... you have a gift! Wake as many as you need, get them up to speed, and get this done. I'm depending on you. No one else can do what you do... you're a born leader! Can I count on you?"

She stood up straight, and saluted him again, this time without the sarcasm. "Aye, Sir, you can." She nodded and turned away, then walked off toward the door opposite where she came in. It opened automatically and she stepped up to the threshold, turned to face the room, and bowed, hands at her sides without looking away, then turned again and walked out.

Voices were scrambled in the darkness. First, a pair of women, then a man joined the conversation. He couldn't discern the language at first, but after a few seconds, he realized they were speaking English. He fought to open his eyes, but gave in to the pain and cold. So cold. He fell unconscious again, speeding through some sort of abstract dream in a matter of seconds. He awoke suddenly to voices again, unsure how much time had just elapsed.

There was an excruciating pain in his chest and forehead, similar to an ice cream headache, but a thousand times more painful. He cried out. Somehow the action seemed to help the pain. He yelled again, this time much louder, straining to move his arms and open his eyes. He could see light, and started to make out the form of a person above him, looking down. He remembered the clinic. It felt as if he was just there.... *Was there a malfunction? Early shutdown? Am I getting busted?*

He tried to look around, but gave in to the pain again. Everything was fuzzy. He became aware of his breathing.... *What's wrong? Breathing too shallow... got to get up!* He struggled to sit up, but something was stopping him. Nausea. Intense pain across chest. He couldn't tell for sure, but it felt like he was in restraints. Now he could hear the doctor talking to the woman above him. "How's he doing?" he said calmly.

"He's further along than I've ever seen, this soon.... He's coming around," he heard her say in a soft, familiar voice. He strained to see her face. She laid her hand on his chest and leaned a little closer. He could almost make out her eyes. "Hang in there... you're OK." She stood up and disappeared from his field of vision.

He started to feel a burning in all his extremities. He tried to move them, little by little, and the pain started to subside, replaced by tingling and warmth. This was encouraging, so he fell back on what he knew. He began to concentrate on his breathing, and the concerted controlling of muscle movement, group by group. He was starting to enjoy a fair degree of success when he was overcome with a sudden attack of uncontrollable shivering. He shook so hard that sounds started coming out of his voicebox that he could not control. He could definitely tell that he was in restraints, and now he understood why. His pain nearly doubled before it finally started to subside. He could finally move his mouth enough to articulate the finer nuances of the English language. "f-f-f-F-F-F-FUCK!"

This was the doctor's cue. They removed the chest strap and the arm restraints, then lifted him onto a heated table covered with some sort of deep foam-rubber that allowed more of his body to sink into the heating solution to speed his recovery. He could now see the same woman's face more clearly. She leaned over towards his face, speaking very softly. "You're almost there. Sorry about the first phase. I know it's long and painful, but if we rushed it, you'd probably die of cardiac arrest."

"You shouldn't talk to them!" the male doctor snapped.

"I shouldn't talk to *you*. Mind your business," she snapped back, turning her attention back to Thor while they both continued to hook up electrodes and diagnostic equipment to his shivering body.

Thor kept blinking his eyes, trying to get a better look at her. He cleared his throat with a little success, then started coughing hard. This hurt him pretty badly, and she rushed to get him a cup of water. "Room temp, only!" the doctor yelled.

"Here, drink slowly," she said, holding the cup up to his lips while lifting up on the back of his head. He sipped a little, then coughed it up. He immediately strained his neck toward the cup for more, eyes widening. She carefully tilted the cup and he drank the rest, still breathing a little shallow, but slowly recovering. "Good job!" she cheered, looking at the doctor for his reaction. "He's pulling out faster than anyone we've seen yet... don't you think?"

"What?" the doctor said, fumbling with one of the larger machines, "oh... yeah, sure. Well look at him, most of the others have been old codgers. This guy's ex-military or something. You didn't get scars like that back then from programming computers and driving your Bentley!" He laughed over zealously at his own joke, snorting a bit through his nostrils. "Maybe he was one of those sports stars... I heard they made lots of money!"

Thor was starting to find this doctor's bedside manner just a bit strange for a professional. Then there was the comment about "not talking to *them*" that made him a little uncomfortable from the moment he said it. He had a crushing headache, but he could feel some medicine that they administered through an IV bag starting to work. "I've had some hangovers in my life, but this is fucking ridiculous!" he grunted out, trying to smile.

The doctor just ignored him, but the woman cracked a big smile, looking down on him again. "I see your sense of humor thawed out as well...." She gave him a little more water, then joined the doctor, who was already working diligently on another patient. "We'll be back with you in a bit... just relax and breathe," she called back to him from one of the beds he couldn't see. He could hear them getting a little frantic about something. A nearby machine started beeping an alarm sound of some kind at them. "He didn't make it either!" she said, slamming something metal against the wall. "Dammit! I need all I can get! Do you understand?" She suddenly got real quiet and almost murmured, "We have a situation brewing outside... believe me when I say, all our lives might depend on it!"

"I'll do what I can. They've been down a lot longer than the rest... hell, most of them weren't in good shape when they were frozen!" the doctor tried to explain.

Frozen? We weren't supposed to get frozen. Maybe he's just using a figure of speech... also not really the defining trait of a schooled physician.... Thor's mind was starting to race a bit. "What year is it?" he called out. Nobody replied. "Hey! What year is it?" he yelled louder, his voice crackling and forcing him into a coughing fit.

"Shhhhhhhh," the doctor said, peering around the machine. "The answers will come, just relax for a bit while I help these others...." He added some kind of shot to Thor's IV line, causing him to doze off before he could even ask what it was.

He awoke to a loud crash and some sort of impact or earthquake. The lights started to flicker, and he sat straight up, still hurting, but feeling a lot more like himself than he did just a while ago. "Lay down!" the woman yelled at him with a push backwards. He still didn't have the strength to repel it, and fell over backwards onto the bed like a ragdoll. "You still need 20 more minutes!" She scrambled to remove his electrodes and IV line and turned to the doctor, still yelling, "Get the others back into pre-incubation, now!"

"But..."

"I know the risk! We may need everybody at their post... that includes you! We don't know it's over," she explained. Thor looked around. There were many others out on tables; groaning, moaning, and gasping for air, all at various stages of early recovery. The doctor was scrambling to comply with her order. He could see now that she was an officer of some sort. This sort of surprised him. This company functioned in the private sector on huge amounts of money from its clients, alone. Why it would have ever become militarized? The doc was obviously military, as well. That explained his strange mannerisms. He knew there was much he didn't understand, but he didn't want another knock out shot for asking questions, so he decided just to play along.

Suddenly he was being wheeled on his bed very quickly down some hallways and through a couple of doorways. Halfway through a large sliding door there was a second crash and oddly enough, everything shook but him! He had been in a few earthquakes on the west coast, and though it seemed similar, something was very different. The initial sensation was too abrupt. Then there was the fact that it didn't keep moving them... just a hard impact, a little sway, then a quick recovery. He speculated immediately that they were onboard a large boat, or some kind of military ship, and they were rescued out of the ocean, like the scenario Dr. Casey painted if they were ever dropped from orbit.

Another one hit hard, this time slamming his incubator bed into the door jamb sideways, after which it dropped straight down, almost to the floor, rising back up after the lights came back on. It was then that he realized that his bed was hovering in midair, suspended only by some kind of ship generated electrical field. *That would explain why the quakes felt different*, he thought.

Through the doorway he could see an octagonal room with some kind of corresponding core in the center, glowing with a blue light, and spanning from floor to ceiling. He was quickly pushed into the room and was circled around the core to the left past a series of cells recessed into the walls, some with people in them behind a glowing blue field of energy across the entryway, some empty. She pulled right up to one of the empty ones and he quickly struggled to get free of the bed. He was almost sitting all the way up when she shoved it into the cell, causing him to fall backwards from the acceleration, legs sticking straight up in the air. Just when he was back up and about to jump off, the bed flipped lengthwise out from under him and back out the doorway, causing him to drop down hard, right on his ass. He spun around on the balls of his feet and one fist just in time to see her turn on the energy shield. She punched a few things in on a keypad on the wall and moved on.

He cracked up laughing, unsure if it was drugs or delirium, then forced himself to stop when it hurt too much. Sitting back against the wall in his birthday suit with the worst headache he could remember, and picking up the pieces of his shattered ego after the only girl he had seen in at least a hundred years just dumped him on his ass in an 8 foot square metal cell, he had to admit... this didn't look good.

CHAPTER 27: BATTLE ON DECK

She quickly reacquired her weapons from her locker and charged outside by way of the cargo room bay door, which was just in the process of being closed and locked down to keep the inside of the ship sealed off from attack. The ship shook violently every few seconds, the result of the bombardment of the underside by mines being placed in their path and then sucked up into the ships own magnetic collection device. People were running all around the deck, looking to the sky, across the vast horizon, and over the side, down toward the surface of the planet, trying to prepare for the next wave.

For the most part, the ship remained unscathed due to its own defense shield: a transparent field of energy that displaced and repulsed all solid matter, preventing it from passing through. The ship's shield generator, consequently the same device that was responsible for the operation of all of the interior cell doors, the generation of its artificial gravity, as well as many other of the ship's benign functions, created an elliptical bubble of protection around the entire ship that the indigenous creatures could not send any projectiles through.

They had, however, developed the ability to pass through it themselves, and were getting bolder and bolder with apparent suicide runs at the deck and the bridge to test their defenses.

The mines were more of a nuisance than anything else. As part of an earlier campaign, surface rovers were deployed to explore and assess the mineral content of the small planet, and were initially greeted by all manner of hostile worm and burrowing insect. They were forced to drop mines in front of, and behind themselves, just to keep from being swallowed or pulverized by any of a dozen different burrowing creatures. What had, by most of their early assessments, seemed to be a barren wasteland, rich in resources but nearly devoid of life, turned out to be quite different indeed.

The numbers and movement of the indigenous was masked from above by the fact that everything lived almost entirely underground. With Sigyn, a neighboring colossus of a planet, three moons, and the binary sun, Algol, making passes every three and a half days near a third star, there was so much seismic and electromagnetic activity that it was impossible to do an accurate sub-surface scan. There was also a constant threat of meteor activity from the suns on the other side of Sigyn, such that they needed to be capable of evasive maneuvering at a moment's notice, ruling out any kind of time-lapse analog scan.

The large planet shielded them for all but the end of each three and a half day cycle, but when they neared the third sun, the orbital ellipse of Sigyn widened for just long enough, while Algol endured additional strain, to make the little planet vulnerable to magnetic disruption, solar flares, and bombardment by meteors pulled in toward the augmented gravitational field. Though this cycle had apparently been going on for millions of years, the planet shook with such intensity during those hours that every time it happened it seemed to be the end; as if it was coming apart from the inside out.

The truth is that the complex blend of situations here existed nowhere else in the universe, leaving the scientific community nothing to base their hypothesis on, meaning they really had no idea how long this system had existed, or would continue to exist.... The only thing they seemed in agreement on is that it was highly unstable, but had worked itself into some kind of uneasy equilibrium for eons, and that it was on a decaying spiral of uncertain length and magnitude. Under constant threat, the rest of the Fleet was forced to spend impulse fuel to "hover" just out of orbit in the least affected zone nearby while a mining ship harvested the radioactive crystal they used for all their fuel and energy production; a substance found in abundance in the acid-rich orange sand of this planet's dry, wind-torn desert plains.

Fire erupted twenty feet into the air on both sides of the deck, not two feet out from the knee wall from the exploding mines pulled up into the magnetic field that the giant harvester generated to extract mineral in large quantities from the surface, and though they didn't damage the ship from underneath at this magnitude, they did offer a degree of cover fire for the strafing attacks from the one real threat they had encountered... Sand Dragons.

The most advanced life form found on the planet, thusly named by the humans because of their appearance, had figured out that they could collect unexploded mines and group them together in bundles, then place them directly in the path of the ship to deliver a significantly larger payload. They had even learned to camouflage them within large deposits of crystal in order to appeal to the humans' greed and lure them straight in over the explosives. This suggested not only intelligence, but strategic and analytical thinking, as well.

Little else was known about them, aside from the fact that they lived underground in vast networks of caves, and seemed to respond to each other's behavior and flight patterns in much the same manner as bees or bats. Though no language had been detected, or communication with them attempted, they obviously communicated with each other somehow. It had been speculated that they used some sort of pheromone, possibly in conjunction with the crystal, which was definitely organic in nature, but the growing complexity of their actions suggested something much more advanced. One theory was that they functioned through a collective intelligence; a form of telepathy, possibly generated by a leader, much like the queen of a hive. In any case, they were regarded with fear and treated with hostility, without much provocation, and this had always put a bit of a wedge between Sky and Captain Parnell.

Sky was a warrior, and would kill without hesitation to defend her ship and her people, but every time the smoke cleared, she was left standing with a bad taste in her mouth about the means by which the Captain accomplished their goals. This wasn't the first time they walked all over a lesser species to steal resources they needed in the name of Humanity and its short-sighted goals, but it was getting harder and harder to abide for her. Though little was known about their "hosts," she sensed their connection was much deeper than anyone here realized.

Just when it seemed that maybe the attack was subsiding, they got hit from below so hard that the concussion knocked several people right off their feet. They scrambled to get up while the rest either grabbed onto something nearby, or dropped into prone position, nervously staring at the sky and the flame wall. The ship shook intensely and pitched hard forward before leveling out; the flames radiating so much heat from all around them that they had to cluster toward the middle of the deck, disorganized and distracted, shielding their faces.

"Spread out and form ranks!" Sky yelled at the top of her lungs. "Now! We're sitting ducks!" They scrambled to obey, but it was too late. Just as the flames dissipated into a smokey haze, a flash and a roar came out of nowhere and took the head right off the man standing closest to the edge. It rolled across the deck, stopping face up, to the horror of his comrades, and before they could digest what had just happened, the winged creature snatched the man standing opposite of him, pulled him right over the edge, then disappeared straight down into the haze.

The return fire from the ambushed troops was grossly late and over-reactionary at best; a few of the less experienced soldiers firing randomly over the side, yelling like angry children at the loss of two of their friends. Sky fired one shot into the air to get their attention. "I said form ranks!" she yelled in their ears, "Two circles! Backs to the center! They're coming from above.... Center circle, cover high! Outer circle, cover the rail!" she ordered.

Just before the men were quite in position, as if to taunt them further, it came up from underneath the vessel and swept straight in sideways, cutting the circle in half by flying low and fast. It knocked over several men right down the middle, then dropped out of sight, right over the opposite rail, before they could fire a shot. Now that they were all facing each other, it struck again in exactly the same manner, from exactly the same direction, without hesitation, causing one of the less disciplined soldiers to shoot one of his own in the chest; the plasma discharge from his rifle blowing apart the young man's armor and tearing a 6 inch diameter hole nearly all the way through him in one ferocious blue bolt of lightning. It was gone again before they could blink. The body of the dead soldier slid to a stop about 10 feet out on his back, leaving a large swath of fresh blood on the deck.

In the distance, hazily obscured by vapor clouds released from the ship's pull on the soil, the being rose high above the surrounding hills, slowed to a stop and hovered with instinctively timed wing flaps. It stared at its prey, still kicking and squirming in vain like a mouse caught in an eagle's talons. It lifted him up to face level and paused, staring deep into the young soldiers eyes with a penetrating gaze, and the man froze, petrified with fear and sure that he was about to die. The creature stared at him silently... *intently.* He could almost hear it trying to ask him something, but there were no words, no sounds, nothing but those dark, penetrating eyes.

"What the hell do you want from me? You fucking freak-show! What??!!" he screamed at the creature, now kicking and thrashing again. The creature's eyes slowly closed, as if it was saddened by the whole thing, and giving up on them quickly. Slowly, they reopened into a full, intense glare of absolute rage, and the creature discarded the little human with a small preamp followed by a powerful backhand toss to the right. His scream faded off as he flailed downward through the cloud cover.

Back on deck, Sky looked up just in time to see the young soldier being tossed into the hazy abyss below, and the creature diving straight down and to the left, toward the tallest cluster of hills in the distance. In the aftermath, four men were helping to carry off their fallen comrade while others stood post, looking nervously about. She was apparently the only one who saw the body fall and truly knew it was over. As she looked around, unable to spot the creature anywhere, she lowered her eyes, saddened for her friends and for her situation. "I want no less than four of you outside at a time tonight! I mean it, nobody gets caught out here alone!" she ordered, then turned to walk back inside, tapping on her belt com to report to the Captain.

As she entered the bay door back into the cargo hold, she ran into three of the men, talking very one-sided about the creatures and how they should be dealt with. This always pissed her off about them, as she knew damn well there was a better way of dealing with other species, even after their careless exploitation of indigenous resources brought on natural hostility. Try as she may to impart even a shred of decency or higher level thinking on the very people she risked her life to defend, her words always fell on deaf ears. They didn't get it. They wouldn't get it even if it was finally happening to them.

It was this very tendency that put her kind in the position they were in; homeless scavengers roaming the cosmos looking for the next meal-ticket, but too nearsighted to create anything sustainable out of it when they finally found it. Frustrated at the simpleton barbs and brainwashed, alpha-male, jerk-off clichés, and still not convinced at all that the actions of this one creature were as random of an attack as was perceived, she made her way to the bridge to bark a little higher up the ladder. It couldn't hurt to try *one* more time.

"Captain, I witnessed strategic behavior out of one of the creatures this time..."

"Sky, I know. We've been over this... they're quite clever, but there's no reasoning with them, and if we don't finish what we set out to do, every one of us will die out here. It might come down to us or them!" the Captain reasoned, not wanting to hash up any previous debates at this point in the game.

"Sir, with all due respect, that's just it... *us* or *them?* What makes you so sure it will be *us* if we push them that hard? I mean, we have no idea what their *true* numbers are, but I saw one rogue pick us apart like we weren't there, and it could've kept going! It wasn't *attacking* us, it was *testing us!* I think it even tried to communicate with one of us!"

"By ripping a man's head off? Nice way to start a conversation!"

"They didn't start the conversation! Anyway, hear me out... The bullshit on deck was a ruse! It *took* one of us! One of its own choosing, then got to a safe distance and tried to interrogate him. It may have found out what it needed to know... or maybe it was trying to see if there was something more to us besides the obvious. I don't know, but I watched its reaction, and it was one of frustration, not blind aggression. Even its attack was elaborate and premeditated. If they possess strategic reasoning, they possess a culture, and we're destroying it without any plan for their sustained survival after we're gone!" she yelled, slamming her fist down on the map table they were standing over.

"Look, Sky, you know I respect you, and I know you're probably right about this, but need I remind you how little *control* we actually have over this situation? There's a whole Fleet of brass a lot heavier than mine who are losing power and fuel daily waiting for us to get this done. They're even sending another Carrier to help speed things up. I am a little concerned that this action will bring about unprecedented hostility from the natives, but the decision is not ours to make. What *control* do you honestly think we have?" he posed, trying, for what it was worth, to remain diplomatic with her.

"We're the ones down here right now... *not them!* If we spent some time focusing on a larger solution, maybe we could all win... *maybe not*... but I believe we are morally obligated to try!"

He put his hand gently on her shoulder, looking deep into her ice blue eyes. "Your mother would have been so proud of you. Your father too. You're a fine leader. Don't let the bastards bring you down."

"Which bastard?" she mumbled, started to leave to go bring up more workers from the Cryo-pool, when she remembered Stanton. "Hey, by the way, there's one particular Cryo you might be interested in seeing. I think there might be something special about this one. He had a ridiculously fast recovery, I mean, I've never seen one recover anywhere close to this fast. He's in the brig right now, at least until we interrogate him and find out who he is."

"I don't know, Sky, you remember what happened last time we tried to trust one of them with something that mattered... that suicidal basket case almost got all of us killed!" he reminded her with a skeptical look in his eyes. "Just give it a while. We'll see what happens. There's too much going on right now, anyway. Besides, we need as many as possible out and working the crystal stores right now! If he's as strong as you say, maybe that's where he belongs! Remember, most of these assholes were criminals, be it violent or in business...."

"Aye," she saluted, walking off feeling like she usually did after talking to him... *like trying to clap with one hand....* "Let's just give it some careful consideration and keep a close eye on him. It's not like we couldn't use to replenish the ranks a bit... we're getting shorter and shorter on good personnel," she added, smiling, mainly just trying to see if she could get the last word in.

"You've got a point there, we'll see."

CHAPTER 28: ACCLIMATION

She stopped by the Cryo wing on the way to the brig. All the incubator beds were empty and accounted for, so she assumed the thaw out effort, at least insofar as the original numbers were concerned, was a success. She opened a storage locker and loaded numerous grey coveralls of varying sizes into a large hamper-style cart. She opened another one and grabbed a bunch of shoes, threw them on top, then proceeded out the double door and down the corridor toward the brig.

As soon as she came through the door she knew something wasn't right. There were still many empty cells, and some of the people who were coming out of Cryo when she left to go upstairs weren't even here. The two nurses were standing next to the doctor in front of one of the occupied cells. She started to walk toward him, but he met her halfway, just out of earshot of the newer patients. "This has been a grave day," the doctor started explaining, "we've lost more than half! 11 souls out of 20! Tell Captain Parnell we just can't do this on an augmented time table! It's fucking unethical!"

"Well, Doc," she prepared him with a cynical smile, "it's about to get worse before it gets better." She looked around a little, then proceeded a little quieter. "We needed 20 more than that, so that would be 31 more... ASAFP!"

"As soon as fucking possible? Shit, how about a month, just to keep the death toll under 50%, for a starter, and have you seen most of these sorry bastards? My great grandma looked better when she died! I mean, Jesus Christ! Didn't anyone exercise back then? And what the hell did they eat? Animal fat and sugar wrapped in a carbohydrate shell so your body stores it like a time-bomb? Hell, this guy over here is the only one who looks like he's been grazing wild, and look at the chart on his lungs and liver! Survive thaw out? Shit, I'm surprised any of them needed Cryo in the first place with all the preservatives in their bodies. That one over there is probably still drunk... I'm surprised he froze at all!" The doctor shook his head in comedic disgust, then tossed her the paperwork on them. "20 more? I can hardly wait to see 'em!"

She was laughing so hard she had to hold her side from cramping. "Are you finished? God damn, Peter, they have feelings, you prick! Haven't you ever heard of bedside manner?"

"I'm a military doctor, screw bedside manner. Haven't you ever heard of triage?" he grinned devilishly.

"Look, all bullshit aside, we don't have time to do this slowly! Parnell said another Carrier is being deployed tomorrow and we need all usable hands up to speed and ready to go immediately! Just get them down here to me as quick as you can... I'll take it from there. If they're as bad as you say, try to be a little more selective right out of the gate, Doctor *Triage*...."

"I'll do that." He stood up tall and saluted her, then turned his attention to the two nurses who were helping the last patient into her cell. "Come, my concubines, we have much work to do!" he bellowed in melodramatic tenor. He left the room with one of them in each arm, his hands dangerously close to their buttocks, as she walked slowly around the octagonal center core of the cell block, looking judiciously into the eyes of each and every one of the "new recruits."

When she got to Thor's cell, she could immediately tell something was definitely different about him. There was a calm sadness in his eyes she had not had time to notice before. He was wise beyond his years, and she would have little trouble explaining much of anything to him, but getting him to accept his new status as a slave and a second class citizen? Probably another matter entirely. She paused for quite a while, reading him, but also openly allowing herself to be read. She already knew they owed him this much. She dropped his energy shield and tossed him a pair of shoes and coveralls.

She started to speak as she walked around the room again, this time handing each person a set of shoes, coveralls and a towel. "As I'm sure you all are becoming painfully aware, the details of your arrangement with CryoKinetics have changed. In short, you are now part of a coalition of survivors of what was once The United Nations. You may have been the fortunate ones back in your day, but now you are considered fortunate to have the rare opportunity to earn your place among us. You are *fortunate* to have missed out on the calamity and chaos of our recent past, and to become a driving force behind a solution. And yes, you are extremely fortunate to be alive at all! Most of those who did not share your wealth and vision are not! You are being given a chance to work with your hands and your mind, and depending on how much you put out, you will ultimately be rewarded with citizenship. Nobody here gets a free ride! If you become a problem, you become expendable. Believe me when I tell you, you don't want to become expendable...." Despite the fact that her speech was obviously well rehearsed and had undoubtedly been given numerous times before, no one questioned her sincerity. The stoic authority of her tone said it all.

The reactions from the people were as different as their backgrounds. Most of them didn't take this news very well, especially after spending their entire lives ordering other people to do their bidding, then spending their entire life savings to take this chance. One particular man, a medium sized athletic looking fellow in his 40's, became enraged, launching himself at her. Thor, already dressed and standing just outside the barrier plane for his cell door, took one step toward the two to help her. Her eye caught Thor's movement, but she reacted only to the attacker, who, by this point was almost on top of her.

She timed her defensive such that the very second he was putting all his weight down onto his lunging left foot, she spun 270 degrees around to the left with her right leg outstretched for a full foot sweep, sending him reeling straight over backwards like a board, his feet completely leaving the ground as his unprotected head sped toward the steel floor. Still squatted down in perfect form with her leg outstretched, she instinctively reached out behind her with her right hand, palm up, and caught his head one inch from impact. "Do we have a problem?" she yelled out for all to hear.

"N-n-nn-n-no, ma'am," the man stuttered, shaking in fear and embarrassment at how easily he had just been beaten.

"Good!" she said, giving his head a shove out of her hand on her way back up to her feet. "You can spend the rest of your day in your cell, thinking about it... Everyone else, please come with me." She turned and looked directly at Thor, who was standing against the core in the center of the room with his arms crossed in an unthreatening manner. He was smiling. "Your questions will all be answered soon."

He could tell she was withholding much information about what had happened that put them in this position, and that their situation was probably graver than she was making it sound. One thing was certain... they were not prospects, they were slaves; taken from a state of cryo-sleep or suspended animation and put into deep freeze status for God only knows how long, then thawed out when the technology permitted. Thawed out, not out of moral obligation, but probably out of need as a source of free labor.

He knew, in any case, that she was probably his best hope at any kind of fair treatment or advancement into any real status as anything other than a prisoner. She wasn't one to be trifle with, that much was obvious, but she treated people fairly. She was a warrior at heart, and in every other sense of the word, he could see that much the very moment he locked eyes with her. "Tyr" or "Teiwaz," the warrior's rune, was in her every mannerism, her very breath, and she wore it proudly. She was just like himself, and she could see it too. Just like his mother. Just like Uruz and Tyr... *Just like Kait.*

She put the troublemaker peacefully back in his cell, then led the rest of them down a corridor to the right, and through a set of locking security doors. As they crowded into the 10 x 10 foyer in between, waiting for the first door to lock so that they could open the second, Thor laughed out loud. He had seen security doors so many times before that they had become standard issue in his own dwellings. Yes, they were definitely prisoners.

"Is something funny, Mr. Stanton?" Sky asked.

Yes, my ridiculous last name, he thought. "My friends call me Thor," he admitted, not seeing any harm in dropping a little baggage, at this point in the game. "I just thought this looked a little more like Super-Max than a naturalization office, that's all, Miss...?" he prodded, still smiling.

"*Lieutenant*... Lieutenant Commander Davies. Well, *Mr. Stanton*, it's kind of run that way, as well. Discipline is what keeps us alive. There's no room on board for rogue

227

behavior of any kind. It simply won't be tolerated. We apologize if it seems a bit oppressive, but as I said, your questions will all be answered soon. Now, please, line up along the far wall." She gestured to the wall opposite the door which just slid open. Everyone made their way over; some physically fit, others barely able to walk and at their physical limit already. "Keep your backs to the wall and *don't move...*" She lifted one old woman who fell to one knee as she was approaching the wall. As she got closer, the woman stumbled again, this time close to Thor. He jumped forward to help her and was stopped painfully by a blast from the energy field between them.

Sky already had her supported from under her arm this time and yelled, "I said, don't move!" Thor stood up straight, a little pissed off, and backed up a step with an angry look on his face, re-centering himself as she helped the woman to a nearby chair, instead.

"Please stand as still as you can, with your hands at your sides and your back touching the wall. The scanner is going to record all your physical data: height, mass, age, organ diagnostics, etc.... This will help us determine what job you are most suited for. After that, we have a series of aptitude and psychological tests, as well." She reached up and placed her hand on a transparent scanner, then a small orb about the size of a melon floated out of a slot in the wall and began to pass in front of each person, scanning them from head to toe. It was a fairly time consuming process, and while it was running, Sky helped the injured woman up, and carefully walked her to an adjacent room where she was quickly escorted off by two soldiers dressed head to foot in chemical suits.

"Who are you people? Where are you taking me?" she asked frantically as the door swung shut... and then nothing.

There were now a total of six of them standing along the wall: a couple in their late 50's, staying absolutely quiet and never letting go of each other's hands, a young man in his 30's, probably an entrepreneur type, fairly intelligent, but too skinny and probably useless in battle, and then a single man and a woman, both in their 40's, both scared out of their minds, and both dangerously close to doing something stupid.

Thor kept his composure and simply watched and waited. Lieutenant Davies was obviously too intelligent to be manipulated directly, and until he knew exactly where and, more specifically, *when* he was, there wasn't much point in starting a rebellion, just yet. So far, other than the fact that they weren't being told nearly enough for his taste, they hadn't really undergone any bad treatment. For the moment, Thor decided, he would take them on their word, keep his head down, and keep prying for information. Given the nature of most of the people who could afford CryoKinetics in his time, he couldn't really blame these people, whoever they were, for dealing with them with skepticism and control. They must have run into some real eccentric blue-flamers already.

He was more than a little perplexed by the technology he was seeing in front of him. This "orb" was operating on multiple frequencies at once, using x-ray, magnetic resonance, and some kind of sophisticated sonar he had never seen before. It emitted an audible hum that almost made him sick. He could actually feel the combination of that and some kind of high pitch energy scan effecting tests on each of the organs in his chest, as well as muscle groups. In turn, it projected a holographic image toward the technician, who happened to be the Lieutenant, that they could use to see diagnostic mapping of any system in the body, in real time, through the use of a clipboard sized control pad that allowed them to toggle through different organs, systems, body parts, etc., and combine what information they wanted with anything else in 3D layers. Even in reverse, he could see her scrolling through information such as blood type, triglyceride levels, white blood count, etc. with nearly zero invasiveness.

Things could be worse, he thought to himself, at least he didn't wake up on a spaceship getting an anal probe from some alien race.... As far as he could tell, these were still the offspring of good old fashioned, red blooded Americans, even if America didn't exist anymore, and they were currently onboard some kind of nuclear submarine, which would explain the jolts and bumps earlier, without the wobbliness of riding across surface waves. Even something as large as an aircraft carrier moves on the water in its own way, and he would have picked up on it.

The energy field was simple enough, in fact, the one in front of him that he couldn't see ran on the exact same pitch as the one in his cell. He was quite sure that with the slightest effort, he could pitch shift and pass right through it. He was just waiting for the right time to test the theory. Most of these idiots would probably roll on him thinking they were going to receive some sort of special treatment. He knew he had to be very careful who he trusted if he was going to get himself out of this.

When she got to the couple she paused, staring for quite a while at the clipboard, then smiled for a second at them both. "Please excuse me for a moment... " She punched in a series of commands on her clipboard and the field in front of them changed pitch. Suddenly they all became aware that they could no longer hear any ambient noises outside the field. The Lieutenant's lips were moving as she held down some part of her lapel and she was pacing the floor, but they couldn't hear a thing.

"Captain Parnell."

"Captain, this is Sky... Two of the Cryos are married, the man has advanced malignant adenomae in both his lungs. Other than that, they both seem healthy."

"The treatment is too time consuming for use on Cryos... Suggest liquidation and replacement immediately." She cringed, closing her eyes, and tried to think of something quick.

"Sir, if we do that, we will lose both of them. They seem like strong candidates for advanced mining ops... The man was military trained... And she was a chemical engineer." She closed her eyes, wincing, waiting for his delayed reply.

"Understood. Good catch, Lieutenant Commander, begin cancer treatment immediately. I want him in the mineral holds training within 48 hours. Anything else?"

"That's all, sir. Davies out." She exhaled and bent over for a moment, supporting her body weight with her hands on her knees. "Jesus..." she said softly to herself.

The woman was terrified, clutching the man's hand so hard she drew blood with her fingernail. "Just take it easy, this doesn't mean anything," he said to her, pretty much accepting his fate already.

"What do you mean, doesn't mean anything, she's on the phone right now talking about how to get rid of you! That bitch doesn't care about us! We're a damn liability, nothing more! She could at least have the decency to say it to our faces, instead of hiding behind this shield!"

"Hey!" Thor snapped at her. "That bitch just saved your husband's life! They can cure his cancer! Now shut up before you offend her and she changes her mind!"

"How the hell do you know, can you read lips?" the man asked.

"Yes, actually I can," he replied, matter-of-factly. "By the way, were you ex-military?"

"I ran a bookstore. Never served. Why?"

"Yeah, like I said, she just saved your life." He smiled, staring at the young Lieutenant with a bit of newfound respect.

She stepped back in front of the couple an held up her device so she could see their anatomy again. She punched in a command and the field returned to normal. She smiled at them, then spoke quickly. "Mr. and Mrs....?"

"Kensington," the man spoke up.

"Mr. Kensington, this is your lucky day. We have a procedure that will cure your lung cancer. We'd like to get started immediately." The man's eyes widened, and he looked over at Thor in disbelief, then at his wife, who was holding his arm tighter than ever, tears coming to her eyes. "After that, you will begin training as a mining supervisor and refinement specialist." She shifted her attention to Mrs. Kensington. "And what exactly did you do before?"

"I was a homemaker for thirty years," she said proudly.

"What do you mean, *homemaker*... you used to build homes?" she asked, confused.

"No, I managed our household: bought supplies, planned and prepared meals, planted and tended our greenhouse, and did all the housekeeping and cleaning."

"Well, my boss thinks you are a chemical engineer, so we'll be trying your hand at developing this skill. You'll be able to work with your husband in the mineral hold, if you can absorb the knowledge quickly. If its too hard to digest, we'll see about side-stepping you into an area that fits, but that will mean different bunking arrangements and you will scarcely see each other, if at all."

"I can learn it! I can learn just about anything!" she desperately asserted.

"Just remember, time is of the essence," Sky said, with a serious look. She hit another key and a tone could be heard for about two seconds, then it stopped. Three technicians, each escorted by an armed guard, entered the room. "You three," she addressed the remaining prisoners, "will be taken to the next room and given a series of tests. Give the tests your best effort, as the results are taken *very* seriously. You two, go with them," She gestured at the two nurses just entering the room. "I'll be back to start your training, Mrs. Kensington, but for now, go with your husband."

"Thank you, Miss Davies, thank you very much." Sky just nodded, still entering information into the device. She turned her attention to Thor, who was staring at her and smiling just slightly, trying hard not to lay it on too thick just yet.

"You... come with me," she said coyly. "I already know exactly where to use you...."

CHAPTER 29: PLACEMENT

As things quickly unraveled, Thor became more and more confused. He was left intentionally in the dark and didn't, as of yet, have any clue just how far from home he truly was. *Who were these people?* If he was meant to take everything at face value, and believe their every word, than they were, in fact, the last humans on the planet, isolated from God only knows what, on a ship of some kind. Then there was the fact that they were being attacked. *Attacked by who?* In any case, he appeared to be a slave here, at least for the time being. Was this because the ones that used this service were considered the enemy, or the possible cause of the fall of man? If so, it might be in his best interest to explain his true identity sooner than later. *She would listen. She is Teiwaz... She is Tyr... the warrior sign... a kindred spirit. But could she convince the others? Would they even care?*

The real problem was that if this is what it's come to, and humanity can't see past its own greed and intolerance *once again*, then what would be the point? Maybe the ones attacking them are the righteous ones, and it is they that are his only possibility for freedom.... *Too little information. Must remain quiet and probe situation from within....*

He couldn't stop thinking about Kait. The Lieutenant was so much like her. She had her strength, her decency, her integrity, and above all, her sense of justice and fairness. *Tyr.* He could see this ancestral source of strength and power all over her... she practically wore it on her sleeve. He was already irrevocably drawn to her. He missed Kait madly, and in all fairness to this woman, he had to do his best to separate the two individuals in his head, but dammit, *she could be Kait reincarnated!* Save for her eyes, she looked nothing like her, but her spirit was so much the same. He found himself concerned suddenly with whether or not she was spoken for. This actually made him laugh out loud for a second.

"What's so funny?" she asked him as they walked through a sliding door onto an elevator. He just looked at her and smiled, shrugging his shoulders. He suddenly felt like he was in high school again, with a crush on the new chick. He couldn't help but laugh again. "Now what?" she asked more firmly, this time smiling herself.

"I'm sorry, Lieutenant, you just remind me of someone... *a lot*," he smiled, "I was just thinking about her." He suddenly grew somber, more than a little depressed by the realization that his friends were all dead, and Kait would be now, too, even if she had somehow managed to escape a grisly fate back in 2047. A slight tear started to come to his eye, which he immediately choked back, but not soon enough for her not to notice.

"What was her name?" Sky asked, genuinely interested, with an honest touch of compassion in her voice.

"Kait. Short for-"

"Kaitlyn... means *The Pure* in Gaelic," Sky finished for him.

"Wow!" Thor smiled, astonished, "I'm duly impressed! Not all that many people from *my time* would've known that... *seriously,* well done!"

"Mr. Stanton, I'm going to be frank-"

"Don't be Frank!... Be Lieutenant Davies... and don't call me Mr. Stanton. My name is Thor." He smiled broadly, his cheesy charms having little affect on her demeanor at the moment.

"Thor... I can tell something is definitely different about you than any of the other *recruits* we've used over the years. I don't know if that's because you're a danger, or just different, but I'm willing to give you the benefit of the doubt for now, because of the vibe I get from you. I always trust my instincts, and my instincts tell me I can trust you. *Don't prove me wrong!* We're going to start you off doing some mining and shipping work. It's very physically demanding, but I think your recovery is going a lot faster than anticipated, so why not? I got a feeling you can handle it just fine," she said to him with a wink and a smile. "How are you feeling?"

"Kind of like a slave. I'm a little confused as to why the cells are necessary, to be honest, *Lieutenant.*"

"My name is Sky," she conceded, finally shaking his hand. He returned the honor, looking her straight in the eyes and shaking her hand the way he was taught, *just like your word*, firm and true. He knew now that even though she was obviously his best card for rising beyond slave status, or escaping if he couldn't, he could never openly manipulate her to do so. He would have to wait for an opportune moment and prove his worth beyond that of another set of hands and a strong back, or create a set of conducive circumstances to show them sooner.

"Good to meet you," he said with a polite nod.

"The cells are temporary. I promise," she answered, making a point, even though they were walking, of looking him directly in the eye when she said it. "All I can really say, is they have proven to be necessary, time and time again, for our safety, as well as your own."

"Our own? From who?"

"Mainly each other... This reality is extremely hard for some to swallow. There are also those among you who seem like they were ready to die *before* they were frozen," she shrugged, opening the final door leading to the mineral hold. "They don't usually treat others with the same respect that you seem to show everyone. Have faith, you won't be in there for much longer."

"I hope not. Respect has to work in both directions," Thor warned politely.

"Absolutely! Anyway, here's work. The mineral hold. This is where we process, store and ship all the crystal we mine from the surface. Go ahead and report to Ensign Bellows," she said, pointing at a tree trunk of a man who was standing near three men in grey coveralls while they shoveled through piles of an orange sand-like substance and filled up one large metal cylinder after the next while he looked on.

Other workers were wearing full face respirators and sucking up bags of the finer, dust-like residue that accumulated in every nook and cranny of the large room with large, portable, backpack vacuums. Based on the care they were using in handling and storing these bags, this substance probably had some serious value to these people, even in its crudest form. It seemed to be coming down from some kind of giant sifter above, then piling up right out on the floor of this dimly lit, high ceiling warehouse and wafting out from there into every crack and crevasse in the room.

The large chamber, probably 200 feet across and about 50 feet deep, was devoid of interior structure, save for a series of 8 large steel columns arranged in semi-circle across the front half of the room where the crystal fell through. They had something to do with the support of the sifting apparatus and collectors, but inside, helped serve to quantify the crystal by way of mathematical metering painted on the sides of each one, showing depth, and consequently the rough volume, of the substance. There were a couple of lockers, and then a large utility closet next to a booth that contained some computer equipment and two more guards, leaning against the wall and talking to each other like they didn't have a care in the world. There was an ambient hum coming from the equipment that seemed to permeate the air, but it was bearable enough to still carry on a conversation.

"I've been really meaning to ask you this, Sky, because it seems it's been avoided in every conversation so far, for some reason.... What the hell is the date?" He turned around to face her directly, intent on getting a straight answer, but she was gone. "Oh, nice trick!" he yelled, wondering how long he had been standing there by himself, looking stupid. He started walking over to Ensign Bellows.

The air in the room was a bit musty, and sort of rang on with a peculiar odor, something like burnt celery, or hot brakes from a stolen sports car, he thought, smiling mischievously. As he got closer he realized that there was something odd about all four of the men working in here. Their skin had a violet hue to it, as did the "whites" of their eyes. Some more than others. The Ensign seemed to be affected the least, while one of the workers, a frail looking man, probably in his 50's who stood with a real hunch, was so dark with it that he almost didn't appear to be human at all.

Thor walked up to the Ensign and introduced himself. He offered his hand and was met with autocratic rudeness. "I'm Ensign Bellows. I am in charge of this facility, and from now on, you will speak only when spoken to. Grab a sifting shovel from the utility locker over there, and then follow me. You'll be working first stage." He pointed to a large pile to the right that seemed multicolored compared to the piles they were standing in. "It seems we have a new sort of "dragon egg" to deal with. Sky says you're smart, so let's find out if you're smart enough!"

Thor sighed. He suffered no delusions... at least this served to remind him which side of the tracks he lived on.

Later that night, he leaned against the wall of his cell, staring across the soft blue plane of energy that kept him bound like a prisoner, thinking about everything. Thinking about her. Fate, it seemed, was inescapable. The tests placed before you were there no matter what happened. You can rewrite the test to fit your answers, but in the end, you either understood the lesson or you didn't. It was never about the test. It was never about your score.... It was always about understanding the subject matter. If you run too far south, the same questions will simply reappear in Spanish.

Here in this new place and time, with a fresh slate, wiped clean of all his worldly transgressions, he found himself, oddly enough, in the exact same situation as before: stuffed into a cell with nothing but his wealth of knowledge and untapped potential, grappling with his own conscience about which way to go. He went from struggling to survive as a second class citizen, to stumbling onto an unimaginable fortune while his life was being ripped apart right before his eyes, to struggling to survive as a second class citizen. He knew he couldn't ride this train in any conventional manner. He needed to push the timetables forward just a bit. Too many things were still unanswered about his "hosts."

He relaxed, tuning his mind in on his own breathing... his own heart beating. He expanded his awareness to include the field of energy in front of him. He waited until he could feel it, even see it, with his eyes closed. He slowly opened his eyes, but let his gaze fixate a thousand miles away to the point of blurred awareness, accepting the energy in its suchness, understanding it in *its* full place in the spectrum; the ebb and flow becoming one in the same… feeling its *true* vibration.

He breathed inward, pulling air deeply into every corner of his being, then released it; allowing it to find its own path of least resistance out of his body while focusing only on the vibration he was feeling. He released himself… *allowed* himself to speed up to its vibration; first, his heart rate, then his entire being… then slowly, confidently, he raised his left arm up and extended it out as far as he could reach, pointing toward the center of the room with his palm up. Slowly, he raised his gaze to include the room, itself, clearing back into full focus. His arm was outside the barrier! He lowered it back down to his side, smiling. He knew exactly what he needed to do.

CHAPTER 30: RECONNAISSANCE

For the next several days, he kept his head down and did nothing to draw attention to himself… at least not negative attention. His work was grueling, and was providing him with some much needed physical therapy, considering the atrophy that long term cryostasis had inflicted on his muscles. Almost every mundane, repetitive action can be harnessed and utilized as a tool for isolated muscle building work-outs and stamina building conditioning. The beautiful irony of doing this at work is that as you train harder and harder for rebellion, you look more and more like a team player, and thus, are trusted more and watched less. He worked twice as hard as was expected of him.

Not having the time to participate in conversations at work also gave him the opportunity to hear everything. His coworkers were not to be trusted anyway. Two or three were already broken, and would undoubtedly report anything that was said just to increase their own standing. There were two new guys, both of which acted like scared rabbits, also not to be trusted, and then there was the senior member, Reyes, an insufferable cynic with a big mouth. Even though he would love nothing more than to get out of this trap one way or another, he didn't know when to shut up, which pretty much meant he lacked the real courage to pull it off. Not a good partner, but useful, in his own way.... Useful for the experience he had.

The crafty picking of his brain for information about their captors was a daily pastime for Thor. He simply needed to get the man started on a subject, and he would ramble on long after everyone but the guards were finished listening. He liked to talk to those who seemed the most affected by his drama, so it usually looked to the guards like the two newbies and him scheming again. At some point in the near future, Thor figured this man would probably make a pretty good diversion.

At night, Thor practiced conditioning with the shield. He would wait for everyone to go to sleep, then tune in to it, over and over. Passing completely from one side to the other, and back. He finally got himself where he could adopt its frequency from memory. Now all he needed was to see it coming, and he could pass through one of these shields on a whim. This was extremely important, because as much as he could tell, everything on board was run by the same shield generator, and thus, operated at the same pitch.

Everything else about this busy little world, it seemed, revolved around schedules: nurses in and out with meds at all hours of the day or night, eating schedules in the daytime, guards doing rounds, and of course... *security cameras*. He had cadence figured out for every rotating camera from his cell to the mineral hold to the mess hall, and he could time them to a drum beat with his eyes closed. On the fourth night, he decided it was time to find out the full breadth of his dilemma. He waited until just after the last guard patrol for nearly a four hour block, then he made his move.

When the small orbital camera that circled the top of the column in the center of the room passed by his cell, he slipped out of the bedding on the small mattress he slept on. He approached the energy field, staying close to the wall in the direction the camera was moving. Taking a couple deep breaths, he expanded his awareness through the field, accepted its energy, then passed through it without incident. Realizing that he only had moments before the camera was back around and his window would be closed, he bolted through the unlocked doorway and down the dark hallway.

This time of night, after the final guard had passed, there was never any movement in this hallway. He could hear this perfectly from his cell, but no further. When he got to the stairwell by the elevator, he was flying blind. He gave a long listen, then started winding up the stairs unsure what he would find, as they always took the elevator to work. He passed by the door at the mineral hold level and went strait for the top. After passing two more doorways on the way up, he reached what he was looking for. The stairway emerged into the side of a corridor that went to the left and right. To the right he could feel the presence of several individuals behind a large sliding door, so he tiptoed toward an opening off to the left.

After about 30 feet, the corridor had a large opening on the right; a cargo ramp leading into a large warehouse with an obvious bay door at the other end. He still didn't understand exactly what sort of building or craft this "ship" was, but at this point, he was pretty sure he could safely rule out a submarine. Maybe he was wrong. Maybe it was some kind of aircraft carrier, but such a large one that they didn't feel buoyant at all... He had the feeling the answer was on the other side of that bay door. *But how to open it without attracting any attention...?* Maybe he wouldn't have to. He waited for the small security camera panning the opening to go far left, then he sprung through the door and rolled to the right, out of view.

The warehouse was almost pitch black, obviously deserted for the night, and easy to navigate, as there was a wide forklift lane right down the center. Most buildings had egress besides the means by which they were loaded, especially military buildings, because in case of attack, they had to be able to come and go with the main door shut, otherwise they could be trapped and overrun. He was looking for a smaller door on either side, hopefully without an alarm. His eyes were starting to get used to the dark, so he branched off to the right and took a little look around as he approached the back wall and bay door.

The place was supplied like they were getting ready for Armageddon. Stacked floor to ceiling were crates upon crates of weapons, explosives, food, clothing, medical supplies, building materials, etc.... He had run into some well supplied fortresses in the underground before, including their own, but this was something to behold!

He was standing in one isle out of what must be thousands, and he could support a small army for months on what he could reach out and touch. He could see now that their numbers must be more vast than he had originally guessed. He heard some commotion coming from back the way he came. It sounded like 3 or 4 people talking and laughing; possibly coming his way. He proceeded down the isle toward the wall and headed left, toward the bay wall again. He paused for a moment, heard nothing, then walked silently along the wall toward the door.

He came to a small door on his right, just before the bay door, no bigger than the opening for a closet. He examined it carefully, not wanting to trigger any alarms. He could see by close examination that nothing was attached to the inside that could trigger an alarm, and the walls were solid steel bulk heads, so it was unlikely that there was any internal wiring. The door had a hand crank right in the center, similar to what one would see on a submarine, yet far more advanced. He got up the courage and gave it a crank to the left. The door sighed as if an air seal had just been broken, but no water gushed in. Guessing this was probably a good thing, he proceeded to open it the rest of the way.

It cracked open to a breath of odd smelling air hitting him in the face. It was cool and refreshing, but he was suddenly having a little trouble breathing. It was noticeably thin and seemed to contain something he didn't normally breathe, similar to the smell in the mineral hold. *Had they finally poisoned the very air we breathe? And why were they at sea? And what was this substance they were mining off of the surface?* The questions were welling up in his head faster than he could build up the courage to step through the door and reach out for the answers.

He peeked out, seeing the aft deck of what looked to him to be a large, flat mezzanine or roof top with a waist high knee wall protecting the perimeter. It was dark outside, but he could see violet in the small patch of sky he caught out of the corner of his eye as he slipped outside, his back to the open deck, and pulled the door carefully closed behind him.

When he turned around, his jaw dropped open. Straight ahead, over the edge of the knee wall, taking up a good portion of the night sky, was an entire planet! It appeared to be blue, purple and pink all at once, with swirls of weather cascading across its face like brushstrokes from God. Even as far in the distance as it must be, he could see only about half of it setting behind a ridge of mountains. There was an intense halo emanating from behind the large planet; a large light source setting with it, as if it there was a sun behind it in a state of constant eclipse. The breathtaking view drew him right to the edge of the knee wall, where he instinctively looked down.

There were plains rolling as far as the eye could see, becoming more defined foothills out toward the mountains, but shallower fields directly below. It was dark, but he could just make out the orange hue on the surface, sparkling here and there from the reflection cast by the setting bodies. As near as he could tell, given the distortion created by the ship itself, combined with the cover of night, they were floating nearly a full half mile above the surface of what must be the large planet's twin!

Looking up in the sky, he counted two moons, dangerously close to each other, apparently locked in some kind of eternal melee, like two wolves fighting over the same piece of meat. They seemed to rotate around each other as they crossed the sky on their way around their orbital path. Staring upward at them in awe Thor felt the ship bank slightly to port, and he caught a glimpse, little more than a shimmer, of a field of energy encasing the deck he was standing on. It appeared to terminate right into the outer edge of the knee wall itself. His eyes widened as he realized he almost stuck his head right into it when he leaned and looked down.

Starting to readjust his eyes to focus further out on the horizon, he thought he could make out, through the shadowy fingers reaching out across the plains as the haloed planet disappeared entirely behind the jagged peaks, a row of over 50 creatures... perched, but not entirely motionless; watching intently as the ship passed by on its course. They were but silhouettes at this angle, and he couldn't really tell how far out they really were, so their size was still a bit of a mystery, but they sat like a murder of crows, and though they seemed to be about the size of a large human, he was sure he could make out wings on several of them. Much to his surprise, as if this whole scene wasn't already too much to take in, he started to get the sensation that he was being spoken to, though not audibly, nor in an actual language of any kind... but simply hailed. His mind was racing! This could be what he had dreamt of his entire life....

He was suddenly cut off by the sound of the giant bay door starting to roll... open, and a swath of light permeating the deck from inside the cargo hold. He turned his head to see four sets of legs showing through the growing gap. He gasped. There was no time to get clear. He was totally out in the open. He looked at the side again, noticing a small drip groove along the edge. *Good enough*... he almost whispered to himself, then he took a deep breath and adjusted his own energy level, praying the field was the same pitch as inside, and hurled himself over the edge, holding on with both sets of fingertips as his body dangled off of the edge of the ship. The door opened the rest of the way, revealing four men in officer's uniforms, shining hand held spotlights around the deck.

"I don't see anyone... those old motion detectors all need replaced. They go off all the damn time," one of the men said, shivering just a bit.

"We never got a proximity alert, either. I was on bridge when the alarm went off.... Captain's just jumpy since that smart one handed our asses to us on a plate the other day," his diminutive comrade suggested, pointing his spotlight and pistol all around the deck as he spoke. The two others, wielding rifles, fanned out and walked to the stern and back, at last waving a signal broadly up at a command tower high up on a series of catwalks leading to the aft entrance to the pilothouse and bridge.

Thor hung silently, trying to concentrate only on his breathing and pitch, because he knew that if he faltered for one second, his pitch would drop and the field would repulse him right off the side of this ship to his death. He started to feel the hail of the creatures in his head again. He carefully accepted what he was feeling, but continued to focus only on his pitch. He could feel now that his efforts were actually being reinforced by the signal in his head. Staying at this pitch was becoming effortless! For some reason, someone was helping him.

"They do seem to be getting wise to most of our tricks," commented the large one. "Hell, did you guys hear about the rover bomb pulled in by Prospector-5 during the last bum rumbler?" The other men shook their heads. "They found one of our old rovers, and actually rigged it to work unmanned. P-5 thought they were rescuing some survivors from the early jobs, and pulled up the old rover full of our own mines. It went off in their first screen mineral hold and almost took out the whole Carrier! It was pure luck that the compartment was so full it didn't have the oxygen or water necessary to set off a chain reaction. Damage Controlmen were able to put the fires out first.... Thank God!"

"D.C.'s gonna have their hands full this whole next week... I hear were going in close to the nests where the Crystal deposits are richer. Now they're sending in *two* more Harvesters. The Sand Dragons are not going to like that at all. They're gonna take it as an attack, there's no doubt." They started walking back inside, but he could still hear the conversation waning as the door slowly rolled back down.

"Fuck 'em! Remember Cheops? That dark planet in the outskirts, just before we left? If we have to, we'll firebomb every one of them to clear the way! We need this shit to survive! We'll never make the next system without a very full load-up on all ships, and it sounds like we're running out of time..." His voice was cut off instantly as the large door sealed shut against the deck.

The creatures watched, as the light extinguished on deck to reveal the lone human, hanging by his fingertips on the outside of the large vessel. One of them grunted and stood up, focusing on the little man from across the abyss, apparently about to take flight and try to snatch him off the side. The large one next to him quickly stopped him with an arm across his chest, then looked at him in disapproval, letting him know his reason for helping him. The man was obviously an enemy to the rest of them, but he apparently had their own species' knack for telepathy, as well as manipulation of energy. He had only seen this in one other human... a woman. He quickly took flight, careful to stay up and back, clear of their scanners, and followed to make sure the man made it back up. Although he appeared to be exhausted from hanging there for so long, he did so with relatively little trouble.

Thor caught his breath back on the deck, staring back toward the ridge top with the creatures. It was too dark now, and he couldn't make them out, so he walked carefully back to the door he had stuck open with some translucent tape-like material from one of the crates inside. It opened right up, and he slipped inside.

The large creature nodded contently, sure that he had not seen the last of this one. There was something about him. There was something about the woman, as well. Their energy was more familiar to him than the energy of his own kind, and this bothered him immensely. He had to find out why. He gracefully arched upwards, then barrel rolled off to the left and back to the ridge. The rest of his brethren whooped and cried in disapproval, but he cared not. He banked to the right, just past them, snorted as he flew over, then shot straight into a hole in the peak.

Back in his cell, unnoticed, Thor laid back with his arms behind his head and sighed. This was something worth coming to the future for. Suddenly his mind was filled with thoughts of other civilizations, space travel, alien races, and of coarse, Sky. He knew now that it was more important than anything that he prove himself and rise up out of his bondage to a place where he could make a difference. He had a pretty good idea what he needed to do to accomplish this. He smiled, for the first time in a while, not because of a sarcastic joke or retaliatory satisfaction, but because of a genuinely renewed sense of hope.

CHAPTER 31: ESCAPE TO WITHIN

Since childhood, the dream never changed, but lately it was starting to evolve... to expand. Every time it happened, new details were becoming clear, new progress being made, and every time it happened, it seemed more and more real.

It was chilly and the sky was grey and darkening... standing on a tundra covered hillside, basketball sized rocks scattered here and there... rolling into the distance. Suddenly a loud squawk from up above... following the huge eagle out over the crest of a nearby hill, and up to the abandoned cabin. The dream always used to end here, but not any more.

Now, there was the creeping inside to investigate, then suddenly becoming aware of a giant wolf coming out of one of the back bedrooms. It was black and stood chest high at the shoulders. Its head was slightly down and it kept its distance, but continued to follow. Though truly unafraid, there was always a calm decision to avoid it and find another way out of the house. After a prolonged sequence of cat and mouse throughout the house that seemed to differ from dream to dream only slightly, there was always the turning back to see the wolf enter the room slowly, baring its teeth, and the wolf's teeth beginning to fall out onto the floor, bouncing around and falling into cracks in the hardwood until all of them are gone.

Upon looking back up, the wolf is gone, or rather, has transformed into the eagle, sitting on the ledge of the open window. It suddenly flies off, and then comes the chase. Running to catch up, the hills widen, eventually turning into a vast network of fjords and islands. Without realizing where the transition takes place, the dream continues to unfold through the eyes of the eagle, as if they are finally one.

It swoops down, flirting with the tips of the tallest trees; reaching up like fingers desperately trying to touch the sky itself. It sends out an ear piercing shriek, letting the entire world know of its dominion over the heavens, then continues down through the top of the valley, heading toward the ocean. Seeing the smoke rising up from a series of small fires, it follows the edge of the fjord to investigate.

A small village is peacefully going about its toils for the day; fishing boats sailing into the small harbor with the morning catch, while people dressed in almost Viking attire scurry about, preparing to receive them. It banks to the right, out over the inlet and lets out another song, this one a warning to the ravens and gulls converging here and there over the village, waiting for their scraps.

Suddenly a loud noise and vibration comes without warning from behind. It is swept quickly into a vortex of turbulence by the passing of a group of flying ships: manned fighter jets possessing technology far beyond that of the peaceful villagers, swooping down in attack formation, then opening fire with some kind of blue light plasma weaponry and nearly eradicating the entire village in one strafing attack. Explosions, screams, and the roar of the fighters echo off as real as any waking experience, then once again there is the sensation of being pulled by a giant rubber band back into the real world.

She sat up, gasping for air, and looked around quickly to get her bearings. It had been quite a while since she had this recurring dream, but for some reason, this time was one of the most vivid, and definitely the most progressed. She was drenched in sweat. She got up and slowly paced around her small quarters, unsure what, if anything, to make of it. Unable to get back to sleep, she decided to get dressed and check out the ship. Something was slightly amiss, and she couldn't quite put her finger on it.

Thor stood up in his cell, finally giving up on trying to get to sleep. He needed to do something to improve his situation, and he sensed he needed to do it now. For some reason, he could feel that time was absolutely of the essence. Something big was about to happen, and from where he was now, he'd be powerless to influence it, one way or another. He knew he didn't have enough information on this ship, their enemy, or where they were to escape in one burst, there were just too many variables. Instead, he decided he must make a statement... raise some eyebrows and get some attention for the skills and knowledge he possessed. Hopefully this would lead to better positions, rather than getting made an example of, and restricted further. He would need to be extremely cautious.

He quietly raised his pitch to match the field again, calmly slipped through it, then walked softly into the darkness of the corridor without waking a soul. Once again, he would have approximately 4 hours before a guard's scheduled rounds would reveal him to be out of his cell. This would be ample time to make a big impression....

Down on the small planet's surface, deep within the catacombs of the Sand Dragon's lair, the large creature sat up quickly out of a restless sleep, wide eyed and uneasy, and took in a long pull of air before relaxing just a bit. In this warren alone, there were literally hundreds of them curled up here and there, over and under each other, sharing space and warmth like a giant wolf pack.

Phosphorescent algae dimly lit the cavern, and a steady trickling sound from a subterranean stream of fresh water echoed in the chamber, creating a mesmerizing effect on its inhabitants. He leaned over to the pool of clear water next to the wall of the cave and completely submerged his head. He began to pull in water through his clenched teeth, using his teeth as a filter to avoid sucking up a school of transparent fish swimming by. Watching closely as the smallest fish desperately struggled to catch up with the larger ones, he managed a smile, snorting a short laugh underwater before he pulled his head out and dripped dry over the pool.

He was one of the oldest, most powerful beings of their kind, and was the one who had witnessed and followed Thor on his midnight prowl last night. For some reason he had been very edgy and had barely been able to sleep a wink since. There was something about this human. First and foremost was the fact that he appeared to be an enemy of the humans, or at least an escaped slave. How he came to be on the human ship was a mystery, but he seemed to them to be free, at least for now. Then there was his ability to manipulate the shield, just as they do. So far, he had not witnessed this ability, or any level of telepathy in any others, except maybe the female. He had observed her on numerous occasions.

She was a warrior, to be sure, but she did not enjoy bringing them harm, and was definitely conflicted. She had not shown ability with the shield, but he heard her cries and felt her compassion for them. Perhaps they didn't need to eradicate the humans in order to survive this incursion... He knew in his heart there must be another way, but nobody else would listen. They were all convinced that this savage race would stop at nothing short of genocide in their campaign to strip their planet of all its resources. They were convinced that a mass "awakening" was in order, and peace would be achieved through total numeric domination, or not at all.

He alone saw another way.... He alone seemed to care enough to try. He looked down at the young child curled peacefully at his feet, oblivious to the transgressions of his elders, sleeping soundly without any fear for tomorrow. *How could any of them not care enough to try to find another way? It was their moral obligation for the survival of their race, as sure as defending themselves in the first place....* One look at any of the young ones sleeping throughout the dimly lit cave and he knew he had absolutely no choice. He must take action, and he must do it soon.

Morning rounds came, and the door slid open to the octagonal cell block. Two armed guards entered with a serving cart loaded with food for the inmates.

"Rise and shine ladies! Grub's on!" one of the guards called out. A few people stirred and groaned, slowly coming to life. The other guard deactivated the first field, walked into the cell, and handed the man a tray of food. "Come on, sleepy heads! If you're not sitting up, you don't eat!" the guard persisted, getting a little more rude this time.

"You heard the man! Wakey, wakey, hands off snakey!" the other guard shouted, looking around the room.

"Nice one," snorted his partner.

Suddenly, the guard's eyes locked on Thor's cell. It was empty. "What the-" He rushed over and killed the field, looking all around, instinctively, even though there was nowhere to hide. The other guard dropped what he was doing and hit the com on his lapel.

"Captain, did prisoner 7C get moved last night without our notification?" he asked, tilting his head slightly toward the side his communicator was on.

"No!... There were no authorized transfers at all. I'll wake up Sky, maybe she knows."

Her voice came across next, without any hesitation. *"Sky here. What the hell are you talking about? He's gone?"*

"Yes, Lieutenant Commander. No trace."

"Why didn't anyone wake me when the field alarm went off? How long ago did he escape?" she asked.

"That's just it, Sky, it never went off. The field was up when we got here... According to record, it was on all night... uninterrupted!" the man yelled.

"What the- I'm on my way. I'm in the dome. Give me three minutes!" Sky yelled.

The Captain's voice came over a ship-wide, central loudspeaker, *"Security breach! Lockdown protocol! I repeat, Lockdown protocol! Security, report to Lieutenant Commander Davies in cell block C immediately! There's been an escape!"*

Thor smiled to himself. He could hear the tension in the Captain's voice as it came booming over the loudspeaker in the fuel stores area of the mineral hold. He had only minutes to mentally prepare himself before they would undoubtedly figure out where he was. The only thing he was very concerned about was the possibility of security completely over reacting before he had a chance to peacefully surrender. He kept plugging away at his work, fully centered and ready for them.

"Ship's scans indicate there is someone in the mineral hold!" the Captain's voice yelled out of the small speaker on Sky's communicator.

"I'm already there. I'm going in with my two sentries, order our backup to stand post just outside.... Do NOT come inside! I repeat, stand post until I say! We can handle this better without more variables!" Sky ordered.

"Gotcha... Sky... be careful! You saw his scars... this man's a fighter! Wait for backup to proceed. They'll be there in less than a minute!" Parnell requested, his tone changing to that of a concerned friend rather than a commanding officer.

"Roger that. Davies out." She turned to the two sentries next to her. "You guys stay tight and keep a respectful distance from him. I don't want him ending up with one of your weapons. Other than that, *follow my lead!* This man shouldn't be a threat.... I'm not sure what the hell is going on, but I don't think he means to hurt anyone!" They both nodded in agreement, then she stepped over to the door and waited for backup.

He was literally knee deep in crystal when the door slid open about 50 feet behind him. Using the combination rake/ shovel exactly the way he was taught by his new supervisor on his first day, he kept up the charade, working through the pile as they approached him from behind. To Sky's astonishment, he had already worked through most of the day's quota single-handed, and didn't even seem fatigued. She couldn't help but smile, then she forced it back and put on her game face. "Freeze!" she commanded, drawing down on him with her pistol from across the room. "Drop the shovel and turn around slowly, with your hands where I can see them!"

He tossed his shovel to the side, nonchalantly, then slowly turned to face her with his hands out to the sides, palms up. "What? I couldn't sleep!" he said, smiling coyly. "I thought we needed a bunch of this shit...."

She motioned for the two guards to apprehend him. "You're lucky I found you first! Are you trying to get yourself killed? What the hell are you doing out of your cell?"

As the first guard closed in on him, he spoke up. "I told you, I couldn't SLEEP!" On his last syllable, he intercepted the man's right hand with his own, handshake style, twisting under his arm and behind him, and shoved him off balance directly into the face of the second guard. The two collided hard, one of them grabbing his mouth in pain and the other holding his head, struggling to stay on his feet. They both shook it off, then turned and charged in a rage, yelling something that when combined, sounded like a different language entirely.

This time it was effortless. S*nake creeps down.* Left leg outstretched and well below their already elevated centers, he parted their energies around himself, grabbing the lead hand of the one to his right and pivoting just ahead of him, causing his body to spiral down and to the right, head first around behind him, until his upper body hooked around just in front of the feet of the already over-committed second man, sending him reeling into a steel column as Sky swooped up from behind and zeroed in on her target from only a few feet away.

Before the deep "thunk" had even stopped echoing in the deserted chamber, he had completed the circle with his human shield and had him propped up like a puppet, strategically between himself and the gun, with the defenseless man's right arm bent upside down and inwards on himself, and his left hand in a death grip on the man's left shoulder and neck, manipulating a pressure point that had his whole left side in paralysis. Using a silly, high pitched puppet voice, and bouncing the guard around with each syllable, he mocked,

"Don't shoot me... I'm actually a really nice guy!" She had an extremely hard time pretending not to be amused.

"Drop him or I'll kill you both!" she threatened, stepping once to point blank range and cocking the strange pistol. The guard's eyes widened with fear.

"I'm sorry, can I go back to my cell now? I'm bored," he asked, sarcastically discarding the beaten guard to the floor like a child, bored with a toy.

"Sure, " she smiled, both relieved and sarcastic, and then lowered her pistol to his chest and coldly pulled the trigger. He flew backwards about 10 feet from the blue light discharge, twitching on the ground, but still breathing. She tapped her belt-com and said, "I have him... We're in the mineral hold." She paused, looking around the room at the aftermath, then smiled, shaking her head "Bring three gurneys...."

CHAPTER 32: DISCLOSURE

The darkness and haze slowly crumbled away and was replaced, piece by painful piece, by the razor sharp realization that things did not go *exactly* as planned, and he was, in fact, strapped down with unforgiving, very conventional restraints to a chair in the middle of a brightly lit room with five very serious looking people in his face. Though this wasn't part of the original plan, it wasn't entirely unexpected, so he took a deep breath and mentally prepared himself for what was probably coming next.

There were two men to his left he recognized from his orientation: the enforcers in the zoot suits, as he remembered. In the middle was undoubtedly the Captain, judging from his over-embellished uniform, and the way he even *stood still* with a purpose. His eyes seemed genuine, as was his projection of strength, but there was an inquisitiveness in them that was driving him to the point of need…. The man wanted something from him for the good of his ship, and Thor knew what it was.

It was the entire reason for the obviousness of his escape. He had a talent they did not possess, and that would either make him valuable, or make him dead. To the right of the Captain, Sky stood by with the doctor who helped thaw him out. An impersonal prick, if his fuzzy memory of that day was correct. Thor made an effort to clear his throat, but it felt more parched than it should be. He wondered how long he was unconscious. The blue light he saw just as she blasted him was the same pitch as the outside force field. *If only had he only seen it coming.*

"Give him some water," the Captain spoke up. Everyone looked at each other, unsure who the request was being directed at. Sky broke off first and started to pour a cup from a small built in console by a wall of computer screens. Thor turned his head further, realizing he was on the bridge of the ship with his back to the main viewing screens. "Eyes front, Mr. Stanton!" the Captain ordered. He paused for an uneasy moment of steady eye contact , then spoke again while Sky held the water up to his lips and let him take a long drink. "How did you get out of your cell?" he asked, getting right to the point. "Our security records show you leaving, but the field never stopped.... How did you get past it?" he demanded.

"Magic," he stated, calmly. The Captain merely glanced at the two men to Thor's left, and one walked behind him and held his head back while the other proceeded to punish his mid section with menacing uppercuts, ending with a right cross to the left cheek bone, snapping his head back and making him a little dizzy.

"Lets get one thing straight right now," the Captain spoke up, considerably louder and more forceful than before, "I could kill you and thaw out two more before lunch... "

"But...?" Thor added. The Captain glared at him, more than a little disbalanced by his presumptuous aire and apparent insight regarding their intentions. Thor gave him a second, then finished the sentence for him. "But, you have a similar problem with your enemies, and you want to learn more...?"

"How do you know that?" the Captain asked.

"How about some more of that water, " Thor suggested, spitting a bit of blood indiscriminately on the floor next to him. She came over with another cup, in front of him this time, and looked deep into his eyes as she hooked him up. She gave him a look of concern, shrugging her eyebrows while widening her eyes, begging him to comply, for his own good. He conveyed back, without a sound, that he knew what he was doing; a slight nod, almost a wink, a very subtle smile, but the message was received, unbeknownst to the rest of the staff. She stepped back, letting things take their course, but looking for a way to help him. She knew his plight, and respected that he was willing to do something to try to free himself, for better or worse. Somehow, she felt connected to him already.

The Captain looked at the guard behind him and raised one hand up, with one finger loosely pointing up. The guard backed off, but the other one stepped up and pulled out his pistol. It was exactly like the one Sky stunned him with in the mineral hold. He leveled it right at Thor's chest and cocked it. He heard a hum just like he did down below. He had it on the same setting....

"One last time. How did you get through the field?" the Captain demanded again, getting ready to drop his hand to give the order to fire.

Thor looked to make sure Sky was further away from him than the guard, took a calm, deep breath, raising his pitch to the very same level he remembered from the blast in the mineral hold, the generated shield outside, and the field in his cell, then said calmly, "Shock me again and I'll show you." He smiled just slightly, then winked at Sky, who was giving him the same skeptical look of concern that Kait used to show in times like these. He wasn't entirely sure as to the wisdom or outcome of this course of action, but somehow that made him feel a lot better.

Thinking this was another taunt, the Captain gritted his teeth and gave the signal to fire. Thor completely accepted the blast, and it passed right through him, arcing out to the nearest grounded receiver, which was, of coarse, the guard himself. He froze, being shocked and unable to let go of his pistol or even the trigger. Everyone stood wide eyed, unsure what to do to help the man, except Sky. She jumped up in the air, scissor kicking the guard in the shoulder, causing him to fly into the wall, dropping the weapon and breaking the circuit.

Before they had enough time to misinterpret this as an attack, rather than an example, Thor spoke up, giving them the quick and dirty explanation, "You have to raise your own vibration to the pitch of the energy field, then accept it, rather than resist." They all looked at him intently, surprised by his sudden complexity. "Now I have a question..." He glared, looking each of them deep in the eyes, but stopping on the Captain.

The fallen guard, semi-unaware what just happened, aside from the fact that he was just beaten by a man in restraints, struggled to his feet and lunged at him. The Captain reached out with one arm and stopped the smaller man in his tracks, nearly clothes-lining him with his powerful forearm without ever taking his eyes off of Thor. Thor paused for a moment, glancing briefly at the guard, then continued. "Who are you, *really,* where are we, and who attacked us the other day?"

"We'll answer all your questions, but we have a lot more to talk about before we know if you're a threat to our security... please bear with us," Sky interjected with a timely flare of diplomacy.

"If you attack anyone else, the conversations are over. Permanently!" the Captain added sternly.

"In all fairness, Captain, Mr. Stanton never attacked anyone. Not once. In every instance, he was defending himself *from* an attack... even in the mineral hold," Sky said in his defense.

"Noted. Now answer me this.... Why didn't you try to escape? You had all night to do it."

"I've never exactly stood up to be counted with those you have me locked up with. Most of them aren't worth their salt. They were the decadent pieces of human garbage that drove my country... hell, my whole *world*, to the brink of uninhabitability. It's kind of a fluke that I was in cryo with them to begin with. Anyway, I just want to know why I'm here.... The *real* reason why I'm here. I've been out of my cell a couple of times now, just to see what's up for myself. All I know is that I'm a *long* way from Earth, and I'm not a guest, or a trainee, or a team member... I'm a fucking slave!" He looked directly at her, showing her the sincerity, and urgency in his eyes. "I have never been able to handle stagnancy, or mediocrity, but incarceration is a death sentence already! I value freedom above all else, and would die before relinquishing it to anyone! I'm here before you because I think we can help each other...."

She could see the integrity in his eyes from the moment he opened them in the recovery room after hibernation.... He could be trusted, but they would have to deal with him straight. The Captain could see this too, in his own right. He looked Sky directly in the eyes for a moment, then nodded.

"Untie him," the Captain ordered.

"Sir?" the guard asked, puzzled.

"I said, untie him!" he yelled, slightly agitated.

"Yes, sir!" the guard responded, immediately proceeding with the task. Sky glanced over at the Captain through the corner of her eye and noticed him slide the frequency lever on his pistol to maximum power; a death sentence to even the resilient creatures below.

"Let me show you something," Captain Parnell said to Thor, now fully unrestrained and rubbing his wrists as the doctor tended to a cut under his left eye. Parnell turned his back to him, holstering his weapon, and started to walk towards the door. Thor rose slowly, unthreateningly, and started to follow, the two guards falling in behind him. Sky stepped purposefully in between Thor and Parnell, and the doctor brought up the rear.

They walked through a wide corridor, around a bend with several angles of security cameras in place, then a double door airlock, very similar to the North Clan stronghold. When the last door opened, the view instantly took Thor's breath away. He saw the surface of the planet in the dark of night, dimly lit by reflecting light on the moons and neighboring planet, but today was absolutely amazing. Looking out over the bow of the massive ship, high above the planet's surface, he could see everything. The orange sand hills stretching out into the plains, being shaped by the wind right before their eyes. Shadows cast like swirling apparitions fight their way onto the flowing canvass by the light shining from around the giant sphere overhead.

The colossal protector, Sigyn, was high in the sky, blocking the deadly firestorms of the binary sun, Algol, from scorching all life from this tiny planet. Her thick gas rings exploding in a vibrant 360 degree full spectrum rainbow, made immeasurably more intense by the approach of the 3rd sun, Skaði. In a state of nearly eternal eclipse, Sigyn remains in position, except for the end of each 3 1/2 day cycle, when the pull from Skaði causes Sigyn to bend her protective orbit just enough to temporarily expose the planet to solar flares, magnetic interference, and a barrage of meteor showers causing major earthquakes and surface damage until it passes. Ironically, what keeps the planet from escaping this fate and falling out of orbit all together, is the balance created by its own twin moons, Vali and Nari, orbiting the planet, and each other in its tilted prison, always overhead, trapping it in a centripetal warble, much like a coin spinning at half-decay, held from falling by a magnet.

When Parnell explained the system to Thor, he immediately recognized the names of the large planet and the moons from the Norse story of Loki, tricked by the goddess, Skaði, by binding him to a rock using the entrails of his own murdered son, Vali, who was ripped apart by his twin, Nari. Skaði hung a venomous serpent, in this case, Algol, the demon sun, over his head, dripping poison into his mouth. His wife, Sigyn, stands over him, bound to his fate for all time, until the beginning of the Ragnarok. When he shared this legend with Sky and Parnell, their reaction was one he didn't expect. They looked at each other more than a little strange when he spoke of Ragnarok and the destruction of the planet. He decided not to pry at this time, but he had to wonder if maybe they were aware of something that he wasn't.

Though he knew a little about a lot of things, astronomy wasn't something Thor was extremely well versed in. It was a rare night in the underground when he was able to see any stars at all, so their relevance to him was fleeting, at best. He knew from what he was hearing and what little he was taught, that they were in another solar system entirely, and from the looks of things, it was quite some distance from home. He was almost afraid to ask the real question on his mind. He gazed over the side for a while, trying to gauge about how much time had probably elapsed since that fateful day at CryoKinetics when he paid for 100 years. That would make it around the year 2150 or so, but with things in the state they were in, where could they have reached in just a few short years, he wondered. He looked back up, then turned to them and nervously joked, "Well, I knew we were on some kind of ship, but I thought it was a boat!"

"What's a boat?" one guard asked Captain Parnell. Thor looked terrified upon hearing his question. Sky looked down and avoided his eyes, obviously hiding something, so he looked to the Captain. He looked away as well. That was when he realized they were a lot further from home than he thought.

"Let's talk inside," Parnell invited.

Back on the bridge, Thor took a seat and the Captain laid it all on the line. He spoke of an exodus that led mankind to live on space stations orbiting the Earth, then a fleet of ships left to search for another inhabitable planet, occasionally orbiting a prospect long enough to gather resources and raw materials, then setting off again for a while, on and on, until the present time. None of the planets so far have fit all the required criteria for prolonged settlement, so no new roots have been planted. The lines between races, social status, and even power have all but completely deteriorated. The Fleet works and is run under a military style hierarchy, but power is spread out evenly among a judiciary panel of elders, and these seats grow or wane as representation is needed, that is, as the population grows or declines. Reproduction and education are strictly regulated, as there simply isn't room for exponential population growth to occur. For the most part, people are only allowed to replace themselves, though there are a number of criteria that allow for exceptions.

He explained a bit about their mission here, about their timetable and about their problem with the indigenous creatures penetrating their energy shield, which he had already become intuitively aware of due to the circumstances on deck the other night, and the officers' conversations about the *smart one* who defeated them on deck.

This is where Thor started to stray a little. A society devoid of money, races, classes... sounds almost utopian... *except what about all the indigenous life they affect everywhere they visit?* To refuel alone, with a fleet this size, must strip a planet of nearly all its surface detail in order to unearth what they need in the time-frame they probably have to deal with.... *Had mankind become nothing more than interstellar planet-parasites?* And what of Earth? Did anyone stay behind?

"What brought on the need for this exodus?" Thor asked.

The Captain poured himself something out of a fancy looking bottle on a ledge, then proceeded with what sounded like a well rehearsed speech.

"In the 25 year Arab war of the late 21st century, most of the world's resources, especially in the smaller, more anarchic countries, had been depleted in the chaos. In an effort to guard themselves from extinction, several countries brought the conflict to nuclear capacity, ironically feeling it was the only way for their particular race to survive. The Earth fell into a nuclear *autumn* that lasted 3 long years, at the end of which, the world's population had dropped to less than 1/3 that which it was at the beginning of the century. Some died in the war, some died of radiation sickness and disease, and many to the increasingly severe weather patterns created by the environmental disruption, but all of this paled compared to the carnage that followed.

"The chaos and desperation quickly turned an already violent race of divided people into roving bands of nomadic pirates that swept from city to city, and across the countryside, raping, killing, and taking whatever they wanted; destroying the cultures and lives of the scattered patches of defenseless victims they left behind. As food supplies became contaminated, and livestock fell prey to disease, they turned to the only food source they had left... *other humans.* With most of the world's soldiers dead, and those that remained placed to guard the palaces of the wealthy, there was little to stop this onslaught of devastation. It seemed mankind's lack of foresight had finally brought about his ultimate demise.

"It was then that the Alliance For Gaia came down from the hills en masse upon every stronghold in the western hemisphere and took them by storm. Not only weren't there sufficient numbers to defend against such a force, but they took them completely by surprise. The status quo had long since written them off as any kind of a threat. They had no idea the AFG had been preparing for this exact scenario all along, and were stronger than ever. They grew, not in numbered pockets that could be identified and stopped, or branded as a cult of extremists by the government, but rather as an idea; a ghost in the machine, living among those who didn't care, and quietly waiting for the right time to strike.

"Their strength was their anonymity. They used every manner of underground communication to spread the ideals of their cause like a brushfire... music, art, television, the internet... planning only in vague hypotheticals, until at the right time, when it was the only remaining option, the revolution gave birth to itself! Those who were tuned in to the cause knew exactly what to do.

"With the downward spiral the environment was taking, a new plan took root. A new alliance was formed with the superpower from the East to build and launch a fleet of self-sustaining eco-ships to allow the escape of civilized man from this dying planet. All remaining resources were exhausted to meet this goal, and miraculously, it was accomplished. The Exodus had begun.

"Much equipment was salvaged during the construction process. Since it would have been far too inefficient to launch a fleet of this magnitude from the Earth, it was built almost entirely in space, orbiting around the Earth, while salvage crews collected everything of any use. Communication satellites, spy satellites, missile defense satellites, weapons, fossil fuel, just about everything left on the planet or floating around in space was collected, dismantled, then put to some kind of use or storage.... *This included you people!*

"The company that put you in orbit had long since deteriorated and had clientele from every corner of the world, so your lives became subject to international salvaging claim law. The Fleet's first notion was to leave you there, or shoot you down. After some debate, they chose to put you all in a state of deep freeze, excluding only the parts of the brain and soft tissue that would be irrevocably damaged, then bring you along, and thaw you out as needed. This would allow for indefinite cryostasis. To most of the Alliance, just as you said yourself, you all represented the upper crust of the *elite* whose distracted self-indulgence helped bring the Earth to this state of unstoppable decay. Within one year of star mapping, and improvements to ships for extended self reliance, all signs of civilized life on Earth had disappeared, and the Fleet decided to move on."

"You sound like you just read that out of a book," Thor joked.

"What's a book?" the Captain asked with a puzzled look. Thor's jaw dropped open and a strange sound came out of his throat that he wasn't entirely sure he had any control over. He was completely and utterly at a loss for words.

"I'm just kidding!" Parnell said, chuckling like a used car salesman, "You're not the first one to ask me these questions. I've had to study my history...."

"Just how long ago are we talking about?" Thor asked, holding his head up with one hand to his forehead, braced with his elbow on the edge of his armrest as he stared blankly at the floor, slumping down in his chair and starting to look genuinely worried.

Parnell became very quiet, then cleared his throat and looked Thor directly in the eye. "It's the year 2749.... According to our data, you've been frozen since the mid 21st century." They all grew silent, watching to see his reaction to this news. He stared at the floor for a little while with his eyes closed, saying goodbye to his family one final time, in his own way. *They would have loved this shit! Especially the part about the AFG catching everyone with their pants down,* he thought. 2749... born in 2023, that would make him 726 years old! *What a mindfuck!*

He looked up at Sky and shook his head, pausing for an uncomfortably long moment before saying anything. "I... can't believe it," he sobbed, "I thought for sure it was only about 2745, maybe 46 or so! God dammit!" he yelled, facetiously, waving his fist in the air. The Captain looked genuinely shocked at his reaction, which made Sky burst out laughing all that much harder. Pretty soon they all joined in.

"Sir, would you believe me if I told you that my grandfather was one of the founding members of what became your alliance? It was him and his brothers that *started* the original AFG! They disappeared after being hunted for a while by the government, but it sounds like they created an unstoppable wheel that finally served his goals."

"What exactly were his goals?" Parnell asked, a little skeptical.

"To provide mankind with a future. To free slaves. To fuck the corporate whore! Most importantly, to protect Mother Earth by whatever means necessary," he said proudly.

"Is that so," Parnell said, a little taken aback. "What cause do you serve?" At this point, Thor realized they were fishing for his story, and as much as he wanted to dump on someone right now, he decided to keep things a little more candy coated, for the moment. If they knew the whole truth, they might perceive him to be just a standard criminal, or a dangerous liability. At the very least, given the circumstances, it might be a little too hard for them to swallow half the things he had done just to survive.

"Cause? I'm no activist. My causes rise up as they may, and I deal with them, just like anyone else. I've been on my own for much of my life, and I had to grow up very early, so I never really had the privilege or the time for youthful idealism. We must all make it as a race, or not at all. It was the self serving elitists, with their idealism and uncompromising nature that killed our planet in the first place! We have to coexist, and we have to remember the mistakes of our past. Those who cannot remember the past-"

"Are condemned to repeat it," Sky finished for him. "That's one of my favorite quotes of all time," she smiled, looking him deep in the eyes.

He smiled at her, opening himself up to be read, but only by her. "My father disappeared when I was fairly young. He left me with nothing but my survival skills, and a good business name, so after trying the streets out for a while, I quickly learned the value of blending in with the upper class," he intentionally mislead, though only a little. "The chaos you referred to started on all fronts well before the wars you described. We were in a state of overpopulation and unimaginable social decay. You can't imagine some of the things I've seen people do to each other just to survive. I decided to use the skills I had acquired to get a leg up on life, and still maintain my moral beliefs in the process."

"What *skills* are you referring to?" Parnell asked, with a strange look in his eye. At this point, Thor knew they had researched his identity, and probably knew Stanton to be a self-made computer tycoon.

"Adaptability and problem solving with computers, as well as the ability to think outside the box and redefine the parameters by which a conventional game is played...." He realized this was probably the most important job interview of his life, so he wasn't pulling any punches. Captain Parnell clapped his hands together once, rubbed them together quickly, then blew into the space between them while holding them up to his mouth. This, Sky came to know, was his mannerism for when he was about to make a judgment call about something. He stared at her hard for a moment, still rubbing his hands together, then spoke.

"Escort him back to his cell," he ordered Sky, then he looked at Thor and finished, "Tomorrow you will have a chance to try something new and prove that you have the potential to be something more than just a thorn in my ass. If you prove otherwise, *or leave your cell again*, you will be part of tomorrow's waste drop. Is that abundantly clear, Mr. Stanton?" he asked, suddenly as serious as a heart attack.

"Aye, Captain," Thor nodded, standing back up and stretching a little at the tight and uncomfortable jump suit he was clothed in. Sky put her hand on his shoulder, with a slight push toward the door. In that moment, he felt comfort he had not felt since the night he ran down the alley away from his burnt home. He walked calmly, resisting the strong urge to look back. Sky was directly behind him, then the two guards the Captain ordered to fall in behind her. The doctor stayed behind. Undoubtedly, the validity of his story was still under some scrutiny. He could only hope, at this point, that he would have a chance to prove himself valuable before it could be poked full of too many holes.

Not a word was said until they were on the elevator, heading down below. Sky reached around the back of her belt and produced a pair of odd looking handcuffs. She held them open toward him. "Humor us.... This is for the others. The last thing we need is a rebellion." He looked her in the eye, then held out his wrists, confident that this was a temporary arrangement. She put them on him, a little more carefully than she probably would have in the past, and spoke softly, "I'll be interested to find out the rest, *Mr. Stanton*...."

"So will I, my angel, so will I."

When the elevator door opened, she pushed him toward the cell block guards with her pistol drawn and pointed at the ceiling, shouting, "If he so much as looks at you wrong, you are to notify me immediately!" She turned, holstered her gun, and stepped back into the elevator with the two guards. This wasn't the cell block he came from. There were twice as many cells, and each one was half the size, and without a bed. The guards shoved him into his cell and hit the sensor on the wall. The moment the shield was generated, the cuffs popped open.

"Slide them through," the guard ordered. They slid right through the field, confirming another question Thor had in his head, but previously lacked the means to test. He sat down with his back to the opening and meditated. So far, so good, he thought. That could have gone much, much worse.

CHAPTER 33: OPPORTUNITY IN CHAOS

He had just faded off to sleep after being up most of the night. Not having a bed in the cell wasn't the half of it... he simply couldn't shake her off! He needed to keep things in perspective. She was deep in their ranks, loyal, a person of some standing. If things ended badly for him, she would probably be more of a hindrance than a help. He needed to stay focused. There was just something about her he couldn't get out of his head. Their meeting, even 700 years into his future, seemed, with every fiber of intuition he possessed, to be preordained by fate.

The lights came on and voices started in immediately. Work assignments were being called out, and people were being escorted off to their jobs. The place eventually emptied out, leaving only him. He started to relax, smiling because he thought he had the place all to himself, and started to fade back to sleep. She came around the corner just then, smiling with relief, as if she was almost half expecting him to be gone again. "We have something a little different for you today... come with me."

On the elevator, she stood noticeably closer than she needed to, and he instantly became infected by her beauty more than ever. She seemed stripped of some of her stern front, such that all that was left was her natural charm and humor, her dark, semi-long hair, perfect body and ice blue eyes. Maybe it was because it was just the two of them, and he hoped she was feeling it too, but he was definitely growing increasingly infatuated with her at a very alarming rate.

"As you seem to have overheard, we are having a bit of a dilemma getting   our   shields   to   stop   this   planet's creatures from attacking us," she said.

"Creatures? You mean that ruckus the other night wasn't a human attack?" he asked, starting to understand.

"No." She looked at him closely. He could tell she was holding something back. *It had something to do with these creatures....* He decided not to pry. She looked like she would probably tell him soon enough on her own. "Since you have about 700 years of catch-up to do," she evaded, "this session will be mostly educational, with a few tests to analyze your potential for adapting to our technology."

"Sounds good," he said, smiling broadly. He did enjoy a challenge. "I'm a little rusty but I'll give it my best. It has to beat working in that pit with all of those assholes."

She stopped the elevator at a point that seemed like halfway, then hit a series of keys on the keypad, each having a different tone that he committed to memory without looking and alarming her. The elevator slowly adjusted its height to an exact elevation, and was now moving laterally. It gradually slowed to a stop. "Before I open this door, there's something I want you to know," she said, suddenly very serious. "I see honor in you, and the strength to succeed at whatever you choose to do, but the key to our race's survival has always been cooperation. Be cautious."

He erupted into a fit of nervous laughter, hoping all the while that she didn't take it the wrong way.

"What's so funny?" she asked, looking a little offended.

"I just had the biggest fucking deja-vu I've ever had in my life off of that!"

"Shit!" she said, smiling and smacking him in the chest with the back of her hand. "You asshole! I thought you were laughing at me!" She grinned, hit the pad, and the door slid open.

What he saw was absolutely amazing. They had entered what must be the heart of the ship. It looked like an entire civilization consolidated into one city block. She started to walk him through a tour of the place, first sidestepping into a dormitory area and into one of the fitting rooms along a lavatory wing.

"Sit here for a minute," she said, pointing at a bench along the wall across from some mirrors. This was the first time he had actually seen himself since he was brought back from cryostasis.... *He looked hideous!* He walked over to a small sink basin on the wall, presumably for pouring drinking water out of, and washed his face and hair as good as he could with just water. Looking at the soiled farmer Ted coveralls in the mirror, he snickered, assuming that much was just a lost cause... just then, Sky returned with a stack of clothes in her arm. She handed them to him, admiring the quick job he did on his hair. "Nice," she commented. He went into the lavatory and came back out dressed similar to the officers on board. His new uniform had no rank stripes, of coarse, but it was infinitely more comfortable and less putrid smelling than the suit he had been wearing around the clock and working in.

They passed through another room on their way to the dome he saw on the way in. It appeared to be some sort of break room where several people were congregated, eating food and talking about this and that. Thor instantly felt that "small town" vibe as they all stopped, almost in mid-sentence, and gawked at the two of them as they passed through, before resuming their previous banter. Though he was tempted to say, *"Take a picture... it lasts longer,"* he bit his tongue and just nodded at them, smiling somewhat pretentiously. He could almost understand the phenomenon... after all, how often did they ever encounter a new face in this society that wasn't wearing coveralls?

Most of the interior walls, except around the chow hall and dorms, were made of some kind of high density clear plastic or glass substitute, so he had a fairly good idea of the general layout of this level already. It kind of reminded him of a high tech version of Jerrick's place. Everything had a purpose, and not one square foot had gone to waste. The futuristic bio-dome was a living, breathing exercise in the *art* of efficiency.

Walking into the thing was like landing on another planet. There was a system of perpetual balance set into motion in here that Mother Nature herself would have keenly admired. Green plants of all kinds and trees were growing right inside the ship. There was a small stream flowing through the ground level, meandering through the vegetation, providing water to everything. It pooled up in places where fish and other forms of life could be seen swimming about, totally oblivious to the fact that they weren't on the surface of some planet.

There were small fields of crops laid out at nearly every stage of growth; fruit trees and bushes, medicinal herbs, and even limited livestock. Chicken, it seemed, had still remained the number one production animal for humankind.

Off to the side, but still visible there was a separate room for the growth and production of eggs, chickens, and even a large apiary; live bees controlled through pheromone manipulation, producing honey to be used for sweetener of every kind, as well as many other things, including royal jelly, beeswax, and yes... *mead!* This nearly brought a tear of joy to Thor's eye... *yes, there was definitely hope for these people, after all!* More than for drinking, it was being regularly produced for the use of the pure, combustible alcohol obtained by distilling the mead to higher and higher concentrations. Thor smiled broadly, and started to explain his other talent to her, but got sidetracked and decided to save it for later.

She explained how the dome produced all the oxygen needed for the population of the ship, and in turn, their CO2 was filtered back into the dome to feed the plants, as well as a certain amount of solid waste nitrogen from the ships composting wastewater filtration system. The entire engineered bio-system, which was coincidentally standard issue onboard every ship in the fleet, was set up to provide total sustainability with as close to zero waste as possible.

The basic premise was, that aside from fuel, anything taken onto the ship had to have a counterpart of equal mass going out, otherwise the ship would continue to take on weight indefinitely. By contrast, anything going out would represent a loss or depletion that would also have to be balanced out eventually for survival. Because of this complete independence, all functions of the ship and her crew had to be analyzed and engineered for zero waste. Matter cannot be created or destroyed, it can only change forms.... Even the means for heat, gravity, air, power, etc. had to come from some other form of waste recycling that was already onboard the ship. By universal law, this very concept is impossible, there can never be 100% efficiency, but when a group of people's lives suddenly depend upon how close to that number they can get, it's absolutely amazing how much attention mankind is willing to pay to things they used to take totally for granted. *If only we had thought this way as a race when it still mattered,* Thor thought, absolutely humbled by the engineering genius that lay before him.

She took him through the recreation wing, where he was very relieved to see that they still appreciated art, music, sports, leisure games, etc., and he got a bit of a charge to his usually optimistic outlook on things. Until this point, he was starting to worry that things had become sterile and pointless, devoid of the things that made humans what they were; becoming an entire race of idiot savants, flailing through the cosmos on a wing and a prayer, only showing their true potential when life forced their hand.

They had a meal that he could not identify, but it tasted infinitely better than the gruel they were feeding him down below. After a bit of dinner related small talk, she then proceeded to take him to the post he was going to attempt to occupy. One level below the dome, but wired into the engineering level below that, was the computer control room. It was here that all the real brainwork and navigation took place.

There were groups of highly educated minds plugged into the same terminals in threes, forming think-tanks that were responsible for the analysis and research and development of every aspect of ship life. Tied into all the other ships in the Fleet, their research and input was immediately assimilated into the group collective and analyzed by the best minds in the Fleet, onboard the Helios, Admiral T. Alexander Reid's flagship. The ships were independent of each other, but stayed in constant contact, giving the Fleet the benefit of independent speed and versatility with combined intellect allowing for exponential technological growth. Their constant scrutiny and development of star maps and potential courses of

Fleet deployment based on the probability of inhabitable planets in neighboring systems, as well as potential resource hotspots within reachable radii was, thus far, hugely successful, due primarily to this system.

During many of these sessions, Sky explained, many facts and theories have been proved, disproved, or discovered. One such theory was the widely accepted belief that the universe is expanding. The dating of light from a now extinct group of stars, using the ship's known position relative to a third reference point proved that the light from these stars was actually much older than the universe itself. This led to closer analyzation of many of the oldest galaxies in the fleet's field of vision, and the ultimate conclusion that the universe is not expanding, but *contracting*!

This was considered, but then conveniently ignored back in the 20th century when a group of scientists led by Wendy Freedman discovered the phenomenon, but now that they were able to witness this movement from a third point, considerably further away, the data was indisputable. Along with Tod Lauer and Marc Postman, the young scientists reached the astonishing conclusion that rather than expanding outward in a stately fashion like the rest of the universe appeared to be doing, a collection of thousands of galaxies, including the Milky Way, spanning a billion light-years of space or so, may be speeding en masse toward a point somewhere in the direction of the constellation Virgo.

Needless to say, this turned the entire scientific community into a state of upheaval. Debunking the linear concept of time entirely, we clearly see that eternity can easily be explained as ebb and flow, or vibration. As above, so below. The crudest form of matter in the universe still has atoms, which are composed mostly of dead space, and still have a vibratory pitch, as slow as it may be. They differ only in frequency to the highest pitch of energy achievable by light itself, and everything else is in the middle, running the full spectrum; simply different speeds, or vibratory pitches, of the same thing... *energy*. Matter *is* energy. Once this is clearly understood, the laws of physics cease to govern with the iron fist of our elders, and we see that *everything* is subject to reconsideration. *Energy* can not be created or destroyed, *it can only change forms....*

After a long philosophical discussion that had both of them smiling and respecting each other that much more, she started down the hall with him toward the engineering rooms, continuing to brief him in more detail than the Captain may have intended or desired, on their modes of travel, sleep cycling to enable crew members to reach far away systems with as little aging as possible, fleet location and numbers, as well as ship types and capabilities, etc.... She had already answered many of the questions he intended to find the answers to when he had gained access to a computer, and the day was still young!

He had instinctively felt the need to gain knowledge in the event that he become separated in purpose from his captors, especially after the way he had been treated so far, yet the more she explained to him, *the more she trusted him*, the more he felt he would probably never need to use any of it against them anyway... it was mostly just academic at this point, albeit exceedingly intriguing. Still, coming from a background such as his, where nothing was ever predictable or stable, he believed in covering his bases and looking toward any possible outcome leading to a worse case scenario. *Hope for the best... plan for the worst.* This simple philosophy had kept him breathing this far.

Upon seeing the engine room and trying hard to understand how the ship's systems were powered, things started to come together in his head. It was like all the things he heard about when he was a child, the things that the oil cartels kept under government repression, all rolled into one highly efficient, beautiful symphony of engineering genius. Magnetic frictionless couplings and bearings, flywheel generators, solar, hydro and wind power all rolled into one giant system of internal regenerative energy production designed to reduce waste of all kinds to nearly zero, while turning even the waste and byproducts of their environment into more energy.

She explained the brunt of their technology to him. The acid and iron rich mineral they mined from the planet acted as a sort of catalyst for a secondary combustion, producing a burn off of hydrogen from a tiny amount of H_2O, and the remaining oxygen then supplemented the air supply for the ship. As with any combustion, the byproducts are always CO_2 and water... both of which were needed for continued growth and maintenance of the plant life in the dome, directly over the engineering department. Even the ambient heat from the engines rose efficiently to keep the dome at a certain temperature, while the excess was channeled through turbines to produce electricity, aiding temperature control shipwide. High efficiency, pole on pole magnetic couplings and bearings were integrated into every moving part on the ship, reducing friction, and thereby, the need for oil, to almost nothing.

While in a planet's atmosphere, the Harvesters used an advanced form of this magnetic repulsion technology to suspend themselves above ground at different levels, depending on the planetary composition. The key was iron. The higher the density of iron deposits in the crust of a planet, the less power it took to stay "afloat." Lateral sway, yaw, and pitch were controlled, in part, by small impulse burns, but mostly by a combination of "old school" solar and wind harnessing: drogue chutes, rudders, wings, and even sails to harness apparent wind, allowing the massive ship to tack upwind with no resistance. The key to the seamless implementation and collaboration of all of these systems to keep a desired coarse was a barrage of high tech sensors and dish arrays on key points of the ship. Luckily for all on board, the creatures from the surface hadn't figured that out yet and started targeting them directly, as they were strong enough to do some real damage once inside the shield.

He fished for information directly regarding the parameters of the mining assignment, but she seemed unwilling to talk about something, and stayed pretty vague on the subject in general. He couldn't put his finger on it, but he didn't want to pry, so he decided to leave that one alone for now. All she could really tell him was that they lacked the material to get to the next system successfully, and that more Carriers were on the way to help just as soon as they could be prepared for the task and get rigged as Harvesters for this planet's unique conditions. She sounded like she was just repeating that part of the answer as it was told to her, but not completely at peace with some aspect of it, so he took a shot in the dark. "You think they're sending a lot more than just mining equipment, don't you?"

…And just like that, the flood gate opened. "They're sending an armada of single manned fighters to firebomb the resistance if we start to fall short on our time frame! There, I said it... I'll probably end up in the brig, myself, but God dammit, this is the way it always ends up, and I'm sick of it! There *has* to be another way!" she exclaimed, somewhere between a whisper and a yell.

"There's *always* another way," Thor added, getting pissed off as well, "it's just *easier* to do the wrong thing! These bastards haven't changed a bit!" he scowled, staring at the floor. "What the hell is the *time frame* all about?"

"Command is insisting that the binary sun is becoming unstable. One twin is ripping the guts out of the other, and the rate has very recently accelerated dramatically, due to the slow collapse of a third sun's orbital ellipse. They think the three will become one, and when they do, they will supernova! If this happens, that beautiful planet you see out there, Sigyn, will not hold sway the shockwave that will follow... _nothing will!_ It would consume the entire system. These creatures would die anyway. Our problem is that if they're right, we wont be far enough away when it happens to fully escape the blast, and our whole race will be destroyed as well." She sighed, slightly rolling her eyes. He could see that she didn't entirely buy it, at least not insofar as the predicted timetable was concerned.

"So we commit genocide in the hopes that our race isn't killed too, is that what they're selling?" he asked.

"That's about the size of it.... Only problem is that these creatures aren't just mindless monsters, as they would like us to believe! I've sensed a presence there, and I've witnessed a capacity for learning... shit, they might be smarter than us! Who the hell are we to play God with them just to save our own skins!" She was starting to get genuinely upset. He could see, now, the source of the conflict present in her energy that he noticed before. This was huge. He could also see that she could be trusted. She had the spark of genuine humanity that the rest seemed to be lacking, and he admired her deeply for it.

"I couldn't agree more... The question as usual, is what the hell can the little fish do against the sharks?" he posed, wanting any talk of rebellion to first come from her.

"I don't know," she said quietly, wrapping her arms around his muscular frame for the first time. She stayed like this for a while, finally relieved to have _someone_ onboard that thought the way she did. Deep down inside, she really wasn't all that surprised that it turned out to be him. "First things first, I need to show you how to operate our computers... maybe you can help me double check their math. Lets just say I need to see it with my own eyes."

"Sounds good," he said softly, staring into her eyes. He almost lost his breath entirely when she locked her fingers together behind his neck and kissed him exactly the way Kait used to. He closed his eyes and it was her, down to the last detail; down to the core... *it was her*. Nevermind her physical appearance. Nevermind her hair color, her voice, her conditioning in this new world. It *was* her. He suspected all along, but wouldn't allow himself to entertain such a crazy thought, but now he could feel her with every fiber of his being. Now, for the first time in his life, he *truly* believed anything was possible.

Back on the bridge, Captain Parnell wiped a bead of sweat off his brow as he broke away from a meeting with his navigators and first mate about their new course revision. The young communications officer at the helm handed him a small earpiece. "Its Fleet, sir," she explained.

"Thank you," he replied, motioning with his eyes for her to return to her post. She complied and he paced back and forth, answering only in short, one or two word answers, then simply said, "Yes, sir. Parnell out." He handed the communicator back to helm, then stared out the front viewing window for a moment, stretching his arms, chest, and back. He turned around to face the already interested crew, and made every one of them jump, yelling, "SHIT!" as loud as he could, and throwing his empty coffee mug across the bridge at the wall with a crash. "Those   assholes! It's gonna be another genocide! Now they're sending three Carriers, one rigged as a Harvester, one with a fighter squadron, and one with bombers!" He paced a few more times, deep in thought. "God Dammit!" he concluded.

"Here we go again," one of the older helmsmen muttered as the Captain hit his belt communicator.

Sky was just sitting Thor down at a terminal in a quiet corner of his own, and was booting up the main drive, when her communicator beeped. She hit it to reply, "Davies here."

"I need you up here right away!" the Captain said quickly.

"Yes, sir. On my way." She turned to Thor, rolling her eyes. She quickly set him up with a tutorial screen and showed him how they used a combination of an electrode visor and a holographic touch screen combined with 3D holographic imaging. "Play around with this for a while," she said, patting him on the back of his shoulder, "I'll be back."

She quickly walked off toward the elevator. Thor started browsing through menu after menu, finding his way quickly through the operating system to files upon files ship schematics and technical data. He glanced around the room to make sure nobody was watching him. He intuitively picked up on their computer system almost immediately, but didn't want them to know just how fast he really was, lest they perceive him as a threat to their security and cut off his access. He would let them see steady progress, but he could definitely see how holding back what he showed them up front might be in his best interest... even where she was concerned. At least this way, if something was to happen that forced his hand, she would still have deniability.

Once on the bridge, Parnell briefed Sky on the impending situation. She did her best to hide her outrage, since she pretty much saw it all coming days ago. The Captain was still pretty upset, but he was all business now. "How is your prodigy doing?" he inquired.

"So far, so good," she smiled, not wanting to say too much. "He seems to be right at home with our technology."

"Yeah... I noticed," he said sarcastically. "We need to pick his brain a little more forcefully... I don't think we have time to beat around the bush. They're sending bombers, Sky, it's gonna be a massacre!" She put her hand on his arm to steady his temperament.

"I'll do whatever I can to speed it up. He seems willing to cooperate."

"Good. They'll be here in 48 hours. They're only waiting for the next passing of the third sun to insure safe re-entry. When the quakes and showers are over, they'll drop in right on our heels. That's why I need to know how to keep the Sand Dragons out of our shields. If they can't hurt us, command might not unleash hell on the surface, but the presence of three more ships this close to the nest is certainly going to attract aggression. They will undoubtedly attack us with everything they have!"

"I'll work on it with him. We'll find out what he can do," she assured, walking back toward the door.

"Just don't say too much," Parnell warned. "We can't afford for him to have a moral dilemma. He's not even bound by a sense of alliance or duty yet."

"Is that what it takes to do the wrong thing? A sense of alliance or duty?" she jabbed, "I think self preservation will be enough, Captain, but I'll stay vague anyway...."

"Thanks," Parnell said, matching her sarcasm.

Sky left Thor pretty much to himself for the last 24 hours, after a quick briefing about the interlocking nature of their shields, and how the defense grid applied to the other harvesters as well, not just themselves. He had instructions to access and modify their shields, on a trial basis alone, with the intention of keeping the Sand Dragons from penetrating their defenses and boarding the ships. He could do this on his own, but to do it through a computer, and in reverse; disallowing other sentient beings from being able to identify and accept an energy field he would be tapped into, rather than simply passing through.... That was certainly going to be a stretch.

Surprising to even himself, he had already managed to find the shield parameters and the management software for the generator, and had worked out the beginning of a system of reverse manipulation, using the visor as an interface controller. He had already done his homework regarding their present location, range of the ship, probable next destination, and all available data on this planet and this solar system, and was working through the math on the impending cataclysmic event when she finally made it back down to check on his progress.

"How much have you been able to find out?" she asked right away, skipping the pleasantries.

"Well, I know where we are. We're about 93 light years from Earth, in the Algol system. Algol is the demon head binary star on the other side of Sigyn from us. The third sun in the system, Skaði, is on a decaying orbit, but it will not come to a point of impending collision in our lifetime, so long as Sigyn holds up from the constant bombardment. I'm guessing your Fleet Commanders know this, and have their own reasons for stepping up the operations here, but for now, the safety of the human race is not in question.... Still, I'm noticing a direct relationship between the Crystal mass on this planet, and the core stability of Sigyn. I think the binary nature of the planetary bodies in this system goes much deeper than it appears. The suns are connected, the moons are connected.... I think these two planets are codependent, as well. Probably at the core, and at a magnetic level, just like the two moons, Vali and Nari. At one time, this planet probably looked a lot like Sigyn, but has since then been stripped down to its mineral face. The problem appears to be balance. These creatures use the Crystal for life, mirroring the natural erosional depletion and replacement of matter that is happening on Sigyn from the solar bombardment, thus, keeping them in balance. Now, add humanity... carelessly strip mining, at accelerating levels, every bit of Crystal we can obtain. I believe *we* are the ones disturbing the balance, and thereby putting additional strain on Sigyn. "

"And if Sigyn doesn't hold up?" Sky asked.

"The Norse observed this over two millennia ago. These planets, and their situation were foretold in a story about Loki, the God of Mischief. It was said he was betrayed by the gods when one of his sons, Vali, was turned into a werewolf. Vali, after turning into a wolf, ripped the guts out of his own twin brother, Nari, and those entrails were used by the goddess, Skaði, to bind Loki to a rock beneath a poisonous serpent. The serpent slowly and constantly drips poison into his mouth, causing him untold pain and torment. His wife, Sigyn, stands above him with a bowl, catching the poison, in an act of mercy, keeping it from reaching his mouth, but periodically the bowl fills up, and she must pour it out to make room for more. When this happens, some poison gets by her and lands in Loki's mouth, causing him so much pain that he thrashes around hard enough to cause massive earthquakes across the entire planet. She is bound to his fate out of loyalty, and this pattern he is doomed to repeat until she can take no more, then he will be unleashed in his pain and fury, signifying the beginning of The Ragnarok."

"Ragnarok?" she asked, puzzled.

"The Battle of Armageddon.... The End of Days."

CHAPTER 34: RENDEZVOUS

Thor worked through the night trying to write a program to govern their shield parameters, but the root of the problem wasn't creating a fluctuating pitch, it was deceiving those who would be intuitively reading and penetrating it. He had to assume the indigenous beings were able to penetrate it in exactly the same way as himself, so that made it easy to create a model in which to test each new program. Unfortunately, he struck out time and time again when it came to an active and random test. He finally came to the realization that this situation called for a manned operator... himself. He was the only one who could feel where the pitch was at, and adjust it manually to keep them out. He could only hope that their probing could be felt by him in reverse, through the shield's energy field, otherwise he would be flying on blind intuition alone.

Just as he was about to contact the bridge and talk to the Captain about his new findings and suggested course of action, Sky returned. She looked worried, obviously anxious about the impending rub with the natives, but she also looked as if she had something to tell him that she really didn't want to. He decided to beat her to the punch with some good news, figuring it might be just pressure from above she was supposed to impart on him.

"Hey gorgeous, check this out! " He waved her over. When she got to his terminal, she put her hand on his shoulder, squeezing a little bit as if to console herself more than him. "I've got this down to a workable routine... the only thing is, it'll probably require me to run it manually while we're under attack. Watch the screen." He put on the visor and hit a button to start a simulation. "The blue field represents the shield outside. The red bogies are the indigenous trying to get in." He closed his eyes. She watched in awe as the simulator ran for about two minutes without one penetration.

"That's all well and good, but you said yourself, penetration is accomplished intuitively, by feeling the pitch of the energy field.... Would this not also apply to the Sand Dragons? It seems this simulation is assigning them random energy signatures, and you simply have to keep the pitch fluctuating to stop them," she speculated.

"Not exactly. I've got them on a quasi-predictive routine, capable of reading each new signature within a few seconds and actually learning from their mistakes. That's the part I can't really know for sure, as I've never dealt with *them* before.... I really have no idea how fast they can adapt to my pitch changes. I'm relying on being able to feel them as they *intend* to change their pitch, just a split second before coming into contact with the field. That's when I can pitch shift and repel their attempt without any chance for a correction on their part."

"What makes you think you will be able to feel them?" she asked, more genuinely curious than skeptical.

"Because I already have."

Her eyes widened. She looked as if there was something she really wanted to share with him, but time wouldn't allow it. She squeezed his shoulder and smiled, then patted him on the back. "Good job, Thor. Are you ready to present this to Parnell? He'll be very relieved to hear this! He's wearing grooves in the floor with his nervous pacing! We rendezvous with three other Harvesters in 30 minutes!" She stood tall and walked toward the door, waving him to follow.

"Let's do it," he said confidently, realizing whatever her worry was, it seemed to have been quelled by his new progress. This technique could very well save them all, regardless of the Fleet's real agenda. It wasn't in anyone's best interest to be slaughtered on the eve of their exodus. All they could hope was that their leaders would maintain their humanity through whatever was about to transpire.

When they arrived on the bridge, things were anything but orderly. The Captain was running around like a chicken with his head cut off, barking orders at his crew, most of whom were handling things with a much more even keel than him. Sky took it upon herself to try to lighten the mood with some good news. "Well, Captain, it seems our prodigy is a lot more adaptable than we could've hoped!"

Captain Parnell stopped what he was doing and turned toward them both with a quizzical look on his face, but said nothing. Thor decided to lighten the mood *his* way. "Hey Captain... Why did the dog cross the road?" he asked with a smile playing on the edge of his mouth.

"Why?" the Captain played along.

"Cause he had his dick stuck in a chicken!" he yelled loud enough for the entire bridge to hear. The Captain stared at him with a completely stoic look. All at once, laughter erupted from a couple crew members, and one of the helmsmen, who had just taken a drink of some water, burst out laughing through his nose, nearly choking as the water sprayed all over the front of his lapel. Thor just smiled as Sky looked nervously at the Captain, waiting to see his reaction. He stared at Thor for almost 20 straight seconds, then burst into an uncontrolled fit of boisterous laughter, not only at the joke, but at the levity it created for his overstressed crew. Smiling at Thor, he took an unbalanced step and approached, slapping him hard on the shoulder.

"What have you figured out? Please tell me you got something we can use! Look up there," he said, pointing at the monitors above his console showing three Carriers like the one they were piloting entering the atmosphere and slowly moving into position behind them. They were roughly 20 minutes away.

Thor explained the entire procedure to the Captain, who listened intently. When he got to the part about how this couldn't work on any kind of logarithm, but rather, needed to be completely manual, random, and controlled by Thor directly, he acted worried. They had a very firm policy regarding lockdown of all Cryos during high alert... *for any reason*. He thought maybe Thor was making that part up to suit his needs, but insofar as opportunism goes, if that was indeed the truth, he had to give Thor props for creativity, as well as believability. This situation would keep him out of the brig during the final phase of harvesting... perhaps indefinitely!

"Good work, son! Good goddamn work!" He praised, finally looking genuinely relieved. "Can you do this from right here?" he asked, pointing at an empty navigation terminal to his left.

"Probably not. The main issue is probably going to be focus. It would be like trying to take a long distance call at a heavy metal show!" The Captain looked puzzled at his analogy, but seemed to at least understand the point.

"Well, set him up with whatever he needs, including an open, two way com-link directly to me, and a separate one to the bridge as a backup, in the event that our connection gets severed. It is imperative to our success that we be able to communicate at all times, wouldn't you agree, Mr. Stanton?" the Captain officially inquired, seemingly testing his devotion to their cause.

"I firmly believe communication may become necessary for any number of reasons, but even if left completely in the dark, I can control the shield with or without any human feedback, so long as I have uninterrupted access to the scanners, and a direct uplink to the other three ships. I'll simply need for them to integrate my program into their shield matrix, and we're good to go."

"Good man," Parnell nodded, "so be it. Sky, go with him and help him get set up and strapped in, just in case of an early attack, then assemble the guard and meet me in the hanger with them... locked, loaded, and ready for combat. I'll contact the other ships and get them working on the programming. Put me through to Fleet Command," Parnell ordered, still beaming at Sky and Thor, "I've got some good news to tell them." He was genuinely smiling for the first time this morning.

"Aye, sir," she saluted. Thor just nodded, respectfully, never losing eye contact, then took one step backward and pivoted around to face the door and started to walk off the bridge with her. He got about half way to the door when his conscience finally got the best of him. He stopped in his tracks and turned back around toward Parnell.

"In case of an attack by who?" Thor asked, boldly.

"Oh, shit, here it comes..." Sky murmured under her breath.

"What?!" the Captain exclaimed, still half smiling, "Who do you think?"

"What I mean is, who will be attacking who? It seems to me that we're preparing for a massive attack that, with all due respect, I believe we are bringing on ourselves. Have you ever tried to negotiate with these creatures?" Thor boldly suggested.

"These *creatures* are more like savage monsters, and while they do possess a tactical intelligence and some form of control over their environment, be it conscious or intuitive, we have seen nothing to suggest that they are a civilization or are in any way capable of growth," he replied, as if he was blindly quoting some generic response he had been programmed to say.

"Capable of growth? Are you shitting me?" Thor exclaimed, growing seriously irate in a hurry. "Is that the accepted standard for judgment of worth? Look where *growth* got our species!" Sky put her hand on his shoulder, as if to shut him up, while looking at the Captain with her eyebrow raised, as if to imply that he was right. "Anyway," he said, taking it down a few decibels, "I know for a fact that they are capable of some form of higher communication... telepathy, or something, and there is no doubt they rely on Crystal for some form of sustenance, otherwise they wouldn't be so threatened by what we are doing, but the real problem, and you can do the math for yourself, is that there is a symbiotic relationship between the planets and suns in this system, and I'm pretty sure that the Crystal is the key! The instability in the core of Sigyn is being *caused* by the unnatural depletion of Crystal on this planet....

"The long standing balance is being tipped too far to one side, and I fear the end result will be catastrophic! The repulsive characteristic of the Crystal that you use to keep yourselves off the surface and in low orbit is present on a planetary scale between all the twin bodies in this system. Right now they are in a state of very delicate, very fragile balance, but we are upsetting that balance! I would *implore* you to reason with your superiors before it's too late, but somehow I think they probably already know exactly what they're doing, and are willing to sacrifice this entire system and commit genocide to support their own interests!"

"That's enough!" the Captain yelled, obviously frustrated by his position in the whole thing, but not completely numb to the truth. "Wouldn't you be willing to sacrifice everything for the lives of everyone in the Fleet? If we don't leave with enough Crystal to get to the next prospect, *WE ALL DIE*... it's that simple!"

Thor took a deep breath, looking around the room at the astonished faces of the bridge crew, then exhaled long and slow. "Please excuse my frustration, sir, I just think there has to be another way, and I don't see anything that would give me the idea that Fleet Command has exhausted any other avenues of possibility. I truly believe they are taking the low road because it is faster and simpler, and putting an acceptable spin on things to make it easier for people like you and me to swallow." He stared deep into the Captain's eyes. "You know, mankind really hasn't changed at all in 700 years, has it? As far as my position, Captain, don't fucking worry about it!... This situation is what it is... I don't like it, but it's not currently in my power to change it *by myself,* and as soon as we are threatened by an attack, *for any reason,* I will continue to protect the lives onboard all four ships, with everything I've got in my arsenal, for as long as I draw breath," he insisted, never losing eye contact, then added, "Warriors are seldom afforded the luxury of soldiering in an honorable fight..."

"...And soldiers are seldom afforded the luxury of a conscience." The Captain said coldly, just staring at him for a moment, then at Sky. He nodded without saying another word, but with a hint of respect that wasn't there before, then turned and started talking to his helmsman.

"Let's go prepare ourselves," Sky said softly, patting him on the back. She pointed up at the rear view screen at the three Carriers falling into position behind them; the heat mirage of re-entry still radiating from the outer shell of their shields. "Their presence here will undoubtedly bring on a shit-storm from the natives."

As they walked down the corridor toward the computer room she set up for him above engineering, he paused, looking troubled. "Let's take a little detour," he suggested, gesturing with his chin toward the stairwell leading to the mezzanine level, out on deck.
"Sure, I guess.... What's up?" she asked, a little puzzled with his timing.
"I don't know...."
"I think I feel it, too," she said, opening the door for him with the handprint scanner on the adjacent wall.

Down on the surface, the wind was howling. There were dust devils whipping through the foothills, chasing each other in a relentless game of cat and mouse, crashing into the rock walls and each other in a violent explosion of random expression; nature's symphony, resonating a crescendo in perfect time beneath the flickering lightning show of static electricity randomly darting around the horizon and over the dust filled plains of orange sand and grass. The third sun, now well out of sight from its brief, but tumultuous visit, laid just below the horizon, casting an intoxicating reflection on the twin moons overhead, which, in the twilight state of the surface, amplified the intense tone of the already brilliant acid veins that crawled across the plains through the lowlands like a blood red road map painted across the face of the entire planet.
The dust being kicked up by the turbulence created from the small convoy finally reached the far away ridge and

he blinked his outer eyelids, carefully keeping the transparent inner lids closed as he watched intently. The three new ships were drawing nearer and nearer to the first one, the one he had been assigned to watch ever since it came down from the stars. He turned his head, lowering his right wing joint slightly to gaze into the eyes of his comrade who sat next to him, still as a statue, blending in like Earth's chameleons with the rocks and soil around him.

They exchanged glances, and with it, a premonition... vague, but frightening, of fire raining down from the sky from a myriad of flying vessels intent on destroying their kind in one fell swoop. The elder closed his eyes, bowing his head and meditated for a moment, then looked at him with tears of sadness and rage welling up in his eyes. He nodded, then lashed himself out to the southwest, straight up high, then down through an unseen hole in the hilltop to warn the others.

He sat for a moment in the wind, turning himself orange and gray, most likely without even realizing it, simply by tuning in and acclimating himself to his surroundings in an attempt to heighten his focus. He forced his inner eyelids open, in spite of the wind, and pulled the image of the first ship into vivid view. Things appeared normal, but toward the top level, he could see two of the beings standing outside, leaning on the rail.

The female he had seen before. He had even tried to speak to her, but in the end, she stood to defend her kind and the connection was severed. He could tell she was a leader among her people, but she was different than the rest. She was a natural empath. He couldn't make her understand him, but he could feel her emotion, and he knew she could feel him. Right now, she was crying. There was a man standing next to her. He had seen this one before, as well. *It was the other night....* He was the one hanging off the guardrail, hiding from the others! There was something unique about him, as well. He seemed to be aware of them that night, at least on a primitive, instinctive level. Something told him these two still had some part to play in all of this.

He looked back at the other ships and saw many men walking all over the topside structures of their ships, most of them carrying the devices that they used to fire on him and his brothers; the very same devices that cost him the life of his mate. He glared at them, closing his inner eyelids, then slowly and proudly flew up and out over the plains, then back into the caverns to join the others, making sure he would be seen.

Thor spoke to her of human history as he understood it, much of which had been lost to the times. He spoke of Hitler, of Manifest Destiny and the American Indians, and of the corporate oppression he witnessed first hand in his lifetime... *and for what?* The good of the masses? What a joke! Where were they now? Full circle? What looks like full circle, often times when observed from the side, from outside the situation, reveals itself to be nothing but a full blown downward spiral!

Teary eyed, she explained everything to him. She told him how worried she was for these creatures, who, in her honest opinion, had done nothing but defend their own territory, and certainly deserved a chance to live on after they left. She knew there was an intelligence far greater than anyone imagined about these beings; she had witnessed it first hand. On deck, in the middle of a quick skirmish with one of them, he paused and looked right at her. When they locked eyes, she swore she could *hear* the creature inside her head. She was so pumped with adrenaline at the time, that it kind of caught her off guard, but she could definitely feel its intention. It was asking her to stop! *It was asking them all to stop....* She tried to tell Parnell, but he wouldn't hear her. No one would. Until now....

She spoke openly of another campaign where the fleet, realizing they had uprooted an entire race of subterranean creatures in a strip mining effort and pulled them onboard amidst the mineral stores, decided it was too late to return them to the surface of their planet, and jettisoned them with the organic waste out of the airlock after getting the minerals they needed to produce fuel. A retrace of the lost ground would have caused a catastrophic fuel loss, but would have prevented the complete genocide of a semi-intelligent, peaceful species whose only crime was being very small, good at hiding within their surroundings, and completely undetectable by infrared scans or the naked eye.

They were an absolute marvel of nature, able to rearrange the atoms of their body however they needed in order to pass through or around solid objects or dissimilar materials. They took on the actual physical characteristics of whatever medium they were surrounded by, and could exist at a tremendous range of temperature. So much could have been learned from watching them in their natural habitat, and now they were utterly extinct... an effect mankind seemed to have on nearly every species they came into contact with. She had just begun to tell him about a more recent, even more heinous crime, when she suddenly realized there was a docking sequence being initiated and had to postpone the conversation.

"They must be coming over on a shuttle to go over the Captain's plans. We better get below and work this thing out, Thor.... Most of our ranks still aren't keen to the idea of being open partners with Cryos!" She smiled softly at him, starting to feel a true sense of trust.

"I understand," Thor said somberly, "most of us smell funny." She burst out laughing, slapping him on the arm on the way in.

Captain Parnell was going over some new data revisions with the bridge crew when a call came in from the largest of the three Carriers, the Flagship, Helios. It was Parnell's mentor and C.O., Admiral T. Alexander Reid. "Put him on screen," Parnell yelled out loud, looking up from the drafting table at the main screen.

"Good day, Captain. I trust you're all ready to present an updated strategic map to the tribunal?" said Reid, getting directly to the business at hand, as was his reputation.

"Yes, Sir, we are. We were just going over some revisions based on the most recent scan for acid density hot spots. We also have a revision to our defense strategy that you will undoubtedly find most interesting. Please bring shield parameter access codes for all three vessels.... We have one among us who has found a way to reprogram the shield pitch using a subroutine he operates manually. It's going to optimize our efforts here, without a doubt. It may not even be necessary to fight at all," he proposed, hoping for the best case scenario.

"Nonsense, Captain. Even if it works like you say, our deep scans have located an army massing for an attack, less than four miles to the southwest, deep underground. Their numbers have doubled since we arrived. No, I think it will take a lot more than a strong defense to fend off this kind of attack.... We'll still need that shield, so have him briefed, but I think it's going to be a shit-storm, my old friend, the likes of which we've never seen! Anyway, our cooling sequence is complete, and we have a stabilized, corresponding orbit. We're going to dock with you in three minutes. We'll talk more about this then."

"Yes, Sir."

"Have there been any attacks from the hostiles?" Reid asked.

"Not in about a week, but he was particularly cunning... "

"What do you mean, *he*, don't you mean, *it*?" Reid asked with a very hateful tone.

He had definitely worked very hard on making them his enemy, Parnell thought to himself. He cleared his throat before responding. "Yes, Sir. Anyway, I'll meet you in the conference room. Have your guys send those codes to our bridge, directly. We'll work it from there. Just have one good programmer ready to patch it all in on your side, and we'll be ready for anything they throw at us," Parnell added.

"Sounds good, Reid out." The screen flickered from the lightning show outside, then went black, followed by a reboot to the front surface view they had been using prior to the transmission. Parnell rolled up his maps and started to head off the bridge, then turned his attention to the helm.

"Transfer all surface data to the conference room main screen, along with the codes when they transmit them. Helm, you have command! Broaden the life form scans to include density changes in underground voids.... I want to see them coming!" He marched out of the room, followed by his second in command, hitting a certain key on his communicator on the way out.

"Lieutenant Commander Davies," she responded.

"Sky, I'm going to need you in the conference, after all. Get him up and running and get up here... please," Parnell ordered, sounding a little worried.

"On my way, Sir. Davies out."

The conference room of the Phoenix was set up with the expanse of space travel in mind, but it lent its esthetic flare quite well to the events of this day. One whole wall was covered with a thick pane of glass, showcasing the stunning scenery of the planet's surface, and, coincidentally, a built-in early warning system by way of the expansive view in the direction of the creatures' subterranean lair, hidden throughout the ridge of lower mountain range. They would be hard pressed to make it all the way across the plains without being spotted.

Captain Parnell was already waiting in the conference room when the others were escorted by a security detail, led by Lieutenant Davies, from the docking bay to the meeting. She ordered the two guards with her to stand post outside the door, then formally gestured for Admiral Reid and the two other ship Captains to be seated. To his left was Captain Daniel Ellis of the Achilles, and Captain Loren MacGregor of the Icarus was on his right. The three sat down immediately after exchanging pleasantries, but it was Reid, of coarse, who jumped straight into business.

"Before we get started, my old friend, I would like to reiterate the pressing need to adhere to our newly imposed timeline, due to the findings of our observatory group regarding the decaying orbit of Skaði, the third star in the system that we have charted as '3S1', and the inevitable cataclysmic affect this is going to have on this entire system. When Sigyn is destroyed, 3S1 will be pulled into Algol. and the binary sun will supernova, destroying this entire system, and all of us, as well… *if we're still here.* Our minimum safe distance has been estimated to be twice that originally calculated, due to the singularity that will result from such a massive supernova. The immediate birth of a new black hole in this sector will cause unimaginable repercussions. We need to make sure we are clear of its potential heliopause well in advance.

To that end, we are going to adopt a three pronged attack: a high speed, high efficiency, and high yield approach to the mining operation. It has been estimated that we have 3 days to retrieve as much Crystal as we can carry and be off of the surface, headed toward our next destination, or we'll never reach our estimated M.S.D. and outrun the shockwave from the initial supernova. Nothing but the outer rim planets in the system will remain, and soon after, not even those.... They will be pulled in from orbit and become part of the singularity," Admiral Reid pointed out in very matter-of-fact sort of way, leaving little room for argument.

. The Captain took a deep breath, bowed his head a little, then exhaled, unrolling a large map onto the cartography table, When the corners were locked in place and three index pins inserted, a 3D holographic image of the topography rose up from the table for isometric viewing. There were streaks of red throughout the map at different elevations, obviously beneath the surface, and they varied in color intensity from light pink to blood red, depending on mineral density for the specified scan... in this case, Crystal content.

"Here's our plan, Sir. We stick primarily together, following the hot spots, as marked on the map with a solid black line, fanning out over the wider veins out on the plains, and coming in single file over the deeper, more concentrated veins, so as to provide multiple pass refinement in one single, concentrated effort. Traversing the mountain range in this manner will provide security and efficiency, and according to our calculations, if we keep with the planet's rotation, we should be almost directly in line with the Fleet by the time we're done mining everything we need." The Captain took a long pull off of his coffee, then sat the cup down purposefully, almost with the authority of a judges gavel... unfortunately, everyone was not impressed. Reid looked skeptically at the holograph, pushing a few buttons to turn the view this way and that, then exhaled his apparent discord, staring at Sky first, then Captain Parnell in a presumptuous manner, primarily because he knew damn well that Sky had pressured his old prodigy for the application of the most unobtrusive route possibility to minimize indigenous casualties.

"This will take too long," Reid complained, "I'm sorry, Captain, I just don't share your optimistic appraisal of the timeframe we are operating under.... Why aren't these paths linear?"

"They are designed to take us *around* the nests.... " He pointed at three different areas of deep, concentrated Crystal density. "We are almost certain to encounter violent opposition anyway, but the last time we encroached on one of these hot zones, we barely made it out alive! We lost 40 crew members, and spent two weeks repairing the ship! We were overrun in a matter of minutes! Even with Mr. Stanton's shield revisions, we would surely be swarmed and lose our ability to see.... We'd be hard pressed to navigate our way out to get free," Parnell informed them, covering a little for the fact that there were those among them who were simply and adamantly opposed to a clean sweep, preemptive campaign for obvious humanitarian reasons.

"We don't have any choice. We lack sufficient fuel to reach our next destination, and this whole system will probably destroy itself in less than a week! *That includes this planet and all its inhabitants!* They're probably dead already, so before we allow ourselves to be overrun, we need to clean-sweep the entire region! It's the only way to be sure that we don't seal the fate of our entire species," Reid iterated, utilizing his authoritative air of self entitlement stemming from years of near dictator-like unquestioned leadership and his own personal flare for the dramatic.

"With all due respect, Sir, there *is* an alternative that won't seal their fate or ours." Parnell looked at Sky with a wink, then back at Admiral Reid. "Our man downstairs is more than just a programmer. He can actually block them from coming into contact with us at all, so long as he is *plugged in* to the shield control." The Captain told them everything about Thor's abilities and his innovations with the shield in the hope that they would understand that he wasn't just planning on reprogramming the shield parameters, but virtually thwarting their entire attack, and that they might see it as a viable alternative. Sky was dying to bring up Thor's findings on what was really causing the unbalance between the planets, but her heart told her that they already knew, and it may do nothing but serve to defeat even the possibility of avoiding a fire bombing to bring it up.

"You're sure he can be trusted?" Reid asked.

"In short, yes. He's got nothing to lose, but everything to gain by cooperating.... It's not even a matter of *trust*. His life is at stake too," Parnell said, looking at Sky, who was nodding in agreement.

"Okay," he agreed, finally taking a deep breath and pausing in apprehension before letting it out and continuing. "We'll use him at the onset of the confrontation and hope for the best, but if anything goes wrong and this doesn't work out, we're going to firebomb the whole area and do this the easy way! Tie your program to all four ships once you've tested it. Do it tonight. We'll be in position to proceed at 0600," the Admiral stated, standing up from the table and stepping back as if to adjourn the meeting.

Captain Parnell, Sky, and both the other Captains stood up as well. "Yes, Sir," Parnell said, saluting the Admiral. He saluted back, and the other three followed suit, preparing to leave the room. Parnell turned to Sky. "Take Mr. Stanton to the live station we set up for him in engineering and help him finish. Call me when it's ready to test."

"Yes, Sir," she smiled, promptly leaving the room. The two other Captains held back, as did Parnell.

There was a long silence, then the Admiral slowly looked up at Captain Parnell. "Do you think she suspects anything?"

"I don't think so, and he will have to be isolated in engineering to pull this off, so he should be none the wiser after it begins. God willing, he will pull this off for us without finding out and having a stroke of conscience, because even firebombs will be useless against the ones who take flight, and there could be way too many to defend against with just our fighters," Parnell said with no sign of remorse on his face.

"If we wait to start mineral extraction until the first attack wave, we should have the element of surprise," Captain MacGregor added coldly.

"Time will tell," the Admiral commented, staring out the window toward the darkening ridge top, "Time will tell. Wait 'til I get back to my ship, then set the new course. Remember, 0600 sharp."

"Yes, Sir."

Sky reached out over Thor's chair and put her hand gently on his shoulder as he sat alone in his computer room working up a system for installation of the program on the other ships. She leaned over his right shoulder, bringing her face right next to his ear, and whispered, "They're going to give you a chance to prevent a catastrophe! Can you really do this? Even if we're overrun, I mean?" For the first time since he met her, she was smiling with her whole being, absolutely and unequivocally in the moment.

"Yes. I _know_ I can." He leaned back in his chair, reached backward over his shoulders, and fondled the side of her hair, pulling her head against his with his hand open wide on the side of her face and neck. He could hear her breathing start to get heavier as her open lips brushed by his ear and softly slid down the side of his neck; her left hand now locked in his.

"Let's go down to engineering," she mumbled through a passionate kiss, unable to pry her lips from his.

Admiral Reid always chose to pilot himself in any shuttle he was riding in. Being a lifelong military man in a mobile fleet, he had spent more than his share of time in the cockpit of just about every type of craft they had, and was damn good, but the main reason he always took the stick was that he was an insufferable control freak. He was actually incapable of letting anyone else become responsible for him in any way. This was a quality that occasionally served him well, but most of the time it only served to pissed other people off.

Captain Ellis and Captain MacGregor were already back onboard their respective ships, and Reid was coming around for final approach behind the Helios, when there was a sudden flash of something passing very quickly right in front of the forward lights! His attention instinctively snapped to his radar screen, which he had been neglecting for a while and just enjoying the manual control, but nothing showed up. He shrugged it off as a small vapor flash from a passing cloud or something and was just starting to drift off and enjoy himself again when it happened again, this time seeming to come from above and flash downward very fast.

"What the... " Reid said aloud, standing up and looking out the small shuttle craft's front window, trying to see downward at what blew by them. His face was almost pressed on the glass when it hit straight on... a massive Sand Dragon slammed into the front of the craft and clenched its window frame from the sides with its huge clawed hands! Reid jumped nearly out of his skin, finally landing almost directly on top of the control stick, causing the craft to pull straight up in a gravity bending vector with the Admiral pinned over the controls and onto the pilot seat on his back, with his neck still bent toward the window, staring the creature right in its huge, penetrating eyes.

Caught in a giant back-flip with the Helios below him, and the Icarus and Achilles coming up from behind, the Admiral couldn't even blink. He was involuntarily caught in a mind-lock with the creature, sharing thoughts completely out of his control. The entire course they had laid out flashed through his mind. Firebombs, fighters, sweep mining, the supernova... all of his knowledge on what was really causing the planetary degradation and everything else of any strategic importance had now been compromised.

He had a flash in return of large groups of indigenous creatures living in caves; wonderful caves, with waterfalls, rivers, phosphorescent light, etc.... Whole families of these creatures coexisting with all other life forms down below.... They were not at all as he'd imagined. They had a sophisticated language, albeit not verbal, but very advanced, art, structure, and even a sense of humor! To his surprise, he also picked up on the fact that they weren't, in spite of their monstrous appearance, even carnivores! They absorbed their nutrients entirely through the water and air of the planet, something to do with the Crystal in its acidic form... as it existed in the deep of the planet's caverns; permeating the water, soil, and air to the point of near saturation.

A proximity alarm started going off. As they reached the top of the long arc backward, he could see, just entering his field of vision, that they were set on an immanent collision course with the Icarus, and coming down fast, right on top of her! The creature, almost as if it had seen the image through his eyes, gave the ship a mighty shove to his right, sending the small craft spiraling in a downward barrel roll in between the two large Carriers, narrowly missing the Icarus's bow. Alive, but now spiraling for the ground, the Admiral rolled backward over the console, grabbing the stick. He focused hard on the terrain farthest away to eliminate vertigo, then pulled hard to the opposite angle and back, slowly correcting the roll and pitch at the same time.

With no more than a few meters to spare, he managed to pull out and back around toward the Carriers. His eyes were instantly and instinctively combing his entire field of vision for the creature, who seemed to have disappeared completely. It was not showing up on radar, and was nowhere to be seen. His heart was racing as he pulled in and locked course right behind the Helios, hailing them to start the docking sequence immediately.

The Captain burst into engineering in full battle dress uniform, unsure what to expect after failing to reach Sky on her communicator, only to find them set up and working through the first live test. While hooking him up with full body electrodes as he insisted, instead of the 4-point visor, she briefed the Captain on their plan. He set up the table top holographic monitor from upstairs to display a graphic representation of shield frequency showing a visual change in color and intensity consistent with what pitch it happens to be vibrating at during that very moment.

"Okay, Captain Parnell, I need you to raise the main shields. I'm going to walk though the entire spectrum."

"Very well," he replied, hitting his belt com, "Shields up, no alert, this is an engineering test."

"Yes, Sir!"

From where they were in engineering, they could hear the hum of the shield generator firing up, reaching maximum in just a second or two. Thor closed his eyes, quickly adjusting to the pitch of the shield. Above the screen, the 3D holograph of the ship was quickly surrounded by a transparent, glowing representation of the shield. The Captain and Sky watched in awe as the color of the shield on screen transformed from a dull yellow-green to amber, then on to purple and deep violet, all seamlessly.

Thor found this connection with the generator to be kind of like an amplifier, broadening his ability to feel his surroundings to a much larger radius than the edge of the shield itself. Though not entirely unexpected, he had no idea how big this was, and it only stood to broaden further once the other ships were tied in. As it was, he could almost feel the planet's surface; the plains, the foothills and mountains in the distance… all were almost visible to his mind's eye.

He felt the sudden sensation that his focus was actually being picked up on by someone else, and then the presence was upon him. He felt it draw near; so clear that even the decision to pull away from the shield at the last second was "audible" to him. The whole thing seemed to work on a similar premise as the common reversal of a speaker into a microphone. They were essentially both the same thing, just different in size and output. He smiled, temporarily shutting down, and told Sky and Parnell about the fly-by, excited that he could read it blind from that distance.

The Captain looked instantly skeptical. "Impossible, I would have gotten-" Just then he was interrupted by the bridge hailing him on his belt com.

"Captain, we just had a fly-by. It looks like he was repelled by our shield before he even touched it!"

The Captain looked at Thor and smiled broadly, "Well I'll be damned! We may just keep you around for a while!" He turned to Sky, "Here's the access codes for the other three ships. Once each set is entered, hail their Commander and get them to accept implementation on their end, then you can add them as a subroutine." He shook Thor's hand, "Good job, kid! Stay sharp, let's get this right the first time! With any luck, we may just get out of this! Sky, you'll be with me. You'll be needed in the cargo bay. If any of them break through, that's

312

our last line of defense! 0600, kids!" He marched out of the room, and Sky paused for a moment, then turned toward Thor to say something.

"What's wrong?" she asked Thor, who was leaning against the wall with a strange look on his face all of a sudden.

"Just a strange feeling... I'm not real sure," he said, a little confused, "There was a presence I felt the night I escaped my cell. I could swear it just touched the shield...."

"But you're not even plugged into the shield right now," she smiled.

"I know! That's what's so weird about it! I guess the field has some degree of continuity throughout the entire ship, but wow, their telepathic energy must be tremendous!" They sat back on the large recliner-style office chair together, looking up through slots in the floor at the level above where he had been working the last several days on this project. This department was actually very comfortable, with dimmer lighting so the instruments and LED's could be read easier, only a small amount of ambient heat and noise; basically just a hum from the shield generator and a few degrees of temperature controlled difference to keep expansion and contraction of the silver encased EMP shielding on all the circuit boards to a minimum.

"Tell me, Thor, was the creature's energy malignant? In any way?" she prodded, pretty sure she already knew the answer.

"Not at all. In fact, I'd go so far as to say it was quite the opposite! Almost as if it was yearning to be understood...." Thor looked at her modestly. "I know what this must sound like," he added.

"Not even! I know *exactly* what you're saying! The one I told you about that I locked eyes with up on deck was the *exact* same way! I tried to tell anyone who would listen, but just got ignored by everyone!"

"Are you kidding? They *want* these things to be monsters! It makes it easy to justify slaughtering them for their resources! To look at them as reasonable beings, worthy of respect, or even fair treatment, slows us way down! Hell, it would mean we would have to actually be fair and humane to these creatures in return, instead of just taking whatever we need, freely, and killing anyone in our path! It makes me wonder sometimes, *what the hell are we fighting for?* Maybe the universe would be better off without our kind in it."

"I don't know, Thor, I just don't know. Maybe it would. Who knows? I guess we fight for the chance that things might one day change... that they might get better, and people will finally have a *real* renaissance," Sky dreamed, staring at the ceiling with a smile on her lips.

"I think you're right. For that to happen, though, we'll need to shed a lot of dead weight and archaic habits," Thor added, yawning. "A big splash of bleach in the gene pool...."

"To be sure," she murmured, slipping off to sleep in his arms, momentarily secure in a completely insecure universe, and for the first time in her adult life, she didn't feel alone.

CHAPTER 35: CRY HAVOC

"Blood and destruction shall be so in use
And dreadful objects so familiar
That mothers shall but smile when they behold
Their infants quarter'd with the hands of war;
All pity choked with custom of fell deeds:
And Caesar's spirit, ranging for revenge,
With Ate by his side come hot from hell,
Shall in these confines with a monarch's voice
Cry 'Havoc,' and let slip the dogs of war;
That this foul deed shall smell above the earth
With carrion men, groaning for burial."

-William Shakespeare

The dream unfolded much as it always did. It was chilly and the sky was grey. The hillside was devoid of most plant life, save for a short tundra covering on the ground with the occasional small flower or patch of weed. Large rocks scattered here and there broke the monotony of the landscape, which seemed to roll on into the distance, unchanged, but for some reason he could not focus on it. Suddenly a loud squawk sounded high above him and he turned his head to see what it was. A majestic bird flew right overhead, gliding smoothly on it's tremendous wingspan, and headed out over the crest of a nearby hill. He quickly followed. Upon clearing the hilltop, he could see a small building standing alone in this barren diorama. He started up the hill toward it.

Almost as if being yanked off his feet by a giant rubber band, he was jolted straight up the hill, stopping abruptly at the front door of the cabin. The door was cracked open a bit, and the house was obviously abandoned, so he entered. The house was cold and dark, but enough light made it in to see around.

A few steps down a dark hallway, he became aware of someone else in the house. It was dark and he could tell that the man was aware of his presence, but did not attack or run. Instead, he seemed to work his way toward the back of the house. For some reason, he did not fear the man, but rather, made a decision to approach him. He kept his distance, turning right as the man went left into a large room, but kept a constant eye on him, as if not wanting him to leave.

He could see his head through the interior windows and over a knee wall, here and there, always looking at him. He seemed to be looking for something. He entered the room where he was standing, and as they locked eyes, he could see that the man was no threat. His curious suspicion was replaced with a genuine desire to communicate, but for some reason no words would come. All at once the man faded into a haze and he was pulled forward again, this time through an open window and back out over the tundra. He looked back to see the man running to catch up, but he couldn't make progress, falling further and further behind until he faded completely into the blur.

He flew on; the hills widening and eventually turning into a vast network of fjords and islands. He swooped down, flirting with the tips of the tallest trees; reaching up like fingers desperately trying to touch the sky itself. He sent out an ear piercing shriek, letting the entire world know of his dominion over the heavens, then continued down through the top of the valley, heading toward the ocean. Seeing the smoke rising up from a series of small fires, he followed the edge of the fjord to investigate.

A small village was peacefully going about its toils for the day, boats sailing in and out of the small harbor while people scurried about. He banked to the right, out over the inlet and let out another shriek… this one a warning to the ravens and gulls converging here and there over the village, waiting for their scraps. A lone child lifted her head to see where the noise came from, shielding her eyes from the sun with one hand as she squinted to make eye contact with him.

Suddenly a loud noise and vibration came without warning from behind. He was swept quickly into a vortex of turbulence by the passing of a group of flying ships… manned fighter jets possessing technology far beyond that of the peaceful villagers, swooping down in attack formation then opening fire with some kind of blue light discharge of energy, nearly eradicating the entire village in one strafing attack. Explosions, screams, and the roar of the fighters echoed off as real as any waking experience, then he is hit. Straining through the pain and smoke, he could see the strange world spiral closer and closer as he descended toward the water, out of control.

The pain was excruciating as he made contact with the surf near the shoreline, pulling up into a shallow enough angle just in time to save himself from a devastating impact. He started to sink, unable to move, then a hand reached out to him. He reached up to grasp it, and saw her through the hazy surface of the water. Once again, there is the sensation of being pulled off balance by an invisible force, then jarred awake in a cold sweat, breathing heavily.

His outer eyelids opened suddenly as he sat up, at first unable to get his bearings. He had this dream many times in the last year or so, but this time was definitely the most realistic and the most progressed. There was almost no distinction between the dream and the very fabric of his reality. He finally realized the hand he saw, the girl just above the surface, was her! The one from the ship. The one who looked at him with empathy. The one who was different....

As the phosphorescent light from the algae in the water and fungus growing on the stalactites and stalagmites of the cavern gradually became bearable to his photosensitive eyes, his inner lids slowly opened and things finally came into complete focus. He looked down at his waist. The young child that he was blessed with when the strangers took his mate from him was curled into a ball, purring loudly as she slept; utterly peaceful and content in the nescience that everything they knew, their entire existence, was about to be forever altered.

Thor was jarred awake to the sound of battle sirens and flashing lights. He had been dreaming the same recurring dream as always, but this time he fell, hit by the fighters, and was pulled out of the water by Sky. Though he had never had the dream progress to this level, he realized that he had dreamed of her before... probably many, many times. To see her in this dream not only seemed right to him, but it seemed extremely familiar, almost like a very clear déjà vu.

The room came into focus, and he realized her hand was really on him, shaking him awake, not pulling him out of the water. He was a lot further under than he thought. He nodded at her and she bent down, gave him a quick kiss, then stepped back, tightening her utility belt. She was already in full battle gear. Thor smiled, a little taken aback at how sexy she looked like this.

He shook his head, forcing his eyes to focus, and pulled both hands through his hair to straighten it out of his eyes. He took a deep breath, realizing the responsibility level that was upon him, then exhaled loudly, centering himself. Out the various windows and catwalks around and above them, people were running this way and that on their way to their respective posts, all of them seeming very focused and single minded in their efforts, much like worker bees in a great hive. Thor was immediately impressed with their apparently high level of professionalism and efficiency.

This was the first time in his entire life he had been part of anything this big, and he couldn't help but feel a little bit of pride; a sense of unity and purpose much different than the closeness and like-mindedness of the North Clan. It was a bit humbling. She could see the difference in his eyes, the difference in his very aura, and actually mistook it for fear.

"Stay focused... you'll do great! I'll be holding the main cargo bay... *don't worry!* I'll see you after," she insisted, hugging him tightly. "Good luck!"

"You too... be safe! I *better* see you after!" He shouted at her as she darted out of the room. He stood up, tightening the limited gear she had brought for him, then sealed himself in the room and started putting on the electrodes as they had decided. Once he was finished, he hit the belt com attached to his uniform, and hailed Parnell.

"Captain, Stanton here... I'm ready to go. Green lights all the way," Thor said loudly, not sure how sensitive the communicators were.

"Parnell here. What lights are green? What do you mean?"

319

He suddenly realized these people had never seen a car, let alone a traffic light, and wouldn't get the analogy. "Sorry, that's a figure of speech. A little before your time. All systems go! Proceeding as planned. How's that?"

"Roger that. We'll only contact you if we have a problem. Bridge out."

"Stanton out."

Sky entered the bridge, armed to the teeth, with full body armor and head gear on, reminiscent of the militarized riot cops of the late 21st century. She marched directly up to Captain Parnell with extreme purpose and stood fast, saluting him. "You hailed, Sir. Where do you want me?"

He returned her salute. "Lieutenant Commander Davies.... Plans have changed slightly. I want you outside. I want you to hold the deck. Only fall back to the cargo hold if we're overrun. Coordinate as many men as you need.... If the shield fails, nothing gets through!" He paused for a moment, taking a deep breath. "Look, Sky... just keep 'em locked and loaded and in position. With any luck, we won't have to fire a shot."

"Yes, Sir," she said, saluting again, then taking a step back, pivoted on her heels, turning 180 degrees and walked off the bridge, hailing her subordinates to meet her with a detail of 50 of their best soldiers on the main deck.

"Captain, we're coming over the last set of dry hills now. We'll be in range to start mining in 8 minutes," said one of the helmsmen.

"Very good. I'll notify the Fleet," he said, stepping over to the communications terminal.

Thor was sitting in seiza in the center of the room, hooked up to the electrodes, manipulating the shield slightly in order to get the feel of things in preparation. He was only tweaking the shield parameters ever so slightly, just enough to establish "contact" with the system. He was mainly trying to feel *outward* the same way he was tuned when felt the presence before it hit the shield last night. He expanded his focus and sense of awareness to the point that he was almost able to *see* the surrounding terrain.... *Something wasn't right.* He was suddenly overcome with the awareness of being read himself... and not by just one entity.

Captain Parnell watched on screen as they soared slowly over the last row of hills. He noticed what looked like a very dark cloud stretching across the sky in the distance. Squinting hard, he started to realize what he was actually seeing. "Oh my God," he said, quietly, closing his eyes and taking a long, slow breath. When he reopened them, he had to blink a couple times just to be sure he wasn't dreaming. Hovering about 500 feet above the surface of the planet were literally thousands of the creatures, waiting directly in the path of the Carriers, as if they anticipated this exact course of action. Before he could give the order to warn the other ships, they started to move. He hit his belt com for Sky. "Lieutenant! Form ranks! It's an ambush!" he yelled.

"We see them! Give me all guns on deck! Prepare to defend yourselves!"

Parnell hailed Thor on the com, "Stanton, I hope you're as good as you say you are... " he paused, and Thor interjected, already on top of things.

"I know! I feel them! Just keep the ships close together... If we separate, I'll lose contact and can't help them! Tell them to stay with us!"

The massive swarm had advanced and were moving fast toward them, blacking out the entire sky. The Captain was arguing with Captain Ellis, who didn't understand the full nature of the protection Thor brought to the table. *"Sir, with all due respect, this is suicide! We should regroup and rethink our strategy! We can still outrun them!"*

"Negative. Hold your course!" Parnell yelled back.

"There's too many! We need to retreat!" Ellis desperately whined one more time.

"HOLD YOUR COURSE! That's an order!" Parnell shouted, losing his patience. "Stanton... how are things looking?" he asked with growing concern.

"I feel them... Captain, and they're aware of what I'm doing!"

"What?!" the Captain yelled.

"Yeah! Anyway, I'm gonna beat 'em, I got this... just let me stay focused!" Thor said, a little frustrated already.

"Roger that. Remember, failure is not an option! The cost would be catastrophic!"

Sky stood on the first level mezzanine, just above the cargo hold bay door, and rallied her troops, as well as the soldiers of the other two crafts, via com link, quickly briefing them on their strategy, but only mentioning the dynamics of the shield defense in vague detail. "...Suffice it to say that we need to stay on guard for isolated breaches or complete failure, but shoot to kill *only if threatened within the shield!* We only need to buy enough time to get what we need and leave. For all others within range, aim for a wing shoulder! When one is injured and starts falling, another one will catch him and take him away... This gets two of them out of our hair. We can't possibly get them all, so choose your shots wisely!"

Halfway through her speech she saw a squadron of fighters take off from the flagship in a strange formation and head straight at the oncoming swarm. A squadron of bombers took formation right behind them, arrayed around a central one, then another squadron of fighters, hanging very close behind. *What the hell are they sending bombers for,* she thought, *they've   already taken flight.. They must be headed for the nests as a decoy to draw them away from the Carriers....*

The fighters tightened their formation around the bombers just as the two opposing forces slammed into each other 500 feet above the surface like two medieval armies rushing the battlefield. The ships broke right through the center of the swarm, using their stronger frontal shields and a barrage of artillery as a battering ram. The sound was horrific. The crushing of bones and tissue, combined with the cries and roars of the creatures and the engines created a demonic symphony the likes of which no one on board any of the Carriers had heard before.

One of the fighters near the front made the fatal mistake of trying to bank left and dodge a particularly large one and failed catastrophically as the creature slammed into his underside, causing a wide fuel explosion that caught three of his comrades on fire; spiraling down to the planet's surface engulfed in flames and thick black smoke. The sharp ray of light from the third sun, coming up over the ridge, was just enough to distract another pilot who didn't get off a stunning shot to the creature in front of him, resulting in a collision that penetrated his shield at a combined speed of over 700 mph, causing the creature to emerge through the backside of the skewered craft in pieces before it even exploded.

From the decks of the ships, as the crews watched on, the swarm looked like a funnel, turned in on itself in the center as they gave chase to the pack of ships doing the frontal damage. At first it appeared to be working, and the first mining preparations were being made, but before anyone could so much as sigh with relief, the outside of the swarm had begun to roll back out, spreading as wide as the sky itself, and closing in fast.

Thor tensed up with the sudden realization as they advanced, then closed his eyes and prepared himself... he breathed in through his nose, out through his mouth, re-centering himself yet again. *There were so many....* He could keep most of them out, *but for how long?*

Inaccurate gun turrets from the side walls were already blasting randomly into the vast haze of attackers, but even divided nearly in half, there were more than the eye could see, swooping down beneath them to attack the underside of their ship while the bulk of them swarmed around the convoy in a circle, much like the Indians of the American Plains circling a wagon train. The soldiers stood vigilant, watching in awe as the overwhelming force closed in around them, choking their view of the outside, until all at once, they were upon them.

The battering was comparable to a major earthquake as they smashed into the energy field and the underside of the ship, causing a number of soldiers to lose their footing entirely and flail around the deck of the ship like fish out of water. Those still standing or kneeling in prone position opened fire maniacally, completely stripped of the clarity of mind necessary to aim at all. Death blows were being struck left and right, but they just kept coming, slamming incessantly into the shield like golf ball sized hail on a convertible.

As much to its own surprise as to the surprise of the crew, one of the creatures broke through the shield, disbalanced with hostility, followed immediately by another, also seemingly surprised by its own success. It flailed across the deck in a frenzy of blind rage, slamming into machinery, structure, and soldiers like a pinball before coming to its senses and grabbing a soldier who was close to the edge by his head and yanking him over the railing. Sky's pistol shot pierced him square in the back of the head, but it was too late. The others, pulling the man from the other side of the shield, already had him in their grasp and ripped him in three different directions before disappearing into the swarm, narrowly evading a barrage of fire from the enraged and horrified crew.

The second creature was coming right for Sky at a hellish rate of speed. Keeping herself absolutely centered, she locked eyes with the creature for just an instant before blasting him right in the face at point blank range with her high powered plasma rifle. His head exploded in every direction as the decapitated body slammed into her so hard it sent her reeling right through the line of soldiers behind her, and into the closed steel doorway to the cargo bay. Dazed from the impact, she scrambled to her feet, shaking off the soldiers that were trying to help her up. "Help *them!*" she yelled, pointing at the front line, who were still frantically trying to blast through the solid canopy of creatures glued to the shield over the bridge tower.

Out over the orange sand, now riddled with the fallen, the remaining fighters, having broken through the bulk of the swarm, pulled in tighter to the bombers who were tail-gunning hard at the concentrated mass pursuing them like a heat seeking tornado. They hooked upwards, and slightly back on their previous course, rolling over to reorient themselves to gravity, then started dropping bombs, not at the nests, but directly on top of their pursuers, seriously disorienting them as the bombs hit them head-on, annihilating five to ten of them per hit; their line degrading as fast as the ships climbed. The ships reached a plateau elevation and leveled off, still dropping bombs, but concentrating their forward fire on the swarm in the direction of the Carriers. It was then that the center bomber, an unmanned drone, broke away from the squadron, completely unnoticed, and shot up to an elevation far above the battle, where it came to an abrupt stop, hovering in the clouds and mist.

On the deck of the Phoenix, they were taking a beating. Shield breaches were happening with greater frequency, each time claimed more and more lives, some even due to crossfire from the panicked and fatigued soldiers desperately trying to hang on against a seemingly perpetual flow of aggression.

The Captain gripped the console anxiously, eyes glued to the monitor; unable to help as he watched his men torn to shreds by the relentless foe. He could hear the call come across the radio to the Helios from the returning fighters... *"Coming in for final approach. The package is in place."*

"Roger that, Leader. Spread out and strafe close to all the ships on your way over... Try to draw them off of us, then get as far away as you can!"

"Roger."

Her eyes widened as she heard the sound of the approaching fighter. "Cease fire!" she ordered, afraid of stray shots hitting the ship. The sound was deafening as it roared right over the deck, within a few feet of the shield, still crawling with creatures. All at once, they peeled off like a blanket, giving chase to the pair of ships who were already splitting up and veering toward the opposite horizon.

The Captain hailed her on her com, *"All hands inside! Clear the deck and seal the doors behind you!"*

"Roger that. Davies out," she called out, then waved toward the main entrance, yelling at the top of her lungs, "Everyone inside! NOW!" Seeing their growing reinforcements already closing in, she was a bit puzzled, but did not hesitate.

The control had been hit for a Fleet-wide, high priority announcement, as the voice, most likely that of Admiral Reid, was emanating from every loudspeaker, room com, and personal com on every ship. The message was unmistakably clear, and got everyone's undivided attention immediately....

"Attention all personnel. Detonation in 10," the Admiral called, and hit the button, causing a small light to start flashing on the control panel of the drone ship, still hovering high in the clouds above them. Thor gasped as he became aware of what was transpiring.

At that very moment, down on the surface of the planet, the lone creature had the same *exact* notion. It was clear to him that this was not just a vague coincidence, but a very localized phenomenon of mental connectivity between himself and the human. It was stronger than the hive-based collective intuition he shared with the rest of his race.... Somehow, they were of one mind. He could see clearly in his mind's eye what was about to happen, and could even *hear* a voice counting it down. He looked straight up and saw it, glistening high above the clouds. He knew he couldn't get to it in time. He scooped up the fallen comrade he was assisting and fled for an opening in the rocks, leading down into the catacombs below.

"Power down!" the Captain shouted over the ship's loudspeakers. She had just escorted in the last soldier, wounded badly and being helped by two others, when she heard the Admiral's voice over the speakers.

"Five... Four... "

"What the...?" she mumbled as the lights went off.

"Captain, this is helm! The Achilles is not where she's supposed to be!"

"Three... Two... "

*"*Mother fuckers!*"* she could hear Thor yell as he ripped off the last of the electrodes in a rage, his com still on and tuned secretly to her frequency as well as the Bridge.

"One."

There was a flatline tone sounding in the cockpit of the drone bomber, then an unimaginably bright flash and a spherical halo displacing the vapor forming the clouds. It shot out instantaneously in a radius of pure destruction, reducing everything in its path to particle matter. It blew away the tops of some of the peaks and foothills to form a giant, perfectly concave crater corresponding to the bottom part of the spherical shockwave.

Then, from within the explosion, another reaction had begun. A massive fireball emerged, billowing outward with plumes of smoke and ash that kept expanding outward in every direction, well past the initial radius of the shockwave. The initial electromagnetic pulse disrupted the anti-gravitational properties that kept the giant ships afloat and they dropped suddenly, then were slammed sideways by the force of the blast, which literally fried through several layers of creatures before hitting them.

Onboard, all who weren't secured in harnessed chairs instantly floated about five feet off the floor as the ships began to drop, then were slammed sideways into walls, doorways, control panels, and each other. The Achilles, having drifted out of position just before the blast due to the overloading of its shields by the flood of creatures swarming upon them during the fight, reeled sideways, directly into the belly of the Icarus, who was busy trying restart their engines after the initial EMP. They were literally cut in half, giant pieces of the flaming ship flying in multiple directions, causing the catastrophic explosion of the Icarus, as well. Both ships exploded in a fiery cataclysm, jarring the Helios and the Phoenix back the other way.

The engines re-fired, almost in unison, on both ships. With antigravity and internal environmental controls back online, the lights flickered on, and people scrambled to their feet, having been knocked back down by the secondary blast, and started running to their respective posts. Sky staggered up, lifting one of her men to his feet as well. Injured and dead bodies riddled the corridor. She started walking for the bridge when the Captain hailed her on her belt com.

"Sky, do you copy?"

"Right here, Sir, go ahead!"

"Stay where you are and stay battle ready! We may still need you on deck.... There may be survivors!"

"Survivors? Captain, what the *fuck* did we just do?" Sky yelled, stopping in her tracks.

"You have your orders, Lieutenant." Sky slapped the belt com, turning it off, and winced, closing her eyes with her jaw and fists clenched. She knew damn well what happened, and he never said a thing to her about it.

The cave was collapsing all around him, as he leaned over the small child, still shielding her from debris as she drew her last breath, and slowly but painfully exhaled. He looked up, his eyes turning nearly black, and stared into the cave, roaring so loud he caused it to tremble all over again. There were dead and dying everywhere, trapped and bleeding under broken stalactites, boulders, and piles of loose rubble. Some of the ones who got caught outside at the beginning of the blast made it inside, half scorched and dying, only to have the cave in finish them off. The smell of burning flesh was overpowering.

The ceiling started to rumble again and he took flight deep into the cave; the mouth having already collapsed completely and sealed him in. He flew with amazing precision through the maze of underground catacombs. He worked his way sideways, then up through a series of smaller shafts, eventually emerging into a large chamber, lit with phosphorescent algae, to find a disoriented and furious group of survivors. He made his presence known as he approached them, but seemed to have little or no affect on their level of focus. Laying in the middle of the floor, surrounded by her lamenting children, their queen was dead.

Without her collective subconscious binding they were lost, for the most part, reduced to emotional and instinctive thought processes. He was different. He was of her very bloodline. He possessed the power to reason, strategize, adapt, and even wait, when necessary. He possessed higher thinking to a degree rivaling the most prominent human intellect, though only in capacity, as in practice, their race was still considered quite primitive. The others did not, and it was obvious to him that they were about to lose it completely, probably turning on each other when they realized they were trapped down here.

It was then that he saw her. A young female was sitting in the corner of the chamber, shivering with fear. She was obviously with child. He approached her, locked eyes long enough to calm her down, and led her quickly out one of the passages that used to lead outside, opening to the backside of ridge. Since it was shielded from the blast geographically, there was a chance it might still be open to the outside. He was getting all different images from the others as to what had happened, mostly scattered and fragmented flashes of a violent nature, and there were no more injured coming in from outside…. He needed to see with his own eyes how bad it was.

Captain Parnell and his Chief Engineer were scrambling around the bridge pushing buttons and running diagnostic tests. All at once, the picture on the main screen lit up, and communications were restored. Though it was daylight on the planet's surface, tons of dust and debris had kicked up from the surface, forming a thick haze with random beams of light penetrating through the gaps. Just below and to the right, he caught sight of the Helios, crippled and smoking, with crews already on deck performing damage control and standing watch. There appeared to be no creatures in sight. He looked all around the ship, on each of the corresponding monitors and on the radar screen as well, now also up and running, but no Achilles. No Icarus. He quickly hailed the Helios.

Unsure how to best explain what happened, the Admiral sent them their last transmission from the front screen before the blast. The video message was broken up pretty bad from all the solar activity and the tremendous amount of static in the air, but with some effort, it was cleaned up enough to be visible. They had all watched in horror as the two ships exploded right in front of them! It was actually on a collision course with the Helios first, and would have probably taken them out, but for the second blast that suddenly shoved them all straight back and caused the smaller two ships to collide.

"Something caused the Achilles to stray off coarse, or none of this would have even happened. We'd be brushing ourselves off and getting busy mining right now!" the Admiral squawked through the interference. *"It's possible they had a breach, like we did.... One of the bastards got through the deck door prior to the blast and killed over 40 of my men and thrashed our control room before we could finally take it down! We're stable, but unable to move for probably three days. I want you to begin mining ops around the clock with double topside watch on high alert! When you're full, transfer your load to the Helios, then go back out for more. I've notified the rest of the Fleet of our situation and we're bringing in all available ships, but they won't be here for two days because of the 3rd day storm. Immediately after it passes

again, we'll have backup, but you're to proceed until then as planned."

"Admiral, what the fuck happened? This is grave! How the hell did they know we were coming, and in time to mount such a defense?" Parnell asked, desperate to make sense out of this. The Admiral turned his head, hiding his shame. He knew the beast on his shuttle window that night read him like a book, and that this costly mishap was probably due to the fact that he didn't tell someone about it, and change strategies. Instead, he did what any politician would do at a time like this... blame-shift.

"Why don't you ask your touchy-feely shield energy guru... if he can read them, maybe he allowed himself to be read right back!" he accused, trying to offer up Thor as a Patsy. The Captain knew better. He knew Reid for too long to not know when he was hiding something.

"With all due respect, Sir, he didn't have a clue what our strategy was. Neither did Sky. Only the four of us did. Who knows what these *things* are capable of.... I just hope we crippled *them*, because we won't withstand another wave like that!"

"Roger that, Johnny," the Admiral said in a more personal tone, *"Anyway, you have your orders, but please shuttle me all the nonessential maintenance and engineering personnel you can spare.... We've suffered tremendous damage."*

"Aye, Sir... Parnell out."

CHAPTER 36: ALL BUT ONE

Thor finally made it to the elevator after working his way through fallen machinery, injured crew members, and dead bodies. He realized now that he had been used to facilitate a planet wide genocide that could have been avoided with some diplomacy and careful, creative thinking. He sensed that Sky was still alive, but he needed to know if she was in on it. His heart told him that she couldn't be, but she *was* bound by a lifetime of conditioning.

Suddenly he got a chill that he couldn't shake off. It was kind of like before, but this time, something was definitely different. There was a mass of bad intent, the likes of which he had never felt in his life, and it was coming at them fast! He knew that another wave was coming for them... soon. Rather than returning to the shield controls, he continued up. "Fuck 'em!" he said out loud. He needed some answers.

The two of them were almost outside the cave when they heard the noise coming down the corridor behind them.

He scooped her up and shielded her with his body inside a small cove to their right, just as the mob shot by them and out of the mouth of the cave in a blind rage. Their war cry was answered a couple seconds later by another pack, descending from a nearby ridge. He instructed her to stay where she was and rose slowly out of the cave to see a horrific site.

The setting suns cast a hazy light on what appeared to be the entire valley floor and surrounding hills riddled with the corpses of their fallen comrades. Thousands lay scattered about, and hundreds of thousands were missing entirely, their scent morbidly branded in the acrid smoke that still filled the air. Two of the ships made up a smoldering pile of wreckage lodged in the orange sand below a third, still in the air, and a fourth one that was moving away, up the valley on their original heading, pulling a steady stream of minerals out of the soil, up from around the bodies, as if they hadn't missed a beat. He didn't know what they needed this for, but there was no mistaking what they were willing to do to get it.

The pack had divided, half headed for each ship. He knew with the power the humans possessed, these disorganized raiders didn't stand much of a chance, but as he watched patiently, thinking of his fallen queen, fallen brothers and sisters, and shattered race, he silently cheered them on... looking for a sign of hope... *looking for a weakness.*

She was halfway down the corridor when the battle sirens started going off again. She rushed back to the bay to regroup with her men. The Captain hailed her directly.

"Sky, we have incoming! Get your men back on deck and watch the aft! Shoot to kill! Something's wrong with our shields and I can't reach Stanton!"

"Roger... Davies out." Just then, the elevator door opened and he was standing there, staring right at her. She held up her hand to him as if to get him to hold on, opened the outer door, then relayed the order to her men. She turned to him, relieved, and smiled a little nervously. His face did not change.

"Is this what our race has evolved to become?" he yelled, with his arms sarcastically out to the sides, gesturing at everything and everyone around him, "Planetary parasites with no regard for life? Why didn't you tell me?" She stood before him with a confused look on her face. The blue twilight combined with the orange sand from below and painted her smooth skin with a violet glowing hue that made her even harder for him to read. He realized then that he had seen her this way in a dream, and the feeling of betrayal was amplified by the surreal memory coursing through his mind. In his dream, she was his captor, and had forsaken him for her own standing very similarly to what he was now feeling.

"I didn't know!" she sobbed, tears filling her eyes. Cocking her weapon, she choked it all back and asserted, "We're still under attack, Thor, *please* man your post and help me save the ship, we'll talk later!" She bolted out the door, instructing her men to form a circle, facing outward and watching the back of the man on their right. The door sealed shut between them and it became dead silent in the cargo bay.

He found his mind rolling through every atrocity man has committed throughout history.... There were countless wars, fought under the guise of nobility, necessity, or humanitarianism, but after shoveling through the endless layers of propaganda-based bullshit, the motive was always greed. Be it for money, power, land or resources, it was still greed, and the part that made it the sickest was the ease with which the people with the real power brainwashed their pawns into doing, without question, all their dirty-work without even so much as an independent thought.

Duty. No need to wash their hands of anything, because they were never dirty. A built-in mechanism for justification without accountability. In mankind's entire existence in this universe, nothing has changed except the amount of destruction we are capable of unleashing in one blast. We still take whatever we want, need or fancy, and destroy everything in our path! He felt sick. These creatures were doing absolutely nothing but defending themselves against an unwelcomed, pirate race, stripping away the very balance of their ecosystem. They destroyed their own planet, and somehow hung on to a parasitic existence destroying others, as well. Do your duty for the good of the *whole*. For most humans, *mankind is the whole*. This is as far as they will ever see....

Outside it was nearing dark and they had spotlights searching madly about. Panning around off the aft end of the deck, she spotted them. They were coming in direct, and a lot faster than usual. She waved her hand out over the knee-wall, feeling nothing. She hit the com, "Captain, do we have shields yet?"

"Negative, something must have happened to Stanton. I can't reach him on the com! I sent two men down to investigate, but you're on your own for now... Brace for a hard fight, Sky, there's around 20 of them!"

They were already in range of her plasma rifle. "FIRE!" she yelled, focusing intensely on one of them. She did not miss. The blast hit the oncoming creature directly in the forehead, and he dropped just enough to slam into the steel knee wall instead of her. He hit so hard, a portion of his body detached completely and struck one of the men behind her in the back, inadvertently saving his life, as one of the creatures that was zeroed in on him missed his mark by only inches, and grasped nothing but air. She quickly fired two shots just above the soldier's head at the frustrated dragon, but missed both times.

One of them to her right swooped low and flew directly at one of her best men, who was firing straight at it the whole way in. It seemed completely uninterested in its own safety, as it pummeled straight into him, driving him directly into one of the steel exhaust ports sticking about four feet up out of the deck. He was crushed by the force; his weapon flying sideways and backwards out of his hand. A huge exit wound was showing on the backside of the large dragon who dwarfed him in stature, covering everything but the dead man's head. The fallen dragon was still making an effort to get up off the soldier when Sky let her rifle hang from its strap and unloaded an entire clip from her pistol at the back of his head as she continued to walk toward him, yelling at the top of her lungs in anguish at the loss of her friend.

She had never witnessed them attacking in this manner before. They seemed completely without strategy, fighting far more aggressively than ever before, but randomly diving in, head first, as if they no longer cared if they lived or died. Some of their diving attacks were nothing short of a Kamikaze run, taking their opponent with them on a direct, frontal suicide attack. They were coming from everywhere at once, and were inflicting heavy casualties on the tiny humans. Looking up toward the rising moons she saw one coming in fast.

She raised her rifle upward and wrapped her left forearm into the strap to steady her aim.... Mere seconds before he would have achieved impact, she took the shot, sending a blast of blue plasmatic energy swirling forward, straight into his exposed torso as he opened his wings and extended his talons for attack. The blast hit him directly in the soft of the chest, just below his ribcage, and blew most of his entrails out of the back of his body through a gaping exit wound, but his angle and speed of approach didn't change an inch!

The skies were clear and the remaining soldiers watched in horror as she spun around to try and dive free of the impact. Unbeknownst to the distracted handful of soldiers, one remaining dragon had climbed over the opposite side and was rushing across the deck straight at her! She turned around and almost ran right into it, fumbling her rifle as she jumped to the side with it hanging from her arm by the strap; the enraged beast snapping at her exposed abdomen as she dove, and missing her by only a fraction of an inch. The sound of its teeth clamping together sent a shockwave of adrenaline up her chest toward her neck as she flopped face down on the deck, scrambling to gain control of her rifle and turn over to face him.

Just as she made it onto her back, his enormous mouth descended upon her again, this time from too close to evade! She closed her eyes; her reality reduced to slow motion as the moment unfolded and she attempted to make her peace with the universe. Instead, the only thought on her mind was Thor. She was sick with regret. She opened her eyes again just in time to see the dragon's mouth closing upon her, then was nearly blinded by the intensity of the blue blast as it wiped him right from her view; his head flailing off to the right as time instantly sped back up to normal.

It took a moment for the sound in her ears to return. First, it was just a murmur, then the voices of her men could be heard over the whine of the engines. They were trying to figure out who took the shot. She rolled her head to the left and squinted through the smoke, blood and bodies and finally saw him…. Standing nearly 100ft away in the doorway to the cargo bay with a plasma rifle in his hand was Thor, staring at her without saying a word. He tossed the rifle out onto the deck and turned back around, stepping inside and shutting the door.

"Captain, he's not down here! But the equipment appears to be functional!" the young programmer reported to the bridge, from Thor's post in engineering.

"Try to re-route the computer to the original shield settings by bypassing the new program! Let's get those shields up, NOW!" he yelled, desperately.

"Roger, Captain! Not a problem," the rookie boasted, sounding quite sure of himself, given the time constraints.

Parnell turned toward the helmsman, pulling his hand over his sweaty brow, and exhaled, "Jesus Christ, where the hell is-" he stopped, turning quickly to see Thor standing in the bridge doorway, staring at him with glazed eyes, as cold as space itself. "Why the fuck aren't you at your post?! Our people are *dying* down there!" He pointed forcefully at the monitor, showing the aftermath of the battle on deck.

Thor took a step toward him and snarled, "Y*our* people are dying down there.... *My* people are *already dead!*" The door quietly whisked shut behind him.

"You-"

"Why the fuck did you do it?" he interrupted, "Why didn't you tell me I was being used to commit genocide?!" he demanded, a step closer.

"You-"

"Why didn't you assholes try to find another way?" In his own cadence of speech, he advanced toward the Captain, who didn't notice him taking two more steps, bridging the gap between them in a single, smooth movement, and breaking his nose with an open palm blow right on the last syllable. He flew up and backwards, sprawling onto the control console. One of his legs twitched involuntarily as if he was on the very cusp of unconsciousness as it hung over the edge of the countertop.

The dumbfounded bridge sentry, standing with a surprised look on his face, hesitated just long enough to find himself without a weapon, and lifted his hand to feel the swollen imprint of the butt of his own rifle across the left side of his face. The helmsman just to his left backed off; arms out to the sides. "Different century, same damn disease," Thor muttered, lowering his weapon and shaking his head in disgust; seemingly unconcerned with the rest of the bridge personnel who looked on with pale faces and gaping mouths. The Captain covered his face with both hands, moaned, and slid off the console to the floor, mumbling to himself unintelligibly.

The freshly uncovered deck monitor revealed a hellish site. From this angle Thor could see the bodies of both human soldiers and the indigenous creatures blanketing the deck. One remaining rogue, a particularly large one with one wing shot almost completely off, was slowly and fiercely ripping one of the soldiers apart with its huge talons. Another soldier, who was rushing in to try to help him, got backhanded so hard that his lower jaw bone caved in completely as he sprawled across the deck on his back, stopping only when he collided into the knee wall with his head.

Then he saw her, struggling to her feet from underneath the decapitated body of the creature he killed, unarmed and stumbling as she tried to rise to her feet, and holding the side of her ribcage with her hand, but rushing to help the screaming man anyway. "Shit!" He yelled, bolting out the door and down the corridor, fearing the worst. If she could put her life so totally on the line for the life of just one of her men, knowing damn well she had no chance for victory, maybe she was worth something, after all.

"Get him!" the Captain yelled, spitting blood and trying to stand, "Get him and bring him to me!"

Before the elevator door was even open, he was running again. *One last turn, and then....* There she was, standing in the doorway, badly injured, but still more concerned with helping her fellow soldiers. She had stopped after the immediate threat had passed to drag two of the injured inside before another wave hit. "What's wrong with the shield?" she asked, painfully, dazed and disoriented, but already moving back through the open doorway toward the deck.

"You're the only one," he stated, his voice steady and completely at ease.

"What?!" she asked, confused as hell, with her attention being pulled back outside, even though it appeared to be over. "Look, just stay out of sight! Security is up in arms about something, so keep that gun out of sight! This may not be over!" He heard footsteps running down the corridor toward the cargo bay, so he ducked just out of sight. There were fifteen armed security soldiers, followed closely by the Captain, still bleeding and twitching his nose and eyes. She glanced at Thor quickly, then back at the Captain, who was approaching her fast.

"Where is he?" Parnell demanded, not ten feet from Thor's hidden position.

"Who?" she asked, actually somewhat puzzled, but starting to piece it together.

"Stanton! He is guilty of high treason, and he's going back to cryo, or facing a firing squad... the choice is his! Now where the fuck is he, Sky?!"

"You people are the ones who should be shot!" Thor said calmly, leveling his rifle at the Captain's head. The others responded quickly, spreading out slightly, and drawing down on him from every angle with their weapons.

"You don't get it!" the Captain snapped, "We've survived this long because we don't question our leaders' decisions. We may have taken a lot of damage today, but without this Crystal, we would *all* have died in space, trying to reach another planet. As it is, we *still* have our work cut out for us!"

Thor threatened him with the point of his gun, raising his voice to near rage, "Do you have any proof of a time limit? Did you ever try to communicate with these beings? You self-serving bastards did nothing but repeat the mistakes of a thousand generations interested only in the bottom line! Question your leaders? Your leaders have the judgment of a pack of rabid dogs, you spineless Kerr! Question your leaders? You should question yourselves!" He threw his rifle on the ground, and spat in disgust.

"Arrest him!" the Captain ordered. Sky stepped forward, reluctantly, eyes showing deep sadness and fear... fear for him. Her gun, which had been at her side, slowly raised to hip level and stopped on him. Her eyes were glazed over with blind obedience. This was the only life she had ever known, but he already meant more to her than anyone had before... in fact, at this moment, she knew that she loved him. She knew she needed to help him, she just didn't know how. For the first time in her life, she had no control.

"Please," she whispered with her eyes closed for a moment.... It was then that he realized he was wrong about her. For as much as it pleased her to find a kindred spirit in this shallow excuse for an existence, he knew she could never be torn from her duty. Her ideals stopped at talking, just as they did for so many others in his life. So very few were the warriors who were willing to throw it all to fate... to take a leap of blind faith in order to substantiate a true revolution for mankind.

No one was willing to risk that pathetic little rock they desperately cling to year after meaningless year and take a chance at manifesting some real change. To challenge the status quo on every level, not just a philosophical debate, like the coffee house sages and the sidewalk commandos he laughed at all his life. She knew he was right. She made all the same points herself, and he thanked God for the soul mate he honestly thought he found, but when push came to shove, he found himself right where he always did.... Standing alone.

He paused just long enough for her to reconsider, then jumped as high as he could, turning 180 degrees and just barely grabbing the lower rung of the guardrail on the mezzanine above the door. She threw her arms out sideways and yelled, "Hold your fire!" He calmly pulled himself up, and walked around the side of the structure that supported the aft watchtower, the tallest point on the ship.

"There's no other way in, he'll have to come back sooner or later," the Captain asserted, arms crossed.

He gradually ascended the 300ft tall tower, pausing occasionally as if to take in the view, both moons casting a violet hue on the planet's surface, as well as the surface of their skin, the same violet skin he had seen on her in his dream. Now the dream made sense... *it was her betrayal.* She traded him for her place among them. He grew enraged at the way everything he cared about had been stripped from him again, then his rage turned to disappointment as he felt his very future dissipate like a breath of smoke into the warm air of this strange place where he would never belong. *Damn, he needed a cigarette....* Halfway up he paused again, feeling the agony of a destroyed race filter its way into his mind. He shifted slowly from disappointment to deep, sullen sadness: the kind that makes one sick from the inside out.

Upon reaching the top, he sat in seiza, facing the oncoming breeze, and meditated on the betrayal his race perpetrated upon this otherwise peaceful species, as well as the loss of his entire family back on earth. It felt like just yesterday he was sitting on top of the tower on the waterfront, feeling just as alone as he did now. She was the one thing that made this situation worth rectification, but now, it seemed, even she was beyond his grasp. She had made her choice. Slowly, he stood, gazing deeper across the plains than he ever had before; deeper within than ever before.

My way
Stand on the platform and breathe
Silence, my only reprieve
Sober looks from the ones who enslaved me
turn to shock as I dive with an arrow's grace
toward a fate much kinder than to keep on living
for the good of a people who see nothing but hate

Perched high on the rocky ledge, just below the ridgeline, with the female nearly asleep from exhaustion at his feet, he watched closely and waited, as one after one, they were struck down. Somehow they were able to penetrate the barriers, but their rage had disbalanced them, and their attack was random and clumsy. Still, by sheer aggression they were able to inflict a pretty impressive amount of damage. Out on the deck of the ships, very few of the invaders were still standing. What he still didn't know was how many were inside.

The pack that attacked the hovering ship was nearly cut in half as they approached by some kind of large deck cannon, but managed to take out about 1/3 of the humans and the last two fighter ships that were still trying to land before they finally fell prey to heavy fire from the soldiers' weapons. The pack that attacked the ship that was still moving up the valley toward him didn't do as well, due mostly to one warrior on deck with a particularly keen sense of focus and determination. He had seen her before. Her energy was more pure than the rest, and at one earlier encounter, he could feel that she was an empath.

She was in great conflict about their presence here, he could feel it. He had let her live, hoping she might somehow get through to her kind. That time was past, he thought, as he watched her deal a death blow with a large knife to the last survivor, who was trapped on deck with a broken wing, still grappling with two other men. He saw her look around quickly, grab one of her injured comrades, then drag him, wailing, through a doorway inside. A couple remaining men looked hastily around, pointing weapons nervously as she emerged to grab another one.

She lingered in the doorway for a moment before emerging on deck, followed shortly by a group of armed soldiers who started looking around for something. There was one in the back who carried himself like a leader. He was covered in blood and yelling something. Then he saw him.... Pointing a weapon at their leader was the one who tuned into the energy field. He was sure of it. He had seen this man's soul, as he was sure his had been seen. This exchange of life energy was commonplace among his people, but he had seen only disjointed traces of it among the humans until recently. He was also present on the deck last night with the female warrior. *But what was this that was transpiring?*

First, it looked like the soldiers were going to kill him, but now he was climbing the ship's tower, his aura rapidly changing in pitch and becoming more pure and more visible as he ascended. The others stood and watched as he kneeled at the top and meditated, stripping away the tones of anger, hatred, fear, and doubt, and at that very moment he could feel what this man was feeling... it was clear. His eyes showed no more sadness as he stood with his arms out to the sides, then dove straight off the tower.

The female let out a horrified scream and rushed to the side, crying out hysterically as he passed by, straight as a meteor, nearing terminal velocity before he even cleared the bottom of the ship's hull. The entire decision making process took less than a second, and he bolted downward off the rock ledge he was sitting on, straight down the rocky hillside on a direct collision course. If only the man was going a little slower....

Thor was finally free. The planet looked absolutely amazing from here, as the ground rushed in, blanketed in violet twilight. He digested the beauty of this place, and then became part of it, merging with his surroundings, until there was no longer any attachment to his earthly body at all. He was finally aware of what it *truly* was to exist unequivocally *in the moment*. He decided to slow his decent by letting his arms and legs out and arching his back. Stricken with a sudden case of delirium, he reached over and pulled an imaginary rip cord, then said, "Oh, shit!" when a chute didn't pop out....

He laughed out loud, suddenly realizing he better start looking for something to aim for. He spotted a particularly nice set of boulders, and was just starting to tilt back into a dive when he felt a familiar presence. Out of nowhere he was abruptly knocked sideways like he had been broad-sided by a truck. A truck with large talons... digging into his legs and ribs, arm and neck. After almost pissing his pants, he quickly realized he had been picked off by one of the dragons.

Leaning almost all the way over the edge of the ship, she had completely lost sight of him. She closed her eyes, wincing in pain, as her cry still echoed through the valley in the distance.

"Stupid asshole! Probably best for him this way, though... Reid would've had him shot by morning," Parnell gloated with a shit-eating grin on his face.

Sky slowly turned to face the Captain with a wicked scowl on her face. "You have no idea what you've done, do you?" she asked, not even waiting for an answer.

"He-"

"He was the most honorable man I've met in my life, you bastard, and you, you brown nosing, boot licking, piece of shit, corporate WHORE! You used him like an expendable pawn, knowing goddamn well he was right about EVERYTHING!" On the last word, she came absolutely unglued, nailing him right across the left side of his head with her right boot; her left hand slapping the right side of his face, trapping him in the attack. Blood shot out of his mouth, along with a couple teeth Thor had loosened earlier, as if she was popping a large zit. He started to crumble forward from the shock in a defensive tuck, so she came down on the top of his skull with her right elbow, flattening him out face down on the deck. To her surprise, and the surprise of the on looking guards who were unsure whether or not to get involved, he immediately started to recover and muster up the strength to get back up. She pulled off her gloves and threw them on the deck, pushing up her sleeves.

"Come on! Get up, you sanctimonious, lying piece of two-faced shit!" she screamed at him, circling around with her fists up while he clambered back up to his feet. "Kill 'em all and let God sort 'em out, huh? Sounds good, asshole! Let's start with YOU!" She lunged at him with a scissor kick intended for his solar plexus, but he blocked it, making her land a little too close to him as he came over the top with a strong right cross to the face. She ducked just out of the way, pivoting away from the punch and under it, and drilled him with a reverse elbow to the lower jaw, immediately followed by the other hand hitting him square in the nose with her palm, breaking his nose further and sending him down again, this time on his back, where she ruthlessly followed up with a football style kick to his exposed groin before he even finished sliding to a stop.

She walked purposefully up to him on his left side, grabbed him up by his lapel, and drug him, beaten within inches of his life already, over to the knee-wall on the opposite side of the deck. She lifted him up like a ragdoll, and draped his limp body hard over the edge until he could see the ground going by below, and stopped, holding him there. "You wanna see who's better off, you prick?" she yelled in his face as he started to regain consciousness, his eyes tearing up, but clearly fearing for his life. "You wanna see who's better off?"

He was trying to mutter something through all the blood, but at this angle, he was practically choking on it as he tried to speak. She pulled him up to her ear. "What's the matter? Got something important to say and no one will listen to you? Oh, you poor thing!" she said sarcastically, throwing him with disgust onto the deck at the feet of the guards, who were now pointing their guns at her. "What are you waiting for?" she yelled at them, "Do it, you brain-dead robots!" She started sobbing, then walked back over to where she left her gloves, and started to put them back on. The Captain was far from coherent, but managed to utter one order to his guards.

"Arrest her!" he said, choking and spitting up blood, "ARREST HER!"

CHAPTER 37: OUT OF THE ASHES

Hovering high above the planet, with the ship far out of sight, the huge dragon slowly lifted Thor up to eye level and opened its inner lids, staring deeply into his eyes. Thor had been borderline telepathic his whole life, able to feel the emotions of animals and strangers alike, having never laid eyes on them before, and then have complex ideas form out of them... in some cases, even words. This was something else, entirely.

His head was instantly filled with thoughts as complicated as any he himself had ever conjured up... images of a civilization of these creatures feeding off of each others' experiences through some kind of collective subconscious... images of a leader: a queen, ruling them and caring for them as if they were all her children. He saw an earlier ship, similar to the one he was just on, indiscriminately dropping bombs on top of a large nest full of females and small children, and he could hear their screams and smell their burning bodies as if he was actually standing there right now... and yes, he could feel their pain.

One of them was this creature's mate. At first she was badly burned, but still alive, then as he hovered over her, trying to console her or help in some way, she convulsed painfully and died right before him. She was *very* pregnant. Locked together telepathically, Thor and the creature simultaneously let out the same gut wrenching, agonizingly loud cry for her. He could feel every bit of this creature's heartbreak and loss. He realized right then that they were not so very different at all. He was choked up with sorrow for this creature, and for his species, after what had just happened. His body went limp in the creature's grasp, as if he no longer felt anything... anything except the shame of an entire race upon him.

"I'm *so* sorry...." he said, out loud. He locked eyes with this creature for a long time, pouring over with a heartfelt show of genuine emotion. The dragon was obviously able to read his thoughts and intentions, and therefore understand his words, because just as if it had already consigned itself to even an inkling of forgiveness or understanding for him, it looked deep into his tear-soaked eyes, relaxed its grip just a bit, then swooped slowly down toward the ridge top it came from.

He came gliding up on the rocks he had been perched on earlier, and Thor, even in the relative darkness, could tell they weren't alone. He didn't get the impression he was being taken as food, or as a prisoner, but since he really didn't understand exactly why, his worst concern on the way down was being seen by a lot of them at once. Upon seeing him, she tensed up and let out a squawk, then backed herself into a niche between two rocks, shaking dramatically. The large one released him, setting him down on his feet out in the middle of the small clearing in the rocks, beside the tunnel.

He immediately turned his attention to her. He held out his hand in much the same way you would introduce yourself to an animal, not meaning any disrespect, but wanting to give her a chance to check him out a little bit before he approached her. The large one stepped toward her, lowering his head to her level, looking her straight in the eyes. She immediately calmed down a bit and stopped shaking, reaching out to touch his outstretched hand with hers. Thor stared deep into her eyes, and could actually see the point at which her feelings were influenced by whatever the large one was saying. He could also tell that she was pregnant. He took a slow step back, so as not to alarm her or put her on the defensive, then smiled. "Congratulations, Mom!" he said, also looking at the male, who was staring at him, obviously surprised that he could tell just by looking in her eyes. The old one nodded at him, then let him know that there was something he had to show him....

Thor was blown away, every time this being attempted to communicate an idea with him, it "sounded" more and more like verbal communication, but *directly into his head!* He continued to speak back in vocal sentences, figuring that maybe this was helping the creature to understand his mode of communication better.

"My name is Thor," he said slowly, pointing at himself, then he gestured at the creature, "What is *your* name?"

The creature nodded in understanding, then tried to respond, *"I am called Erük'FahSallat' Mouldaemom Ar'Khab, or..."* and he nodded, projecting just a notion, or feeling, of very distinct order, that apparently, to his people, meant the same thing. *"Although, we exist on a collective mentality and seldom recognize each other as individuals. Only in mating rituals, birth, and death prayers...."* For some reason, it surprised Thor to hear him speak of prayer. Thor was "hearing" this directly into his head, without the creature uttering a sound, and yet he had his own voice, mannerisms, etc. just as if he was speaking a new language, and improving rapidly.

"Erük'FahSallat' Mouldaemom Ar'Khab, your name is nearly beyond my ability to pronounce... would you mind if I called you *Erük*, for short?" he paused, waiting for a reply.

"No. You may call me whatever you wish. It does not matter."

"Thank you. How long until she has her baby?" he asked, genuinely concerned for their safety, given everything that had happened.

"Soon," said Erük, appearing in body language to be smiling proudly, though it was hard to tell from looking at his predominantly reptilian face, save for his intensely focused and telepathic front viewing eyes. Though they had lived on the sustenance from Crystal and mineral rich water and air for the last several thousand years of their evolution, at one time, eons ago, they must have been carnivores, as would be suggested by their mouth full of sharp teeth, which they now used almost exclusively for fighting. He had a twin row of spikes growing from the front of his face, almost right between his eyes, then spreading out into full blown horns as they crossed over the top of his head to join up with the back-scale spikes between his twin sets of wings. The younger female did not, having considerably smoother skin and only one set of wings, she more closely resembled a sandy-orange colored dragon from the myths of early man on Earth. Both of them had deep, penetrating eyes that seemed to be opaque and dimensionally endless windows to the oldest souls in the universe.

Though not fully able to stand 100% upright, full grown, they stood over 7 feet tall when perched on their rear legs with their back arched upward, as in attack position. Their hind legs were massive, capable of jumping or attacking with extreme force, and their balance was enhanced by the existence of a thick tail, large enough to be used as an effective close range weapon, and the males were covered from head to tail with thick, armored, exoskeletal plates and scales, earning them the nickname "Sand Dragons," among the humans.

"Can all your kind sense things as you do?" Erük asked.

"No. There are others, though," Thor tried to convey without speaking.

"The female?"

"Yes."

"Is she your mate?"

"I thought so. I think she chose them over me...."

"Is that why you jumped?"

"Not entirely."

"Then why?"

"I couldn't bear my part in what was done to you all. I couldn't bear to live for the good of those who did it. That's no future. Then she chose them over me. I had nothing left to lose."

"You have your life. Your life has a destiny. It wasn't meant to end here...."

"How do you know?" Thor said aloud.

"Because I saw you and you are alive," he said out loud in a bizarre voice, blending growls and windy, guttural sounds from deep down in his diaphragm. Thor was blown away. He laughed in amazement, astonished at how seriously bad these beings had been underestimated.

"Can all your kind adapt as fast as you?" Thor asked.

"No. I am from the Queen's direct bloodline, as is she," he said pointing at the female, who was still staring at Thor skeptically from the niche in the rocks. *"Most of the others only function as a hive. I fear for them. The Queen is slain. They are fierce and erratic. We must remain quiet."* Thor felt sad all over again, realizing the irreparable damage the humans had inflicted on these creatures' entire culture... their very future. *"You don't need to carry the guilt of your*

people," Erük insisted, feeling his guilt and probing his mind for the cause.

"Oh, yeah? And why not?"

"Come, I have something to show you," he said, scooping Thor up under his arm and flying down the hole in the ground next to them. Erük flew him through tunnel after tunnel, cradling him tight in his large front arms through the darkness without so much as a bump until the whole labyrinth started to light up. They flew for what seemed like miles, deeper and deeper into the planet's core until Thor could feel an almost total shift of gravity. He all but lost his internal sense of direction and distance as they proceeded until time itself seemed to slow down. Thor guessed that they were very close to the core itself, and though there was no magma or solid iron to be seen, things seemed to also be slowly heating up.

He could see up ahead that the corridor they were in was about to open up into a large chamber, full of light. Erük flew out into the center of the great chamber where there was a large pillar made of clay that spanned the entire height of the room, floor to ceiling. Around it, there was a small pool of water, or river, that seemed to be flowing fast... *in a circle!* Thor stared in amazement. Looking all around the large cave, there was evidence of it everywhere... they had to be in the actual center of the planet!

Water from the river pool was flowing in small streams *up* the pillar, and as he looked higher and higher up, Thor suddenly realized everything he saw around him, the pools of water in the floor, the stalagmites, the holes to corridors leading out, and even the river pool itself, were mirrored on the ceiling, some 100 ft above, yet somehow remained in place from the planet's unique gravity and centripetal force. In all his studies, he had never considered the possible effects of a hollow planetary core, but it seemed that due to its unique composition, over the eons, that is exactly what this one had become. The ironic part was that because of the increased algae in the water, he could breathe better here than on the surface, where he constantly felt out of breath.

"Follow me," Erük said out loud, since he in no way had Thor's undivided attention. Thor looked like a kid in a candy store, but he snapped out of his wondrous daze and followed him. Erük walked toward the column in the middle of the chamber. Thor was amazed at how light he felt in here. The pressure in the air was a little intense, but he felt like he could jump and never come back down. The more remarkable question may have been, why was there any gravity at all?

To Thor's shock and amazement, when he reached the column, he simply adjusted his angle of approach and started walking right up it. Thor leapt over the river, and was right back on Erük's heels. Once on the surface of the pillar, he gained great perspective. The illusion of the room subsided, and now, it appeared to be more of a bridge between walls, with gravitational anomalies and random streams of water covering their surfaces entirely. They walked all the way out to the middle of the bridge, carefully staying out of the water. Something told Thor, without even asking, that it was sacred to them. Erük was treading lightly, as well, and when he reached dead center he stopped, slowly turning to face Thor.

"Look up," he said, pointing Thor toward what now could be considered the ceiling. To his amazement, he saw a series of stones and stone tablets floating in midair around the core of the pillar, not visible from either floor, due to the irregular shape of the pillar itself. They were slowly rotating around the column and spinning around on their own axis. Thor squinted and looked as close as he could at one of the larger ones. It appeared to have some kind of writing on it.

"What are they?"

"Come and see for yourself...." Erük stepped right off the column and floated effortlessly out toward the tablets. Thor followed, and couldn't help but laugh out loud, as the sensation of zero gravity made him feel giddy for a moment. He had wanted to feel this his entire life, and now that he was here, he had to force himself to be serious.

He came out of a nice full front flip with a half twist right behind one of the largest stones, to realize they were covered with some form of hieroglyphics, and elaborate artwork depicting a series of events in their history. The stone in front of him depicted some kind of large flash of light, or an explosion, with many of their kind caught inside the perimeter of the flash. They were on fire, as were many who were on the ground, and in the hills. His heart sank. He rushed over to the next one he could reach, back in the direction they were orbiting from.

It was a depiction of four large birds in attack formation flying toward a large array of their kind. They had an airborne army of small offspring following them, and the two armies were about to collide in the sky above the hills under a dawn sky. He was not seeing a depiction of events of their past... these were prophecies carried by this race for God only knows how long! This wasn't their history... *it was their future!* Erük was hovering, just staring at him intensely, waiting for his interpretation.

If these were in order, he thought, then the next one should be in the other direction from the one he saw first, that one obviously depicting the weapon that Fleet Command set off in the air over the nests. He shoved himself in the direction that the slab would be coming from, both arms outstretched to grab hold of it as it came around before him. His giddy mood was quickly replaced with a recurring sense of guilt and remorse. Erük put his taloned front hand on Thor's shoulder and chest, *"I told you this was not your fault... now there's a very serious reason why we're here...."*

They were both interrupted by the loud sound of wings flapping intensely. Thor pulled himself in tight and ducked behind the massive stone slab from the direction of the noise. Two large males entered the chamber, one chasing the other in a rage. He flew into one wall, bounced back, hit a large outcropping, then darted into an adjacent tunnel, their sound fading away as they aimlessly ran amok. The tattered survivors were turning on each other. "We don't have much time," Erük warned him aloud, waving him over to look at the last stone.

Thor pulled himself around to the front of the giant stone tablet to see what at first looked like Leonardo daVinci's famous artwork of the geometrical formula for ascertaining height based on the measurement of arm span, middle finger to middle finger, as depicted in his four armed and naked Vitruvian Man painting, but with an angel, instead. After looking a little closer, he realized that it was more of a depiction of something of a phoenix, very much human, but also merged with characteristics of *their* race, with it's arms extended toward the heavens, and two more arms out to the sides, rising out of a pile of bodies made up of both species.

He squinted, feeling like maybe he was missing something. The artwork was very coarse, and had weathered hard from condensation, heat and humidity. Looking a little closer, he realized that this probably didn't depict one creature at all, but two or three, as there was a third set of arms with talons for hands, holding the front creature around the waist! These carvings were obviously extremely old, yet very detailed, and Thor couldn't help but notice the strong degree of accuracy with regard to anatomical proportion that had been paid to their detail for a race that had never met, or even seen a human being before their meeting a few short months ago.

"These prophecies have been here since before any of us can remember. It is said they were carved by the very first of our kind, a traveler from the future. It is said that a great seer will come," Erük pointed at the picture of the winged humanoid, *"and he will deliver our race from out of the ashes, to salvation on a whole new world. A world that isn't doomed to destruction by the vengeful hand of the trickster, Li'Ökhí! Once his bonds have been severed, and balance disrupted, he will tear asunder the very stones beneath our feet, the water, drop from drop. The very air we breathe will be swallowed up and consigned by him to oblivion! We are running out of time...."* He pointed a shaking hand at the last stone, an elaborate depiction of what Thor could only guess was the twin Demon Sun, Algol, going supernova, and blowing the entire solar system to pieces. This planet, its moons, and its loyal companion, Sigyn, reduced to nothing but subatomic particles of nuclear waste before Algol turned back in on itself, and imploded into a dense singularity, a new black hole, sucking even the very memory of its existence into the abyss.

Thor wanted to believe that the prophecy stood for something important, something in his control, but he just couldn't wrap his mind around what he and his people had done to this peaceful, intelligent race of beings out of sheer greed and impatience. "You are saying this 'Great Seer' is *me*?" Thor asked, out loud again.

"Who else could it be?"

"How can I save a people who we've already all but decimated?" Just then, the female flew into the chamber, and she was his answer. She was flying toward them across the large open room, looking terrified. Erük looked at him, and as Thor began to understand, he nodded.

"We are a vastly telepathic race, with communal and collective retention, as well as function. If but one of us lives

on, we survive, and will replenish ourselves over time. If one survives, we all survive."

"But that would take centuries of inbreeding... Isn't this a genetic problem for you?"

"Females of our kind are born with child. In order to replenish quickly when our numbers are low, we reproduce, unhindered, until a pureblood mate is found. For us, mating is a process to instill balance and stability, and control our numbers so we don't overpopulate.... When times are good and we are at peace, we each produce and teach to a higher degree only our own replacement, our natural child, which, because of fertilization from a mate, is genetically superior to the others in every way." Thor was absolutely fascinated, especially realizing how large of an effect such a built-in safeguard would have had on the human race's troubles. He had to wonder if maybe God wasn't still experimenting....

They were interrupted by the female, winded from fast flight in her panicked state, coming up to them quickly and trying to convey a message to Erük. He put his front talons on her shoulders, leaned in toward her face, and calmed her down with his mind. Being also of noble blood, she had the ability to conduct herself fully independently of the snare of the collective, which meant her thoughts were her own, as were Erük's, but without the output of the central mind, the Queen, the rest were now leaderless and unpredictable, at best, or so Erük thought.

"There is a large group of survivors coming from across the valley! They were on Hël'Aliil during the attack, and are just returning. They are being led by M'ahk Kaesir Ar'Goevnihiila, the natural son of the Queen, herself!" she conveyed to Erük in their native manner... more ideas than words. He turned to Thor to fill him in. He was staring at the last of the stones before the final explosion: a picture of three humanoid figures, the one in the center with wings, holding

359

hands on the back of one of the large birds from one of the first motifs, probably signifying their ships, but this one is literally rising up out of the flames below, like a phoenix, and heading toward the third planet out in a single sun system. This was the final prophecy still to unfold before the great explosion consumed the solar system, and he was starting to understand it.

"The Queen's natural son returns with a large group of adolescents returning from *Hël'Aliil*... a M'ahk Tehríll rite of passage. We need to leave quickly and carefully." He wrapped Thor under his right rear wing, completely covering him from sight, while still maintaining the ability to maneuver through the dark, twisted passages that led them here.

Thor noticed fairly early on that the air was actually much easier to breathe the *deeper* into the labyrinth they descended, as now that he neared the surface, he found himself short of breath again. This was due, in part, to the acres of phosphorescent algae that not only supplied oxygen, but light to his new friends, as well as the many transparent creatures swimming the pools and streams, and the myriad of different life forms crawling and flying about down here.

It seemed the indigenous life forms of this planet had more shielding from the binary sun than just Sigyn, as most of its species seemed to be subterranean, and due to the soil's complex chemical structure generating it's own heat, it became almost unnecessary for any of them to expose themselves to the dangerous surface, giving them the greatest natural defense of all... obscurity. This single factor was largely responsible for the grossly inaccurate assessment of the quantity of indigenous life on this planet by the invading humans. Without subsurface scanning being operational, there was simply no way for them to know just how many of what kinds of creatures called these catacombs home.

The gravitational anomalies present here and on the surface kept them blind to the use of scanning equipment, but it also made physical navigation nearly impossible for anyone who wasn't raised here. Even with the benefit of a native guide, Thor was getting totally turned around. At times, it was hard to know which way was up and which was down, due to the erratic gravitational flux present in the system, not to mention the fact that they were navigating their way back out from what was undoubtedly dead center of a planetary mass about 1/2 the size of Earth. Instinctively, he was still doing his best to memorize the course anyway.

The streams from just below the surface seemed to pour down through the caverns, then pick up centrifugal momentum as well as heat, and simply rise back up another channel in the form of a spring or geyser, adding to the conductive nature of the planets interior furnace, but making it difficult to tell which way they were traveling. Sometimes they would be flying at what felt like a nearly horizontal vector, then suddenly plunge into a pool of water, then back out the other side. It was a maze that even the most intuitive of creatures found himself second guessing.

They managed to work their way out without incident, staying away from the other party by heading out a series of old tunnels that would put them just behind the Harvester by nightfall. If he understood what they were up to, it would mean they would be on their way back with a full load by daybreak, keeping close to the other Harvester in a tight, elliptical tour. Thor knew now, if they were to have any hope of escaping the fate that now lay before them, they would have to get onboard that ship.

They cautiously emerged from the catacombs to a gorgeous site. There was a haze just to the east that after close examination turned out to be the Phoenix heading out for a final sweep, as anticipated, leaving behind the still crippled and fuel-drained Helios to wait for their return. This just added to the profound beauty of the sunset that was transpiring before them. Thor saw a particularly tall peak, sticking up out of the ridge they inhabited, and immediately started climbing to the top, where he could see a perfect outcropping to use as a crow's nest, as well as a possible bed for a couple hours.... In places, the rock was softer than anticipated and he almost called out for help to Erük, who was watching closely, but after pulling it off on his own, the view was all that much sweeter.

As he centered himself and became part of his new surroundings, he might have figured this to be unlike anything or anywhere he had ever seen. Not so. In fact, as daylight gave sway to more and more pronounced silhouettes and long shadows over the plains, he was suddenly light years away... back home, sitting under the high point of the overpass, thinking about Kait. She and Sky were so much alike that they seemed to be the same person, and he missed her terribly. He wondered where her head was at... if she was still alive, and what would happen if he saw her again. He couldn't help but feel a little sick for judging her so harshly.

Standing high on the top edge of the natural precipice, overlooking the wilderness of colossal peaks and valleys with his back to the open plains, he relaxed his eyes and let the scene become what he truly longed for: what he actually missed with a sense of home-sickness he had never felt before. The tops of the tallest mountain peaks became buildings, shrouded in a neck-high ring of hazy cloud cover and detailed with windows to a thousand little dramas that had long since closed their doors for the day. The mesas and plateaus of sand and rock twisted and worked their way toward the underground like the overpasses and viaducts that made up his sky for so much of his life.

He stared into the deep valleys, blanketed in darkness, and they, too, were still alive, radiant with the energy and unseen movement of nocturnal predators going about their rituals in the shadows. The foothills of the foreground became a blur of waterfront structure, marinas and coastline shops thinning out into the sand and boulders of the coastline. As he gave in to gravity and found a comfortable niche in the outcropping to rest his head, he stared deep into the heavens of this alien world. Looking up, he could only remember one time in recent history when he could see so many stars! Staring off, deeper into space than ever before, he wondered how many worlds have come and gone without our influence, without our infection, and how many more we would still be allowed to influence. *How many more would we need to destroy?*

He allowed himself to linger in between worlds for a long time, imagining what it would be like to live in a world as pristine as this one was before *we* came; a world whose value was never quantified, but rather nurtured in symbiosis by every inhabitant fortunate enough to call it home. The wonders of its true nature had been unmolested by humanity for so long, frozen in still life artistry, yet alive with vibration; the ebb and flow of its collective spirit resonating in perfect pitch the harmony of thousands of individual tides, each no less grand than the whole, itself, alive for eons in perfect balance, yet brought to the very cusp of annihilation in the relative blink of an eye.

He stared far into the night, past the tops of the towers to the edge of the rings of Sigyn, and caught sight of something rare and wondrous, indeed. Flying gracefully, as if under the oceans back on earth, he saw dozens of creatures flowing in a graceful flock upward toward the rings of the planet, itself. He could tell, even from this distance, that he was seeing something of tremendous importance....

They appeared to be an ethereal, spirit-like version of the manta rays of Earth! Coming from somewhere down in the planet, they made their migration under cover of night all the way across the space between planets to the very rings of Sigyn, herself, where they seemed to glow intensely, then blend into the color of the rings, as if they were but water being assimilated into a larger pool. It was purely magical, and drew him into a deepened trance, totally calm and at peace with his surroundings, even though their success or failure meant not only their lives, but held in the balance was the very existence of both species. Leaning back onto the inclined ledge, he slowly faded off, high in his nest, with his mountain range as camouflage for their impending ambush.

Chapter 38: The Open Arms of Madness

He felt like he did little more than doze off for a couple minutes, but it must have been hours. He yawned, opening his eyes to a most intense sunrise. The system's third sun was looming ever brighter out from behind Sigyn, who was in full view overhead, casting a strong violet hue on everything in sight. Her rings were visible as a halo, evenly spaced for 360 degrees, and brighter than he had ever seen, with sunlight filtering through them, nearly engulfing the entire sky. The light that permeated the sand was being reflected back down from Sigyn, herself, as Algol was in a state of total eclipse. This was the start of a new solar cycle, and the intensity had been increasing due to the relentless mining upsetting the balance between planets.

Thor realized this tall rock tower was probably not the place to get caught when the quakes and meteors started in. He looked far out on the horizon in search of the Phoenix. He didn't see it right away, because it wasn't letting off a distortion haze into the air, which he quickly realized meant that it *wasn't mining anymore. It was carrying a full load!* He spotted it on what appeared to be a return trajectory to the Helios and smiled, as this meant it would be passing right in front of them very soon.

He started sliding down one of the more gradual faces of the tower on his feet, positioned as if he was riding a snowboard and carefully keeping his toes out of the loose dirt as he slid on his heels, faster and faster. He turned his feet sideways, realizing the tower was about to drop off straight down and he was about to run out of road, when Erük suddenly appeared from below, flapping his giant wings softly, so as to just hover at his new level, offering him his backside. "Nice timing, my friend!" Thor called out to him.

"I've been listening to you since last night," Erük assured, slowly gliding down toward the ground with Thor sitting proudly on his back, *"but how do we get on board that thing without being seen?"*

"Dragon Eggs," Thor exclaimed, telepathically.

"Dragon *what*?" Erük asked quizzically, with just a hint of defensiveness in his voice.

"Sorry, I forgot. On board, when I helped with the mining, we were bombarded from time to time with what they referred to as Dragon Eggs," Thor explained, *"I can see now that you give birth to your young, and do not lay eggs at all, but they thought that was what they were. They explode when they come in contact with our shields.... We kept running them over and sucking them up from underneath, causing many fires... ring a bell?"*

"Yes. They are the eggs of the V'eíshnioü Larva. An extremely important worm that later makes an exodus to the halo of Sigyn to become one with the rings, and die. There have been those among us who have used these eggs as a weapon against the ships, but to most of us they are sacred, and protected at all cost."

"Ahhhhh, the Manta Rays I saw last night! I've never seen anything so beautiful! Why are they so important?"

"It is they who produce the Crystal. The acid veins are solidified bile produced from eating the blades of grass that grow on the sand, then excreting the sand back onto the ground. We depend on this to survive!" Erük responded, *"Even their exodus plays a part in the delicate balance that keeps this planet in harmony with its sister."*

"Yes, I can see it clearly... what is given from one side must be replaced. The shards and meteors broken loose from the solar storms! They would cause the planet to continue growing in mass while the other was depleted, it's not just about the mineral content and magnetic anomaly... It's just like what is kept in check between the two conflicting sides of Algol by Skaði!" Thor looked like a giddy scientist, discovering a new element. He looked over at Erük, who didn't share his enthusiasm, then said out loud, "Then it pains me to say it, but we may need to sacrifice a few to pull this off, because I can't think of any other way to get onboard without being noticed!"

"Nor can I," he responded, "but how will they get us onboard?"

"Whenever they start getting sucked into the shield on the underside of the Harvester, they explode, causing a lot of damage to the collection device, as well as the undercarriage of the ship, itself. In order to avoid this, they always order the shield to be diverted away from the bottom until they are clear of the problem. The eggs are then sucked into the dividers for waste removal without exploding, then separated from the rest of the soil, along with any other large debris. We enter through the mining ports when the shields are down, then take the ship from within." Thor held his hands out to the sides, palms up and shrugged, "What do you think?"

"I assume you know how to get free of the equipment once inside, right? Is this dangerous?"

"Not as dangerous as not doing it! I know what we have to do. It's just a matter of timing... trust me." Erük looked at him scornfully, one eye squinted, and the other one right on him, open wide, brow raised high. "I know. I fucking hate it when people say that to me, too," he laughed. Erük nervously imitated his laughter, which made Thor laugh even harder.

They waited quietly, as still as the surrounding rocks, covered with sand to hide their heat signatures from the infrared scanners onboard the Phoenix. The young female, Ar'Yiisah, carrying in her womb the future of their entire race, was staying close to Erük, who had taken on the role of high protector of their royal bloodline, now consisting of himself, and her, the future queen, and her unborn child. As long as there were at least two, her metamorphosis could be completed, and their race could live on, the entire knowledge gained by the race through the ages passed on through the collective subconscious to each new subordinate, along with the instinct and experience of every individual who ever existed.

This was what made them special; unique in a vast universe. This was their immortality... *their link to God.* To them, there was no Heaven, no Hell, and no real afterlife. They found purpose in their existence through the understanding that everything they learned, everything they experienced in life, essentially everything they *were,* would live on through the others and be added to the collective. Even their bodies quickly became part of the ecosystem, and were inadvertently ingested by the living in the form of Crystal and minerals in the water and air.

As the ship drew closer, she became frightened, and began trembling. Thor reached out, trying not to unearth himself too much, and put his hand on her shoulder in an attempt to manipulate her energy level and calm her down.

The moment his hand came into contact with her, he was overcome with a flash: a vision of violence taking place involving Erük... He was being hurt badly, and was in excruciating pain... then it was gone. Just a one second premonition with no real detail, but it seemed as real as any memory in his head. He gasped, wide eyed, and turned to Erük, unable to speak.

"I've seen it too," he said, *"I'm not sure what it means, but she is a seer."*

"Not sure what it means? I'll tell you what it bloody means! It means we better come up with another plan!" Thor exclaimed.

"There's no time... besides, whatever happens, it is my karma. Sometimes the reason for a vision isn't to stop it from happening."

"Then what is the reason?"

"To choose to accept it. You cannot be a martyr and a victim at the same time...."

"Don't be a martyr! You're race needs you. Fuck that... I need you."

"Need me... For what?"

"You're the only friend I have." Thor smiled at him, and for the first time, he saw what felt like a genuine smile come from him.

"Don't worry, my friend... I'll be fine. Now, let's get this done!"

The hum of the ship was almost deafening now. Its giant hull starting to black out their view of the sky as it loomed overhead with its colossal engines pulling in loose, Crystal rich soil and expelling spent sand, stripped of all fuel necessary for the continued repulsion from the planet's gravity. An energy shield was in constant place underneath the ship, shielding it from large debris, coincidental ground contact, etc., but unfortunately, Thor could never get a steady read on its pitch, due to the constant flux of static electricity that bombarded the field. He was sure this would prevent them from being able to just "tune in" and slip through their defenses, so the plan was to hit them with a series of buried eggs, wait for them to drop the bottom shield and pull them onboard, then slip through undetected into the material hold. They had the eggs all laid out along the course they knew the ship would be bottle-necked into following through the foothills, and were simply waiting out of sight for the right chain of events to occur.

They saw the first two rise up out of the sand and explode into a fiery mess on the bottom of the ship, turned volatile from the high voltage of the shield. The ship heeled slightly to port, then swayed back to nominal, so far undamaged from the blast. It was common for them to run into these, especially this close to the foothills, that was why the humans assumed they were "dragon" eggs. It usually wasn't until they had been hit several times, and it looked like it was going to continue, that the decision was made to temporarily drop the shield.

They were coming up on the second wave of traps when a loud shriek came over the hillside. It was the Queen's son, and Ar'Yiisah's brother, M'ahk Kaesir Ar'Goevnihiila, and his juvenile band of rogue warriors, coming in for a ferocious ambush! The ship banked hard to port, drifting out of the foothills, and away from their trap.

"God dammit!" Thor yelled out loud, realizing this blew their one chance to get onboard without a fight. He started to scramble to his feet, brushing off his cover.

"Wait!" Erük yelled, stopping him with his powerful arm, "Stay with her!" He flew up out of the ravine, hoping to stop them before it was too late. The very existence of their race was in the balance, so it did not bother him in the least to sacrifice a few of his own kind for the good of the whole.

Their attack would mean nothing in the grand scheme of things, and they would all still be extinguished.

He came up from underneath two of them who were hanging just back from the shield, and drove himself straight up so hard that they were instantly impaled on his giant talons. He roared so loud it sent chills up Thor's spine, then slammed the two together and threw them in different directions, limp and lifeless. This got the attention of the others, and they started to fly toward him, ignoring the ship.

Just below the ability of either species to detect came another sound, a low hum at first, causing some dust to fall off of some of the surrounding formations, then it gradually intensified until it began to shake the very ground. It was the Helios. It appeared, apparently to the surprise of even the people on board the Phoenix, just off their port bow, on a collision course with them. The Phoenix banked hard to starboard, resuming its original course, and narrowly evaded a total disaster. Soldiers on the decks of both ships had to grab onto the knee-wall to keep from falling over the side as the massive ships simultaneously took emergency evasive maneuvers to avoid each other.

Erük flew straight up, spiraling out of sight as the others were caught in a tremendous crossfire coming from the decks of the two ships. Down below, three more eggs exploded into the bottom shield of the Phoenix, who had maneuvered back into the ravine at the base of the foothills. The massive ship started to pass right over the top of them and Thor felt the pull of the giant magnetic turbines lifting him right off the ground. He reached out, grabbing Ar'Yiisah's front arm and taking the young dragon with him.

She instinctively started to flap her wings, trying to escape the pull and control her flight in another direction, and Thor grabbed her other arm, pulling her toward him... reassuring her that they would be okay. Two more eggs exploded, this time burning their skin from the blast as they floated about half way between the ground and the ship. If the shield wasn't lowered, they would probably be incinerated, and Thor knew this, but after seeing them exercise this protocol over and over during his work detail, he had faith in their plan.

A large cluster of eggs, meant to turn the tides if the commander was having trouble letting his guard down floated past them, just smaller in mass, so they traveled faster. Thor hadn't really calculated this factor into his plan. It was going to hit the shield just before them, and create the largest explosion yet. Ar'Yiisah covered Thor in her wings, sacrificing herself to protect him. He struggled to get free, not wanting her to die in his stead.

"Its *my* job to protect *you!*" he screamed, kicking and thrashing about from within her protective shell, "You *have* to live!"

The blast started toward the front and instantaneously erupted into a large fireball, engulfing the entire bottom of the ship. She closed her eyes, hoping she could hold on long enough to protect him from the fall as well. Just as the force of the explosion hit from above, they were knocked sideways by another force, carrying them to safety. She opened her eyes, expecting to see Erük's beautiful eyes, but instead realized it was M'ahk Kaesir Ar'Goevnihiila, her half brother!

He was surprised to see her alive, and held her out in front of himself as if to get a better look at her. This opened her chest out, causing her wings to open just enough to expose Thor, who was still dangling in her talons. He roared ferociously, right in Thor's face, and when she pulled Thor out of his way to protect him, he looked at her with the same shock, and roared twice as hard at her, throwing them both at the ground in a rage. He flapped proudly in the air for a moment, hovering over them as they hit the sand in a cloud of dust, writhing in pain and shock.

M'ahk Kaesir Ar'Goevnihiila was defeated in his charge at the ships, turning his head to see the last two of his scouts fall from the edge of the ship, but needed someone to blame this on... *someone to unleash his fury upon!* He drew up his wings and shot toward the injured human and his treacherous half sister in full attack mode, too young and hormone driven to see past this even for a moment to hear her out. She struggled to get to her feet, determined to protect Thor from him at all costs.

Two feet away from tearing them limb from limb, he was broadsided himself by what appeared to be a rocket from above. He slammed into the sand a few feet from Ar'Yiisah's head in a cloud of dust and debris. As it cleared, a silhouette stood tall above them, wings spread out to the sides, and talons outstretched, ready to attack again. It was Erük, alive and well, and just in time.

The hum above them suddenly stopped. They looked up and saw a small cluster of eggs pass through the material dampers without exploding. The last blast had convinced them to turn off the shield. Thor turned and smiled at Erük, who was already helping Ar'Yiisah off the ground, checking to make sure the baby was undamaged. He looked back at Thor, smiling as well, and Thor knew they were okay. He started running for the ship, already a little past them and picking up speed. Suddenly Ar'Yiisah screamed! It was a deafeningly shrill cry the likes of which Thor had never before heard in his life! He spun around to see Erük knocked to one knee, his arm trapped with one set of claws, and the giant right talons of M'ahk Kaesir Ar'Goevnihiila's bloodied arm wrapped around Erük's throat from behind.

"Go, NOW!" Erük yelled, turning in on him with a lightning fast twist, and striking down on him hard with his right arm and wing. They were locked into a whipped frenzy of sand, dust and flailing bodies, as Thor and Ar'Yiisah scrambled to get clear of the violent clash between the two titans, both twice as large and twice as strong as either of them. She took flight as soon as she was free of their reach, scooping up Thor on the way to the bottom of the great ship, hurrying to get inside the damper hatch before they gave the order to turn the shield back on.

Captain Parnell paced the bridge, bandaged heavily from the fight with Sky. He looked out over the deck at the soldiers who still stood fast. There were only about twenty left out of the hundred they had at the start of the campaign, and the Helios, even less. He turned to the helmsman, pointing at the screen, "Put me through to Admiral Reid."

"Aye, Sir." The helmsman complied, and the screen flickered, then displayed the Admiral, busy putting out fires on his own bridge.

"Yeah, John, What can I do for you, I'm kind of busy... we have another breach! One of them is tearing up our -" The screen flickered, scrambling the video and sound due to some kind of distortion. *"- for damage control... Send a shuttle with enough Crystal, and another with -"* It broke up again, but this time, it shut off completely, then came back on. *"Did you experience that? I think the planetary changes are accelerating.... We need to hurry! Send me men and fuel. We'll take one more pass together, then we're out of here! Reid out."*

"Aye, Sir. Parnell out." He turned his back to the bridge and picked up the com, "Lieutenant Chambers, I need a shuttle ready to go to the Helios with a full security detail onboard, another one rigged and loaded for in-flight refueling! Ready the material stores for another run."

"Yes, Sir."

They were crawling through the in-feed tubes when the ship shook violently, the blast coming from underneath again. *"They must have turned on the shields again.... There's only a little time to get clear of the main turbines. We have to move!"* he instructed her. She went scrambling by him like he was lying still, scampering down the tube toward the large fan blades. "Wait! Hold on!" he called out loud, trying to keep up with her.

"Well, make up your mind!" she called, impatiently waiting for him with her arm resting on her hip. He scrambled to catch up, laughing at how similar their races actually were. They made their way through the large turbines praying that they didn't engage with them inside, as they would be cut into pieces. Halfway down one of the large condenser tubes, Thor knew they were in the clear. He had cleaned out the tops of the hoppers that sifted the large debris before, and recognized where they were.

"Follow me close, and don't make a sound," he instructed her, pulling off his boots and tying them to his shoulder. He stuck his feet to the sides of the tube as hard as he could to create friction, then slid slowly down the tube, keeping pressure on the sidewalls. As soon as he got down to the top flange of the hopper that sifted small material away from the large debris, he caught his feet on the edge, then started down the ladder on the outside of the container. It opened into the mineral holds that he started working in when he first awakened, so he knew exactly where they were. He looked around and saw that the room was deserted, so he waved for her to follow.

Halfway down the ladder a loud clunking sound startled him, but it was followed by the warm drone of the turbine engaging. He realized, just then, how insanely close they came to not making it. They reached the bottom of the ladder, looking for somewhere to hide as they heard the shuttle bay door opening from outside the room. There was a large pile of eggs already separated from the rest of the large debris in between themselves and the door, which was already open about two feet and climbing, revealing three sets of legs: one in uniform, and two wearing the suits that they used for the prisoners. They scrambled behind the pile and waited silently.

"Take cubes from those stacks until you've loaded the shuttle to capacity... human cargo is pilot plus one. Fuel up the other one and equip it for a security detail. Small arms only," the stern Sergeant ordered, pointing to the piles of Crystal, already stored for loading and quick assimilation into the fuel intakes of all of their ships. Luckily this took them off to one side and away from them, as there was nowhere else to hide that was close enough to reach quickly.

Thor absolutely did not want to lose any fuel to the Helios, but loved the idea of freely sending a dispatch of soldiers over there without even a fight. He looked at Ar'Yiisah, hoping for some input. She concentrated her gaze on the larger of the two workers. Suddenly he doubled over, holding his abdomen and groaning loudly.

"What the hell is the problem?!!" the guard yelled at him, almost out of the room already on his way to round up the security dispatch.

"My s-stomach... I... I don't know... I -" he grunted.

"Come with me! ...And you," he said, turning to the other one, who was standing there with a dumb look on his face, "Get busy stacking them here until I get back with more help!" he pointed at a spot on the floor close to the bay door, then walked off with the sick worker, tapping his belt com, "Medical unit two, we have one incoming... possible stomach infection..." The bay door slid quietly closed, locking the worker inside securely until the guard's return.

"Well done, my friend, well done... How did you...?" he thought.

"It's easy to make someone think they feel a certain way, especially if they don't know you're there... "

`*"What about him? I want to-"*

"I know. Replace the fuel crystal for the same weight in spent sand and V'eshniou eggs to sabotage the Helios... I'm one step ahead of you." She pointed at the other worker, who was walking slowly over to the wall like a zombie, completely entranced while they were free to do what they pleased with the shipment.

"Can he hear us?" Thor asked.

"It's as if he was not even here. When he snaps out of it, he'll have the memory of doing the work himself. He'll even be sweaty and out of breath, if we hurry."

"Well, let's hurry. The brig isn't very far away... we don't have much time." Thor started working through the stack, grabbing cases upon cases from the work line and filling them up with scoops from the refuse pile nearest the door. *"Do you have any kind of read on Erük? I haven't been able to sense him since we came on board,"* he asked, not sure he really wanted the answer.

"No read at all... which is strange..." She paused, looking at Thor, somewhat concerned, *"But nothing on M'ahk Kaesir Ar'Goevnihiila, either, and he's my half brother. I can almost always feel his presence. It's as if they both disappeared completely."*

"Let us pray that's not the case! " Thor thought, sincerely.

"Why does it matter to you?" she asked, not meaning to be offensive, but genuinely curious why one of their kind would matter so much to a human.

"Because he's my friend! He saved my life! But it goes beyond that... I've already bonded with him on some other level.... He's more honorable than almost any of my kind, and

I value that above all else. Loyalty is everything! He is family!" Thor snapped back, somewhat defensively.

"Please do not be offended! I merely wanted to know. You're the first human I've ever known."

"No offense taken! I'm just worried... I just hope he's okay, I've lost a lot of friends lately." He sighed, then all at once, they both realized the guard was back! They were more than done, the stack obviously taller than one small shuttle could possibly carry in it's cargo hold, but there was sand and dust everywhere! Thor looked panicked, jumping back behind the pile as the bay door started to open. He stared at Ar'Yiisah, who simply smiled, took a deep breath in, and blew hard in the direction of the work station they had erected for the task. Everything instantly and effortlessly blew away, into the back corners of the room, leaving no trace of spent sand anywhere near the freshly stacked tower of fuel cases, ready to ship out. The only problem was the other worker, who supposedly did all the work single handedly, was still standing in a trance, facing the opposite wall. Ar'Yiisah stared at him, concentrating for a moment, then the man opened up his pants, just as the door was open far enough to see, and started pissing directly on the wall without a care in the world.

"What the hell are you doing, asshole?!!" the guard yelled at him, walking toward him for a second, but then stopping in his tracks when he saw how much work he did.

"Sorry, I... umm," he mumbled, quickly re-fastening his pants.

"Forget about it! Nice work! Wholly shit, man! I underestimated you! You're a maniac! These two can go and unload the shuttle over there and stay and help out... You're staying right here and helping *us*!" The Sergeant slapped the man hard on the back, laughing. "The three of you, get this shit on the shuttle and let's get these ships out of here! The Admiral needs this ASAFP!" He pointed over to the puddle by the wall and scowled at the man, "Clean that shit up first! What the hell is wrong with you?" He tapped his belt com, "Get the security detail loaded, we're ready to leave in 5."

They stayed out of sight until the crew finished their task, shutting the bay door. Thor overheard one of them saying they were going to re-commence mining procedures side by side with the Helios, and that's what they needed the fuel for. Basically, it was just enough to get them moving and into full production, then they would have enough on their own to proceed. This meant they didn't have much time at all, the Helios would find out there was a traitor onboard as soon as they tried to fire the first case of fuel. They needed to move fast.

He snuck out of the material hold and into the corridor. Since they didn't really have a plan, at this point they needed to know who they were up against. How many armed guards were still on board, and where were they located. He wished like hell Sky was still with him, and he truly hoped he would not have to go against her. Not only was she a tremendous adversary, but he was quite sure that he loved her, and would die before laying a hand on her. He didn't know if a lifetime of conditioning could be broken so far as to get her to join them, but if she could only hear what Ar'Yiisah or Erük had to tell her, maybe... just maybe.

They crept into his old station in engineering without so much as a noise or sign of anyone else. It seemed that they were already functioning on a skeleton crew, and the last altercation thinned out the staff all that much more. This just made things all that much easier. Thor had spent many long hours on this very computer, educating himself as to the flight protocol and technical systems of this ship, half the time with this kind of eventuality in the back of his head as an ulterior motive. Since he was a child, he had always spent a lot of time planning worse case scenarios out in extreme detail, usually to the detriment of his relationships with friends, girlfriends, etc., who deemed him "paranoid," but this would turn out to be one of the rare instances when it was all worth it.

He accessed a general roster of active personnel, and realized that they just put in the order to send 20 soldiers over to the Helios, leaving the Phoenix with only 5, and according to this information, they were all bridge personnel! He smiled widely at Ar'Yiisah, who was reading him as fast as he was reading the file. He started bringing down the personal file on each one of them, but his heart missed a beat as he dropped down the file on the last one, and it wasn't Sky! He got physically sick to his stomach when he realized this must mean she was dead....

He staggered backward, all the blood rushing from his face, and knocked over the chair he was using. His knees got weak. Ar'Yiisah caught him in her arm, wrapping a wing all the way around him to comfort him. No sooner had he digested this information, as there was a low rumbling noise and an impact that knocked them both off their feet.

The lights dimmed to emergency power, and an alert siren sounded over the intercom. There was no way this could have been the Helios bomb, yet. It wasn't likely to be that big of an explosion, anyway, simply an incapacitating blow to their fuel intake system, crippling them so they couldn't give chase. It was too soon. They would scarcely be back with the "fuel," and loading it in place for an initial burn... no, this was something else.

Thor grabbed the edge of the table to balance himself and started punching up planetary data on the holo-screen. "Holy shit!" he exclaimed out loud, punching through page after page, then re-checking everything twice. "Sigyn is coming apart much sooner than we originally thought! She's pulled wide out of orbit, and we're getting pulverized by Algol!"

"That happens every three days, Thor. Why are you worried?"

"Because this time it's not going to stop!" he said out loud, heading for the door, "Follow me. We're taking the bridge. We'll all die if we stay out here much longer!" He wiped the tears from his eyes, stretched his arms out to the sides to prepare for combat, and opened the door. As soon as they were both in the dimly lit corridor, another blast took them off their feet again, but slammed them both into the wall, sideways. The whole ship seemed to be heeling over from a strong force coming from below and to the left, not above them. This time it *was* the Helios, and the shockwave was massive!

Thor looked at Ar'Yiisah with wide eyes, realizing from the size of the blast that they must have inadvertently caused a chain reaction in their fuel intake cells that brought about the total destruction of the Helios. Unsure how many innocents were onboard, he couldn't help but feel a sudden wave of guilt. Ar'Yiisah cried for him, but then put her taloned hand on Thor's forehead, inciting a vision, clear and vivid, of the nuclear blast that wiped out almost her entire race....

"This is war. They had the firepower to stop us... then my race would be extinct forever. You are doing the right thing, my friend. Follow your heart.... I can't do this without you!" She held her other hand over her abdomen, allowing an energy channel to open between her unborn child and Thor. He smiled, feeling its energy, pure and innocent, becoming part of him, and his focus was returned to him in a big way.

Suddenly he heard footsteps marching down the corridor from around the corner. They hadn't been seen yet, but he was sure it was the security detail from the bridge... and they would be armed to the teeth. They must have already deduced this as an act of sabotage, and were after the workers who loaded the shuttles. He grabbed Ar'Yiisah's hand and started to run down the hallway in the opposite direction, toward the brig.

Not a great place to head if you're trying to stay free, he thought, but it was probably the last place they would go at a time like this. The workers they wanted were still in the material hold, preparing for another mining effort. They ran down the hall, around another corner, through another doorway, and there they were... the double doors he passed through coming from the recovery room after being thawed out. They entered the doorway into the octagonal chamber, still fully operational and loaded with prisoners.

As soon as the prisoners saw Ar'Yiisah, a couple of them screamed. "What the hell is that thing?" yelled one old man, sitting in the corner of his cell, trying to back up even further out of total fear.

"It's a fucking Sand Dragon! He brought it in here to kill us!" one young man, obviously ex-flight crew, screamed at the top of his lungs.

"I did NOT bring her here to kill anyone! She will not harm you! There's a revolution going on, and I need to know right now if we can trust any of you," he offered, not really expecting to recruit any trustworthy help, though he was considering setting them all free as a diversion.

"Thor?" The voice came in through the background noise, as if he was hearing it only in his imagination. He started looking around at the individual cells. "THOR!" she yelled, staggering up to her feet. His head spun around to the left from around the core in the center of the room. His heart stopped for a beat again when he realized it was Sky! He rushed in, almost forgetting about the energy field between them. He closed his eyes, took a deep breath, exhaled it and centered himself to its pitch, then took a large step into her cell, grabbing her and hugging so hard her feet came up off the ground.

She had been beaten up pretty bad by the guards for sedition, but luckily, due to her family ties to the Captain and the Fleet Commanders, she had not been put to death. In spite of her bruises and cuts from head to toe, she was the most beautiful thing he had ever laid eyes on. He grabbed the back of her hair in a bunch, pulling her face tight to his right cheek, and listened to her breathing, his mind racing through all the things he wanted to say to her.

"I love you." It was the only thing that mattered in this moment. In this moment, the entire universe, the war, the ship, the hostile sun blasting the planets with its fiery angst all ceased to exist, and all that was left was her. He could feel the moisture on his face from her tears mixing with his. He could feel her lips move as she tried to speak, but kept softly kissing the side of his face instead.

"I love you too," she softly replied, her eyes still closed as if she was afraid to open them and find out it was a dream. "God, Thor, I thought you were dead...."

"I thought you were dead, too. I guess this explains why you're not on the active duty roster!" They both started to laugh out of nervous delirium and relief. Thor reached down, holding her hand in his while staring deep into her ice blue eyes. He noticed something that surprised him on her hands. He pulled one of them up for a closer look. She had burns all over both hands, deep into the skin.

"I tried to do what you taught me," she smiled, gesturing at the energy field, "several times." She looked up at him, childishly embarrassed.

"Jesus, Sky. Shit. Okay, we need to get you out of here," he said, scratching his chin.

"I know what to do," Ar'Yiisah said, emerging from behind the core.

Sky had been trying to see around the corner after someone said "Sand Dragon," but even knowing of her presence, she jumped almost out of her skin at the sight of her this close! "Did I just hear you *inside* my head?" Sky asked, absolutely blown away, but not too surprised at her intelligence. She looked at Thor, eyes wide open with excitement. Sky had suspected all along, but nobody would listen to her. Suddenly the ship was slammed from above with another fireball from Algol. Mostly gas, and mostly absorbed into the shield, it did little but remind them of their time limitations.

"We have to go!" he said, starting to get worried. The last thing he wanted was to lose her now and cause the extinction of an entire race due to bad timing. Ar'Yiisah walked effortlessly through the shield, causing Sky to back off a little bit, out of habit. Even as a smaller, younger member of their race, she still dwarfed any human. At 7 ½ feet tall while up on her back legs, she was pretty intimidating to stand next to. She walked over to Sky and held out her arm. Sky grasped it, immediately feeling a warm sense of relief. She could actually feel her internal energy change from second to second, like someone was turning a knob.

"Now just relax.... Trust me," she said telepathically, curling her up into her wing slowly and gently.

"I fucking hate it when people say that," she thought to herself.

"I do, too. But you need to trust me completely for this to work," Ar'Yiisah said.

"You can hear me?" she smiled.

"Yes... Now relax, and just breathe...." She waited a second before pulling Sky's vibratory pitch up to match her own, then stepped through the field, followed by Thor. As soon as she unraveled her wing, and the rest of the prisoners saw what she had done, they all started to chime in, wanting

384

help getting out, agreeing to do anything in return, promising not to tell anyone, etc.... Thor decided pretty quickly that it would be in everyone's best interest if they stayed where they were at until this was over, then they could be freed and shuttled back to the Fleet, if they wanted. Suddenly, they heard the Captain's voice over the intercom.

*"*Proximity alert! Brace yourselves for incoming!"* Thor looked hastily around the room, and saw nothing but trouble in every direction. If they got thrown, it would almost surely be into an energy field.

"Lock hands around the core of the room!" It was a 3 foot diameter pillar of electronics and energy condensers, but despite the matching blue glow, it didn't actually radiate any energy, it was all contained. They rushed to comply, and just made it, as the shock was tremendous! They flew off their feet as the ship was slammed down from above with what must have been a good sized meteor, broken loose from Sigyn.

As they brushed themselves off from the fall, they heard the moans and groans of those who slammed into the field on the way down and were rendered nearly unconscious. Rushing for the door, Thor turned to the prisoners and said, "Hang tight! We'll be back for you!" Sky walked up to the closest cell, an old woman who was badly hurt from the shock and the fall. She put the palm of her hand on the pad and the field dropped. She smiled. "Hey Thor! I still have clearance!" She walked around the room clockwise, dropping all their security fields. "I want you to stay in this room until we return.... Someone help this woman!" They walked out the door and she turned around and placed her hand on the outside sensor pad, locking the double doors from the outside.

They started down the corridor toward the bridge, stopping briefly at the engineering terminal where Thor laid it all out for Sky. To make a decision as grave as the one that faced her now, he figured she needed to see the facts for herself. "Now, you know I intend to take this ship, don't you?" he tested her, "It's clearly the only chance there is for their race to endure this travesty, which was caused by *us*!"

"What about all the innocent families in the Fleet who won't make their next destination? Do we leave them to their own devices?"

"That's exactly what we do! Their idiot leaders have driven this system to the brink of supernova, and if we don't get the hell out of here, we're dead! We can't save them! It's up to the resourcefulness of the assholes *they* put in power to get them out of this! All we're doing is trying to right the biggest wrong they perpetrated, and survive this mess ourselves. Believe me when I say that they knew this was coming! They gambled lives on being able to greedily take everything they needed without a hitch, and now they're paying the price for their ignorance! They could have avoided *all* of this shit! If you ask me, they've been dodging the same bullet for over 500 years, anyway... How long can a race get away with this shit? Maybe it's for the best if they don't skate out of this one! Maybe they *need* to be stopped! What they did to these peaceful creatures was pure evil, and I can't abide it."

"I'm sorry. I agree with you, it's just harder for me to swallow... I grew up on those ships, with those people," she said, a slight tear in her eye.

"If this was easy for you, I wouldn't want to know you." He wrapped his arms around her trying to soothe her pain. "If they are meant to, they'll survive this... they'll find another way. Your people are nothing, if not resourceful."

"They're no longer my people... my place is with you."

CHAPTER 39: ONCE MORE UNTO THE BREACH

Running toward the cargo hold on the way to the bridge, Sky took a quick turn to the right. Thor and Ar'Yiisah followed, not sure where she was going. She entered a locker room and popped open a large cabinet, revealing several rifles and several pistols. Thor smiled. "Now were talkin'!" They both grabbed one of each and strapped the rifles over their shoulders. She was about to shut it, when Thor reached in and grabbed another pistol, stuffing it in his boot. "For luck...." he said, smiling with a wink. She smiled and reached in, grabbing another one, herself.

They were on their way back out, when they were cut off at the door by Ensign Bellows, the asshole Thor was lucky enough to meet on his first day of work in the mineral hold. Ar'Yiisah had sensed him coming, and hid herself off to the side of the doorway, where she waited. He was standing in the doorway with a self important look on his face, holding a pistol on them and smiling, so Thor backed up a step, holding his pistols loose and unthreatening, with his hands up and to the sides. Sky set hers on the ground and kicked it over to him. She already had the second one tucked in her pants behind her back. He bent down to pick up the pistol, leaning just inside the door, and just caught a glimpse of her as she came down on the back of his head with her powerful talons, decapitating him instantly.

"Nice touch!" Sky said to Ar'Yiisah, smiling at her. She picked her gun back up, wiping some blood on the dead Ensign's backside. "He never used it anyway!"

They made their way to the cargo hold, knowing the Captain would have undoubtedly secured the fire door on the main entrance to the bridge, making it nearly impenetrable from that side. They would have to climb to the pilot house on the mezzanine from outside the ship, then use Sky's access to get inside from there. As they rounded the corner into the cargo hold from the hallway outside, they heard the sound of soldiers running down the corridor towards the open door.

Thor motioned for them to fan out among the darkened aisles, and for Ar'Yiisah to go high and wait for an ambush. There was a large open aisle right down the middle of the giant room, large enough for docking shuttles to be loaded and unloaded. They split up, one on each side of the room, hiding back a few aisles from the entrance where the aisles started to become randomly spaced and oriented.

They were all in position when the soldiers came around the corner, weapons drawn. Thor waited until they were all inside, then he took the easy shot he had from behind a row of medical supplies, and made it count. Three men were in prone position, down on one knee, out in front of the other two, while the two that were standing were scanning the room with some kind of sensor, probably infrared. Thor lined up his shot carefully, aiming for the narrowest tissue on the soldier's body. His rifle was set to maximum, the recoil knocking Thor back a couple of feet as his shot rang true, severing the kneeling man's head at the soft point of the throat, then proceeding to drill the man behind him square in the chest. The soldier was picked up by the blast from the rifle and thrown out the door and across the hallway into the opposite wall, his chest wide open and smoldering.

Thor dove down the aisle as they returned fire, rolling forward while shielding his rifle from impact with the ground, in an evasive technique know to the Japanese as "chugari." Their shots erupted just behind him, sending supplies flying apart all over the aisle as he slipped into darkness. Their leader waved for them to cease fire and spread out, still unaware that Sky was on the other side of the room, hiding in the dark.

She was holding back for some reason.... He couldn't figure it out, then looking a little closer at the one who was in command, he realized why. The man was wearing her uniform! He had not just been promoted to replace her as Lieutenant Commander, but was actually wearing her very clothes! Thor was about to take the shot, when he realized Ar'Yiisah was directly over the top of him... *waiting... watching.* From where she was hiding, Sky had a perfect shot. She took aim and exhaled, steadying her rifle, then slowly squeezed the trigger. The hapless officer was looking the other way, toward Thor's side of the room, and didn't even see where the blast came from, but suddenly found himself unarmed, with his rifle blown to pieces all over the place, and his hands and face badly burned from the explosion. He was staggering around with a blank expression, losing his balance from obvious shell shock, when his comrade tackled him to pull him behind cover, to safety.

As soon as the man had him off to the side and out of the view of the last remaining soldier, Ar'Yiisah swooped silently down from the ceiling, landing directly on top of the puny man, and literally tore him limb from limb. She wasn't sure why Sky had spared the other one's life, so she decided to respect her decision, and merely rendered him unconscious. Hearing the fallen soldier's muffled screams, he knew there was only one left, and he wasn't running away. Thor nodded and doubled back around to flank him.

There was a click that echoed through the otherwise silent hanger sounding like a lock being disengaged. Thor backtracked, figuring he needed to get even wider with his arc, lest he be flanked himself. He was working his way around the outside wall of the room, when the bay door started to open. He could hear footsteps scamper, than it was silent. There was bright light from outside shining in from under the door, casting a shadowy, surreal haze on everything in the room, and the movement of the long shadows cast from Skaði's direct glow while the ship turned about made it very hard to tell what was what.

Everyone froze, madly looking about. Thor wanted to give chase so he couldn't warn the Captain, but something told him this was a trick. He closed his eyes, trying to hail Ar'Yiisah....

"Hey, sister, can you see him? Is he still here, or did he go outside?"

"Thor! Watch out! He's still here, but so is-" She was cut off flat by gunfire erupting in Sky's direction. The soldier emerged from behind an arms crate with a Dragonfire Cannon, one of the most destructive, high power/ high RPM weapons in their small arms arsenal. It was cutting down everything in her direction in a fiery cataclysm of smoke and flying debris. One whole shelf blew apart, then another. The gun shot pulses of energy so rapidly, that it looked like it was breathing some kind of electric fire, earning it its name. It even projected a built in shield that covered the user from almost all frontal fire, but the man must have thought Sky was the only one left,

because he left his backside completely vulnerable to attack, and even started walking toward her as he attacked.

Ar'Yiisah flew back up toward the ceiling in an effort to get close enough to the gunman to do something, but just as she was directly overhead, Thor, frustrated with not being able to get in a clean shot at him that wouldn't jeopardize Sky even further, launched himself across the open bay, jumping up in the air for the last ten feet, and scissor kicked the man in the middle of his back with the strength and focus of a battering ram, breaking the man's spine and folding him almost completely in half, backwards; the dead-nerve grip his disconnected hand still had on the weapon causing the hellish destructive blast to continue spraying randomly out the bay door for a few more seconds until it was empty.

"Sky!" Thor yelled at the top of his lungs, unable to see her right away from under all the debris and smoke kicked up from the cannon fire. There was a whole shelf full of crates that fell right at the onset of the attack, right in front of the last place he remembered seeing her.

"I'm alright!" He heard her grunt, moving debris off of her legs and standing back up. She was nearly completely covered in some kind of dust, as were most of the broken shelves that buried her, probably saving her life. She picked up her rifle and started dusting herself off.

"Oh, Sweet Jesus Jefferson! Thank God," he yelled in total shock and relief, after what he just witnessed. He bent down and started prying the maniacal weapon out of the broken assailant's hand, being as careful as possible not to set it off again, since it was probably recharged by now. He pulled the man's twitching hand out of the arm-sheath and threw him back down at the ground in disgust. Marveling at his new toy, he holstered his pistol and slipped his arm inside the sheath. It automatically tightened to perfectly accommodate his arm. He smiled.

He was checking out the different levers with his arm stuck inside the gun when he saw the shape come around the corner and into the cargo hold. It was Parnell, still bandaged and bloody, carrying a rifle, which he immediately raised right at Thor. Sky was looking the other direction, toward the open bay door, and saw something entirely different. The massive creature, almost twice the size of Ar'Yiisah, swooped in out of nowhere, and was heading directly at Thor with its talons extended. Without a moment to spare, Sky lifted her rifle, and zeroed in on him, leading just in front of the target, knowing she wouldn't get a second shot.

"NO!" Ar'Yiisah shrieked, swooping straight down from above as Sky pulled the trigger. Parnell fired at the same time, sending another blast of deadly energy directly at him from another angle. Just before Sky's shot hit the giant creature, Ar'Yiisah opened her wings, passing directly in front of it and catching the full force of the blast right in the chest, sending her sprawling over backwards as Erük snatched up Thor just in time to keep him from getting hit by the shot from Parnell, which slammed into the bulkhead, instead. Before he could readjust his aim and fire again, Erük swooped in with Thor in his talons, and let him go at the last second, allowing Thor to use his whole body weight, as well as their combined momentum as a weapon.

He flew through the air, poised for attack with the focus of a hawk, and drew back his huge rifle as if it was a sword ready for a straight thrust. He landed with all his weight and the force of his momentum combined with the power and timing of his most menacing punch and drilled the Captain with the point of his gun right through the chest, almost running him completely through as they slid ten feet back, slamming him into the door jamb. As he stood there gasping for air with blood starting to drip from his mouth and bubble up in his throat, Thor closed his eyes and saw, through the

Captain's eyes, the flash that killed nearly every one of Erük's people, and heard in his head the excuses that made it so easy for him to justify it.

He slowly opened his eyes to see the fear and horror he now reflected, knowing his very life, the life that he so selfishly protected with the death of countless others, was about to end. Without saying a word, Thor spit in his face, grabbed the top of the rifle with his left hand as well, and dug deep with the barrel of the gun into his chest cavity, lifting him completely off the ground, then pulled the trigger, blowing his entire torso all over the doorway.

The sound of the rifle was surreal, mixing eerily with the echoes in the giant room of a battle winding down into silence. One scream didn't fade into memory. It was Sky. *Something was definitely wrong....* He spun around quickly to see her huddled over someone, sobbing hysterically. She was nearly hyperventilating, on her knees, rocking back and forth, mumbling.

"I didn't know... I didn't know... I didn't... God DAMMIT! WHY?!!" She started crying hysterically, Erük crouching calmly beside her, one taloned hand outstretched to Ar'Yiisah; her breath becoming shallower and shallower, and the other on Sky's back, trying to comfort her and relieve her guilt.

"No, no, no, no, no... GOD NO!!!" Thor yelled as he came scrambling up on her other side, sliding up on one knee beside her. He pulled his hand out of the rifle's control sheath and set it on the ground off to one side. "Oh fuck, no... fuck, no WHAT THE HELL HAPPENED?!" he demanded, not understanding how she got hit.

"It was an accident," Ar'Yiisah said out loud, for the first time, ever. She looked at Thor. "She was trying to save you... she is a great woman.... Love her... love-" She coughed painfully hard, then continued, looking over at Sky, and taking her arm with her right hand. "Do not blame yourself... you did not know. I would have done... I would..." She started coughing up blood and convulsing, fighting for the breath to finish her statement in English. "I would have done the same thing.... Now you need to be strong again. *They* need you!" She squeezed Sky's arm, snapping her out of her pity-based trance, and stared at her, imparting her own personal essence, the part of her that made her royalty, the part that made her unique, along with the knowledge necessary to know what to do with it, directly into Sky's head. "*I* need you!" She pulled Sky's hand over onto her abdomen and held it there, right over her baby. "He needs you... "

Her voice was getting faint, and she was breathing shallower. She reached up towards Erük, putting her hand across the side of his face and temple, eyes locked on each other as she gave herself over to him wholly and completely; her light finally fading as she spoke, "You will make us live again... *live... again....*" She exhaled, slowly, trying hard not to cough. "Give Erük your knife," she said to Thor, who was looking straight down, exhausted in every possible way. Thor opened the sheath, and produced the massive combat knife he grabbed out of the armory and handed it over to Erük with a concerned look in his eye.

"My God! Is there no other way?" Sky asked.

"None," she replied, grabbing Erük's hand and guiding the knife around the path he would need to cut in a V shape, then she retraced with him to the point of the V, and plunged the knife in, herself, with a loud gasp. She pulled it back out just a little, keeping the blade depth as shallow as she could get away with, and carefully they sliced from her lower waist to the bottom of her rib cage, at an angle. She screamed as they pulled it out, panted a couple times while mentally preparing herself, then plunged again, this time from the corresponding location under the other side of the rib cage, cutting downward to complete the V. She let the bloody knife fall to the floor with a clang, and winced as Erük peeled back the flap of skin and tissue to reveal the wondrous sight within.

Ar'Yiisah mustered all her life energy at once to gaze upon this miracle one time. He was the very reflection of her; finer, smaller, and smoother, to be sure, but every bit a healthy, vibrant young dragon, already opening his inner lids to see them all, one at a time. She reached out as Erük placed him in her grasp, and she smiled her last smile at him, passing on her dignity, the very seed that would insure the survival of their race, not just their species. Her eyes glazed over, and she was gone. Sky broke down crying, while Thor tried hard to console her, choking up, himself, but it was the sight through the bay door that finally got them to their feet.

What started out as occasional fireballs coming down and exploding without incident into the dome shaped field of energy that shielded the deck, had gradually increased into a violent show of power from the heavens, the likes of which none of them had ever seen. The ship shook as it started getting pulverized with larger and larger projectiles of what looked like massive chunks of solid earth! The chunks were exploding into the shield, but they were wildly affecting its course of flight and maneuverability, and little by little they were wearing down their main power repelling them. They all knew, without even saying it, that climbing the mezzanine to gain bridge access was suicide during this kind of shit-storm, so Sky scooped up the baby, and the three of them started running for the interior door, shutting the outside bay in case there was a shield breach.

"What about the fire door! The Captain's surely got us locked out of the bridge! There's no way helm will open it for me!" Sky yelled over the increasingly thunderous beating they were taking.

"Leave that to me!" Thor yelled back, as they started running across the cargo bay toward the inside doorway.

"Trust you, right?" she half-joked, forcing a smile at him.

"Of coarse!"

When they reached the other side, Thor started looking all around for something. The whole doorway was a blood soaked mess. He smiled, pulling his knife from his hip again, and walking toward the edge of the shelves to his left. He crouched down, and took a hack at something, then stood back up with the Captain's dismembered right hand, still attached to the forearm, cut a strap of material from the dead man's pant leg, and wrapped it around the stump to contain the blood.

"Let's go," he said, taking off toward the bridge. The ship heeled violently a couple times on the way to the barricaded door, and they started fearing the worst, not really sure where they were, or where they were headed. Upon reaching the door, they stopped for a moment to get centered and prepared, having come way too far to simply walk right into a trap, now. Thor pulled back the arming lever on the Dragonfire Cannon, waited for the hum he heard before, then slapped Parnell's bloody hand onto the sensor pad.

At first it looked like they were going to have to try to blast their way through, then the fire door slid quietly open, exposing the conventional, inner door. He hit the pad again, lowering the cannon to attack position as the door slid open to reveal two skinny helmsmen shaking in their boots, one of them armed with a ceremonial gold pistol from the Captain's desk that Thor saw earlier. They fanned out into the room, Erük last, and the shaking from the helmsmen got much worse.

"I suggest you put that pistol down, Sir," Thor said, lobbing the Captain's severed hand over the railing onto the floor by the men's feet, "there's been a change in management!" Thor suddenly noticed the puddle of urine pooling out onto the floor from the man's leg, and looked up to see a wet spot around his crotch. He couldn't help but laugh a little.

"Now... please," he repeated, politely. The man quickly complied, putting his hands in the air and stepping back as far as he could, the other man quickly following suit. Thor looked over at Sky, who was staring in awe at the firestorm outside. "Seal the bridge!" he yelled to her, and bent down to throw the hand in the trash and pick up the pistol. He pulled the cannon from his arm, pulled out the power clip and put in in his pocket, and set it down on the map table, putting the Captain's pistol in his pants. He walked up to both men with his hands behind his back, nonchalantly, and paced in front of them, looking them up and down.

"In case you want to live through the next few minutes, let's get one thing straight. We are now in command. Parnell is missing much more than just his hand. He has been punished for the needless genocide of this peaceful race!" He gestured at Erük. "I don't know where your hearts lie, but I'm going to give you just one chance to make yourselves useful," he said, pointing at their posts, "after that, my friend, Erük, will use you for a chew toy!" He stared at each of them for a second or two. "Is that abundantly clear?"

"Yes, Sir!"

"Aye, Sir!" the second one replied.

"Good! Take evasive action! Get us away from here! We're getting hammered!" They took their appropriate seats, wasting no time doing it, then started punching buttons and checking data.

"Sir, there's nothing on this side of the planet that isn't getting hit just as bad, and there's no cover in the mountains, in fact it looks more dangerous! Whole peaks are getting knocked down."

"Sky, Erük, any suggestions?" Sky walked over to Thor after running several different things through the computer. She pulled him off to the side and spoke to him quietly. Erük kept an eye on the helmsmen, while holding the baby in his arms.

"Thor! Fleet knows what happened. Somehow Parnell had them posted up until he attacked you. They're sending a retrieval squadron. They intend to take back the ship! It contains the fuel for the whole Fleet. Otherwise they're not going far!"

"That's what I'm counting on! We can't have them following us, can we?"

"Where are we planning on going?" she asked, somewhat sarcastically, because up until now, this whole thing seemed reactionary, at best.

"Earth," he whispered. Her eyes widened. She had to admit, she had often wondered, especially when she was growing up, what life must have been like for her ancestors.... Not having to depend on any artificial environment to survive. Breathing all that fresh air, before the planet got so polluted. *Who knows what the last 500 years would have done to a living, breathing planet, especially without the influence of humanity!* She suddenly became very excited. "I've seen the charts on where they're headed, and it looks like a long ride for a whole lot more of this same kind of shit! Mineral rich, hostile moons and bastard planets that are too young or too old to support life without decades of Terra-forming. No, thanks. It's going to be a long ride, but either way, we have to get clear of this system quick! Algol is going to supernova shortly after Sigyn breaks up and throws 3S1 the rest of the way out of orbit! It's inevitable!"

"How long do we have?" Sky asked.

"It will start to happen on it's next return. We are in eclipse now, so 3 days. 3½, maximum," he calculated loosely.

"How fast can we travel?" Thor winced, pretty sure they weren't going to start talking about warp drives and hyperspace.

"We can augment our normal propulsion with our Crystal impregnated solar sails in a *standard* system's termination shock, to get to .98732 the speed of light by the time we breach the heliopause, but acceleration is slow, and with this system's unique magnetic field fluctuations, it might be worse!" one helmsman blurted out.

"Okay, so in English, please, can we make minimum safe distance from a 3 sun supernova in 3 days, then use the sails to harness the power of the blast to speed up the rest of our voyage?" he asked, looking at everyone.

"No," the helmsman said, without a second thought.

"Wrong answer!" Thor yelled, slamming his fist down. "Isn't there a way we can use the magnetic fields here to our advantage? Using our sails for impulse repulsion, not as conventional acceleration, maybe?" he proposed.

"Do you remember the gravity in the chamber at the core of the planet?" Erük asked Thor, but made sure he was projecting to everyone in the room.

"Whoa!" the helmsman said, as they both turned around, surprised to *hear* him.

"Yeah, I do..."

"I know another way through. It would at least solve our immediate problem and give us a place to hide from the beating we're taking and this squadron Sky speaks of."

"How far away?" Thor asked, not wanting either helmsman to hear.

"Just up the ridge." Thor knew that they needed to get off planet as soon as possible, but if Fleet saw them do it now, they'd simply run them down.

399

"Thor," Sky said softly, "If it's Earth you want to head to, we need to leave from the other side of the planet, and we'd have to go right past the entire Fleet to get there!"

Thor looked back at Erük. *"Does the tunnel you speak of go all the way through?"*

"Yes... in a bent path."

"Is it wide enough?"

"Yes."

"Let's do it! Show the helmsman where to go. Shortest route possible! I think I have an idea that might give us the additional speed we need"

CHAPTER 40: INTO THE MOUTH OF THE DRAGON

Thor walked over to the intercom and turned it on, shipwide. *"Ladies and Gentlemen of the Phoenix... anyone still left onboard, free or imprisoned... Captain Parnell is no longer with us. I am Captain Thorsson Krey. Lieutenant Commander Davies and I have assumed command of this vessel and are attempting to make right some of the atrocities of the previous administration. This will take us far from Fleet, who at this time are in the process of trying to blow a hole in the universe and see how many of our ships will fit into it! Anyone who wishes to remain with the Fleet will proceed to the shuttle bay immediately and wait for *Commander* Davies, who will see to it that you are given the opportunity. If you wish to remain onboard the Phoenix, there will be a long exodus back toward Earth, as well as a great reshuffling of current job positions and administrative tactics. If you are detained and unable to get there, someone will be there to retrieve you. You are now free. Those staying with the Fleet, please identify yourself by laying your towel by the entry to your cell, immediately. Thank you very much, Godspeed, and good luck to us all." He looked over at Sky and winked, setting down the microphone.

"Two promotions in one conversation! Nice!" she smiled, only a little sarcastic. "Captain *Krey*...." It occurred to her that this might be the first time she had heard his real last name.

"You deserve even more.... We both know it will really be *you* who will be *Captaining* this vessel, I just didn't want to paint you as a co-conspirator, seditionist, and mutineer all in one conversation, without your permission. Whatever is said to these people *will* get back to Fleet," he warned, not wanting to make this any harder on her than it already was.

"It's okay. Hell, the mere fact that I'm going with you means I'm involved. Let's go. I've made my decision... I already told you, my place is with you."

"Thor, they're coming..." Erük said, spinning around to get his attention and pointing at the approaching lights on the radar screen. He suddenly got a strange look on his face, snorting, then spinning back toward the helmsman who soiled himself earlier. "and a transmission has just been sent to them!"

"From where?"

"From *HERE!*" Erük said, looming above the scared little man and looking almost straight down at him as he sat quivering in his chair with a guilty look on his face.

"Bring it up on screen!" he called out to Sky, who was standing in front of another terminal, checking the shuttle bay surveillance cameras to see how many were leaving. She

402

nodded, hitting a few quick keys. The screen to the right of the large main lit up with a flicker, showing text with a time stamp and terminal number matching the helmsman's chair. *"HOLD FIRE! SHUTTLE LEAVING WITH LOYALS. PLEASE RESCUE. HIJACKED CARRIER LEAVING FOR EARTH VIA TUNNEL SYSTEM THROUGH PLANET CORE. CAPTAIN KILLED."*

The man started shaking in his chair and blubbering, "Please... please... I can explain..."

"Bring him to me," Thor said, coldly. Erük grabbed the back of the man's shirt, along with a bunch of his skin and hair, and threw him straight up and out of his chair, slamming him over the map desk and onto the floor at Thor's feet. Thor stared at him for a second as the man squirmed on the floor, pissing himself again as he tried to get up. Thor reached down and grabbed the back of the man's uniform and started dragging him toward the doorway to the mezzanine.

"Let me get that for you, sweetie," Sky said softly, opening the two security airlocks. Thor drug him out onto the back catwalk and lifted him up over his head, kicking and screaming. Without even a moment's hesitation or a single word uttered, Thor tossed him right over the side onto the deck with a cold, clumsy thump, amongst the shower of fireballs and chunks of earth that were still coming down like rain. He screamed like a little girl all the way down, then crawled around aimlessly like an injured little bug, doomed to death, with absolutely no way back in.

They came back inside to the other helmsman, who was sitting at his post, trying hard not to appear as nervous as he really was. Thor approached him casually, and knelt right beside his chair, looking him square in the eyes. "You'll be treated as fairly as you treat us, but level with me, do you wish to return to Fleet? Now that they know where were headed, it doesn't make a difference to us, either way, except that you seem very smart. Smart is useful.... Smart we can use. So, what's it gonna be, soldier?"

The man paused for a moment, took a deep breath, nodding, while looking at the floor, then replied, "I have no living family, and I have no friends. I've been on this ship since I was born, and I grew up reading stories about Earth from our library. If there's even a chance of us making it, I'm with you. Besides, what Fleet has done here, and in several other worlds has been absolutely inexcusable! I'd rather die than be counted with them any longer!" He extended his hand to shake Thor's and was instantly and openly obliged, smiling broadly and slapping the man on the back with his left hand.

"What's your name, rogue?" Thor asked, standing back up and starting to walk over to Sky.

"Ensign Bjorn Eriksson, Sir" the young man said.

"Bjorn? A fine Norse name, indeed... you'll fit right in," Thor said with a satisfied grin on his face, "This is Erük. Work with him and get us just inside the mouth of the tunnel. Call me on the com when we're close."

The man looked nervously up at Erük, then back at Thor. "Aye, Sir."

"Erük, keep an eye on him. Keep the bridge secure. We'll be right back," Thor told Erük, telepathically, still not yet sure if Bjorn could be trusted.

"I will."

Thor and Sky showed up in the brig and scooped up the only two takers in the room. Several cells had already been emptied out and the occupants sent onboard the Helios to help their mining efforts just before they were destroyed. This only left one in the back wanting to stay onboard.

The voice echoing through the small room sounded strangely familiar. He had definitely heard this man before. "Top of the mornin', *Mr. Krey...* or was it Stanton? So, the NSA sends agents this far into space to dispatch crooked ship Captains, then? I'll go for a ride with ya, but first, how 'bout gettin' us outta this cell, then, eh Boyle?" he said with a thick Irish brogue. Thor walked in a little farther and peered into the cell. Sky looked confused as Thor suddenly burst into laughter.

"McGinn, was it? Well I'll be a cocksucker's lunch! You're a sight for sore eyes! So you don't want to go join the Fleet for the rest of your sentence?" he joked, gesturing for Sky to drop the energy field. "Good... we can use another good man! Hang loose, we'll be back as soon as we can!" They left the room with the two elderly people, locking the main brig door on the way out. "Just in case," Thor muttered to Sky.

"Where do you know him from?" Sky asked, strangely concerned.

"I met him in the office at CryoKinetics... haven't seen him since. Why?"

She looked a little puzzled, then replied, "Oh, it's just that he has even more scars than you do. Do you have any idea what he did for a living?"

"No, but I'll find out. Maybe it's nothing. Those were turbulent times for most of us... Hell, I wasn't who *I* pretended to be." They rounded the corner to the shuttle bay and stopped at the door. "Be ready for anything." He looked at her and noticed she already had her pistol drawn and ready.

"One step ahead of you, love."

Smiling broadly, Thor opened the door, careful to eyeball the entryway for a possible ambush. There was a small group of people hanging about the shuttle bay, including a couple mining workers, members of mining security, several agricultural workers, cooks, maintenance men, and their families. They all looked very nervous and were all packed light and ready to go. One woman stepped up, "What the hell happened?"

Thor gestured for them to enter the shuttle, as Sky unlocked it and opened up the cargo hatch. "Our race committed genocide against a peaceful, highly intelligent species, and has pushed their entire solar system, as well as those around it, to the brink of destruction. The binary sun, Algol, *will* supernova, most likely in 3 days, and the Fleet commanders could have stopped this all from happening," Thor said loudly.

"Then why didn't they?" one of the nurses asked, stepping forward.

"I don't know... Greed... Impatience... *Convenience?* Who knows? Maybe something we can't possibly know or guess.... Why do those with power *always* step all over those without it? Either way, they want our fuel pretty bad, and we're not about to give it to them!

"Where are you going?" the young woman asked, holding her lower abdomen, instinctively guarding her baby from any possible harm.

"We are going to make it back to Earth!" Sky interjected, lowering the ramp with a hiss. "If they keep messing around trying to stop us, they aren't going to outrun the supernova, much less make it to the next system," she added.

The nurse took another step toward them, "I'm going with you...." She gestured down at her belly, protruding through her opened shirt an obvious 6 or 7 months worth of pregnant, then looked back up at them with deep, sullen eyes. "*We* are going with you.... All of my family is gone, and my brother just died in the battle... This ship is the only home I've ever known... but please, answer me honestly... *can we survive this*?"

"If we work together, yes, we can... and *we will!* What is your name?"

She grabbed up her medical bag and stepped away from the others, toward him. "My name is-"

"Nurse Astrydd. We've worked together before," Sky spoke for her, smiling broadly. "She's a top notch nurse, and a good soul, to boot. We'd be honored to have you onboard, Astrydd... you *and* your baby!"

"Well, guess what... now you're *Dr.* Astrydd. Chief physician of the Phoenix, by default," Thor said, shaking her hand while looking to Sky for her approval, which she quickly gave with a consenting nod and a smile. "Anyone else?" A young couple stood there arguing about it, while most of the other's quickly got onboard the shuttle. The ship started to heel hard, as if it was turning abruptly to port and downward at a steep angle. Several people screamed. "It's okay! It's okay! We're there, that's all! Get onboard, now, if you're leaving!" He pointed up the shuttle ramp and the last few people scrambled onto the tiny craft, filling well past capacity.

The call came in from the bridge, *"We're at the site. Situation stable... commencing auto-launch protocol in 1 minute and counting...."*

Sky stood at the entrance and addressed the people onboard. "We've programmed the shuttle for a search and rescue routine... The ship has a homing beacon, and Fleet knows you're here. You'll stay just inside the mouth of this cave, where you'll be safe from fly-rock and meteors, until they come for you, which should be very soon. Godspeed, and God be with all of us." She hit the switch, and the ramp retracted, automatically closing the hatch.

"Commencing auto-launch protocol. Clear shuttle bay immediately!" They ran for the door they came in as the helmsman, Ensign Eriksson, continued counting down over the ship-wide intercom and the bay door opened to the outside, temporarily dropping their shield over that part of the ship. The shuttle lifted off, and gently maneuvered outside, then the massive Carrier swooped back around and immediately started its descent down into the depths of the dark abyss.

When Sky and Thor got to the bridge, things were tense. It seemed the detachment sent to retrieve the Phoenix was a little larger than they had imagined. Still in need of more fuel, the Fleet had sent two more Carriers with the retrieval squadron, and though he had anticipated this, as they neared the mouth of the tunnel, the radar screen was suddenly absolutely teeming with incoming! They must have had many more fighters than he first estimated launch from the Carriers to insure the crippling of the Phoenix, and they were only moments away from the mouth of the cave! Thor paced the floor for a moment, unsure what to do against such a force... Then it hit him!

"Sky, can you give me the schematic to this tunnel system on the holographic?"

"Sure, but it won't show any of the side tunnels in their entirety, just the main shaft," she said, punching it in on the computer. The combination sonar/ radar image rose up off the map table in full 3D, showing a long, snaking, dynamic tunnel, narrowing in several places before widening at the core, then narrowing again in several spots near the other side. Thor pinpointed what looked like an almost impossibly narrow spot, just a couple kilometers from where they were currently flying. He turned to Eriksson, still pointing at the spot.

"Will we make it through this bottleneck?" he asked, as Bjorn punched some numbers in his console. The young helmsman spun back around.

"Barely... and I mean *barely!* We'll have to turn on our side 90 degrees to do it, then another 270 degrees of clockwise barrel roll to complete the maneuver. We'll have to slow way down to pull it off, which, of coarse, will screw us for the shotgun maneuver out the other side.... *Shit!* I didn't see that coming.... Our side impulse thrusters don't move us fast enough to keep up with our current velocity!"

"What if they did?"

"What do you mean? What if they did...? If they did, we'd be fine!"

"Follow me for a second, What if we lost the tower?" Thor proposed, with a scheming look in his eye. "When I climbed up there, all I saw was a homing module of some kind, probably transmitting directly to Fleet. All our important instruments are fore and aft! That entire structure is just a crows nest, really... for terrestrial mining ops. It creates a moment arm that requires a much higher force to be applied near the fulcrum in order for the ship to rotate, so getting rid of it would help, right?" Bjorn started punching in numbers on two different terminals, then smiled, spinning back around.

"Yeah," he said, "it would not only increase our side impulse, but it would probably eliminate the need for the last 270 degree turn, altogether! But how do you intend to be rid of it, though? If we hit it on the cave walls, it would tear us apart!"

"The tall columns are simple I-beams. They used to use magnesium bricks to cut train tracks a long time ago, so

409

we do the same thing to weaken the mast...." He had his arms out to the sides with a casual look in his eyes, as if to imply that this was a simple operation that couldn't possibly go wrong. "Sky, do you know where all the mines are kept?"

"Yeah, but why mines? We have much better explosives than that!"

"Show me, but I'll still need those mines... "

"For what?"

"Trust me...." he smiled, winking at her, "Erük, come with us! Bjorn, you're on baby detail!"

"What?!!" he exclaimed, as Erük carefully handed him Ar'Yiisah's baby; squirming and curling up for warmth while making little baby dragon belching and cooing sounds, as he blinked his enormous eyes at the young Ensign.

They opened the explosives magazine and Thor instantly looked like a kid in a candy store again, going crazy trying to find just the right setup to do what they needed. Since most of this stuff was either made on Earth and stored all these years without many applications, or duplicated, using the original as an exact model, he was able to quickly identify most of the stuff he was seeing. He grabbed several long strips of cutting tape, an effective plastic high-explosive used for making mincemeat out of steel, a handful of remote blasting caps, a remote detonator, and 30 lbs of RDX powder, compressed into bricks with boosters already attached. He had Erük carry an improvised bag full of a cluster of 20 old magnetic-base land mines taped around a large brick of C-4 in the center, and they headed for the bridge.

They took the explosives to the airlock on the mezzanine deck and instructed Sky to blow the tower if anything happened to them, then catch the top of it on the wall

410

during the 270 degree barrel roll that Bjorn would initiate. She took the remote and went back to the bridge as they went outside and began climbing up the structure as the ship sped down the shaft, deeper and deeper into the core of the trembling planet using a series of front-facing floodlights to navigate and the occasional patch of phosphorescent algae growing on the walls as a beacon to keep their bearings in the vast darkness. They stayed focused and alert, with even one tiny mistake spelling almost certain death, they had no room for error on any side and were very soon to have vengeful followers hot on their tail.

"I'm going to wire the base. Can you make it to the top and mount all of those together, such that the buttons on top are facing up, out and forward?"

"I will." Erük started up the tower without hesitation and Thor got to work on the base. He put one brick of RDX inside each of the two front columns that attached the tower to the deck, just above the junction plates. He used the one remaining one on the starboard side, aft, leaving one rear column untouched. He then started wrapping each column, including the bare one, with cutting tape, struggling to hold on in the vortex of wind that surrounded him. The sound was deafening; the ship's engines echoing off of the narrow walls and bouncing right back at them as the wind howled by them, faster and faster. One by one he planted a blasting cap into the boosters attached to the RDX and wrapped one apiece into the ends of the cutting tape, molding it around them with the antennae sticking up in the air.

"Are you almost done, Erük?" Thor asked, relieved that they were able to communicate in this fashion. Just then, out of the darkness behind them, a blue flash enveloped their shield, making him jump back a few feet and cover his eyes.

411

Erük slammed into the deck next to him, almost coming down on top of him.

"Erük!" he yelled, scrambling for the airlock. The giant creature barely moved, struggling to get up at all. Thor stopped, then ran back down the catwalk toward him. He was just starting to get up off the deck when another two blasts hit the shield, causing static electricity to flow over the surface like lightning. Thor suddenly became very nervous about the remote blasting caps getting set off accidentally. "Erük! We gotta go! Is it done?" He was underneath Erük, lifting with his back, trying to get him inside while the ship was maneuvering sharper and sharper through the narrowing labyrinth before them.

"It is done."

They struggled up the catwalk holding onto the railing to keep from falling as the ship heeled almost upside down while following the hard curve of the tunnel, and Thor caught a glimpse of the squadron of fighters right on their heels. They made it inside the first door of the airlock and Thor hit the com immediately.

"Blow the charge! Sky! Blow it!" He pressed his face up to the window to see inner door opened, and they ran for the bridge.

"I don't understand it! Why aren't they exploding? I know they're wired right," Thor yelled, pushing the button again while looking at the bottleneck on the holographic map get closer and closer. "Maybe the shield static is interfering..."

Bjorn spoke up, fast. "Don't even think about dropping the shield! We'd be toast! Look at all of 'em!"

"Let me do it. I can augment the signal strength," Erük suggested. Thor tossed him the box, nervously looking at the map.

"Ten seconds 'til bottleneck! Better do something!" Bjorn yelled. Sky held the baby tight and strapped herself into a chair by the helm. Erük held the box tight, pressing the button continuously, then closed his eyes. Thor started hearing a ringing in his head, then Sky and finally Bjorn. Suddenly, they heard a loud explosion that shook the entire ship and lit up the inside of the cave for just a moment as if it was daytime. They could hear chatter over the radio about a fire on deck, but nothing about the tower. "The tower's still standing!" Bjorn yelled.

"I know! it's supposed to be! Take the 90 degree bend, then fly it straight into the next bend, hitting the top of the cave with the very tip of the tower!" Thor yelled back. Bjorn smiled, finally understanding what he had up his sleeve.

Outside, the two back columns were severed off two feet from the bottom, as was one of the front ones, and the entire structure was being held to the ship by one column, already weakened by a smaller charge of cutting tape. As they came into the first turn, the fighters were hanging close, like a school of hungry piranhas tasting blood. They heeled hard, 90 degrees, then held their course, one of the fighters carelessly careening into the tunnel wall and lighting it up again. The tower was leaning a little, but held on through the maneuver. Thor breathed a sigh of relief. They saw the choke point coming up and gasped, as it looked too tight for them to make it, even without the mast.

The fighters backed off at first, but were right back on their tail as they hit the low point of the ceiling dead-on with the top of the tower, detonating the clustered bundle of mines and causing a huge explosion to rip apart the tunnel walls. The tower broke right off, sending 300 feet of reinforced steel flipping end over end right down the tunnel, taking out many fighters as it bounced around in the darkness. The tunnel, still under the internal pressure of an entire planet, collapsed on itself behind them, taking out all of the remaining fighters and causing their pole-on-pole magnetic repulsion based acceleration to shoot them out of harm's way at a greatly increased rate of speed; something they had not anticipated, but eagerly accepted!

Sky handed the baby to Erük and helped copilot the ship through the planet's core, sealing it up for spaceflight as they came close to the outer crust again. They all cheered as they crunched the new numbers and realized this new development, caused by desperately reacting to an attack by their pursuers, gave them the rate of acceleration they needed to blow right past the unsuspecting fleet and proceed with the ship's normal stage set of acceleration procedures for deep space travel. That, combined with the amplification of a slingshot effect from repelling the gravity of the planet's closing core as they shot out on their new vector like they were being blown from a cannon, was just enough to get clear of the supernova's destructive shockwave.

They fled for two solid days with no sign of being pursued any further, in fact, no sign of the rest of the Fleet at all. Unsure which direction they would choose to flee, they could only pray now for the souls of the many families on board the large armada that represented the last of civilized mankind.

Even at a velocity very close to the speed of light itself, they were still able to see very clearly in their rear viewer as the third sun crashed right through the already

414

splitting Sigyn and was slowly consumed by Algol, creating a brighter and brighter light as the three stars became one; pulling everything in the system, including the planet they were on, into itself. They watched in horror and magnificent cosmic brilliance as it tore apart everything: planets, moons, and even other stars, unsure if the rest of humanity made it to safety, or not.

Once it seemed that the light from the stars could get no brighter, it exploded in a giant flash, sending a shockwave out in every direction that vaporized everything in its path. The pillar of light and unabashed solar energy shooting symmetrically in both directions took form as the shockwave flattened out into only a swirling disc, trying to make it back toward the center as the giant hypernova gave birth to one of the most destructive and wondrous events in the universe... They were witnessing the birth of a new black hole.

Standing on the bridge with Sky by his side, Thor finally felt a renewed sense of hope... not just for himself, but for Erük and his race of M'ahk Tehríll. Looking at the way he carried the newborn as proud as any human father, Thor was absolutely sure that he made the right decision. For once in his life, he wasn't just patting himself on the back for his ingenuity... he was genuinely proud of what they had accomplished.

They locked in a course for Earth, a voyage of almost 93 light years, which, at their top speed, would still take almost a full century to travel, and started working out a sleep rotation plan that would get everyone on board there in what would seem like only a few short years. A journey not without its own hardship, troubles and adventure, it would take them at least that long to prepare for what they would find when they got there.

About The Author

Gunnar Garisson is an old soul, warrior poet living well out of his time in modern society. In addition to writing full time, he spends a vast amount of creative energy designing off-grid, self sufficient homes, medieval weaponry, music and a better and stronger horn of mead.

He has a passion for the wilderness that was instilled at a very young age, and is a devout member of the church of the highest peak he can find. Alongside years of multi-disciplinary Martial Arts training and an Engineering degree, he is an avid swordsman, and can often be found deep in the woods sparring with his brothers, steel on steel. He enjoys loud motorcycles, small animals, and riding pretty much any kind of board, but his deepest love will always be family.

Only without the bonds of family are we are truly alone....

For current, up to date news, new novel release dates and ordering info, as well as contact information, visit:
www.gunnar-garisson.com